The Colours We See

KAISA WINTER

Dear Emily,
So excited to share
this book with you!
Wishing you a life
★ full of colour!

All the best,
Kaisa Winter

First published in Great Britain 2020

Text © 2020 Kaisa Winter
www.kaisawinter.com

Cover illustration © 2020 Dana Young
www.danayoungstudio.com

ISBN 978-1-914118-01-2

Printed on Forest Stewardship Council® certified paper

ONE

Somewhere above the Atlantic Ocean, I thought I was about to die. Just when I was finally about to start living. Our plane hurtled helplessly through thundering strobe light chaos while a single thought looped through my mind: *Mother was right.*

But somehow, without too much fuss, the storm passed and we landed safe and intact in Chicago. Turns out a bit of turbulence is normal. How would I know? I had never been on a plane before. I had barely been out of England.

Walking on unsteady legs through the walkways of O'Hare, I felt like Dorothy taking her first tentative steps into Oz. Here was life and buzz and colour, a whole new world at my feet. I wobbled wide-eyed among the other passengers, together forming a giant centipede that stretched along the winding corridors and contracted into queues at each checkpoint, security and fingerprints and questions, oh my; I hadn't slept in twenty hours but I was here, *I was here* and this was the start of everything.

My convoy dispersed in the arrivals hall and I stopped, unsure where to go. Dazed, I stood watching the whirlwind around me – taxi drivers picking people up, bags wheeling this way and that, phones ringing, people embracing returned loved ones.

"Excuse me, ma'am," came a voice from behind me. "Are you lost?"

I turned around and saw a middle-aged man wearing a big American grin and an *Ask Me* badge. It took me a moment to collect my thoughts, then I gave him a cautious smile. "Um, define lost."

Because the truth was, I *was* lost. Not only in the sense that I was standing bewildered and sleep-deprived in a foreign country, wondering what to do next. No, in every sense, I was way off course with a sodden map and broken compass.

"I mean," said the man, his smile unwavering, "is there anything I can help you with?"

"Actually, there is." I leaned forwards a little to shift the weight of my cumbersome backpack, which was already digging into my shoulders. "My cousin is supposed to pick me up in Lot D. Do you know where that is?"

"Certainly," he said, and gestured to his left. "Take the exit over there and you'll find it just across the road. First time in America?"

"First time," I confirmed. *First time anywhere, really,* I thought, but said nothing.

"Great book you got there." He pointed to my dog-eared copy of *On the Road*, which was stuck down the side of my backpack.

"Oh, right, yeah," I said, still feeling slightly removed. "It's my favourite." I pulled it out and flicked through its pages, highlighted and marked-up from my many years of thumbing through it. "Ever since I first read it, I've dreamed of coming here."

"Well, looks like you made it! I hope you have a fantastic stay."

As he wandered off to rescue more lost travellers, I looked down at the book in my hand, at a quote I had underlined three times. *The road must eventually lead to the whole world.*

The whole world.

My own world had been unbearably small for too long, but now I was at the edge of everything. All of it, at my disposal. The prospect was as terrifying as it was exhilarating. I had finally escaped that house and its monochrome misery; although now I felt like a chick out of its shell, tiny and vulnerable. But it was time. I had to see who I could be outside those walls.

I turned and headed for the exit, compressed under the weight of my backpack. With my five foot two inches, the bag was almost the size of me, but I assumed I would get used to it in time. There was a certain satisfaction in having all my belongings right there, squeezed into a container I could carry with me everywhere. A sense of freedom.

Mother's letter was still waiting in my back pocket, biding its time like a ticking bomb. I could feel it through the denim, burning me like a branding iron. I couldn't bear to open it, not yet. Instead I tried my best to ignore it, just as I tried to ignore the voice in my head that kept telling me I was a fool for coming to America, a selfish daughter for leaving my mother behind, and that this world would never live up to my fanciful ideals.

That voice had pestered me for too long, and I made a pact with myself there and then, as I scurried towards Lot D and my new life – I promised myself I would find a way to bypass that voice. Or better yet, silence it for good. Because it was loud, and far too convincing.

* * *

I found my long-lost cousin leaning against an oh-so-very-Nathan car: an old yellow convertible, boxy and weather-beaten, its top down in the bright spring sun.

"Nath!"

He looked up and opened his arms with a big grin. "Ah, the tenderfoot pilgrim has landed at last!"

All our lives, Nathan had talked about moving to the States. He used his niche biology degree to obtain a work visa, and four years ago he packed his bags and crossed the Atlantic, just like he had always said he would. There was something about Nathan, the way he seemed to create the life he wanted for himself; while I was trudging around in the same old circles I had been carving for years.

"Whose teeth are those?" I teased as I walked towards him. "They're several shades whiter than they used to be! You're not fooling me, mister."

"You always had a keen eye, little Hazel!" he said, gathering me in a brotherly bear hug. "We'd better get yours bleached pronto if you want to blend in."

I laughed. "I think I'm fine, thanks. I thought you weren't the vain type?"

"Not vain, nope. Let's call it... *appearance aware*." He put on a rakish expression as he threw on a pair of aviator shades, the perfect accessory to his faded Pulp Fiction T-shirt.

"Look at you! What a lovely sight for a weary traveller."

He threw his arms out. "I like a cliché, what can I say?"

Nathan wasn't a traditionally attractive guy. He was short and tubby, with ash-ginger hair and a spray of freckles, but his lack of Hollywood Handsome had never bothered him. He had always had this untouchable confidence, and was one step ahead of the school bullies with his bonkers outfits and outrageous hair dyes. By the time Mother pulled me out of school, everyone knew his name and most were his friends. I was the polar opposite of Nathan, and I had always envied his gutsy and easy-going approach to life.

"Right, ladybird," he said, jumping into the driver's seat. "Let's hit the road and we'll catch up on the way. Madison is many glorious miles away and we're going full-on road trip style, wind in hair 'n all!"

I shoved my bag in the backseat and joined Nathan up front. While he guided us out of the sprawling airport bustle and onto a six-lane interstate, I felt myself begin to relax for the first time in a long while. The worst was behind me. Ahead lay the road, and the whole world.

Once the outer stretches of Chicago were behind us, we drove through enormous farm fields lined with rusting water towers, billboards and roadside diners. It looked just like in the movies, and I stared in awe at it all. It was all so *big*. Nathan negotiated the busy roads with effortless ease, chatting away about work and life and America as we overtook trucks the size of my childhood home, great big trundling beasts covering their endless miles.

Then Nathan asked the question I had been dreading.

"So, what's your plan, now that you're here?"

I shot him a nervous glance.

"Um, I don't have a plan, actually," I confessed. "I didn't want a schedule or anything. I just want to take it day by day, see where the winds take me. Is that... stupid?"

"Not at all!" Nathan flashed me a white-toothed grin. "It's the only way to travel, if you ask me."

I drew a breath of relief. "Okay, phew."

"You've got, what, four months here?"

"Yeah." I felt my smile widen at that particularly wild prospect.

"In four months you can see pretty much all of it, if you want. You'll love Cali for sure. It's swarming with ancient forests and hippies. You'll fit right in!"

"Hey!" I laughed. "I'm not a hippie!"

"Oh, sorry," Nathan said, "I meant *artist*."

"Whatever." I looked out over the fields that seemed to stretch forever around us, draped in the soft chartreuse of springtime.

"Speaking of artists," Nathan said, "how's your mum taking it?"

In an instant I felt my stomach sink, reaching for the rough tarmac flying by beneath us.

"Umm," I mumbled. "Not great, I guess."

"What does she think of you coming here? She must have flipped out! Her precious Mini Me finally flying the nest."

"Oh man, she was miserable. She cried for, like, a week. Tried again and again to make me change my mind. It was awful." Nathan let out a little laugh and I narrowed my eyes at him. "What?"

"Well, you know. It's not exactly surprising. She's so possessive of you."

"She's my mum."

"She ain't that way with Amber, though, is she?"

I sighed and stretched my legs over the rubber mat, catching a glimpse of my shoes. I had brought my favourite pair of sneakers, light and summery with stripes in every colour of the rainbow. They always cheered me up when life felt bleak.

"Mum and Amber never got on," I muttered. "I mean, who gets on with Amber? She's such a fuck-up. I'm like, the good kid, you know? That means a lot of pressure on me. And Mother had no one else when... You know. After Dad finally gave up."

"Okay, fair." Nathan shrugged, eyes on the road. "But you're, what, twenty now?"

"Twenty-one."

"Twenty-one years old! Time to spread those wings and

fly, girl! You definitely shouldn't be stuck at home looking after your mum. You still working for her, too?"

I squeezed my eyes shut, a sudden ache throbbing around my temples. "I know it's not ideal, but it was a mutually convenient arrangement."

Nathan shook his head. "Convenient for Eleanor, sure. I bet she would still change your nappies if she could."

I was about to protest, but then I thought about what he had said and felt a little queasy. "You know, I think you may be right."

"Of course I'm right! I think you'll find I'm always right." He flashed me a rascally grin, and I decided to shake the troubles out of my mind. I wasn't going to let her rule my head anymore.

Tentatively, I reached an arm into the rushing wind. I twisted my wrist and felt the foreign air brush against my skin, pushing my hand upward. Then I tilted my head and let the heavy breeze whip my hair into a wild mess. In front of us, the highway stretched endless and glorious, shimmering with possibilities.

* * *

We reached Madison after dark. In the distance a spring storm was brewing, and lightning flashed like phosphorescence in the clouds. The silence was deafening as we stepped out of the car into a leafy neighbourhood lined with sleepy houses. All I could hear was an eager orchestra of crickets and low rumbles of faraway thunder.

Nathan carried my bag inside. I followed him into the living room and flopped onto his sofa, yawning as I lengthened into a satisfying stretch. "House tour tomorrow?"

"Sure thing. Can I get you anything?"

"Some water maybe?"

"I think I can rustle some up," he said, and disappeared into the kitchen.

I let my eyes drift over the living room. It was neat with some quirky touches, random artwork and a bunch of books lying around like he was halfway through reading all of them. It had a bachelor feel, sparse with lots of browns and dark blues, but it was cosy.

Then I spotted a guitar leaning against the wall, surrounded by scattered sheets of paper.

"Nathan?"

"Yeah?"

"You play the guitar?"

"Totally, yeah, there's a bit of a music scene in this town." He reappeared with two glasses of water and handed me one. "And I play the bass, too, in a band."

"Oh, cool! I had no idea. I play, too."

"You do? I thought painting was your thing, following in your mum's footsteps and that?"

I pressed my lips together. "I haven't painted for years."

"Really?" His face dropped. "But you were, like, a mega talent, right? Pretty much a wonder child, I thought."

"Hardly. Maybe I was alright but, you know…" I looked down at the glass in my hand, twisted it back and forth. "Life got in the way, I guess."

I was too exhausted to explain the real reasons why I had given up painting. Anyway, I wasn't even sure I'd be able to articulate it. It felt easier to push it out of my mind.

Nathan showed me to the spare room, with a big window above a double bed that called me like a siren song. I gratefully sank onto its covers and dug my head into the pillow.

"Thanks, Nath," I said, as he put my bag in the corner. "For everything."

"No sweat, ladybird."

"Really, though. I wouldn't be here if it weren't for you."

"Well, taking me out of the equation," he smirked, "you'd certainly have zero reasons to come to Madison."

"Ha, yeah. But also. Coming to America, well… If I'd been by myself, I don't think I would have had the guts."

"Sure you would. You're underestimating yourself."

He closed the door behind him and I lay still for a moment, heavy as lead. Then, reluctantly, I rolled off the bed and brought my toiletries to the bathroom.

In the mirror, my travel-worn face stared back at me, all pale skin and bloodshot eyes. I ran a brush through my brown locks, which were usually thick and full of life, but they seemed as brittle and jetlagged as the rest of me.

As I peeled my clothes off, Mother's letter fell out and landed on the bath rug. I sighed and ground my teeth together. *Fine*, I thought. *Let's get it over with.*

I lifted the envelope by its top corners, as though any disturbance might set off an explosion, and held my breath as I tore it open.

My Hazel,

How can I ever accept that you are leaving me? You cannot understand what it is like for a mother. I grew you inside myself, an extension of my arm, the flower on my stem. I raised you to become the artist you are, whether you see it or not. Everything you are is thanks to me, and yet you walk away so easily. It stirs in me a pain that is beyond healing.

So, I am left with my canvases, always calling me. They are calling you, too, Hazel. You just can't hear them yet. But you will, of that I am sure.

Outside, spring is coming into blossom, but I take no joy from it. Who am I, when for so long 'Mother' was my very identity, and now my children are gone? I am wilting in this unbearable solitude, counting the days until I reach the end of this long and gruelling life.

You have turned your back on all I have offered you, all the opportunities you didn't even earn. I gave you everything. I hope you never forget that.

I pray to the gods that you will never feel the kind of pain you have caused me.

Your Mother,
 Eleanor

I fucking knew it. I *knew* she would do this. Why did she have to pour black paint all over us until we choked on her misery? My stomach churned and I leaned over the sink, afraid for a moment that I might throw up. Guilt was clawing at me, tearing great big gashes in my heart. After all, she had given me everything – more than I could handle – and now I had left her, alone and heartbroken.

Come on now, I urged myself, looking at my reflection. *Don't let her ruin this, too.*

The sight of my red-rimmed eyes made me even more sad and I tried to force a smile, but then my dimples appeared, and they always made me look like her. Or at least back when she used to smile. I hated the way they reminded me of her. I covered them with my index fingers and turned my head sideways, trying to imagine myself without them, wishing I could smooth them out with a touch. If only it were that easy to erase something you didn't want.

I stood pinching the poisonous letter until my breath had calmed and my eyes stopped burning. Then I hurried back to my room and hid it at the bottom of my bag, where I wouldn't have to think about it any longer. I hadn't come all this way to keep living this nightmare.

In bed, I curled up and tried to focus on the cool breeze that came in through the open window, carrying scents of unfamiliar blossoms and dry grass, and soon I drifted off to the pulsing lullaby of the Midwestern crickets.

Ahead lay the road.

And the whole world.

TWO

I woke confused, dazzled by a beam of sunlight poking at my eye. Instinctively, I turned around and burrowed my face deeper into the pillow, before I remembered where I was and flew right up. *I'm in America!*

Through the window I could see pastel suburbs and sprawling oak trees, topped by a beckoning blue sky. My head cleared in an instant and I wanted to run outside and explore. But Nathan was still asleep, so instead I padded into the living room and stretched out on the sofa, letting out a gratified exhale. I was free.

My eyes drifted over to Nathan's guitar. I picked it up and ran my fingers over the curved wood. Back home I had a cheap, second-hand acoustic which had served me well in learning the basics. I knew I wasn't much of a guitarist, but I did enjoy singing.

I placed it on my lap and shaped a few chords with my left hand. I didn't want to disturb Nathan, but impatience got the better of me and soon I began plucking the strings, humming some tune I knew. Soft notes danced with the dust that swirled in the morning light, and I wrapped their harmony around me like a soft blanket.

After a while Nathan appeared in the doorway, squinting and smiling, his cheeks still showing marks from his pillow.

"Mornin', ladybird," he yawned. "No, don't stop, please. You sound great. I'll put on coffee."

He went off clattering in the kitchen and I carried on playing. I could feel a hopeful smile on my lips – the relief of the escaped prisoner, the elation of a blank canvas.

Soon I was handed a steaming cup of wonderful-smelling coffee and I put the guitar aside. I grabbed the mug with both hands and brought it to my nose. Nathan sank into an armchair and rested a freckled leg over his knee.

"You know, I had no idea you could sing like that," he said.

I felt myself blush. I never played in front of people, and I certainly wasn't used to receiving compliments.

"Um, thanks," I mumbled into my mug.

"I'm serious. I go to a lot of open mics downtown and there's not a lot of people who sound like you! Would you want to perform sometime?"

"Perf—!" I began, but in my shock I breathed in a load of coffee which sent me into a coughing fit.

"I'll take that as a yes," Nathan chuckled, sipping his drink like a civilised person.

Once I had regained my wits, I doused him with big eyes. "For *real*? You think I'm good enough?"

"Oh, easy. I mean, open mics are for amateurs, so there's a real blend of talent anyhow."

"Ooh…" I tried to imagine myself on stage and tightened the grip around my mug. "I'd be so nervous, though! What if I go up there and just blank?"

"That's, like, everyone's fear. But it never happens, trust me."

I turned my face to the warmth of the sun pouring in through the window. It did sound like fun. "Well," I said, "I'm already four thousand miles from home with no plan or direction. What's one more terrifying challenge?"

"Ha! That's the spirit. You write your own songs?"

"Dear god, no. I've tried, but let's spare the good people of this town, I think!"

Nathan chortled into his coffee. "If you say so! Get a couple of covers together, and I can sign you up for a set day after tomorrow?"

"So soon? Holy cow. I just need to practice, like, a *lot*."

"Sure thing. We can play together, if you like, when I get back from work. I'm heading into the lab in a bit, and *mi casa es su casa*. Roam free, girl."

Nathan gave me a spare key and some instructions. After he left, I cracked open a window and leaned out to marvel at my new world. I filled my lungs with scents of fresh-cut grass and cherry blossoms and pricked my ears at the sounds of lazy birds, doors closing, engines roaring into life. A new place, a new beginning.

Then I remembered what I had just agreed to and a mild panic settled in my chest. I grabbed the guitar and began practicing.

* * *

Late in the afternoon, when my throat was getting tired and my fingers burned from pressing against the strings, I put the guitar down and stretched out on the sofa. I was getting hungry. Nathan had given me directions to the local grocery store, so I grabbed my key and headed outside.

Madison's lush suburbs were bathing in brilliant afternoon sun, and the smooth lawns looked an impossible shade of green as they wrapped around the giant houses. The air was still and soft, leaving a host of star-spangled flags dangling limply from mailboxes and doorways. I strolled to the store with my face turned upward like a starved flower, squinting against the blinding sky.

In the store I grabbed a small trolley and pushed it down the aisles while ogling all the exotic foodstuff. After a while of musing over the Marshmallow Fluff spread and Easy Cheese cans that looked like yellow whipped cream, I decided to keep it simple and settled for plain peanut butter.

I headed over to the bakery section to find some bread, but paused in front of a display of colourful cakes. Everything was bigger and brighter than back home, all the icing in piercing neons and hot pinks. I leaned forward to study the doughnuts and wondered how many I had to eat before I guaranteed myself a terminal illness.

Then my eyes drifted over to a cake I didn't realise I recognised. It took me a moment before I could place the sudden ache in my gut. The cake was decorated like a beach, with cliffs and rocks and pale sand lining one segment, and the blue ocean stretching across the top, complete with a tiny sailing boat in the middle. Then I remembered. It was the spitting image of the last cake my mother ever made for me, for my eleventh birthday. The last time we celebrated together like a normal family.

I stared at the cake for a long while, my feet cemented to the floor. I could see Mother as she was then – beautiful, smiling, gleaming with joy and hope and all those things that eventually drained from her like paint from a spilled pot. Part of me wanted to walk straight back to Nathan's house and put all this shit behind me.

But another part of me, a deeper and more desperate part, wanted to bring that cake home and keep it forever.

"You after the Ocean Cake?" A tubby, aproned lady had

appeared behind the counter holding a white carton with a transparent lid. "Want me to box it up for ya?"

"Er, well…" I looked down at the cake and felt a black hole open up inside me, closing in with deadly gravity. "Yes, please."

"Alrighty." She scooped it up and placed it in its packaging, stuck a label on the side and handed it to me. I pulled it close to my face, peering at the little boat drifting alone across the ocean. I wondered then, just as I had wondered on my eleventh birthday: was it leaving, or coming back?

A little lightheaded, I placed it in the trolley next to me.

"Happy birthday to me!" said a voice behind me. "How did you know?"

I whirled around and saw a tall, lanky guy grinning down at me. It took me a second to realise that I had put the cake in his trolley. I hadn't even noticed him approaching.

"Oh, gosh, I'm sorry," I stammered, reaching for the box.

"No, no, you can't take it back now," he said, and snatched it up before I could reach it. As he bent forwards, a cloud of caramel curls bounced all over his head.

He twisted the carton around, studying the scene. "That's a killer cake. Good choice." A friendly grin remained stretched across his face.

"It's a good one…" I stared dumbly at the cake, then glanced up at him with a bashful smile. "Er, happy birthday, I guess."

"Oh, no, I'm sorry," he chuckled. "I was only joking. My birthday was two months ago."

"Ah. Duh." I laughed as though I was in on it, feeling more than a little stupid. Why did I always believe whatever people told me?

"So, I'm afraid I must return your generous gift." He handed it back to me and I absently placed it in my own trolley, still foggy with nostalgia. "You're not from around here, are you?"

"Ha," I said, smiling up at him. I mean, I was short, but this guy was a *flagpole*. He had to be well over six foot. "Is it that obvious?"

"No, it's just, this is kind of a small town. We don't get a lot of visitors. Where you from?"

"England."

"Ah, I had a hunch from the way you said 'obvious'," he grinned. "Awbviuss," he repeated, putting on a haughty look with his mouth shaped into an exaggerated O, and I couldn't help but laugh. "Welcome to our humble land!" he said, sticking his hand out. "I'm Lawson."

I smiled and shook his hand. "I'm Hazel."

"It's an honour, Lady Hazel," he bowed, and his twirly locks fell about his face. "May I inquire as to what brings you to Madison?"

"Well, I'm hoping to travel all over the States, but I started in Madison 'cause my cousin lives here."

"Oh, who's your cousin? Someone local?"

"Um, yeah, Nathan Griffin. You know him?"

"Sure, he plays the bass in the Go Go Trolls, right?"

"Oh my god, is that their band name?" I stifled a laugh.

"Yeah, I know, they're just a bunch of clowns, really. Great, though! He's a mean bass player."

I crossed my arms and shook my head. "This really is a small town, huh?"

"Sure is." He grabbed his trolley and spun it around. "Anyway, I better get going. Hope you enjoy your fancy vacation in Madison," he smirked. "Got any plans for your stay?"

"Um, no." I shook my head. "Oh, actually, yes! Nathan said we'll go to an open mic tomorrow." I stood up a little straighter, pleased to be able to announce some sort of plan.

"Ah, well, in that case I'll be seeing you again, Lady Hazel! Save me some of that cake, will ya?"

"Yessir!"

I watched as he lolloped off on his spindly legs. Then I looked down in my trolley, at the sad little cake with its icing ocean. I picked it up and walked over to the bakery counter.

"I'm sorry," I said to the apron lady. "I changed my mind."

That evening Nathan and I sat in the living room, drowsy and content after several helpings of takeaway tacos, and practiced our music late into the night. Nathan listened to the songs I had in mind for the open mic, offered advice and suggested tweaks, and we played and sang until dawn threatened over the horizon. Exhausted, I hauled myself to bed, and dreamed of vibrating strings and spotlights.

THREE

Everything is white and my breath becomes a cloud of mist in front of my face. I'm wrapped up in thermals and I feel safe and dry, even though we've been rolling around in the powdery snow for what seems like hours.

We've made a snowman. I had no idea how to do it, but Amber knew, and she showed me. We gave him eyes made of pebbles and a smile of raisins, and a long, crooked parsnip nose. We made him together, and I love him.

Amber is getting hot and pulls off the hat Mother made for her, tosses it in the snow. Her red hair is a wild mess and a bright contrast against the pristine white around us.

"Let's go on the swing!" she suggests, and I'm right behind her as we run towards the old tyre swing at the back of our garden. I love it when Amber wants to go on it, because I'm not tall enough to use it on my own. Besides, it's no fun swinging by yourself.

"Help me up?" I plead. Amber threads her fingers together, creating a little step I can put my boot in, and heaves me into the air. I squeal with joy and land on the tyre with an oof! Then I pull my legs over and sit up, while Amber stands so that she can push us into motion.

"Ready?" she asks, her knees slightly bent.

"Ready!" I squeak.

And off we go, higher and higher, ever closer to the pale blue sky. I shriek with glee when we reach above the hedge, and the orange glow of the setting sun hits my face. My nose feels like ice and the air is biting at my cheeks, but I want to keep going.

"Higher!" I demand, and Amber pushes with all her might.

Over the hedge I can see the rest of the neighbourhood, the streets and houses covered in new snow, and beyond that, the rest of the world. I grin and stare at the bright sun hovering on the edge, and for a moment, I am blinded.

FOUR

A spectacular sunset burned over Wisconsin as we made our way to the open mic. I sat hunched in the passenger seat, my trembling arms wrapped tightly around a battered guitar case. The inside of my lips had been shredded from jittery chewing, and I had already made peace with the fact that I was facing imminent death by heart attack – and on stage, no less.

As we rolled up to the venue, my last shred of courage quietly disintegrated. Nathan forced his cabrio into a narrow space, where the engine coughed and fizzled into silence.

"Here we are," Nathan declared. "Roll out the red carpet!"

The venue looked harmless enough – a small, red-brick building dressed in posters and strings of lanterns. What worried me was all the *people*. The pavement was swarming with clusters of sophisticated creatures who would surely take offence at my very existence, armed with Lucky Strikes and vintage handbags. I sat frozen in my seat, watching them huddle and whisper about things I would never know.

"Come on, girl," Nathan laughed. "You'll be *fine*, don't worry!"

"Easy for you to say, mister-famous-bass-player!"

"Hardly." He grinned and undid his seatbelt. "Let's go."

"Well," I mumbled, my eyes still fixed on the crowd. "At least I'll have forty-nine other states to hide in, should I embarrass myself beyond salvation tonight."

I stepped outside and slung Nathan's guitar case over my shoulder. Time to be brave.

We made our way through groups of friends and lovers while greetings and name-drops flew left and right over smouldering cigarettes and clinking bottles. They seemed so easy together, like they had all known each other forever. It made me think of school, and how much I had missed out on when Mother forced me to be homeschooled. Here were old friends, new friends, arms around shoulders, all fist bumps and smiles, and I wanted so badly to be a part of it.

Inside, we were enveloped by dark wood and dim lighting. The bar itself was framed by a string of fairy lights and lined with shelves of backlit wine bottles that shone in a rainy-ocean palette. Nathan introduced me to the bartender – old friends, of course – and bought us a couple of beers.

"Find us a table, will ya," said Nathan, "while I go add you to the setlist."

I took my beer and gingerly circled the room until I found a table in the corner. Safely tucked away I could sit and observe the bustling room, breathing in foaming ales and excitement, perfumes mingling in the air, and wafts of cigarette smoke blowing in through the door. This was a far cry from my sheltered life back home.

The makeshift stage, made from black-painted wooden boards along the back wall, was coming alive with activity. Someone was speaking into the microphone, testing sound levels and recoiling as feedback set in with a high-pitched screech. Some guy at the back was plugging in his bass. A drummer adjusted his seat and gave the cymbals a few trial bashes. People were pushing their way through the crowd, bumping into each other and nearly spilling each other's drinks, waving apologies and greetings along the way. It was hot, it was loud, it was sticky and exhilarating. There was something about this night, about this atmosphere and these people. A current crackled through the air and shot down my spine.

"Lady Hazel! What's up?"

I looked up and saw the cake guy from the store towering over my table, bouncy curls falling about his face.

"Lawson!" I squeaked. "Hi!"

"Told you we'd see each other again. May I sit?"

"Sure!"

The chair scraped against the floor and Lawson plopped his ungainly form down next to me.

"Nathan here?" he asked, resting his elbows on the table.

"Yeah, he's here somewhere." I scanned the room but couldn't spot his ginger mop anywhere. "He went to sign me up for a set."

"Oh, you're playing too? That's great!"

"Well, I'll try," I mumbled, pulling at a string that had come loose from my dress. "It's my first time. Honestly, I don't know how I'm going to get through it."

I grabbed my bottle and took a generous sip. Lawson looked at me, and I was waiting for him to tease me or laugh. I knew I was being silly. But he just nodded thoughtfully.

"I'm not gonna lie, the first time is tough." He laced his fingers together on the tabletop. "What you gotta do is, you gotta get up there and just do *you*. Forget about the audience. Forget about expectations. Close your eyes and play for yourself, just like you would at home. Nobody else matters."

I looked from Lawson over to the crowded room,

squeezing my beer bottle with both hands. "Okay." A hint of a smile defied my frazzled nerves. "I'll try that."

A dark-haired guy appeared behind Lawson and put two beers on the table. "Ah, jeez," he sighed as he sat down, "it never gets easier, being back here."

"Liam, hey." Lawson seemed a little tense as he gestured towards me. "We got company."

The guy looked up and saw me, but his gloomy expression remained. "Oh. Hey."

"Hi." I gave him an awkward wave, as though I had barged in on their conversation and not the other way around. He seemed sad and withdrawn, his shoulders slumping slightly as he began fidgeting with his bottle. His hair was a deep brown, so dark it was almost black, short in the neck but heavy on top with a long fringe hanging down in front of his eyes.

"Hazel's new in town," Lawson announced. "From over the pond, dontcha know," he added in a silly Artful Dodger accent.

"Oh, really?" He flicked away his fringe with a little jerk of his neck to reveal a pair of intense, mud-brown eyes that felt as though they could swallow me up forever. His features were soft and boyish, his face pale and heart-shaped, with gently curved cheekbones and dark eyebrows set in a slight frown.

"Liam is the singer in our band," Lawson continued. "Well, the singer, the songwriter, and the brains behind the entire operation. Meanwhile, I bring the looks," he added with a slight bow.

I chuckled at Lawson's introduction. "Sounds like a dream team. Nice to meet you, Liam." My eyes locked with his and I found myself wondering why they looked so sad. "Are you performing tonight?"

It was Lawson who spoke again, and I was becoming very

24

curious about his mute friend. "We're doing a couple of songs, not the full band, just me and Liam, for old time's sake. We don't normally do open mics anymore. In fact, we're in the middle of a tour right now, so you're lucky we're just stopping by in our old hood."

"A tour! You guys must be doing alright then?"

Liam smiled at this, a lopsided smirk that sent my tummy into pirouettes. "We're doing okay." His voice was husky and soft, and it hung in the air like a summer rain. He held my gaze for a second, then nodded to the guitar resting against my chair. "You going up too?"

"Oh." I gulped. "I was going to, but I'm starting to regret it. I'm just an amateur."

"Aren't we all, deep down?" said Lawson, with a broad grin. "Looking forward to hearing what you got! Anyways, no rest for the wicked. We gotta get ready." They stood up with their drinks and Lawson turned to me. "Remember, just play for yourself, and try to enjoy it."

"I'll try!"

"You'll be swell. Catch ya later, Jane Austen!"

As they walked off, Liam turned and looked back at me with those big, brown eyes, and for a moment the whole room went quiet. Then he merged with the crowd and was gone.

The night kicked off with an enthusiastically welcoming hipster presenter, complete with linen shirt, braces and a designer moustache. Musicians stepped on and off the stage, a wild mixture of people, groups and duos and solos, electric and acoustic and the occasional poem. They all seemed to know each other and cheered each other on, requesting certain songs or covers that seemed to be part of their repertoire. Some were very skilled and sent my heart into my throat, but others kind of clumsy and awkward, which soothed my nerves some. Talented or not, it mattered little to this crowd, who kept cheering and encouraging everyone.

Still, I couldn't help but feel small and self-conscious among all these experienced musicians. With music, I never really knew what I was doing. It wasn't like when I used to paint, the way it flowed so effortlessly, without force. The songs I attempted to write all sounded trite and simplistic, and I didn't seem able to create anything real or raw. Instead, I hid behind the relative safety of covers.

Another act finished and the moustachioed presenter took the stage. "Right, folks, we have a new act in town! She's a singer visiting from the green shores of England." I sank deeper in my chair, tightly gripping the neck of Nathan's guitar as a wave of nausea rolled through me. "That's *the* England, folks, not *New* England, so she has travelled far over the seas to grace us with her tunes. Let's give her a warm welcome!"

Everyone applauded and twisted their heads around to spot the new girl. I stood up, and the people nearby clapped and whooped.

"There she is! Hazel Griffin, everybody! The stage is yours."

The walk up to the microphone felt like it took forever. I didn't want to keep people waiting so I hurried, and tripped on the edge of the stage but landed back on my feet. I pulled out the chair, placed the guitar on my lap, and adjusted the mic stand with a squeak.

"Sorry, just gotta…," I mumbled as I untangled the cable, feeling like a bumbling troll who shouldn't be the centre of anyone's attention. Once settled, I got ready to start the first song, and for the first time I looked out over the crowd. Panic tugged at my throat as I saw their expectant faces, but then my eyes landed on Nathan, who was giving me a thumbs up. Seeing his confident grin warmed my insides.

"Hi, I'm Hazel," I croaked. "Well, you know that." I turned away from the microphone to clear my throat. "Anyway, it's my first time in Madison, and so far I love it. Thanks for having me." Deep breath. "Here I go."

I placed my fingers on the fretboard, felt the thickness of the A string and the tiny nylon E string under my fingertips. I wasn't used to having a microphone in front of me and it blocked the view of my guitar, but then I started plucking and there was no more time to worry.

The vibrations came out of the speakers and went right through my bones; that clean, soft sound of amplified acoustic strings, and I felt my shoulders drop. I started to sing and remembered to breathe properly, and although my voice sounded slightly cautious at first, soon I sank into the experience like a hot bath after a long day. It was one of my favourite songs, sad and slow with a gentle melody, and I could almost feel the wind in my hair as the tunes carried me away on their magic carpet. I feared I would break the spell if I looked up at the audience, so I kept my gaze down, flitting between the floor and the fretboard.

The final chorus came and I landed on a soft C-chord, and the crowd erupted in claps and shouts. I let out a shaky breath and looked up past the bright spotlights, where Nathan stood waving and whooping. Towards the back I spotted Liam and Lawson applauding, Lawson cheering and Liam fixing me with a burning, unwavering gaze. My heart tumbled in my chest and rattled my ribs, and I thought *damn*, I could get used to this.

I leapt into my second song, and in a flash it was all over. I leaned into the mic and mumbled my thanks, unplugged the guitar, and floated off the stage on a soft cloud.

Nathan grabbed me in a big bear hug. "Way to go, kid!" he yelled. "That was awesome!"

I felt high and delirious and didn't even notice whoever

was performing next. My mind was busy replaying what had just happened. I had surprised myself. And they had loved it.

After a few more acts, I snapped out of my revelry when the presenter got up and demanded our attention.

"Listen up, everybody! We're all in for a special treat tonight! I'm sure most of you have heard that Liam Riley is back in town?"

The crowd roared.

"Liam is here tonight with bandmate Lawson Kowalski. They have taken a break from their busy touring schedule to come back to their dear old hometown and treat us to a few songs."

Another roar. I looked around for Liam but couldn't see him anywhere.

"So, let's give a warm welcome to our homegrown talents, Liam and Lawson of Object Impermanence!"

Feverish shrieks and applause rained around me as the pair appeared from the corner and walked onto stage, acoustic guitars slung over their shoulders. Lawson waved at the crowd, while Liam focused on his mic stand, raising it a little and re-angling the mic. They plugged their instruments into the amp and tested the tuning. Only then did Liam look up at us.

"Thanks everyone, it's good to be back," he said, although his voice sounded flat and I remembered what he had said to Lawson earlier, something about how it never gets easier being here. I wondered why, because everyone seemed to love them. While the crowd was going crazy, Liam seemed aloof, guarded; and it made me even more curious about him.

Lawson leaned into his mic to greet their fans and plug their album. Then the boys looked at each other, guitars poised, and whispered a *one, two, three, four* under their breath, and off they went.

The room fell silent as their strings began softly

resonating through the venue. Liam's left hand moved swiftly up and down the fretboard like he had scarcely done anything else in his life. His lyrics flowed in perfect and surprising rhymes and rhythms. It was the kind of performance that required one's full attention, and we were all willing to give it.

Something about his timid posture and vulnerable voice made the performance seem so honest and true, and it held us all in reverent awe. Liam didn't try for us, he didn't put on a show. He was just there doing his thing, and the fact that he was in front of an audience was more like an afterthought; like a side effect he didn't particularly want. Close behind stood Lawson with his guitar, strumming a backing riff and occasionally adding baritone vocals, creating a mesmerising stereo dream.

I couldn't tear my eyes from Liam. He wore tight, ash-black jeans and a dark grey cotton shirt with arms rolled up to bare his pale forearms, flexing and releasing as he picked and strummed the strings. His fringe hung down in his face, but this time he didn't flick it away; as though he preferred to hide behind it.

His face was soft in the spotlight, his eyes locked on some distant point somewhere past the crowd, gazing into himself rather than out into the room. I was hoping to catch his eye, but he wasn't there, he was not on that stage in front of us. He was somewhere else entirely, and I was desperate to find out where that was and how I could get there.

* * *

Too soon, the bar bell rang its song of closing time. People poured out of the entrance, congratulating and thanking each other for another great night. Lighters sparked and bike chains clinked. I looked everywhere for Liam and Lawson. I couldn't get them out of my head, and I knew I had to talk to them again before they went back on tour.

I scanned the room for Nathan, hoping to find him or Liam or Lawson or just something to cling to, or else the stars might call me to them and I would drift off and maybe never find my way back.

Then I spotted Nathan near the bar and hurried over.

"Oi, Nath," I said, poking his shoulder. "That Liam fella, do you know him?"

He shrugged. "We run into each other at events and stuff but no, I wouldn't say I *know* him. Their band is sick, though. Went through the roof a few years back. You like their stuff?"

"Yeah, they were incredible! Do you know where he is now?"

Nathan looked around. "Not sure where they went to." Then he narrowed his eyes and a sly smile formed. "Why do you ask?"

"No, no..." I tried to protest but my nervous smile betrayed me. "I—I just... I met Lawson the other day, and—"

I stopped when Nathan cut his gaze to a point behind me. I swung around and was met by Liam's Nutella eyes, his hand outstretched, offering me a beer.

"Hey," he said. "Owner gave me some drinks to say thanks. Want one?"

"I, uh, er, yes please, sure." I glanced in Nathan's direction and ignored his teasing grin.

"Come with me," Liam said, and something surged through me; a peculiar sensation that I would follow him anywhere.

As we criss-crossed the crowd, people greeted Liam with handshakes and thanks and pats on his shoulder. He worked his way through the throng, smiling and thanking them, while superlatives and compliments rained over him.

Out front, we found a quiet corner by the smoking area

and sat on the ground, resting our backs against a wall covered in posters and flyers. A slight breeze tugged at the layers of faded paper with line-ups and band names in bold capitals, like a colourful punk quilt.

"So," he said, "Hazel like the nut?"

I smiled. "No, Hazel like the colour." I shook my hazel-brown hair to support my statement. "My older sister has ginger hair, so she was named Amber."

"Well, Hazel-like-the-colour, I really dug your performance."

"Er, thank you. I mean, I'm not a musician, but—"

"I don't wanna hear it." With that same lopsided smirk, he held a palm up to block my disclaimers. "No apologies. You were great. I had a feeling you weren't going to take a compliment very well."

I smiled at him as I swallowed a mouthful of beer. "Where did you get that feeling?"

"Well, first of all, you're British, right? You guys apologise for everything, including your own talent. I love it, it's really sweet. A welcome change from this country's inflated confidence and in-your-face arrogance." He looked ahead and drank a deep gulp from his bottle.

"Oh, yeah," I mumbled. "Sorry."

He chuckled and looked back at me. "See what I mean?"

My hands flew to my mouth. "Oh, sorry! No! I mean. Not sorry. Oh god." I momentarily dissolved into a giggling fit but took a sharp breath to regain control of myself. I didn't want to come off as an infatuated schoolgirl in front of Liam, but I feared that battle was already lost.

"And the way you held yourself on stage, you seemed kinda shy. I don't know, I just got the feeling. And I was right, wasn't I?"

I felt myself shrinking a little and began pulling at my beer label.

"No, no," he protested, as though he could sense my insecurity. "Don't get me wrong. I loved it, I really did. I love that kind of vulnerability on stage. It's a rare thing."

Our eyes locked again, and a heat spread from my tummy to my face like a flash fever. I held his gaze as I put my lips to the neck of my bottle and took a sip.

"Liam!" Someone was shouting from a car that sat with its engine impatiently running. "Time to go, *chacho!* Lawson's already on his way over to Frank's!"

Liam tore his eyes from mine and looked over to the guy. "Shit," he whispered under his breath. "Look, I gotta go. It was great to meet you." He stood up and offered me a hand, and when he pulled me up I landed just a little closer to him than I had planned to.

"Umm," I mumbled, taking a small step back. "Where are you going?" I was surprised by my own forthrightness. It was none of my business. I just didn't want him to leave, not yet.

"There's an afterparty at my uncle's house, celebrating our homecoming. I don't know, it was organised by some old friends of ours. I guess we have some devoted fans in this town." He looked out over the dispersing crowd, and I could sense a tiredness come over him.

"Come on!" the guy insisted, hanging out of the idling car.

Liam looked back at me. "You in town a while? I'll see you around, yeah?"

I nodded, and as he walked off I returned my attention to my bottle, tugging at the label I had already peeled halfway loose. The car door slammed shut, but opened again. I looked up.

"Hey, Hazel!" Liam said, leaning out the door. "Why don't you come along?"

"Oh!" I looked around for Nathan but couldn't see him anywhere. "Okay!"

I scuttled around the car and slipped into the backseat, next to Liam. We exchanged a smile in the dark and my heart leapt into a somersault. The world felt wild and immeasurable, and here I was, free to partake in the dance. I didn't have to be the person I had been. Everything was new, so I could be, too. The entire world was at my feet, and I wanted to embrace it without hesitation.

We closed the doors and off we went; and those few miles we covered together that night would turn out to be the first of thousands.

FIVE

We drove down the main road, orange streetlights pulsing through the car in beat with my exhilarated heart.

"Guys, meet Hazel," Liam said. "Hazel, meet the band." He gestured to the driver. "This here is Victor, our tour manager and merch wizard. Without him, we'd be lost."

Victor nodded a hello to me through the rear-view mirror. He looked slim and tidy, with a neat haircut and thin metal-frame glasses. Like someone you could trust with your life savings.

"Beware of him!" said the guy in the passenger seat. "Vic's everybody's boss, you'll see. Make sure you do what he tells ya."

Victor chuckled at this, although his eyes remained firmly on the road. "Everyone buckled up?" he asked.

"*Mira*, Exhibit A!" the other guy said. "Yessir, boss man!" He laughed and snapped a salute.

"Right," said Liam, "and this noisy one here is our drummer delight, Mango."

Mango twisted around and hooked his elbow over his seat. "Pleasure to meet you." He looked more exotic than his bandmates, with a round, olive-skin face topped by a buzz cut. An expertly trimmed beard and moustache framed his smile, and a pair of bushy eyebrows danced over his inquisitive eyes.

"Hi," I squeaked, tightly gripping my bottle. I hoped the butterflies would stop their tummy tango soon. "Your name's Mango?"

"Well, it's Manuel, really, but it's been Mango for so many years now, I hardly remember."

He spoke with a pleasant Latin twang, softly rolling consonants and swiftly skipping vowels, far from the languid drawl of his Midwestern mates.

"We call him Mango because he's *so sweet*," Victor said with playful sarcasm.

Mango laughed and landed a punch on his arm. "I'm sweet and you're sour, am I right?"

"Hey, now! No violence when I'm driving."

"But any other time is fine, yeah?" Mango grinned and turned to me. "You're the girl from England who performed, right? You got a great voice!"

"I—" I was about to protest when I heard Liam emphatically clear his throat, and I remembered our conversation earlier. "Thank you," I said to Mango, then turned to Liam with a coy smile.

"I hope we'll see more of you on stage," Mango continued. "So, are you visiting or moving here?"

"I'm backpacking. Sort of. Across America."

"Ay, that's amazing. I'll never forget when I first came here. Biggest decision of my life."

"Where did you come from?"

"*Soy de* Puerto Rico, my friend! Came here on a scholarship for college and got stuck with these losers." A big smile creased his face, which beamed with a benevolent love for his mates and possibly the world in general.

I wasn't sure where Puerto Rico was, but I figured I'd keep that to myself. "What's college like?" I asked instead. I had always been curious about college and uni, leaving home and living life on your own terms, all friends and parties and freedom. I had missed out on all that, but I couldn't be sure anymore whose fault that was.

"Oh man, college was great!" said Mango. "What an experience."

Liam sighed. "It really wasn't."

"Man, I still don't get why you dropped out. You could have stayed, just two more years. We had a good time, no?"

"I never knew what I was doing there," Liam said. "I'm glad it worked for you, but it sure as hell didn't for me."

Mango shrugged and raised his eyebrows with a cheeky grin. "He's a moody one, get used to it."

Liam ignored him and turned to me. "Why did you come to the States, of all places? You could have gone anywhere."

"Oh, you know…" It seemed a strange question, really. "It's *America*," I said with a shrug, as if that explained it all. "I don't know, it's just so fascinating. So big and bold and extreme."

Liam's eyebrows shot up with a snort. "Extreme, I'll give you that. And a fucking mess, if you haven't noticed."

"Here we go, Mister Emo!" Mango howled. "Let's hear it. Let's wallow in the injustice of the world." He twisted around with his big grin. "You know I love you, *hermano*."

Liam laughed. "Don't I know it." He emptied his bottle and chucked it on the floor. "I just don't get it," he said to me. "You have everything in Europe. All those countries and borders and coastlines. So much diversity and, like, actual *history*. And governments that are not literally plotting against you." He let out a heavy sigh and shifted his gaze to his lap. "Everyone in this country is just a puppet on a fucking string, dancing for the clowns and cowboys who call themselves our rulers. It's pathetic. We're, like, two elections away from civil war, I guarantee it. I don't know why you'd choose to travel through this backward hellhole."

"Oh come on, it's not *that* bad, is it?" I said, as Victor steered us off the main road. We drove slowly through a residential area dotted with small houses, barely lit from the sparse streetlights.

"It's not far off," Liam said, looking up at me. "And all this 'greatest nation on earth' bullshit. People only say that 'cause they haven't realised that other countries actually exist."

"Yeah, fair," I said. "Calling it the greatest is maybe a stretch, but it's so entertaining! You're like an experiment."

Liam tilted his head. "An experiment?"

"Well, you know. You're such a young nation, still full of growing pains and angst while you're trying to figure things out. It makes for good drama, what can I say? It's like Europe is a boring grown-up and America is the world's teenager."

Liam coughed out a laugh and his face softened. "The world's teenager... I like that."

"So now that you're here in this godforsaken mess," said Mango, "what's your plan?"

"Not sure yet. Travel around, see what else this world has to offer. Maybe figure out what I'm supposed to do with my life."

"And you've come all by yourself?"

I nodded at Mango, and his smile widened.

"Brave!"

"Well." I folded my hands in my lap with a self-assured pout. "I'd rather die free than live trapped."

"Woo! We got an adventurer on our hands!" Mango threw a fist bump at Victor, but our conscientious driver refused to take his hands off the steering wheel. Mango shrugged. "He loves me really," he said, and shifted his arm to me. "You go, *chica!*" I felt a little silly as I raised my fist and bumped it against his – but, hey, it seemed I was actually making *friends*.

"So, you got no plans at all?" Liam asked, swallowing me up with his quicksand eyes.

"Nope."

He nodded approvingly. "Way to go."

I gave him a warm smile, with something flirty hiding just beneath my eyelashes.

"So," I said, looking over at Mango and Victor. "You guys, and Lawson. Is that your whole band?"

"No," they said, shaking their heads as we rolled to a stop. "There's one more."

SIX

We parked outside a small, one-storey house at the end of the road. The front lawn was swarming with people, and I could see more spilling out of the back garden. In the open windows sat speakers that filled the night with some indie rock I didn't recognise. Along the front of the house sat a couple of camping tables, holding stacks of beer crates and a rainbow of liquor bottles. I walked wide-eyed next to Liam, at once a shy imposter and enthralled explorer.

"This is my uncle's place," Liam said, as we headed towards the house. "He's a legend, you'll love him."

Someone spotted us and yelled something, and the crowd erupted into cheers and applause. Mango and Victor smiled and waved, but most of the attention was on Liam, who didn't seem all that comfortable with the plaudits.

Up ahead, I could see a girl appear in the doorway. She was drop-dead gorgeous, with a pale, doll-like face framed by a cascade of auburn locks. Liam walked up to her, and my heart nearly stopped when he gave her a hug and a kiss on the cheek. She fixed him with a gaze the way a snake stares at its charmer – hypnotised, but also hypnotising.

They whispered something to each other, and I held my elbows, suddenly feeling awkward and out of place. Then Liam turned and found me.

"This is the fifth member of our band. Ivy, meet Hazel."

Ivy. Her name slipped through my mind slick as oil, sharp as vinegar. Before we greeted each other, we took a moment to size each other up in the way only competing females can do. Her style was irritatingly impeccable – new vintage in mustards and greens that perfectly complemented her fiery hair and translucent skin, fitting snugly around her slender figure. It was a stinging contrast to my yellow skater dress and butterfly hair clip, and I felt like a silly primary school kid. A whimsical fringe dangled just above her eyes, lending her a waifish, innocent look. But I instinctively knew there was nothing innocent about her. I could almost hear myself growl, some ancient lioness awakening inside me, before I took a hold of myself and reached out my hand.

"Nice to meet you, Ivy."

"You too, Hazel."

A perceptive onlooker may have noticed our voices scrunching when sounding each other's names, our eyes narrowing, our shoulders pulling back. Fortunately, Liam was occupied with other things.

"Frank inside?" he asked Ivy, who nodded in response.

Liam slipped away so quickly that I missed my chance to follow, and I was left standing with Ivy and a hundred strangers stomping up a lawn somewhere in Middle America. Above our heads a million stars pulsed across the sky, flickering in a multitude of colours as their light cut through the atmosphere.

"So," I said at last, since someone had to deal with the awkward silence. "What do you do in the band?"

"I play the violin, mostly," she replied unceremoniously, looking out over the crowd with a casual indifference. Her voice carried a Southern drawl, lazy and superior. She had the sophisticated air of a rich girl, but I saw something else in her, too, something rebellious. I couldn't compete with this.

Liam appeared with an older guy I figured must be his uncle. The man had his arm around him and they were deep in some engaging conversation, shouting in each other's ears to reach above the music. I couldn't help but smile at the sight of them. They stopped in front of me and Liam looked up.

"Oh, hey Hazel, this is Frank. He's the best goddamn man in this town, if not the country."

Frank chuckled and put on a bashful look. I got a sense that Liam always introduced him that way.

"Well, then, I am deeply honoured to meet you, Sir." I smiled and nodded my head in a modest bow.

"Oh, the manners!" Frank gasped. "Would you look at that! Now where did you find this one, Liam, huh?"

"She's from England, actually," Liam said, and Frank turned to me with wide eyes.

"England! How very exotic."

I laughed. "Yes, I'm quite the alien!"

Frank nodded. "Unprecedented, no doubt."

Standing next to each other, they looked a little similar. Frank was skinny like Liam, but shorter – just a little taller than me, which was rare because I was always the shortest person in the room. Both had deep brown eyes, but while Liam's seemed to be burning with something I couldn't define, Frank's were calmer, brighter, with a youthful twinkle.

"So, traveller from across the oceans," said Frank, and two narrow dimples appeared around his smile. Everyone always looked better with dimples than I did. "May I offer you something to quench your thirst?"

"Yes, please." As I followed him to the drinks table, I

snuck a quick look over my shoulder and saw Liam lean into Ivy and say something in her ear.

"There's beer, punch, or use whatever you like if you want to mix yourself something."

"I'll try the punch, please," I said, trying to put Liam out of my mind for the moment.

"As the lady wishes." Frank grabbed a red plastic cup, filled it with the cherry-coloured cocktail, and handed it to me. "So, what brings you to town?"

I told him about my plan to travel around America. Talking to Frank was easy, it turned out, and I found myself rambling on about everything I was hoping to see and do, how nervous I had been during my performance, and how much I already loved everything about this country. Frank smiled, nodded, listened, and only spoke once I stopped and realised that I hadn't taken a full breath in a while. I filled my lungs with the cool night air and chased it with a large mouthful of berry booze.

"I think it's a great thing you're doing," Frank said.

"Yeah? You don't think I'm being naive?"

"Let me tell you something." Frank leaned closer with a knowing smirk. "Without naivety, you'll never get anywhere in this life. I've travelled a lot in my time, and had I not been a little naive, I probably would never have left my house! Life is better when you take risks."

He spoke slowly and emphatically, in a full, warm voice that felt like sunshine and freshly baked bread.

"Well," I said, "that's not like any advice I've ever heard. Thank you."

Frank looked out over his yard and its boisterous visitors, and something wistful came over him. "I do miss that feeling. When it was just me and my car and the never-ending road."

"Why don't you travel anymore?"

"Times change, I guess. You get older and... priorities rearrange." From his shirt pocket he produced a pack of Marlboros and offered me one. "You smoke?"

"Oh, sometimes with a drink. But not right now, thanks."

"Smart girl."

He flicked a metal lighter into life and leaned into the flame. As the smoke left his mouth, he began to cough.

"You okay?" I asked.

He straightened up. "I'm fine. Dry throat is all." He pulled open a can of beer and took a deep gulp. Then he started up again, a hoarse cough that racked his entire body.

"Whoa, Frank..." I wasn't sure what to do, so I just put a hesitant hand on his shoulder while he stood bent over, hacking up whatever evil was trying to escape his lungs.

"Gee, old man!" said Liam, who had reappeared behind us carrying a sloshing bottle of vodka. "Should you be smoking with a cough like that?" He leaned in and gave Frank a friendly slap on the back. I looked around for Ivy but couldn't see her anywhere.

"It's nothing," Frank croaked. He regained his composure, straightened up and took another drag off his cigarette. "See?" he said, the twinkle back in his eye. "I'm fine."

"Hope so, uncle." Liam threw his right arm over Frank's shoulders. "Man, is it good to see your sorry ass! I wish you could come on the tour with us." He swung the near-empty bottle into the air and took a swig.

Frank let out a wheezing laugh. "I think I'm too old for that kind of life now, as in fact I was just explaining to Hazel."

"Bullshit! You're not old." Liam's mood seemed to have taken a sharp turn upward. "So, Hazel, welcome to the bachelor manor! You should have seen her on stage tonight, Frank." Liam pointed to me, bottle in hand. For a split second I could feel the heat from the spotlights on my face and my insides took another tumble.

"Yes, I heard," Frank nodded, offering me his friendly eyes. "I'm sure it was quite something."

Liam drained his final sip and lassoed me with an intense stare. I felt my knees become a little uncertain.

"We should play together sometime," he said.

"M-me?" I searched his face to see if he was messing with me.

There was his crooked smirk again. "Yeah, you. How long are you in town for?"

"Um, I don't know yet."

"Well, don't make any plans to leave just yet! You gotta come to our studio, we'll have a jam." His dark eyes held me in their grip, sucking me in like a helpless piece of dust.

"Sounds great," I said, but my smile froze when I saw three girls appear behind Liam. Alternative-chic with black and blue hair and dark-painted eyes, they giggled nervously as they surrounded him.

"Oh my god, hi," one of them squeaked. "We just wanted to meet you. We're huge fans!"

Liam threw me a quick glance and turned to his admirers. "Well, hey, ladies. You from town?"

They walked off to chat, and I shifted my weight awkwardly. I tried taking a sip from my drink, but my cup was empty. Frank looked at me and threw his cigarette butt on the ground.

"Can I top you up?"

"Oh, sure, thanks."

We walked over to the table and Frank dipped the ladle into the punch. As the liquid filled my cup, he cut me a sideways glance.

"You know, this is how it's been with Liam since he went

and got himself famous. He can be slippery, but he'll be back soon, I'm sure."

"Oh, it's fine." I tried my best to look unperturbed. "I bet a lot of people want to talk to him."

"They sure do." He handed me a full cup and looked over at Liam and his girls. "I'm as happy as anyone to see him back in town, but lately we all gotta share him round."

Frank felt faraway suddenly, and the wistfulness of earlier seemed to have sprouted into a deep sadness. He noticed me studying him and cleared his throat.

"I'm sorry," he chuckled. "Old men like me get a little sentimental at times."

I gave him a cheeky smile that I hoped would cheer him up. "You're really not that old."

"Well, that's kind of you to say. But it feels a little different from where I'm standing."

I was about to respond when I heard a familiar voice behind me.

"What's up in Wonderland, Alice?"

I swung around and smiled at the sight of Lawson's trademark grin.

"Lawson, hey!"

"I didn't know you'd be here," he said, grabbing me in a friendly hug. "I see you've met everyone's favourite uncle!"

"I have indeed." I beamed at Frank with all the warmth in me, hoping to melt away all the sorrow that lived in his eyes. "Oh," I said, turning to Lawson, "I also met Mango, and – Victor, is it? From your band."

"Rad! Good to see you've been doing the rounds." He gave me an encouraging nod which sent his curly mop bouncing like a set of slinkies. "And Ivy?"

Right. I pinched my lips. "And Ivy," I muttered.

"Care for a beer, Sir?" Frank held out a can to Lawson.

"Thanks, bud." He took it and pulled off the ring with a hiss.

"So, um, Lawson…," I began hesitantly. "Liam invited me to come to some studio, for a jam." The way I said it, it sounded more like a question.

"Oh, up on Edgehill Drive, sure."

"Is that your band's studio?"

"Yeah, kind of. It's not, like, a *studio* studio, like industry level. It's just a house, but yeah, that's where we rehearse and record."

"Sounds cool. But, like…" I scraped my foot against the gravel. "Do you think Liam meant it when he said we should play together? I mean, I'm not very good."

He interrupted a big gulp of beer and had to wipe a drop off his chin. "Sure he meant it! Liam doesn't care about technique or training. He spots raw talent and authentic people. I can see why he's taken a shine to you."

I looked down at my rainbow shoes and tried to suppress another blooming smile.

* * *

Hours later, after Frank's poor lawn had been reduced to mud, people reluctantly crawled home to nurse hangovers and heartaches. I was wrapping up a meandering conversation with Frank while texting a rambling message to Nathan, hoping he could pick me up.

"I've had a great time," I said, my mind swimming in a near-dawn boozey soup. "It's been so good to meet you. Thanks for having me."

"The pleasure was all mine, I assure you," Frank said. "It's been a delight, truly."

"You're too sweet." I chuckled and wrapped him up in a hug.

"Hey." He pierced me with eyes that held more facets than the world's largest diamond. "All the best for your big adventure. I bet you'll have some incredible tales to tell once it's all over."

I returned his gaze and was surprised to feel a sting of nostalgia in my gut.

"I hope we meet again," I said.

"Well, who knows what's in the stars." His mournful smile once again brought out all his lines and dimples, prompting a smile from me in return. Then I felt a poke to my shoulder, and I turned around to find Liam holding his phone up to me.

"Hazel-like-the-colour! Gimme your number and I'll text you the address for the studio."

My cheeks flushed as I punched my digits into his phone.

"Sweet," he said, pocketing his device. "I'll see you there!"

"Okay!" Our eyes met and a shiver sparkled down my spine like a river of freshly poured champagne. Then he was dragged away again, this time by a group of rambunctious lads who had some amazing and urgent matters with their favourite celebrity friend.

With one final wave to Frank, I walked off into the first light as it peered over the horizon with all the promises of tomorrow.

SEVEN

A *fresh April breeze is blowing through my mother's studio. We sit surrounded by her art, abstract shapes that come alive in the glow of the afternoon sun. It has always been this way – my mother and I, an unbreakable team, the chosen ones.*

"You have been blessed with my talent, Hazel dearest," my mother tells me. "It is both a blessing and a responsibility, and I know you will carry on the torch with grace and dignity." I smile and nod with the solemnity I feel is required of the moment.

"I will, Mother." I am not to call her Mum; it is far too common, she says. She is the life-bringer, the light-bearer, the goddess from which all good stems. So I call her Mother, for there is no greater joy than knowing that I please her.

I relish the experience of creating art. To have an image in my mind, and to then bring that image to life with brushstrokes and colours... It's a kind of magic.

"This is how the gods breathed life into all creatures," Mother says. As I watch my imagination manifest on the page, people and animals and landscapes, I wonder if I should have that kind of power.

I am in awe of my mother's creations, which put my own crude drawings to shame. I don't always understand what the paintings mean, but I know they are bold, and carry an ethereal beauty that only makes sense in the soul. At least that's what my mother says. And I believe her, because she knows everything.

"Why can't Amber paint with us?" I ask.

"Amber doesn't want to paint, dear. She's not like us."

"Where is she?" I hadn't seen my older sister in several days.

"She's not interested in being part of this family, and I won't force her. We all make our choices in this life, and she has made hers. Now, put Amber out of your mind and focus on your work."

I am shading a baby elephant poised over a watering hole. In the background, Mummy Elephant looms so large that I couldn't fit her on the page. Mother watches as I work, and I give the grooves of the trunk extra attention, making sure I don't rush any details.

I feel so lucky to have my mother here, to guide and teach me. I cherish our afternoons together, when she takes the time to sit with me; time that she could be using to create her own art. Instead she chooses to spend it on me, and I feel a duty to do my very best. It's the debt I owe her.

As a final touch, I add some wispy grass and reeds along the edge of the water, and then I hold up the drawing to study it.

"I think it's done. Do you like it, Mother?"

"Like it?" she says, fixing me with eyes grey like frost. "Never give away your power to someone else by asking them to like you or your work. Nobody has to like it but you."

She has told me this before, and my cheeks burn with shame. Why am I always asking the same stupid questions? Why don't I ever learn?

Mother takes the drawing from me and holds it up in the light. "But I do like it. It has life. You have given life to what was before a mere piece of paper. You have great power, my dear daughter."

She rises and walks over to her kaleidoscopic wall and pins the drawing in between two of hers. "It will hang right here, so that everyone can see. I am so proud of you."

And my petals open a little wider, twisting and bending towards my mother.

EIGHT

"I'm gonna fuck it up I'm gonna fuck it up oh my god I HATE SHOELACES! Oh, Nathan, I'm going to be *so late!*"

"Don't sweat it, ladybird." Nathan stood leaning against the doorpost, looking disturbingly relaxed while I was all over the place in a twitching, hyperventilating mess. "Anyway, he won't care. It's his studio. He can just chill and play until you get there."

"Yeah, but, oh, but... Argh, why don't people use velcro straps anymore?! Isn't it time for the eighties to make a comeback?" I tugged at my knot one final time, then stood up and caught my breath. "I just," I whirled around to find my bag, "don't want to, you know" – one last mirror check, nothing in my teeth – "don't want to be disrespectful or anything."

"Ha!" Nathan scoffed. "I'm sure Liam won't be *too* offended."

His name rolled off Nathan's tongue like an unpinned grenade, and the impossibility of what was about to happen sent further shockwaves through my nervous system. Me, playing with Liam, at his studio. Dorky Hazel from Folkestone and musical legend Liam Riley, who had already toured the world with his songs. And who also happened to be painfully beautiful, which was a terrible (and exquisite) distraction. My stomach somersaulted. "Oh my god, Nath, I'm going to throw up."

"No, you won't," he chuckled, reaching his arm out to guide my frazzled self out the door before I could commence yet more delaying tactics. "Why don't you try breathing? It's always worked for me."

He led me outside and into his car.

"I'm going to fuck it up."

"Careful," Nathan said, grinning as he twisted the key in the ignition. "If you keep saying that, it might come true."

* * *

We drove along a path that wound its way through a leafy suburb until we reached a house near the top of a hill.

"This is it," Nathan said, and the old engine coughed and sputtered to a halt.

The houses dotted around the verdant neighbourhood were all painted in blinding whites and baby blues, but this house looked like it hadn't seen a lick of paint in at least a decade. And the garden had clearly been left to its own devices many years ago. But it looked charming, the shabbiness a small rebellion against its uppity neighbours.

I stared at the wonky mailbox with its four numbers and tried to will my body to move.

"You know..." Nathan gave me a rare, serious look that made me pay attention. "There's only one way you could truly fuck this up."

I sat up straighter.

"If you mess up a chord or say something stupid, nobody cares about that. But if you go in there and completely forget to enjoy yourself – *that* would be your biggest mistake. What's the point of anything if you don't let yourself have fun?"

I felt my lungs open up, and I gratefully accepted the extra oxygen.

"This is your chance. Who knows where this might lead? These guys are great. They're nice guys, they're successful. And Liam is, as everyone knows, a musical genius. And you've been invited to the party! Do yourself a favour and take some credit."

I looked from Nathan over to the house. I wanted to take his words to heart, but I didn't know how. Finally I decided that if I couldn't be brave, I would at least pretend.

"Okay." I popped open my seatbelt. "Thanks for the lift. And the pep talk." I smiled at my stupid, wise cousin.

"Just have fun," he said emphatically. "You got this, girl."

"Just have fun," I repeated quietly, as if memorising the answers to a test.

Nathan and his stubborn old car disappeared down the hill and I was left standing in a deafening silence, with not so much as a breeze to rustle the treetops.

I started walking slowly up the garden path, swallowing hard in the hope that it would push my heart back into my chest. It was a little too cold for the flower print sundress I had on, but I wanted to look my best. It tucked in at the right places, leaving room for my hips while accentuating my waist. My short, curvy form was the opposite of Ivy's dainty features, but at least this dress did me some favours. I hoped Liam would like it.

Up on the front steps, I stopped to fluff up my hair and run my tongue over my front teeth.

"Holy mother of baloney," I whispered, my heart drumming against my ribs. "Just have fun. Just have fun."

I took a deep breath, pulled back my shoulders, and put

my finger to the doorbell. For about twenty seconds I just stood there, unable to press it. Then it occurred to me that maybe there was a security camera somewhere and Liam was inside watching me standing there like a doofus, and my finger swiftly did its job.

Ding-dong.

There was no answer. I stood up a little straighter and pulled at my dress. Still no answer. I rang the bell again, knocked on the door. A furtive peek through a window showed no signs of life. I turned around and scanned the street. Had I got the wrong time?

I sat down to wait, the concrete cold against my bum. Legs crossed, I leaned back and looked up at the sky, vast and pale and carrying the promise of summer. A plane rumbled past, tracing a white line across the powder blue dome. I checked my phone. No message. I was sure he had said today.

Maybe he wasn't coming. A chill shot through my chest. Had he been messing with me after all? Or had he been too drunk to remember?

"Hazel!"

I swung my head around and saw Liam hurrying up the path.

"Sorry," he panted, "I lost track of time."

"Oh, that's okay!" I shot up and brushed off my dress, hoping I showed no signs of the prolonged panic attack that had preceded my arrival. "I haven't been here long."

"Well, thanks for waiting anyhow," he said as he slowed his steps and pulled out his key. As he got closer a tingle shot through my body, and I had to force myself not to stare at his beautiful face. He wore a tight, black cotton top with three-quarter arms, and a pair of grey skinny jeans, a wondrously casual look topped by that tousled mop and long fringe. While he fiddled with the lock, I tried to quickly figure out how the hell I could appear cool and confident when I was pretty much on fire inside. No strategy came to mind.

"Here we go," Liam said, holding the door open.

"Thanks!" I put on a cute face and slunk past him into the hallway.

"Through there." Liam gestured towards the living room at the end of the hall. It was a large room, sparsely furnished but littered with musical paraphernalia. Over in one corner, a couple of faded sofas sandwiched a stained coffee table, and scattered all around them were several electric and acoustic guitars. Cables snaked their way across the floorboards, plugged into amps or coiled into piles. On the walls, which I thought must once have been white, old band posters and vintage LP covers were held in place by pushpins.

"So, this is where the magic happens," I said, surveying the space. Sunlight poured in through a wide window overlooking the unkempt backyard. The room smelled fusty, like old libraries and museums, and I felt myself relax. Now that I was safely inside, it seemed less daunting.

"Yep, this is it," Liam confirmed. "Our little hideaway." He stuck his hands in his pockets and looked out over his kingdom. "I moved to Chicago a few years back, so this is a handy base to have when we're in town."

I thought of all the music that must have been born and shaped in this place, how many sparks and ideas would have seeped into these walls.

"In here is where we record," Liam said, pointing to an adjacent room. I stepped closer and saw a large study dominated by a corner desk, on top of which sat two computer screens and a mixer board. A couple of microphones sat in their stands, and the walls were covered in blankets and fabrics.

He spun around and ran a hand through his fringe. "What else? Kitchen is that way, and there's a bathroom down the hall and one upstairs." He turned to me with a lopsided smile and my heart picked up a salsa rhythm. "And that's the end of the grand tour. Can I get you a drink?"

"Sure." It was barely noon, but I'd welcome anything to soothe my nerves. "What have you got?"

"Beer, whiskey?"

"I'll take a beer, please."

"Right on. Make yourself at home."

Liam disappeared into the kitchen, and I walked over to an electric Fender resting in its stand. I ran my fingers down the metal strings and over its shiny body, admiring the multitude of dials and switches. I had no idea what they were for, and it all seemed a little out of my league.

"Gosh, I envy this," I mumbled, barely aware that I was speaking.

"What's that?" said Liam, who had returned with our beers and handed me one.

"All this." I gestured at the room. "Having a place and project to share with friends. I've always worked alone, whether playing or paint—" I paused and shook my head. "I've just never had, you know, creative partners. It seems great, to be able to inspire and feed off each other." I looked up at Liam. Lost in my thoughts, I momentarily forgot about my nervousness. "But, like, scary too, I imagine? You'd have to be really close to be able to open up like that, and make yourself vulnerable to the possibility of, I dunno, sounding like an idiot, I guess."

Liam pursed his lips as his eyes drifted over the musical debris. "You're right," he said, scratching the back of his neck. "I guess I've always taken it for granted, but yeah, it's pretty great. I've done a lot of solo stuff, too, but if you play for long enough it's almost impossible not to end up collaborating with people."

I sat down on one of the sofas and took a sip of my beer.

It felt weird to drink so soon after breakfast. "So, when did you start making music?" I asked. "And how did you learn to play the guitar?"

"It was Frank who taught me at first." He sat down opposite me and rested his bottle on the sofa's armrest. "I spent a lot of time hanging at his house. Which was great because... Well, back home wasn't much fun." He paused and took a long sip from his drink.

"That's something I can relate to," I mumbled.

"Oh, really? I guess shitty parents are universal." I wanted to ask him more, but he quickly continued. "Anyway, Frank has this amazing record collection, and he'd play me all these old songs and then show me how to replicate 'em on his guitar." A smile tugged at his mouth as he gazed into his past. "We had some good times, us two. I wasn't allowed to get my own guitar, or play music at home—"

"Why not?"

He said nothing at first, just looked down at the floor.

"I'm sorry," I said, "I didn't mean to—"

"It's alright. My parents are what you would call religious crazies. Fundamentalists."

My eyebrows shot up. "You're kidding?"

"Afraid not."

"Wow, okay. That's... Wow."

"I know, right? I think it's all bullshit, of course, but they were dead serious about it. My dad is a pastor of this small congregation, and in our house, his word was law." Liam took another sip from his bottle, his face cold.

"And he wouldn't let you play music?"

His jaw tightened. "Music was the devil's work."

"How is that even..." I shook my head, stunned with shock.

"I know. It's fucked up." Liam looked off into the corner of the room and took a deep breath. "But then Frank bought me a guitar, anyhow, and I kept it at his for years. That's when I started writing my own songs. It never felt like a choice, really. Like, I had to play or I'd go crazy. I'm sure you know what I mean."

I didn't feel that way about music, really. But I knew what he meant. I had felt that with painting once.

"So." Liam put his beer down and nodded at the instruments. "Wanna do this?"

My shoulders tightened and I wrung my hands.

"I've never…," I began, biting my lip. I felt all the shyness of a musical virgin, barely able to speak. "I've never played with anyone before. Except for Nathan, but we were just messing around. I don't know if I'm any good. I won't know where to begin."

Liam smiled at me like I was a lost puppy. "Tell you what." He stood up and grabbed an acoustic guitar from a stand. "I don't care if you're good or not, okay? Good is subjective, anyhow. Just do your thing."

He held the guitar out to me. I hesitated, then took it by its neck and slowly placed it on my lap. Liam chose another for himself and sat back down.

"You wanna start by playing something, just you? If that's easier."

"Just sing anything? Like, right now?"

Liam leaned back and slung one arm over the sofa's backrest, and flicked his fringe aside with a smirk. "There is only now," he said, looking at me intently.

I shaped a C-chord, pressing my fingers hard against the strings. I had already sung to a venue full of people, but this was far more intimate. The stakes felt much higher.

There is only now. I bit down and started strumming. The sound filled the room and seemed too loud at first, disturbing the dusty silence around us. My throat started seizing up and I began humming to keep myself from choking. Eventually

57

the humming turned to song, and soon it was like cycling; freewheeling along a smooth, downhill road towards a glittering coastline.

Liam's gaze bored into me and filled me with a warmth that spread from my solar plexus until my entire body was glowing. His attention made me focus, and there was nowhere to hide.

After I finished, the room felt awfully quiet; another song absorbed by those yellowing walls. Liam sat unmoving, head slightly tilted, eyes locked on me. My cheeks burned and I shifted my gaze to the floor.

"I love your voice," he said finally, and in an instant my heart burst from its cocoon, wings unfurling. "It's unique. Soft, but with a big range, and when you slip into your head voice your sound becomes so honest, fragile even. You've got something special."

I didn't know what 'head voice' meant, but I decided I'd figure that out later. Right now, all I wanted was to air my wings in the sunshine of his praise.

"So, I was thinking…," he began, and once again that lopsided smile found its way straight into my chest. "We've got one more show to play in town, this Friday. You want to sing harmonies on one of our tracks? I've got a song that would be perfect for you."

A dizzying wave swelled in me, foaming with exaltation and longing and nausea. "For real?"

"If you want." Liam stood up, his jeans stretching over his skinny legs, and I had to will myself not to stare. He ruffled through a pile of papers on the floor, found a sheet and handed it to me. It had hand-scribbled lyrics and chords for a song titled *I Will Be the Dust in Your Hands*. Then he sat back down with his guitar. "I'll play it to you, see what you think."

He closed his eyes briefly, and his shoulders curved as he leaned into his guitar. There was that shift again, the one I had seen on stage; that moment when he disappeared from the room and into himself. His eyes were cast down, off in the distance somewhere in that secret space where only he could go. At once he was obscured and stripped bare, removed but resolutely present as he dissolved into his song.

Gentle strums, every third stroke heavy on the E string, a soft G chord. Once again I was taken aback by his vulnerable voice, like I was witnessing something too private for me to experience this close up. His vocals crawled tentatively out of him and hit my heart like tiny daggers, daggers laced with some powerful potion I was beginning to love the taste of. It was a sad song, like most of Liam's songs seemed to be, and the words carried his sorrow with such power that my own sorrow began to stir in my chest, answering the call of its kin, wanting to come out and dance with a sadness so like itself.

He played it a few times until it started to sound familiar. I looked at the paper, nodding along to the melody, but when I tried to join in I felt a heavy lid over my mouth, a lid I had to push hard to open. I was afraid – afraid to be inadequate, to be ridiculed; but also to be good enough, because I wasn't sure where that might lead.

My voice turned from a shy whisper into song, singing the melody at first but then rising to find a harmony. Sometimes it fitted perfectly, and the resonating sound brought goose-bumps to my skin. Other times it came out all wrong and I had to stop and re-find the tune, which I could if I just relaxed and listened. Liam repeated lines and verses until my harmony had found its shape, adding depth and dimension to his creation. Sometimes I held back, waiting reverently while Liam tackled some of the more powerful lines on his own, and then I would join again. The corners of my mouth curled upward even though it was a sad song, and occasionally Liam would glance up at me and nod and smile approvingly, and I was in heaven, truly.

I didn't notice time flying by or my tummy insisting that lunchtime had long since passed. When our fingertips ached and our throats were dry, we sat back and grinned with satisfaction, and I felt like the last few hours had brought us a lot closer. But, more surprisingly, my fear had finally given up and gone hiding in a dark corner somewhere, and I stretched in the space it had left behind.

"So, you up for Friday? Just this one song. I thought we'll open with it before the full band comes on. Sound good?"

"Sounds great!" I lay back on the sofa and squealed with joy. Liam responded with a laugh, husky and sweet as fudge. His murky pond eyes twinkled with something irresistible, and I knew I had no choice but to go seek it out.

NINE

"Hazel, you all set?"

I was standing on trembling legs in the wings of a large concert venue, watching the stagehands tape setlists to the floor. Lawson, who seemed to be at the epicentre of the pre-gig flurry whizzing its way through the backstage area, had stopped to check on me.

I interrupted my nail-biting and responded with a tense nod.

"Are you sure? Anything you need?"

"I'm okay, thanks, Laws." I braved a smile, even though my heart was running a marathon and I had to gasp for breath to keep up with it. The clock was ticking. Through the wings I could see the colossal crowd, all awaiting the arrival of Object Impermanence. But first, they would get *me*, and I wasn't sure how they'd like it.

I was beginning to regret my choice of outfit. Liam had told me to go casual, so I had carefully picked out something that would feel casual but still look fun. With Nathan's help, I had settled on a striped T-shirt and navy-blue cotton dungarees. Looking at it now, though, I felt like an oversized toddler, and was kicking myself for always dressing like a child.

Suddenly the music stopped and a hush went through the crowd. My eyes widened and a chill spread up my spine. *No, no, no...* What the hell was I doing? I shook my head and took a couple of steps back before I spun around and bumped straight into Liam.

"Whoa!" he said, blocking my escape with an outstretched arm. "Where do you think you're going?"

"I can't do this!" I hissed.

"Yes, you can." He flashed me a teasing grin. "I've seen it."

Someone shushed us from the back. Liam put his hand on my arm and gave it a light squeeze.

"Come on," he whispered. "If I can do it, so can you."

I held his eyes for a moment, trying to believe his words.

"It's time," he said. I turned around and saw the organiser in the opposite wing waving us out. A bright spotlight flooded the stage and Liam sauntered into it like it was nothing, while I scurried closely behind. The crowd exploded.

"We love you, Liam!"

Just keep breathing, I told myself, and focused all my will on remaining upright.

Liam picked up his guitar and slung it over his shoulder, and I took my place by the microphone next to him. He checked his tuning and adjusted the A-string with a slight twang. It seemed like he didn't notice all the people screaming for him. When he was done, he flicked his fringe aside and leaned into the mic.

"Hey." His soft voice filled the venue and brought down another deafening roar. Some girls near the front looked close to fainting already. "Thanks for coming, it's great to be back.

I'd like y'all to welcome Hazel, who's singing a tune with me tonight. Hazel, meet everyone."

I tried to swallow but my heart seemed to be in the way, so I grabbed the mic stand just to have something to hold onto. I mumbled a croaky greeting, and to my surprise they all welcomed me with hoots and hollers, shouting my name.

"Here we go." Liam cast his eyes down and pressed his fingers to the strings. He grazed the microphone with his mouth and for a moment all I could see were those lips, and a surge rolled through my tummy and I couldn't tear my eyes from him. A brief pause hung in the air and expanded to fit all of eternity and all the beautiful, shimmering things Liam had awoken in me, and in that space I took a breath and held it. Then he began.

The instant his voice turned to song and that vulnerable, heartbroken boy took his place, everyone fell silent. We all felt his sorrow keenly; it was our sorrow, too. But he made it appealing, beautiful even, and his words seemed to reveal a kind of meaning or purpose to our pain.

I looked out over the crowd, hundreds or maybe thousands of eyes, expectant or delirious or full of awe, all locked on Liam. And me, next to him *me*, about to sing. This was it – do or die.

I opened my mouth and my voice spilled out the way blossoms open suddenly at dawn, and floated through the air like a twirling satin ribbon. Everything fell away and I forgot all about fear and insecurity. I was fully present in each vowel that escaped my lips, my mind immersed in the resonating notes. The mesh of the microphone smelled faintly of metal under my nose, and the bass of the E-string vibrated in my gut.

We reached the final verse and, as we had practiced, I let Liam take the final two lines by himself while I sat back with the rest of the auditorium, motionless, breathless.

Then they erupted. I broke into a smile and looked over at Liam. He returned my gaze with that titillating glint, and once again my knees began to give way. This was too much for my heart to contain.

"Hazel Griffin, e'rbody! Show her you love her!"

Claps and whistles rained around me. I smiled and waved and figured I probably looked like an idiot, then hurried off the stage before I fainted in front of everyone.

Half-blinded by the spotlights, I walked through the dark wing, hyperventilating and wringing my hands in a dizzying blend of agony and ecstasy, when I bumped shoulders with Ivy on her way onto stage.

"Sorry," I mumbled, but she was already out in front of the audience, her hair ablaze in the bright lights, her slim hips swaying in a long-sleeve dress of forest green silk. She lifted her violin and tucked it under her chin, her graceful arm poised with the bow.

I turned around and walked through the backstage area to join the audience. When I found Nathan, I was still trembling.

"Amazing!" he whispered, patting me on the back.

"I can't believe it!" I leaned my head back to catch my breath, my eyes bouncing all over the high ceiling.

Then I turned to watch the show. They sounded different with a full band. Some songs were slow and sad, but others were more feisty, angry, with Liam spitting his frustrations down the mic, and when he raised his voice in screaming agony I could feel something deep and old inside me stirring.

It irked me how skilful Ivy was with her violin. The long, mournful notes lent the music an enchanting air, and added a layer of emotion that I couldn't help but be moved by. And it was clear that she was moved, too. I had only seen her porcelain face emotionless and cold. But the strings sang her alive, her eyes squinting, her mouth twisting with each melancholy tune, as though her violin were the puppeteer pulling her strings. She was spellbinding, and I found myself staring at her almost as much as at Liam.

* * *

After the gig had finished, I was swept along with the crowd as they drifted towards the bar. Strangers were patting me on the shoulder and saying how well I had done, and I responded with a moronic grin and stuttered thanks.

"A beer, please," I said to the barman, but he couldn't hear me over the clamour. Then I felt a hand on my back.

"I've got a better idea." I turned around and saw Liam, his eyes glinting with mischief. "Wanna get out of here?"

Lightning bolts shot between us and something inside me caught fire. He led me through the crowds, ignoring their pleas for selfies and autographs. We escaped into a hallway and started up a spiral staircase. The night had completely gone to my head and I felt hot and fearless. Liam turned and took my hand and my heart jolted again, and he dragged me further up the staircase, round and round, until we reached the top floor.

"This is it." He pushed open a creaky door and we stepped into a dusty old attic room, its slanted roof supported by wooden beams covered in cobwebs. A couple of moth-filled lamps glowed with an eerie, jaundiced light. "I'm a sucker for secret hideaways."

"Oh, wow!" My eyes flitted about the room. "This place is amazing!"

"Yes! I was hoping you'd like it." He sat down on a beat-up vintage sofa and stretched his legs out, resting one ankle over the other. "I know the guy who owns the building. He put me here once when I needed somewhere to, um, cool down."

I gave him a quizzical look but wasn't going to press. "Well, I love it," I said as I walked over to the seating area. "It smells like grandparents and old times. Just look at these chairs!" I sat down in an old armchair and ran my fingers over its faded leather.

Liam rested his hands behind his head and looked at me, studying me. My eyes shifted nervously to the floor, then back up to meet his probing gaze.

"Are you into coke?" he asked.

"Coke? Like Coke or Pepsi?"

"No," he chuckled, flicking away his fringe. "More like cocaine or heroin."

"Oh." I bit down hard, wishing I could sink right through the creaking floorboards. I was such an idiot. "Er, duh," I said, trying to laugh it off. "Umm, well, I've actually never tried it."

"Do you mind if I have some?"

"Uh, sure. I mean, go for it."

He produced a small paper pouch from his pocket, unfolded it carefully, pulled out a key, dipped it in, and took a sniff. I watched him intently, looking for a reaction or some kind of shift. But he just put it back in his pocket and sat back in his chair. Now I was curious.

"What does it feel like?"

"Coke? Oh, it's the best. Have you really never tried it before?"

I shook my head. It felt tempting and dangerous and scary all at once.

"It…" He thought for a second. "It sharpens you. And it makes everything interesting. It's like it opens up some door that's usually closed."

Now, that got my attention. I was sure I had a whole bunch of doors that needed opening.

"Wanna try some?"

I sat on my hands, nibbling on my lip as my smile widened. This was a trip of adventures and a night of firsts.

"Okay, sure."

He pulled out the pouch, scooped up a small amount on his key and held it out to me. I leaned in, pinching one nostril and aiming with the other, and sniffed up the little white pile. I couldn't feel anything.

I rubbed my nose. "Did I get it?"

"Yeah, you don't feel it go in, it's really smooth."

Then I felt myself take a deep breath and let it out slowly, emphatically. My eyes opened wider, and I sucked on my tongue and it felt *nice*. This wasn't so bad. I felt my heart go a little faster, but then it always did when I was next to Liam. I filled my lungs with air and tasted the dusty decades that had passed in this attic. Then I stood up and, with a sigh, landed myself on the sofa right next to Liam.

"I find you so fascinating," I said, just blurted it out of nowhere, taking myself by surprise. "Oh, sorry! I don't know why I said that."

Liam laughed. "That's okay. You did just snort truth serum, my friend. No, really, it's okay. You know, I find you fascinating, too."

My face dropped. "You don't! Really? How?"

"You're, like, I dunno. You're different to other people. You seem so honest and authentic." He studied me with narrowed eyes. "There's no mask on you. You're just *you*, without any pretence or fakery. It makes for a nice change. Being around you makes me feel like the world isn't completely cynical."

I stared at him, my wild heart beating a rapid rhythm. Liam found *me* fascinating? Glory!

A restless energy fizzed through my limbs and I had to stand up and walk around. I felt present, strong. "I *love* this room!" I said, heading over to a small window where I could peer out over Madison's rooftops. A deep cobalt blue had spilled over the sky like a toppled bottle of ink, and a thin moon was slowly rising.

"Me too." Liam stood up and walked over to me. "When we play here, I always come up here to warm up for a bit, play to myself. I feel comfortable in this space. Like I'm all alone."

I turned to face him. "You like being alone?"

He thought for a moment. "Yes and no. Alone, or in the right company. It's just, these last few years I feel like I'm always surrounded by people. The band or fans or the record label people. There's always someone at my heels. It's nice to get a break from all that."

"I get it. I guess I prefer company. I spent so much of my childhood alone."

"Oh yeah?" Liam took a step closer and my heart picked up its pace. "Why's that?"

I let out a long sigh. "I wouldn't know where to begin."

Liam shrugged. "Anywhere's good."

I thought of all the lost years, of being dragged out of school, a prisoner in my own home. My throat began to seize up and I swallowed hard to keep from choking.

"My parents were, um, less than ideal."

"Welcome to the club," said Liam.

"My mum was very demanding. She needed a lot from me, more than I could give. And when I couldn't be who she needed me to be, she became angrier, more depressed. I always felt that it was my fault."

Liam said nothing, just kept his steady gaze on me.

"I never knew where the line should be drawn. It's like, I

owe her a lot. And now I've left her, and she has no one to look after her. I feel so guilty."

I clutched my stomach, where my duties towards my mother always made themselves known through tight knots. I hadn't planned on talking about my tedious past, but now the floodgates were open, and out poured a torrent of painful memories.

"Would it be okay if...," I began. The rush was already fading, and I wanted it back. Anything to distract my mind. "Um, if I had a bit more?"

"Coke? Sure." He pulled it out and we each had a sniff. I was bolder now that I knew it wasn't going to hurt. I sucked it up and almost instantly felt another wave of heat flushing my ears, and I could feel my pain being shovelled aside like a spadeful of soft snow.

"It feels good," I said, looking at Liam with a tunnel vision that filtered out all the hurt and troubles, and all I could see were his earth-brown eyes and pale skin and the way he smiled at me. A cautious smile, an understanding smile, his dark eyebrows still set in that slight frown. It felt good to have him there, listening to me vent, holding my pain for a moment.

"I'm sorry about your mom." He was so close now, I could smell the alcohol on his breath. "If everyone wasn't so fucking broken, maybe they could be decent enough to raise their kids as they should be raised, with love and compassion... But the sad fact is, everyone is broken. Everyone is mired in pain, and it spills over to their kids. And so the cycle carries on."

I wanted to ask what he meant, what his parents were like, but suddenly I was acutely aware of how close he was, how his eyes were drilling into me, how I could feel his warm breath against my lips. The knot in my gut had turned into a different kind of ache, an overpowering longing, and I had to suppress an urge to touch his face, to run my fingers over his cheeks, to—

Then he took a step back and turned away, and I was jerked out of our bubble like a broken spell. I held my breath, wondering if I had done something wrong.

Liam ran a hand through his hair and looked back at me, drawing a sharp breath.

"There's... something I've been meaning to ask you."

"What's that...?"

"You know we'll be leaving the day after tomorrow, getting back on the road."

Oh.

I hadn't known that.

I had been so swept up in the moment that I hadn't even thought about any kind of tomorrow.

"But, uh, I thought, I don't know..." He scratched the back of his neck. "I don't know what your plans are for the rest of your stay, but I thought maybe you'd like to join us?"

What?

I stared at him in disbelief. I thought I must have misheard him.

"Sorry, er... Are you asking if I want to join you on tour? Like, to help out, or...?"

"No, like, as a vocalist. I spoke to Lawson and he'd be psyched to have you. We've got a few months left of this tour, but it's a pretty relaxed schedule, and you'll get to see a lot of the country. Unless, I mean, you might have other plans."

Did I have other plans? Umm, let's see... Nope!

My face flushed and I yelped as I slapped my palms against my cheeks. I couldn't help myself. Liam laughed and relaxed his shoulders. "I'll take that as a yes?"

I nodded, grinning. "I'm sorry, I'm so fucking uncool," I said, rolling my eyes at myself and giggling. "But, just, wow!"

Liam chuckled, and I thanked my lucky stars that he

seemed to find my bumpkin dorkiness adorable, somehow. My blood rushed through my veins like a flood after the thaw, and I wanted to dive in and let myself be taken wherever that whirling meltwater wanted to flow. The great big universe was infinite and beckoning, and I was at the precipice, ready and willing to jump.

TEN

I spent the following day with my nose in a road map, tracing the routes I'd be travelling with the band. It all seemed like a dream I might wake from any moment. As always, my mother was lurking in the back of my mind, eager to remind me what a naive nobody I was. I tried my best to shut her out, determined not to let her ruin this for me.

She hadn't contacted me since I left. But then, I hadn't contacted her, either. Perhaps we both needed some space. I hoped the Atlantic Ocean would be space enough.

Sunday afternoon, Nathan drove me to the address Liam had sent me. The GPS guided us to a large drive behind a garage littered with workshop paraphernalia.

"Oh, my… Do you think that's it?" I pointed to a vehicle that sat at the far end of the yard.

"Whoa," said Nathan. "Must be."

It was a classic American school bus, painted top to bottom in pale teal, like a summer sky at dawn. It looked like a wonderful vintage dream, my very own enchanted carriage that would whisk me away on unimaginable adventures.

Lawson appeared from behind the bus, carrying two big

coils of cables. He spotted us and waved us over, then went to put the cables into the undercarriage, which was already stuffed with bags and boxes.

"Nooo way!" I squealed in rising falsetto as I climbed out of Nathan's car. "*This* is your tour bus?!"

Lawson beamed with pride and put his hands to his hips, which made him look even more long and lanky. Lovely Lawson, with his big, adorable heart. I was glad he was part of the tour.

"Behold," he bellowed like a circus ringmaster, "the highway hero of the hour, the Interstate Marvel, from school to cool!"

"You *made* this? No! You *did?*" I was nearly skipping with joy, and Lawson seemed pleased at my reaction.

Nathan removed his shades with a low whistle. "Dude, that is one sweet ride."

"Thanks, man," Lawson grinned.

Nathan walked down the side of the bus, checking out every angle, stroking the smooth paint. Then he stuck his head through the open door to check out the interior, and re-emerged with a big grin. "What a job! How long'd it take ya?"

"A few months, give or take. Finished her a month ago and took her on the road right away. Just had her back here for a few minor tweaks and repairs. She's good as new again." Lawson gave his bus an affectionate pat.

"Impressive work!" Nathan looked at me as I grabbed my bag out of the backseat. "Looks like you're about to have a great time. I'm almost jealous." A roguish grin spread over his face.

"Oh, Nathan," I began, and could feel myself welling up. "Thank you so much for everything! This is all thanks to you."

"Oh, don't go all soppy on me now, girl," Nathan said, but

he opened his arms and embraced me in a hug that said he was feeling quite soppy, himself.

"You be good now," he said. "Don't be scared. You can do this. It's going to be fantastic." An uncharacteristic earnestness had seeped into his voice, and a single tear trickled down my cheek. Nathan smiled and ruffled my hair, and then he got back in his car. With one final wave he roared out of the yard, and I was left hovering on the next step on my journey. Lawson looked over at me, and I raised my shoulders in a what-do-I-do-now shrug.

"Welcome aboard, miss," he said. "May I take your bag?"

He heaved my bag onto his back, then held his arm out as though helping a lady onto a horse and carriage. I laughed and accepted his invitation, and we climbed up the steps into the bus.

The driver's seat looked like any other school bus driver's seat, but the rest of the interior had been entirely ripped out and rebuilt.

"Holy baloney, Lawson! You did all this?"

"Well, it was a communal effort, really." He put my bag in a corner and looked around. "I suppose yours truly thought up most of the design, and the little extras and clever storage solutions, they were all mine. I had loads of fun figuring out how to piece it all together. I guess that's just how my brain works. But everyone helped."

His long arms swayed this way and that as he excitedly showed me around.

"Over here, we have the kitchen-slash-chillout area."

We walked up to four sets of double seats facing each other, with small tables in the middle, like little diner booths.

"Most people would build plain sofas lining the walls like this," he said, gesticulating towards the long edges of the bus. "I don't like that. I like the booths, they create a better atmosphere. Sometimes you want to hang out alone or just a couple of people. This way, you don't have to sit all together all the time." He shook his head and his mushroom mop swayed back and forth. "Nah, I prefer this more intimate style."

I looked around and nodded in agreement. It looked very cosy. I couldn't wait to sit in one of those booths with Liam. Just me and him, all close and snuggled up together.

"And here's the kitchenette." Lawson pointed to a small worktop with a tap and sink. "We don't cook on the road, we eat out or get takeout. But there's a coffee maker and a fridge, which is all we need."

A mini fridge and a cupboard were beautifully integrated underneath the countertop, and above it a coffee machine had been fixed to the wall. It was all fresh and new and smelled of sawdust.

Lawson carried on towards the back of the bus. "Here are our storage cupboards," he said, gesturing at two wardrobe-sized cupboards on either side of the aisle. "And finally, ta-daa, the dormitory!"

At the back were three sets of bunk beds – one along the rear of the bus, and two more on either side of the aisle. They were walled in with sheets of plywood, and each had a little curtain you could pull across to create some illusion of privacy.

"This is amazing, Lawson! I am so impressed. So much effort!" I was nearly jumping with excitement and couldn't wait to get on the road in this fabulous ride.

"Worth every drop of sweat," he said, his chest swelling with pride.

"I bet!" I pointed to the top bunk on my right. "May I?"

Lawson nodded with a satisfied smile that linked his big ears. I was much shorter than him and had to climb up by stepping on the bottom bunk. Heaving myself up, I managed to crawl into the little cocoon.

"Oh maaan," I exhaled, melting into the mattress. "I'm never coming down from here."

"Of course, we don't sleep here much. It's only if we're on the road overnight, or for on-the-go naps. Mostly, we stay in motels or with friends."

I peered out over the edge and gave Lawson a dreamy smile. "I think I prefer these to regular beds."

Lawson let out a small laugh, and I noticed his cheeks went a little rosy. He was such a lovely guy, and he had put so much effort into this. I hoped the others appreciated him like he deserved.

"Right, we'll be off soon." He went to grab my bag and placed it in the cupboard to my left. "This here will be your shelf. Go ahead and make yourself at home. I'll make some coffee."

I went to sit in a booth while Lawson put on a pot, and the bitter smell mingled with the scent of fresh wood. Soon I had a steaming cup in my hands, and I leaned back to savour the moment.

Through the window I could watch the ongoing preparations. Victor had arrived with a clipboard and a pencil tucked behind his ear, which he pulled out once in a while to tick something off. He was wearing a chequered, short-sleeve collar shirt and looked every bit the responsible tour manager. Lawson was bouncing back and forth, doing some final checks. Butterflies raged in my stomach.

When I saw Ivy walking across the yard, the butterflies were replaced by a wild stampede. She strutted in on suede heels, copper locks bouncing over her mustard dress. In one hand she held her violin case, and in the other she carried a cute but totally impractical vintage suitcase. Her boots stomped against the bus floor as she waltzed right past me, straight to the back where she heaved her bag into what I assumed was her usual cupboard. I turned back toward the window and tried to make myself small. I wasn't sure how she felt about me hijacking the tour, but I sure felt like an imposter.

"Hazel," she said, icicles dangling from each consonant, and I swung around to look at her. Without invitation, she plonked herself down opposite me and studied me with piercing emerald eyes. Resting her elbows on the table between us, she laced her lilywhite fingers together. Her nails were shiny mother-of-pearl with perfect whitened edges and smooth cuticles. I couldn't help but glance at my own nails, which were all torn from me nervously pulling at them whenever I got a little anxious or excited. Which was pretty much all the time. I sat up a little straighter and hid my hands under the table, feeling like an ungainly beast next to her.

"Hi," I ventured, treading carefully.

"So, you'll be joining us," she said, her face as flat as a closed book.

"Uh, yes. Yes, I am."

"Have you been touring before?"

"No, but... Er. I pick things up quickly."

"Well, this one's a bit different to regular tours, anyhow." She leaned back and ruffled her ginger locks. "Since we got our own bus and everythin', we can take it a bit easier. You'll be fine."

"Sounds good," I mumbled, searching for any hints of what was going on beneath that ivory surface. "I'm, uh, very excited to be here."

"Ladies," came a very familiar voice, titillatingly hoarse from incessant singing and drinking and smoking. Liam came walking up the aisle and sat in the booth opposite. "On the road again!" he said, opening his guitar case. "Good to finally get outta here."

"Hey, Liam," Ivy simpered, curling her coral lips. "I was just welcoming Hazel on the tour."

"Awesome!" He heaved one leg onto the table and leaned back with the guitar against his chest, plucking a melancholy tune.

"Oh, yeah, let's do this," said Ivy, snapping open the latches on her violin case. She didn't bother with the shoulder rest, just tightened her bow and rested it on her strings. Then she locked eyes with Liam, and they nodded to the rhythm until she raised her head and filed out a clear, dominant note which sailed gracefully through the air. Their synchronicity felt like a sort of foreplay, intimate and electric, and I could only sit there and stare dumbly.

After they finished, I offered some awkward applause.

"Don't worry, Haze," Liam said. "We'll teach you all these songs. There's not a lot of time to practice for tomorrow's gig in Salt Lake, but when we get to San Francisco we'll get you up to speed. Sound good?"

I couldn't wait to learn them all so that I didn't have to feel like such an outsider.

"Sounds great," I replied. "I'll work really hard, I promise."

Liam laughed. "Don't worry, you're not an intern. You'll rock it."

"Well, still," I mumbled, picking at my cuticles, but then my eyes drifted over to Ivy's perfect hands and I forced myself to stop. "I hope I'll be of some use."

"You definitely will. I've wanted to add a female vocalist for ages."

I looked over at Ivy, searching her for a reaction.

"Ivy, you—?"

"I can't sing for shit," she said, with disinterest more than insecurity.

"She really can't," Liam chuckled, and carried on strumming.

"Room for two more?" Mango came and sat down opposite Liam, and Lawson squeezed in next to me. Finally, Victor came onboard and put his clipboard to the side.

"All set," he said, throwing a thumb in the air. "Let's go."

And so we started our journey west. Salt Lake City was many miles away and Victor and Lawson would take turns driving through the night. The rest of us spent the evening talking and singing, and after a few beers the night became a blur of laughs and jokes and a sense that I could become a part of this group. As we put the miles behind us, a wildness seeped into my veins, and I felt like the star of some epic tale; the ragamuffin who ran off with the circus.

The road sliced straight as a ruler through the Midwestern plains. After Salt Lake, that same road would take us all the way to San Francisco, the city of love and fog and their iconic bridge. I was going to see the Pacific Ocean for the first time.

Long after the sun had tipped over the horizon and the sink was full of empty beer cans, we crawled into our bunk beds and pulled the curtains for the night. I struggled to rest at first. It was all too much – the fluttering in my tummy, the beating of my hopeful heart, the giddy energy fizzing down my spine. My lips were sore from nervous nibbling, and I had to force myself to relax. I had no idea what lay ahead. But that was okay. That was exactly what I had wanted. No more dreary routine, no more indistinguishable days that all merged into one continuous, drab existence.

Finally, adventure.

Soon, my limbs grew heavy and my mind soft, and I settled into the motion of the bus as it rocked and rolled ever onward beneath the endless sky.

ELEVEN

Nebraska slipped by while we slept. We woke to a cloudy morning over Wyoming, where grassy prairie stretched around us, touching the horizon in every direction. Never before had I seen such a vast land of nothing, and I gazed in awe as we rode on and on through that wild and empty place. I could sense the distance between me and home stretching like a rubber band as we swallowed the miles leading west.

Mid-afternoon, we finally reached Salt Lake City. It lay sprawled in a flat grid that criss-crossed the plains, and we stopped at a motel on the edge of town. I tumbled off the bus, bleary-eyed and lightheaded, grateful to be back on solid ground.

Beyond the low-lying city sat a row of rugged mountain peaks. It looked surreal, like an old-school movie backdrop. We were on the cusp of June, and the air was fresh and soft and just warm enough. I stretched my aching body and turned my face to the sun, oblivious to the cracks that were about to appear in the shiny surface of this new life of mine.

After unpacking and freshening up, we grabbed a late

lunch in a diner with burgundy booths, sizzling burgers and endless coffee refills. After a morning of nothing but biscuits from the bus stash, we wolfed down supersize meals with all the extras. But Liam, I noticed, mostly picked at his veggie burger, and started on the beers while the rest of us were still sipping soft drinks.

"Aaah, life on the road," said Mango, as he surveyed his double cheeseburger. "You go hungry for hours, and then you feast! It's a real rollercoaster. Best get used to it, Hazel!"

I laughed. "It's not too bad so far."

"I swear," Lawson said, with a rueful shake of his head. "Every time we come back from a tour, we promise ourselves we won't go out again for a while. But we just can't seem to help ourselves."

I smiled and slurped my Coke. "How many tours have you been on?"

"Seven or eight?" Mango mumbled through a mouthful of cheesy beef.

"Uh-huh," Lawson said, pointing to Mango. "Like, one a year since we met you, right?"

"Oh, is that how you got started?" I asked.

"Yeah, Liam and I had been playing for a few years when we met Mango at an open mic in Madison." He looked at Mango with a smirk. "Remember how you were all pissed about the singer-songwriters with their guitars?" He turned back to me. "He was mad that drummers can't do open mics, 'cause people don't want to hear a drummer without a band."

"True story," Mango nodded. "Society is rigged against solo drummers."

"So, we joined the battle against this injustice and picked Mango up. Saved him from his tragic bandlessness. And that's how it all began."

"*Entonces,*" said Mango, "it seems we are all here thanks

to *me*." He straightened an imaginary tie and put on a haughty expression, which made me giggle.

"We tried out a few songs together. Liam already had a bunch written." Lawson brushed the salt off his hands and turned to Ivy. "Next, we dragged you into it."

"I met Liam at a party in college," Ivy said, and picked up her drink. She sucked on her straw with an innocent look, and I tried to ignore the images that flooded my brain. "When he found out I played the violin, he practically forced me to play some. He asked if I'd be up for trying out for a band. Turned out it sounded real nice all put together."

I nodded, slurping my drink a little too loudly before I realised it had finished. "Um, so, what about you, Victor?"

Victor, who had been quietly enjoying his meal, dabbed a napkin at his mouth. "I was hired later to do the accounts, but gradually I got more involved in the process, fixing merch and booking gigs. Turns out organising tours is a lot more fun than spreadsheets." He looked at me over the rim of his glasses. "And I *like* spreadsheets, so that's saying something."

"He really does." Mango gave me a faux-serious stare. "The man is a freak."

Victor shrugged and smiled, while placing his cutlery carefully alongside his empty plate.

"And what about the name?" I asked. "Object Impermanence, what does that even mean?"

Everyone turned to Liam, who was sitting at the end of the table. Throughout the meal he had sat there, mute and mulling, barely looking at us. He put his beer down and met my eyes. "Have you heard of object permanence?"

I shook my head. People often seemed to know a lot more than I did, and it made me feel stupid.

"Well, it's this stage where a baby realises that things exist even when they can't see 'em. At first they freak out, 'cause if they can't see mommy they think she's gone forever, until they can see her again. At some stage, they develop enough understanding to say, alright, she's probably around somewhere, even though she's not in front of me."

"Right." I nodded.

"But shit doesn't last forever, and we can't rely on anything to always be there. So, Object Impermanence. Just stating the truth." He shrugged. "Everything ends sooner or later."

* * *

That night, a local ukulele duo had the task of warming up the audience. While their folksy tunes rolled through the venue I hovered backstage, trying to make friends with my usual pre-stage jitters. Liam spotted me wringing my hands in agony and went to get us a couple of drinks from the bar.

"Some oil for the gears," he announced, handing me a plastic cup of foaming lager. "It helps the nerves." He raised his drink to me and took a sip.

"Right," I laughed. "As if *you* ever have trouble with nerves." I expected him to laugh along with me, but he just raised his eyebrows and took another gulp. Feeling a little awkward, I looked down at my drink and grasped for something to say. "It doesn't seem to be getting any easier. Not just yet, anyhow."

"Oh, come on now, Hazel-like-the-colour." Liam leaned an elbow on my shoulder, and I noticed he seemed a little unsteady. Edging closer, he lowered his voice to a conspiratorial whisper. "You wanna know a secret?"

I smiled. "Always."

"It's like this." As he straightened back up, some beer sloshed out of his cup and landed on the floor with a splash. "Your life," he continued, pointing at me, "is determined by the story you tell yourself."

He looked at me as though he had just divulged the mysteries of the universe. I waited for him to elaborate, but he just shrugged and took another sip.

"Umm... What?"

"Look." He shook his fringe aside and sat down on the floor. I sank down next to him, careful to avoid the sticky puddle. "Every day, you live your life based on the story you tell yourself. You wake up and go, 'I'm Hazel, this is where I've been, this is what I do. This is who I *am*.' Thing is, though, that's not the only way to tell your story. It can go however you want it to." He drilled his eyes into mine. "And I get the feeling that in *your* story, you're barely even the main character. Like you're making yourself so small."

"Oh." I didn't know what to say to that, so instead I busied myself with running a fingertip along the rim of my cup.

Liam threw a palm up. "I dunno. But it looks to me like you could give yourself a bit more credit. Make yourself your own headline act."

I drank a mouthful of beer and pulled my knees to my chest, looking at my rainbow shoes. He tilted his head and searched for my eyes.

"Hey. I mean this in a good way. You know that, right?"

"Yeah," I mumbled, avoiding his gaze. "I just... I don't know how to change it, though."

Out of the corner of my eye I could see his lopsided smile grow into a grin.

"It's simple. If you've put everyone else on a pedestal, all you gotta do is build one for yourself, too."

A wave of applause signalled the end of the opening act. Liam stumbled to his feet and held a hand out to me.

"C'mon. Time to get ready."

* * *

Out on stage, the world was once again obliterated by those bright lights and the feeling of everyone's eyes on us. I thought about what Liam had said and closed my eyes as I heard my voice pour out of the speakers. This was *my* voice. It was *me* on stage, in front of a thousand people. Yet I felt so small, exposed, like a tortoise without its shell. Maybe Liam was right.

Halfway through the song, I was yanked out of my trance when Liam suddenly went silent. I carried on singing while glancing nervously at him. He seemed a bit worse for wear, wobbling slightly but still strumming his guitar. I pulled my shoulders back and pushed for volume, now that I was singing on my own. The headline act, with her heart in her throat. Then Liam leaned into the mic and picked up the lyrics, and I stood back in relief.

When the song finished, generous applause filled the room. I gave a modest bow and slipped away to join the audience. Swallowed up in the crowd I could be anonymous again. I found a spot close to the stage and locked my eyes on Liam. I loved watching him perform. All pressure was off and I could just relax and listen, and study him as he slipped in and out of this dimension.

But something was off tonight. He was unusually chatty in between songs, to the audience's great delight. He danced clumsily and twirled the microphone cable around his legs, and I could see the others exchanging worried glances. Each time they finished a song, he bent down and took another swig of his drink. An uneasy feeling settled in my stomach and I whispered a silent prayer. *Come on, Liam. Hold it together.*

I looked over at Lawson, who kept a steady gaze on Liam. Occasionally his eyes would drift out over the crowd, and then straight back to his unruly comrade. Ivy, too, cut her eyes over to Liam, her china doll face just a tiny bit ruffled with concern. Mango seemed oblivious, tucked away behind his drum set. I looked around for Victor, but figured he was out by the merch table.

As they reached the end of a rowdy song, Liam yanked the microphone out of its stand and stepped up to the edge of the stage.

"Well, hell, e'rybody!" he slurred. "What a pleasure to be here." The crowd howled.

Lawson looked out over the room and found me. I raised my eyebrows and he responded with an uncertain shrug.

"I love this tour," Liam continued, his foggy eyes drifting across the space in front of him. "Friends and music on the road, what could be better? And on our own terms, in our own time. We don't have to rush so goddamn much. Everyone's always in such a hurry…"

I squeezed past a few people so I could get closer.

"Big up to our tour manager, Victor, my man, where you at?" Liam shielded his eyes as he scanned the crowd. "Well, he's around here somewhere. He organised this whole damn thing and he's done a fucking good job of it!"

More claps and shouts. Then Liam went quiet and held the mic to his chest. Swaying slightly, he didn't say anything for an uncomfortably long time. Lawson started plucking an intro on his bass guitar in an attempt to get back on track, but Liam didn't move.

"Big thanks to all of you," he mumbled into the mic. "To my band, and our fans, and our new girl, Hazel. I don't deserve you guys."

Then he lifted his foot, and I watched in slow-motion as he tried to take a step, not realising there was no more stage in front of him. I jerked, jumping forward as though trying to catch him. A gasp went through the crowd as he tumbled onto the floor with a crashing thud.

TWELVE

I need to get out of the house. Lydia and the others are waiting for me and I pack my bag in a frenzy, but out in the hall I am blocked by Mother.

"So, you're going," she says bitterly.

"Mother…" I don't know what I can say to appease her.

Her lower lip starts quivering again, and I have to look away. I can't take any more of the crying.

Dad appears behind her, protective hands resting on her shoulders. "Hazel," he says, his voice harder than it used to be. His poor attempts at mediation have become less frequent lately.

"Don't bother, Mallory. She's made up her mind. I just don't see why she can no longer spend time with her own mother, after everything I've done for her."

She reaches into her back pocket and pulls out a pill bottle. I can't tell which one it is, but I'm pretty sure she's not following doctor's orders.

"Eleanor, dear, haven't you—"

"It's fine," she dismisses, and necks a couple of tablets.

I cringe and squeeze past them into the hallway, reaching for my coat. *I can't breathe in this house, I need out. I just want to go see my friends. Is that really so bad? Maybe I am being selfish.*

Dad heaves a frustrated sigh. "Why don't you stay and paint with your mother, like you said you would? Just tonight."

"But Dad, it's not just tonight! It's every night. I can't do it, I'm going crazy! All my friends are—"

Mother interrupts us with a sob. "I'm sorry," she says, though I know she isn't. "It just hurts, is all." She holds her chest in a grip of self-pity and walks off. "Do what you want. I'm only your mother."

I want to help her. I want her to be happy. It's just, I want to be happy, too.

I turn to leave, but I stop when I hear her stumbling into the sideboard. I twist around and see her on the floor, crouching and sobbing.

"Hazel, please." Dad makes a final, desperate attempt. "She's not well."

A familiar, hot fury wraps around my throat and begins to choke me. *Fuck! There's no way out.*

Defeated, I drop my bag to the floor. "Come on then," I say, straining to breathe through the rage that's swelling in me, and I force it down, down and away. I offer Mother an arm and she rises unsteadily, and together we walk down the hallway.

"Oh, my daughter. You'll understand when you get older. Someday, your own children will start to pull away from you. Then you'll see just how painful it is."

"Okay, Mum," I hiss through gritted teeth.

She swings her head around. "Don't call me that. Why do you call me that? You know I hate it."

"Sorry, Mother," I mutter.

Seated in her studio, she gathers her brushes and tubes. "Hazel, darling, I'm so pleased you could stay. I work much better when you're here next to me." The pills must have hit her hard because her eyes are glazed and faraway, and she's squeezing out way too much paint.

I can't pinpoint when the change began. Her shoulders hunch more these days, her head sinking into her body. There is an edge to her *jawline that wasn't there before. Her once-soft features have become harder, more dragon-like.*

She squeezes a black splodge of paint right on top of the indigo, and before I know it, she slips and knocks over a jar of turpentine. I watch in slow-motion as it topples over and lands on the floor in a supernova of shards.

"Oh, dear…" Mother stares dumbly at the mess she's made. A scream claws its way up my throat and I catch it by digging my teeth into my lower lip.

"It's okay, Mother, I'll take care of it. Why don't you go lie down?"

"Good girl, my girl," she mumbles, as I help her up and lead her to the living room sofa. "What would I do without you, Hazel? What would I do without you…"

THIRTEEN

"Liam!" I yelled, as I elbowed my way to the front. A tense silence filled the room as Lawson threw his bass aside and climbed down towards their fallen singer.

"Liam! Hey, bro, you alright? Guys, a bit of room please."

Liam was on the floor, looking dazed but unhurt. "I'm fine, I'm fine," he slurred. I froze when I saw his eyes and instantly recognised that faraway look, while painful memories knotted my stomach. Liam grasped for something solid to pull himself up, but found nothing.

Some curious audience members seemed eager to approach, but Lawson held them at a safe distance. "Don't worry, folks, he's fine," he yelled above the crowd's agitated murmur.

I took Liam's arm and lifted him off the floor. "Hey, you're okay," I said. "You'll be fine."

"Wait, what…?" Liam's unfocused eyes drifted around the room.

"It's me, Hazel."

"Oh, hey," he said, a casual smile breaking through the fog.

Lawson put his hand on Liam's shoulder. "Hazel will get you someplace where you can rest, okay?"

"Sure, yeah," Liam nodded. I wasn't sure how much he was taking in.

Lawson turned to me. "Thanks, Haze. I owe you one."

I leaned in and lowered my voice. "Is he okay?"

"Don't worry," he whispered, his hand on my shoulder. "He gets like this sometimes. It's just Liam, you know? He'll sleep it off."

I sighed and looked at Liam; this beautiful, talented boy, in such a sorry state.

"We'll finish the set and meet you back at the motel, okay?"

"Okay."

Lawson climbed back onto the stage and picked up Liam's guitar. "Sorry 'bout that, folks! Just a few too many of your delicious beers. We've all been there, right?"

The audience responded with hesitant applause and some scattered cheers from people who could relate.

"That's the spirit!" Lawson bellowed. "We got two more songs for ya! Anyone mind if I sing 'em instead?" He strummed Liam's guitar and the crowd roared. Good old Lawson, setting things straight.

Liam leaned on me as we walked towards the exit, my arm threaded around his waist. People stared awkwardly at us but I tried to ignore them. Maybe I should have taken him backstage, but I had been too shocked to think clearly. I just wanted to get him out of there.

Outside, I guided Liam onto a bench. He slumped over with a sigh, burying his face in his hands.

"Fuck," he muttered into his palms.

I didn't know what to say. After a while, I put a cautious hand on his arm. "Are you okay?"

He sat up and exhaled slowly. "Shit's spinning."

In the soft glow of the streetlights, he looked as beautiful as ever. His glorious tousle of dark hair made his face look even paler, and a shadow of stubble said he hadn't bothered shaving today. The intoxicated smirk of earlier was gone, replaced with a remorseful frown. Above us, a sliver moon hung in the sky like a secret smile.

"You want some water?" I asked. "I could get us a cab back to the motel."

He sighed and bobbed his head in a weary nod of defeat.

"It'll be okay," I said, trying to sound reassuring and wanting nothing more than to bring life back to his eyes.

* * *

"Do you have your key card?"

Liam leaned against the brick wall and searched his pockets. The door unlocked with a bleep and I led him over to the threadbare double bed, where he sank down with a groan. I hurried over to reception and got a couple of waters from the vending machine. When I came back, he sat leaning against the headboard, smoking a cigarette.

"Here, drink this." I handed him a bottle, then pointed to his cigarette. "Um, I'm not sure you can—"

"I'm sorry, Hazel," he said, earnest eyes turning to me, drowning me.

I sat on the edge of the bed and unscrewed my lid. "It's okay."

"No, it's not. Haze, I..." He leaned his head back and looked off into the distance as he sucked on his cigarette. A cloud of smoke left his mouth and I decided not to worry about motel policy for the moment. "I'm not that drunk, okay? It's just... I took some Xanax before the show, that's why. It doesn't go with the booze, so..." He ruffled his dishevelled hair and looked at me. "I just wanted you to know."

"Oh, okay." I nodded, and my mother's glazed eyes flashed through my mind. "Um. Thanks for telling me, I guess."

He fiddled with the lid of his bottle. "Fuck. I can't believe I did that again, on fucking stage." He moaned and drank a gulp of water.

"Why…," I began, unsure how much I was allowed to meddle. "Why did you take it?"

Liam pressed his lips together and looked towards the windows, where orange streetlight seeped in through the gaps in the curtains.

"It helps," he said. "Sometimes." He frowned, his sad eyes hooded, and took another sip of water.

"Helps what?" I asked.

But he couldn't answer. He sat up with a sudden jerk and dropped his cigarette. The water came spewing back up, along with everything else he had drunk that night. He heaved and fell onto the floor, holding his stomach while gasping for air.

"Oh my god." I kneeled beside him and rubbed his back uselessly. His cigarette lay smouldering on the linoleum, and I reached over and crushed it under my shoe. Eventually the heaving stopped, and his breathing slowed. He wiped his mouth and curled up into a ball.

"Just go," he said, his voice trembling.

"I'm not leaving you like this. I'll go get something to clean this up."

In reception, I was given a mop and bucket, which I carried back to the room. When Liam saw me, he rose unsteadily to his feet. "Shit, Haze, lemme do that."

"Don't be silly," I said. "You need to rest."

He looked at me for a moment, struggling to focus.

"It's fine, really. Why don't you lie down?"

He squeezed his eyes shut and staggered backwards to the bed, where he curled up with his back to me.

I cleaned up and emptied the bucket in the sink and washed up. When I was done, I walked over to Liam.

"You asleep?" I whispered. He didn't answer, so I sat on the edge of the mattress and leaned over. His breathing was regular but he didn't look restful, his face still troubled with tension.

"Don't worry," I said. I swept his fringe aside and felt his burning forehead. He looked so small and fragile where he lay with his hands clenched in fists against his chest. His Converses were a tangled mess at the end of the bed and I pulled them off, re-strung the laces and placed them on the floor. Then I cracked open a window to let in some fresh air, and settled into an old armchair in the corner. I didn't want to leave him there in case he needed to throw up again. I had heard of people on sedatives choking on their own vomit while asleep. Not on my watch.

Outside, the crickets were singing their usual lullaby, and cool air drifted in to blow away the smoke and sweat and woe of the night. I sat for a long while listening to Liam's rhythmic breathing. As I felt my own body grow heavy, images of the night whirlpooled in my head – the audience's silence when Liam fell off the stage, Lawson's calm face as he got the gig back on track, Liam's mournful eyes as he apologised. The images dissolved into a flurry of dreams featuring me and the band and Nathan and, as always, Mother.

* * *

I woke with a stiff neck, blinking in the morning light. Slowly, I sat up and rolled my aching shoulders. Then I saw

Liam sitting on the bed, fidgeting with an unlit cigarette. His weary eyes were empty, staring into nothing.

"He-hey," I stammered. I glanced at my phone. Nearly five. The room looked very different in the cold shroud of dawn. "How you feeling?"

He lowered his head, twiddling with the cigarette. I waited a moment, but he didn't respond. Perhaps I shouldn't have stayed all night. Maybe that was a weird thing to do.

"Okay, well, I'm gonna go." I pushed myself out of the chair and picked my bag up off the floor. "I'll, uh, I'll see you lat—"

"Do you regret coming with us?" His voice was frail and hoarse. I stopped and looked at him. He was still staring straight ahead.

"No," I said, shaking my head. "Why would I?"

His face softened with a sigh. "Good."

He looked so pale and his eyes were big and helpless, and I felt myself falling, losing grip. I took a step towards him.

"If you mean because of last night, don't worry. It happens, right?"

He snorted bitterly and stuck his cigarette between his lips. "Yeah. Guess it does."

I watched him light his smoke, and when he didn't say anything else, I went to the door and pushed it open.

"Hazel." I stopped and looked back at him. He tore his eyes from that faraway place and met my gaze for the first time since I woke. "Thank you. For everything."

I responded with an awkward shrug. "That's okay." He looked at me, a half-smile appearing through his bleary hangover fog. It was nothing really; I would do it again if he needed it, a thousand times over.

We were in no rush to get to San Francisco, as our gig wasn't until four days later. I crashed in my room and slept until late afternoon, waking only when I heard Lawson and the others packing things into the bus. When Liam finally emerged, quiet and shamefaced, he apologised to everyone and promised to be more professional in the future. Nobody seemed to hold it against him, although we rode mostly in silence that night, heading for the City of Love.

FOURTEEN

I woke to the sight of blue water all around us. We had finally passed the Western plains, crossing the Rocky Mountains overnight, and I was now looking at water touching the Pacific. I could hardly believe it. With butterflies raving in my chest, I jumped out of my bunk and went to sit in a booth.

Lawson was up making coffee, and Victor was at the wheel taking us along a grand, white bridge that seemed to stretch for miles across the bay. At the end of the bridge I could make out a band of bulky skyscrapers, lined up like suspects.

"So, this is it?" I said, staring at the approaching metropolis. It seemed to be brimming with promises of all things new, all things possible.

"Paris of the West," Lawson announced. He placed two cups of coffee on the table and sat down opposite me. "San Francisco is a blast, you'll see. There's no other place like it, at least not in this country. And, as a bonus," he added, blowing on his hot drink, "we've scored free accommodation, so we can chill here for a few days."

"Oh, nice! Free, how?"

"From a couple of friends in town. They're out on tour, too, so their lodger, Max, will host us at their place."

"Sweet! I can't wait to see the city." I inhaled the steam from the coffee and turned back towards the enchanting vista. Tiny speed boats carved up the water on their way under the bridge, and further up I could see long freight ships lulling on languid waves. Green hills swelled along the horizon, and the whole world seemed to be glowing in the thin morning mist.

Lawson wiggled around, trying to find room for his long legs. "Hey, by the way, I wanted to thank you for looking after Liam the other night. I'm glad we could finish the set knowing he was okay."

"It's no problem, really," I said. "Happy to help."

Lawson nodded and looked out the window. Outside, cars were overtaking us on their way across the bridge.

"Can I ask, though..." I hesitated, squeezing my mug between my hands.

He turned to me. "Sure, anything."

I looked over my shoulder to make sure everyone was still asleep. "Does it happen often? Like, does he get like that a lot?"

Lawson sipped his coffee as he considered my question. "Not too often," he replied. "Sometimes he just goes a little too far. But hey, that's Liam. He's always been that way. Daring life at every turn."

"Don't you worry about him?"

He looked into his mug. "I do. Of course I do. He's my best friend. But..." He shook his head slightly and met my eyes. "I don't think he'll ever change. I've tried, but Liam is always going to do his own thing. He's never going to change because of me, or anyone else."

I bit my lip, nodding. I had wanted Lawson to reassure

me, to tell me there was no need to worry. Many more questions bubbled in my mind, but I shut my mouth when Lawson cut his gaze to someone behind me. I glanced back and saw Ivy, looking gloriously gorgeous with a fuzzy bedhead of terracotta locks.

"Mornin', y'all."

"Hi…" I sank deeper into my seat, hoping she hadn't overheard us.

"Hey, Ives," said Lawson. "There's coffee in the pot. Sleep alright?"

"Like a log, as always," she said in her delightful twang. "Me and the I-80 are old friends."

She stretched and yawned and helped herself to a cup. I was struggling to grasp how she managed to look so annoyingly divine after these overnight bus rides, and I didn't want to stare but couldn't help myself.

"Right, nearly there." Lawson clapped his hands and stood up. "Guys!" he yelled towards the bunk beds, where Liam and Mango were still snoring behind their curtains. "Not far now. Rise and shine!"

* * *

We carried our bags into our new home, where our host told us to choose from the free beds and couches. Max looked to be in his early twenties, with black hair in tight curls and a pair of heavy-framed glasses that kept sliding down his nose.

"You weren't here last time, were you?" he said to me.

"Nope, I'm kind of a new addition to the band. I'm Hazel."

"Pleasure to have you." He smiled and shook my hand. "Can I help you with your bag?"

He took my backpack and led me upstairs. In the hallway,

I noticed a collection of abstract paintings in thick crimsons and fiery oranges, and I did a quick double-take.

Max opened a door and put my bag on the floor. "Don't tell the others, but this is our best bedroom. If I were you, I'd pick this one." He gave me a cheeky grin.

"Ha! In that case, I'll happily follow your recommendation. Thank you."

As we walked back past the paintings, I slowed down to take a closer look. Broad brushstrokes cut across the canvases, perfectly blending the vibrant hues and creating exquisite shapes and contours amid the colourant chaos.

"These are amazing," I said. "Who made them?"

"Guilty," said Max, pushing his glasses up on his nose.

"Oh! They're yours? I thought you were all musicians?"

"No, that's Heidi and Teresa. I'm just a humble painter."

"Wow." I returned my attention to the pieces. "Your style is really impressive. Unique."

"Thank you. I've got more downstairs if you want to see?"

"Sure!"

In the living room hung a series of canvases painted in the same style, except they were larger and even more absorbing. I walked up to study them each in turn.

"I don't understand how you manage to paint such chaotic blends, and still maintain this logical sense and form." Max stood behind me, his hands clasped in front of him. "And the colour combinations, they're either perfectly harmonious, where you're separating the cold and warm scales. But some, like this one, are very unexpected, yet they work so well. Oh, I like this one." I rested my eyes on a large canvas decorated with the full rainbow spectrum in a mish-mash web. I tilted my head, squinting. "You can just fall into it. Reminds me of Gerhard Richter."

"Gee, thank you." Max beamed at me. "I take it you're an artist, too?"

"Me? Oh. No. Not anymore."

"Not anymore?" He wrinkled his nose. "What happened?"

I looked back at the painting, drawn into a field of forest green dominating its centre. "It's complicated," I said. "Although I have studied plenty of Art and Art History," I added with a smirk. No need to mention that it had been at home with my mother and tutor, I figured. "So, I'm at least somewhat qualified to critique your work."

"That's cool. I've never studied the theory side of things. I just have to keep painting, you know?"

An old pain throbbed in my gut. "Yeah. I know."

We were interrupted as Liam came stomping down the stairs. "Hey, Haze. Let's set up in the garage so we can start rehearsing."

"Oh, sure." I turned to Max. "Thank you for showing me these. They're really outstanding."

"You're too kind," Max said, waving me off with an artist's modesty.

"Come on," Liam said impatiently, holding open the front door.

We set up our gear in the garage and started practicing the songs I needed to learn. It was daunting at first, especially with the whole band present. I preferred the more intimate sessions with just me and Liam. But in time fear gave way to fun, and even Ivy was supportive and encouraging.

We played for hours, and Liam's lyrics cut through my heart each time I heard them. In that dusty garage he once again shapeshifted into the vulnerable boy he became on stage, the untouchable prodigy who lived in his secret dimension. I joined in harmony and felt my voice begin to form a ladder to that other world, and I sang and sang, kept climbing.

* * *

That evening we all gathered around a campfire in the backyard. The night was balmy and soft, and scents of foreign blossoms tickled my nose. A few particularly eager stars peered down at us through the hazy sky.

Across from me, Max sat talking about the joys of San Francisco. Liam was on my left, his face expressionless as he stared into the flames. Next to him sat Ivy, sipping some rose-coloured cocktail, and Victor and Mango were chatting over to my right.

"I hear ya," Max said to me. "I'm a small-town kid, too. But after I came to the city, I never looked back. Life is just more interesting here. Especially for artists." He paused to push up his glasses. "There's always stuff going on, lots of performances and events."

"It sounds amazing," I said. "So different from what I'm used to."

"I can recommend some places you'd like. Exhibitions and stuff. If you want?"

"Yes, please! Sounds fun."

Liam huffed and got up to grab some beers from the bucket over by the grill. He popped two open, sat back down, and handed me one.

"Oh, thanks," I said, then turned back to Max. "Do you exhibit as well?"

"Sometimes. I've joined a few collabs, and done a couple of my own shows, too."

"Wow, that's great! Were you nervous?"

"Me? Never!" He laughed, and I wasn't sure if he was joking or not, but I laughed along with him. Liam shifted restlessly in his chair and I felt his leg touch mine.

"Did you sell any pieces?"

"Some," Max said, with a satisfied smile that told me he had sold quite a few.

"Impressive!" I said, raising my beer to Max. "Well deserved."

He soaked up my compliments with a big grin. I noticed Liam giving Max a hard look across the campfire, and I couldn't figure out what he had against him.

"Hey, Ives," Liam said, looking over at Ivy. "Wanna play the new song?"

"Oh, sure! I'll go get the spiel."

Ivy vanished in a bright red flurry and came back with a small glockenspiel. She cracked it open and picked up two sticks with little rubber balls at the ends, which she let hover above the steel bars. Then she looked over at Liam, who was settling in with his guitar.

"This is something I wrote a few weeks back," he explained, while tuning his strings. "I haven't played it to you yet, I've only practiced it with Ivy. Here goes."

Why had he only played it with her? A stab of jealousy hit me in the gut as I watched, again, Liam and Ivy playing together, flaunting their secret connection. He was strumming a soft A-minor, looking at her expectantly, waiting for her to join in. She nodded her head, synching with the beat, then brought down the rubber balls and a tinkle of playful notes floated into the air, chiming like tiny church bells. It was a sound that conjured images of falling snowflakes and icicles forming in hidden caves, and I felt myself being transported to some wintry wonderland. They looked at each other with secret smiles, eyes locked in tunnel vision. I wanted to smack her.

Afterward, we applauded them and Ivy took a bow, her red locks falling in front of her.

"Thanks, y'all. I'm just delighted I get to use this little

baby." She packed up the glockenspiel and hugged it to her chest. "Dun't happen often enough."

"I'll write more songs for you, then," said Liam, dousing her with a cheeky smile. My tummy twisted and I tried to look away, but my eyes kept pulling back to the two of them. Liam pointed to his pocket and mouthed something to her, and they both got up and walked inside. The sting in my gut was now burning my insides and flushing my cheeks, and I thought it might be best if I went in there to distract them, wedge myself between them, just—

Fortunately, Max got up and sat down next to me, halting my thoughts.

"So, Hazel. What type of stuff did you paint? Back when you *were* an artist?" He wiggled air quotes around the 'were' with a knowing smirk.

I was at the edge of my seat, but took a deep breath and sat back down. I hadn't noticed before that his glasses magnified his eyes, making them look comically big and quizzical. It was very cute, and I had to suppress a smile. I took a moment to consider his question.

"I guess you could classify me as part-impressionist, part-realist," I said. "I was never any good with abstract or modern stuff. These days, art can be so aggressive and on-the-nose. Everything has to be a statement. But what I liked most was to pick out small moments, tiny things that make up life which we often fail to notice, and freeze those moments in a beautiful picture."

"Like Hopper?"

"Like Hopper! Exactly. The quiet magic of everyday."

"I painted a version of Nighthawks once," Max said, "for an art school assignment. Figurative art isn't usually my thing, but I found it an interesting experiment."

"Nighthawks!" I pictured the late-night scene, the sense of isolation, the few people gathered in silence while the rest of the world slept. Countless times I had stared at the redhead who sits casually studying her nails, wondering where they had been and where they would go when they finally called it a night. Whether she loved the man in the hat. "Arguably his best piece."

"Wanna see my rendition of it?"

"Sure!"

Max led me inside, up the hall and into his bedroom. Only then did it dawn on me that perhaps he was being more than just friendly with me, but I decided to let it go.

Sure enough, next to his desk hung a very different rendition of Nighthawks. The colours were brighter, the texture rougher, the contours popping. But despite the wild colours, he had perfectly captured the stillness, and that iconic light spilling from the diner.

I gave him an appreciative smile. "I like it. You've definitely added your own touch."

"Thanks," said Max, with a dorky grin. "My one and only time painting realism, though. I'm way more drawn to the unpredictability of abstract art."

"Fair, but you know, these realists and impressionists, they deserve our respect. They were the bravest of rebels, dontcha know?" I flashed Max a teasing smile, knowing full well that this would be news to him.

"Rebels?" He scratched the curls atop his head. "I don't get it. They're the ones with all the flowers and bridges and picnics and shit?"

"Yeah, those," I grinned. "You can't fully appreciate them unless you understand the time they lived in. They went against the trends of picture-perfect grandeur and baroque drama to capture the quiet simplicity of everyday life, just for the love of it." I let my gaze drift back to the people by the diner, their blank faces like curtains to a world of secrets. "Poetic and penniless, they rejected the status quo and infuriated the snobs of the artworld as they broke all the rules and created a brand-new movement." I looked back at Max, whose face had broken into an intrigued smile, as I had known it would. "It must have taken so much courage," I said, "just to follow their hearts."

"Hey!"

We swung around and saw Liam in the doorway, glaring at us. I noticed how close I was standing to Max and took a small step back.

"I've been looking for you," Liam said, his eyes burning into mine.

"Have you?" My tone was a little more accusing than I had intended.

"Max, do you mind?" he snapped.

Max threw his hands in the air. "Whatever, dude."

I looked over to Max and back at Liam. "Okay... Sorry, Max. I'll see you later."

I walked up to Liam, and he grabbed my arm and pulled me into his own bedroom opposite, where his clothes and notes lay strewn over the floor.

"Hey!" I protested.

He closed the door and looked at me. "What were you doing with Max?" He ran his tongue over his teeth, his eyes wide and fuming.

I held his gaze and crossed my arms over my chest. "Are you high?"

"So what if I am? Answer me."

I looked at him, incredulous. "Why do I have to answer you? It's none of your business."

"Isn't it?"

"What do you mean?"

He stopped, a sentence caught in his throat. Then his face softened and his shoulders dropped. "Hazel, I..." He closed his eyes, at a loss for the words that usually came so freely to him. I held my breath, waiting. Then he opened his eyes, peering at me from behind his fringe. "I like you, okay?"

Something skipped underneath my ribs and I slowly uncrossed my arms. He tilted his head and took a step closer to me, and I lifted my face to his.

"I like you." He took my hands in his and laced our fingers together. "I want you."

I swallowed hard, dizzy from his sudden confession. For a brief moment I wondered how many girls he had told that to, but then I relaxed and let him come closer, until the heat from his body enveloped me like a magnetic field. This was too good to be true. Except...

"Liam," I said, a hot whisper against his neck.

"What?"

"I just have to know..." I hesitated, looking away. I didn't want to ruin the moment. "What about Ivy?" I put my hands on his chest, not meeting his eyes. "Are you guys, like, together?"

He cupped my face in his hands and lowered his head to catch my eye. Reluctantly, I met his gaze, afraid of what his answer might be. But he didn't answer. He just came closer, until our heavy breaths mingled and soon I knew nothing except his lips and his tongue and his hands all over me.

For a moment I nearly lost myself, blinded by the fireworks that exploded inside me. He felt warm and soft, just like I had imagined, his kisses eager and nibbly, impatiently reaching for more.

But then a cold feeling settled in my gut. I tried to think clearly. Maybe this wasn't a wise move at all. The tour, my entire adventure was at stake, not to mention my heart. But it was too irresistible, the tingles and shivers and his hands, his warm hands on me, electrifying all my nerve endings.

We pulled apart for a moment and locked eyes, his big black pupils boring into mine as though he were already inside me. The closer I got to him, the harder I was drawn in, like an asteroid on a collision course. Now, I had entered his atmosphere and was going up in flames.

He pushed me up against the door and then it was inevitable. He knew his moves like a trained gymnast; perfect coordination, years of practice. Before I knew it, my dress and bra were on the floor and his fingertips were tracing their way from my hips up to my breasts. Goosebumps spread like phosphorescence beneath his touch, sending shockwaves through my body that landed between my legs with a jolt.

Charged with his electricity, all my insecurities evaporated. I grabbed him and snapped his belt open, and he kicked off his jeans while I pulled his t-shirt over his head. As I wrapped myself around him I could feel him rub against me, hard and expectant. I pressed myself against him, filled with an overpowering ache for our bodies and minds to merge.

He picked me up and tossed me onto the bed, and held my gaze with a teasing smile as he peeled off my knickers. Then he grabbed his bag off the floor and pulled out a condom. This was really happening. I stretched my arms above my head, arching my back while the ceiling seemed to be spinning above me.

He crawled on top of me, holding and kissing me like a treasured ragdoll. I gripped his skinny torso and ran my fingers over his ribs. His hair smelled of citrus and it drove me mad as I tugged at it, buried my nose in it.

Then, suddenly, he stopped. Resting on his elbows, he looked at me with a pained expression.

"What…," I panted, trying to collect myself. "What's wrong?"

His eyes bounced over my face and he opened his mouth like he wanted to say something, but closed it again. Instead he shook his head and his fringe dropped down in his face. "Nothing, Hazelnut," he whispered.

There was something in his eyes, like sadness or hesitation, and it worried me. But before I could ask I felt him enter me, hard and warm and perfect, and I tried to just hold on to the moment, to remember all of it – his hot breath against my neck, his fringe tickling my cheeks when he leaned in to kiss me, and the way he looked at me as though he couldn't quite believe I was real.

I was falling, hard and fast; burning as I crashed into his surface.

But somewhere beyond the intoxicating urgency, I could sense that he wasn't fully there. Even with him deep inside me, I could feel a distance between us like a vacuum of light years between stars.

As we lay catching our breaths, I was surprised to feel him hold me, caress me, kiss my forehead. I didn't know what I had expected – that maybe he would get up, light a cigarette, and leave. That seemed like the sort of thing he might do. Yet here he was.

I stroked his chest and belly, the little strands of hair beneath his navel. The glow from the lamp reflected off his skin like sunlight bouncing off the ocean. His breathing slowed and I watched his stomach rise and fall like waves, the light crawling up and down the fine hairs. I wanted to ask him what was on his mind, what this meant, how he felt. But I kept quiet. Wherever we were headed, I was all in.

FIFTEEN

Amber storms out of her room and slams the door behind her. Her bags are packed. Today is her sixteenth birthday and she is out of here forever. She spots me standing in the doorway and for a moment we stare grimly at each other; sisters, and strangers. Then she rolls her eyes and hurries on down the stairs.

"Oh, look at that." I hear Mother's voice from the ground floor. "She's really leaving. How dramatic."

"Fuck you!" Amber yells, pushing past her into the hallway.

"Such a crude character," Mother sighs. "I should have named you Scarlet."

I know Mother is upset, but she doesn't let on. She stopped crying in front of Amber a long time ago, reserving her tears for me and Dad.

"Don't speak to your mother that way," Dad warns, but Amber isn't listening. He's helpless to stop the chaos that's unravelling before him.

I cautiously make my way down the stairs and see Amber pulling on her boots and coat.

"Good luck darling," Mother says. "Don't come crawling back here when you find out just how hard it is to make your own way in this world."

"Don't you worry," Amber says through gritted teeth. "I won't be crawling anywhere near you ever again." She cuts her eyes to me. "Hazel," she says in a level voice, and something twitches in my chest. "Don't let her ruin you. It's not too late."

Mother snorts and turns to me.

"Don't listen to her," she says, piercing me with dagger eyes. "I think we both know whose side you're on."

I swallow hard and look from Mother to Amber and back to Mother. I feel my knees begin to tremble. I turn back to my sister.

"Go," I mumble, looking down at the floor. "We'll be better off without you."

Mother's lips curl into a sneer. "You heard her."

Amber sighs and looks at me one last time. "You won't be her pet forever, Hazel. Count on it."

She opens the door and walks off, and without looking back she takes a left and disappears around the hedge.

Dad closes the door and turns to Mother. "Are you okay, Eleanor?"

"Me?" she snaps. "I'm fine, Mallory. Like Hazel said, we're better off without that snotty little brat."

Dad hesitates, as if there's something he wants to say, but the words seem trapped in his throat. Then he nods and leaves for his study. Mother paces out to the kitchen and I can hear the rattle of a medicine bottle, the tap opening, a glass clinking hard against the worktop.

I run upstairs to my bedroom window to look for my sister, to see if I can spot her walking down the dark November streets. But she is gone. At the bottom of our garden I see our old tyre swing, hanging limp and lonesome in the encroaching darkness.

SIXTEEN

"Morning, Mrs Doubtfire," said Lawson, as he spotted me wrestling with the espresso machine in the kitchen. It was early morning in San Francisco, and Max and the others were still asleep. "May I assist?"

"Please," I laughed, stepping aside. "I still don't know how to work this thing."

Lawson set to work while I leaned against the counter, looking out through the window above the sink. Golden rays filtered through palm trees and magnolias, covering the lawn in shifting dapples of light. The world looked bright and inviting. We had spent the past two days in the garage rehearsing the full set, but I was dying to get out and see the city.

"Feeling ready for tomorrow?" Lawson asked, as he clicked the filter handle into place and pressed a button. The machine hissed and the smell of fresh coffee filled the kitchen.

"Not sure," I said. "I think I know all the songs by now, but I'm a bit nervous still. I don't know if I can hold it together for an entire show."

"You'll be fine. We'll all be up there with you." Lawson inspected some dirty cups and gave one a rinse. "And Liam is great at improvising. He doesn't like it when things get too polished, so a few mistakes would just add a bit of charm. Anyway, you're doing great. You're picking things up real quick."

Good old Lawson.

"Okay, that makes me feel a bit better."

The coffee finished dribbling into my mug and Lawson handed it to me. "Milady."

"Thank you! You're so handy," I simpered. "I'm very impressed."

He placed another mug into the machine and prepared a cup for himself.

"So," he said, keeping his eyes on the pouring black liquid. "I see it's not just our songs you're picking up." He flashed me a knowing look and I felt my face grow hot.

"Oh, um," I stammered, looking down at my drink. I didn't realise we had been so obvious.

"I'm sorry, it's none of my business, of course. I just..." He grabbed his drink and looked me square in the eye. "I just want to make sure you're okay."

"Why wouldn't I be?"

"Well, you know. It's Liam."

There was that phrase again. *It's Liam.* It seemed rock stars could get away with anything. But I knew what he meant, and I didn't need anyone looking out for me.

"I appreciate it, Laws, I do. But I'm fine. I know what I'm getting myself into."

"I hope so," he said, contemplative eyes lingering on me.

I hoped so, too.

"Speak of the devil," said Lawson, and I looked up to see Liam walk in.

"Oh, there's talk about me, is there? By all means, carry on."

He walked up to the coffee machine and glanced over at me. "Hey," he said, a cheeky morning smile on his lips.

"Hey," I replied, my smile growing wider. He tapped out the old coffee grounds, and I tried not to stare at his snugly fitting t-shirt and his wild mess of newly washed hair. Then I noticed Lawson giving me a teasing shrug, and I waved him off with a grimace.

"Haze," Liam said, steam rising from the machine. "I thought we should go over some of the songs that we still need to nail before tomorrow. What are you doing now?"

"Nothing. Let's do it."

"I think the garage is free."

He took his freshly poured coffee and we headed for the hallway. On my way out I glanced at Lawson, and I couldn't help but notice a slight furrow in his brow.

We walked through the hall into the garage, which we had turned into a tangled mess of instruments, amps and chord sheets. Liam took our coffees and put them on a dusty shelf.

"Shut the door," he said.

"Oh yeah, sorry." I turned to close it, and then I felt him behind me, gently pushing me up against the door. He wrapped his arms around my waist and gave me a squeeze.

"Mmm…," he breathed, burying his face in my hair. "You smell nice."

His hands were resting on my stomach, and I took them and wrapped them tighter around me. Then I swung around and looked up at him, my eyes squinting with delight. I put my fingertips against his freshly shaven skin, tracing the curve of his cheekbone.

"Your face…," I whispered.

"What about it?" His dark eyes glittered with mischief.

"It's an eyesore," I teased, with a dramatic eye roll. He

gave me a poke in the ribs. "Oof! Not my fault if you can't handle the truth!"

He looked at me steadily, and I lifted my face to him.

"Well, yours is anything but," he said, sweeping a strand of hair from my face and tucking it behind my ear. I tilted my head, leaning into his touch like a purring cat.

He brought my face to his and kissed me, and I began trembling again, desperate to taste all of him. But after a moment he pulled away and leaned his head to the side, squinting as though he were sizing me up in some way, considering something. I stood still and let him measure me.

Then he turned and picked up his guitar. "Right, let's get started."

A little disappointed, I took a seat next to him, already missing his warm touch and soft lips. But singing together was second best. I leaned into his voice and felt that same intimacy, the same exquisite entangling of souls. And whenever we covered a particularly sorrowful verse it felt like I was lifting his sadness, as though I could help carry some of the burden.

* * *

Later, as we wrapped up and put our instruments aside, I peeked out through the narrow garage windows and saw that the sun had been chased away by grey clouds.

"Looks like rain," I said.

"It rains a lot in this town," Liam said, putting his guitar back in its stand.

"Shame. I was hoping I could see some more of the city before we move on."

"Oh, right," he said, turning to me. "I forget it's your first time here. Want me to show you around?"

We borrowed Max's car and were off into the city. The

afternoon smelled of mist and evergreens, and I pulled my cardigan tighter against the chill blowing in from the Pacific. As we drove along the suburban streets I had to lean out the window to better see the beautiful houses – rows upon rows of pastel-painted Victorian marvels, full of pillars and turrets and elaborate wooden details that made them look more like wedding cakes than houses.

The road climbed higher and higher until I could glimpse the foggy bay in the distance.

"Oh, wow!" I breathed. "This is incredible. I love the hills, and those views!"

"Then you'll like what I'm about to show you." Liam grinned at me, and I gave him a mystified look.

We stopped at the top of a residential street, where the tarmac gave way to a shrubby hill.

"Here we are," he said, a self-satisfied smile on his lips. I looked around, wondering what I was meant to look at. He snapped open his seatbelt and opened the door. "Come on, then."

We left the car in the cul-de-sac and I followed Liam up along an uneven gravel path that lined the hill.

"Hey." He took my hand. "Close your eyes, I'll lead you."

"What?" I laughed. "For real?"

"Trust me."

I shut my eyes and took a few fumbling steps. "Oh my god, Liam, I'm going to fall."

"I got you." He steadied me with his arm around my waist. "It'll be worth it."

Exhilaration fluttered in my chest as I walked by his side towards whatever it was he wanted to show me. I couldn't stop smiling, my cheeks hot from the thrill of being his special someone on this secret mission. I didn't care if he had already taken a thousand girls here. I didn't want to think about that. I was here now.

I was keenly aware of his hand on my hip, holding me tight so I wouldn't stumble over the rocky path.

"Steps," he said, and I stopped and felt for the incline. "There you go." Step by step, we moved further up, and I began to dissolve into giggles.

"Are we almost there?"

"Almost." He squeezed his grip around my waist. We took a few more steps, and he stopped. "Ready?"

I took a deep breath to calm my laughter, then pressed my lips together and nodded with mock solemnity. "I'm ready."

He let go of me and it felt cold where his arm had been. "Open your eyes."

I looked up slowly, my eyes squinting at first, then widening at the sight before me. Miles upon miles of houses crawled over the hills in every direction, like a rolling sea of white debris. Beyond them, the bay faded into grey in the misty afternoon. To my right rose the cluster of skyscrapers we had driven through the other day, and far to the left I could see the top of the Golden Gate Bridge poking into the fog. I held my breath as my eyes ping-ponged across the expanse, while Liam's smile widened.

"There's plenty of viewpoints in this city, but few people know about this one. Everyone's up at Twin Peaks, just over there." He pointed behind us. "I love being high above a city, but I'm not a fan of the crowds."

"It's stunning." I took a deep breath and the air felt fresh and damp in my lungs. "They say that looking at a faraway horizon stimulates the creative mind." I squinted, trying to make out shapes in the hazy distance. "Thanks for taking me here."

We sat on the ground beneath a windswept tree, and Liam pointed out some landmarks along the skyline. He told me stories of when he had visited San Francisco for the first time, having driven by himself from Madison when he was seventeen. Born a vagrant, he said, with a wistful smile. He told me about the many times he had come here to perform, whether solo or with a band. I leaned back on the tree and soaked up his stories, imagining him at all those different ages – a lanky teenager roaming with his guitar, an up-and-coming musician at twenty-one, and now this confident twenty-three-year-old who knew his place on the scene.

I sighed, wide-eyed, awe-struck, wishing I could have been there for all of it. "It sounds so marvellous. What an epic life. I wish my life had even a fraction of the excitement you've lived."

He scoffed. "Come on. It's not so great, really."

"What do you mean? In what way is that not the most thrilling life? Travelling around, living off your music, fans screaming for you everywhere, and the most amazing musicians to work alongside you every day."

He let out a long sigh and fumbled for his cigarettes. "Sure, when you put it that way. It's just, it doesn't feel like that when you're in the middle of it."

I was baffled. "How *does* it feel, then?"

My question hung in the air for a long time. He pulled out a cigarette and lit it, then leaned back against the rough bark and narrowed his eyes as they scanned the vista.

"It gets lonely," he said, at last. "And tiring."

"Oh." His answer took me by surprise, and I searched his face for more clues.

"I don't know." He shook his head, studying the burning end of his cigarette. "I don't know why I'm telling you this."

"Because I asked."

He turned and met my eyes, and his lips curled into a small smile. "Oh, yeah. It's your fault."

"I take full blame." I offered him a warm smile. "Tell me more."

"Well…" He took another drag and blew smoke rings that

hung in the air for a brief moment, then dispersed into the mist. Heavy clouds were blowing in from the sea and I shuddered in the rising breeze.

"Okay, here it is." He looked at me. "Since you asked for it."

"Bring it."

"We go on tour for months at a time. You travel someplace, but you never have the time and energy to see the city, to really experience it. So you stay in some anonymous motel, or sleep on a hard mattress in someone's spare room. The entire time, you're either drunk or tired, or both. You play the same old songs every night, same shit, different stage. A bunch of people have come to see you, but they don't really *see* you. They just see what they want to see. And they don't really want to hear you sing, they just want to shout along themselves. So you drink more to get through the night, take some shit to help you stay awake, then something to help you sleep. Wake up hungover, miserable, alone. Rinse, repeat."

He took one final drag off his cigarette and stubbed it out on the rocky ground.

"I feel like wherever I go, and whatever I do, some piece of me gets left behind. I'm starting to feel hollow. Like a fucking Jenga tower, every day I'm losing a block. I don't know how long I can stay standing."

He stared ahead, clenching his jaw. Then he lowered his gaze and found a twig, which he picked up and began peeling.

"Then, when we're not touring, I fall apart. I need some routine, but then there's this vast expanse of time where there's nothing I *need* to do, you know? I can write songs, I can record, I can plan the next tour. But it's all on me. It's my responsibility to set my schedule and show up for things. And I, well... I tend to just switch off."

I looked at him, the way his eyes danced over the hills as he spoke, and how he held himself, rolling and unrolling his sleeves, absently scratching his arms. The self-assured casanova from earlier was long gone, replaced by this boy who seemed lost and frustrated.

"I'm sorry, Liam. I had no idea."

He shrugged. "It's okay. I can't complain, really. Whatever you do in life, it's gonna suck in some way. I've got it pretty good still. It's just…" He pulled his legs to his chest and wrapped his arms around his knees. "People think I live this perfect life, and it's just not like that. But now you know."

"Now I know."

Gently, I cupped my hand over his and gave him a squeeze. Sometimes, the only thing that helps is the feeling of skin on skin.

Liam shivered. "It's getting cold. Wanna move on?"

We parked in a garage downtown and walked through the evening streets. Liam led me through Chinatown with its lines of bright red lanterns dangling between the buildings, and up and down steep hills that made me stop and catch my breath at every crossing. People had gathered in noisy bars, and hordes of tourists spilled from the cable cars lumbering their way up the hills. Homeless people sat on street corners, asking for change or drawing attention to themselves with makeshift musical instruments, drumming on buckets or blowing into wailing harmonicas.

A crack of thunder rolled across the sky, and within seconds the heavens opened. Rain poured over the city, crashing against the shop awnings, slicking the cobblestones.

Liam groaned. "It was only a matter of time. Come here."

He grabbed my arm and pulled me into a shop, where we stood in the door waiting for the worst to pass.

"I hate the rain," he said, looking out over the wet inferno.

"What? You don't mean that. It's so beautiful!"

"Oh, here we go," he smirked. "Hi, I'm Hazel, and I just love everything!" he teased, poorly imitating my accent.

I laughed. "So? I think that's a good thing."

"What's so beautiful about this?" He gestured at the downpour. "It's just grey and cold and *very* wet."

"I love it, though. I love the sound of it as it crashes against the roof, and the ripples it creates in the puddles. I love how green it makes everything, and clean. And the smell!" I swooned over my beloved rain.

"You go out in it if you love it so much." Liam raised his eyebrows at me, challenging me to prove my point.

Without thinking, I put my hands on his back. "You first!" I howled, pushing him out into the deluge. He gasped with shock, pulling his shoulders up against the spiky raindrops.

I put my hands to my mouth, gaping with delight. "Oh my god! I'm sorry," I wailed, and bent over with laughter.

"You little imp!" He grabbed my arm and pulled me out with him.

The cold hit me like a slap and I shrieked. "Fuck! It's freezing!"

"I know! I'll get you for this!" He came at me and I ran squealing down the street, just outside his reach. A giddiness bubbled in me, tiny explosions like popping candy. We became a couple of school kids, boys chasing girls.

He ran me into a narrow alleyway where he pushed me in underneath an overhanging balcony, and in that quiet place, sheltered from the rain he kissed me, hot and breathy, almost aggressively, and once again I melted into him.

"I can't believe you did that." He shook his head and fixed me with those dark eyes.

"Don't say you didn't like it," I teased.

"Well," he said. "Maybe a little."

"Although, it was a bit colder than I expected," I admitted, shivering.

"Tell me 'bout it." Liam put his hands on my arms, squeezing my soaked cardigan. "Let's get a drink to warm up."

We found a cosy liquor store on a corner. It was warm and comforting, all old wood and dim lighting, and we stood there a while, dripping off and warming up. Then Liam walked over to the counter.

"You alright with whiskey?"

"Sure." He picked up a big bottle of amber liquid. "Er, the whole bottle? But, we've got the gig tomorrow."

"So? That's not till tomorrow night." He looked at me, waiting for my go-ahead. "Come on, Hazel. Live a little." He flashed me a daring grin and I thought what the hell; I *did* want to live a little. I wanted to live a lot.

"Let's do it."

The deluge slowed and we stood in the shop door, holding hands and listening to the fading raindrops. Liam opened the bottle and held it out to me, and I took a deep gulp of the smoky drink. It burned my throat and a heat spread through my tummy. Soon I felt mellow and warm and didn't mind my wet clothes so much.

We walked through the dark streets, slowly drying. We swigged the whiskey, passing it back and forth until I was drunk enough not to care whether we finished the whole bottle. Our laughs bounced between the buildings, our beaming faces reflected in the puddles as we stumbled onward.

Driving home, we shouted along to music loud enough to

shake the streets we passed through. We rolled down all the windows to let the June winds blow in and fool us into believing that life was nothing but beginnings. I knew Liam shouldn't be driving in this state, but I forgot, or didn't care, I wasn't sure which. I felt buzzing and wild, and let the night take me wherever it wanted. I had become immune to the cold, to the wet, to all the risks that lined my path. I leaned out the window and stuck my arms into the damp night, laughing and hollering. We were invincible and the world was ours.

* * *

The house was dark and quiet as we stumbled up the garden path. Liam fumbled with the key and we fell giggling into the kitchen.

"Oh, I'm hungry!" I announced, heading for the fridge in search of a snack.

"Wanna smoke?" Liam asked, pulling out a bag of weed.

"Sure!"

He jumped up to sit on the worktop, knocking over three glasses. "Whoops!" He looked behind him as one rolled into the sink with a crash.

"Guys."

Lawson had appeared in the door, squinting against the light. His hair was even bigger and bouncier than usual. Liam and I froze. I had forgotten that there were other people in the house. Lawson's face was stone cold.

"Bro." He looked at Liam with tired eyes that had seen it all before.

"Hey, man," Liam said, trying to collect himself.

"Look at the state of you." Lawson cut his eyes to me. "Both of you."

"Come on," Liam taunted. "What's the harm?"

"Dude, this isn't our house, okay? Show some respect." He let out a heavy sigh. "You all set for tomorrow?"

"We done our rehearsal this morning," Liam assured him, leaning casually against the sink. "We're good."

"Fine," Lawson conceded, his jawline tense.

"Well, what's this jolly midnight meeting then?" said Ivy, who came waltzing into the kitchen. She was wearing a large sweatshirt that fell down one shoulder, exposing the freckled skin around her delicate neck. "Where y'all been?" She picked up a glass and filled it with water, then turned and looked us up and down. "And why are y'all so wet?"

"Yeah, *Hazel*," Liam said, turning to me with hands on hips. "Why *are* we so wet?"

I couldn't help but laugh and threw my hands up. "You asked for it!"

Ivy rolled her eyes. "Cute." She carried her water past Lawson towards the hall. "Good luck keeping these two in check."

"Yeah, guys," Lawson said, exasperated. "Just... Go sleep it off. I'll wake you up tomorrow when it's time to head to the venue, okay?"

Lawson threw me a concerned look as he turned to leave.

"Sorry, Laws," I said quietly.

I felt guilty that he had to keep us in line. But as soon as he disappeared down the hall, Liam came up behind and tickled me and I had to suppress a howl.

"Busted!" he said, and as he began kissing my neck, I forgot all about Lawson and tedious duties. I turned around and wrapped my arms around him, returning his kisses.

After that night, I no longer needed my own room.

SEVENTEEN

It was time for my first full set with the band. We were playing in the colourful Mission District, in an old church that had been reinvented as an arts venue. As people poured in through the old wooden doors, their voices automatically lowered into reverent whispers beneath the vaulted ceiling. But the moment Liam took the stage, the murmur exploded into an avalanche of shrieks and applause. It didn't help my hangover much, but I was brimming with a bubbly bliss that nearly had me levitating above the noise. And it was comforting to know that Liam felt as rough as I did. At least we were in it together.

The stage felt much more like home when surrounded by the whole band. There was less focus on me and my mistakes, and I could relax and enjoy the gig. I looked over at my bandmates – *my* bandmates! – with incredulous glee, grinning and squeezing my microphone as I caught their eyes in the spotlights.

Liam's usual throng of superfans were spilling over the railings, reaching eager hands towards him, swooning and squealing whenever he came near or kneeled down to reach out his hand. I was embarrassed to notice a twinge of jealousy and tried to shake it off. They were just teenage girls, and Liam was performing, doing his job. Surely there was nothing more to it.

After we wrapped up, we found a small group of dedicated fans waiting outside the old church where we had parked our bus. They patted us on the back and thanked us for a great show, but it was clear that they were waiting for Liam. I recognised the girls from the front as they stood huddled together, tittering, clutching pieces of paper – heartwrenching love letters, perhaps, or somewhere to keep his autograph.

I said my thanks and escaped onto the bus. Obscured by the tinted windows, I could sit undisturbed in a booth and watch the crowd. Their eyes were wide and expectant, and I could see myself in them; the way they raised Liam to impossible heights, ready to worship him.

At last, the doors flew open and Liam walked out. I studied his face, trying to read his mind through the darkened window. He smiled as he received letters and flowers, signed autographs, and hugged each of the girls. My gut twisted at their fluttering eyelashes, their hands all over him, their lips close to his ears as they whispered their girlhood secrets.

Then I heard a pair of familiar heels stomping down the bus aisle. "I see I'm not the only one desperate to get away from that mob," Ivy said, as she slipped into the seat in front of me. Her emerald eyes lingered on me for a moment, then drifted out over the crowd as her lips curled into a knowing smile. "Tedious, isn't it? Kinda part of the deal, though."

I looked at her with raised eyebrows. "The deal?"

She sniggered and tilted her head. "Oh, pumpkin. The deal you have signed up for. The rock star's mistress." Her voice twisted like pouring syrup. "Don't worry. We've all been there."

I hesitated. "You have? But... you're not anymore?"

She extended into a languid stretch and crossed her legs under the booth table. "Liam and I never had a label as such. We were never a *thing*, but then we're not *not* a thing, either." She puckered her coral lips, looking all innocent.

I couldn't help but notice that she spoke in the present tense. I didn't want to believe there was something between them still, but I sure wasn't about to interrogate her. Of course, I could see why anyone would prefer Ivy to me. She was a goddess, talented and gorgeous, and I bet she was a devil in bed. I had nothing on her.

Outside, Liam was still tending to his admirers. Some girls were crowding around him, taking selfies. He dutifully looked into their lenses, his dark eyes caught in the flashes.

Ivy noticed me staring and let out a tinkling laugh. "Well, I know that look," she said, her luminous eyes like mountain lakes; deceptively calm but no doubt freezing and bottomless. "You better enjoy it while it lasts. 'Cause it won't be forever." She looked out at Liam with a dramatic sigh. "Musicians are like tigers. Too large to contain, too wild to tame. Ain't no cages gonna hold him back."

"Anyone here?" Mango poked his buzz cut through the door. "There y'are! Come join the party!"

"Party?" I repeated, a little dazed from Ivy's revelations.

"It's tradition when we play in the church," Ivy explained, studying her perfect nails. "Party in the crypt."

"What?" My eyes widened. "For real?"

"You know it, girl!" Mango grinned at us. "VIPs only, so you gotta be there. See you inside?"

My hangover lifted in an instant and I stood up. I was ready to lose my head once more. "Count me in!"

* * *

We set up a perfect little party space in the damp crypt. Fairy lights and candles flickered across the old brick walls, creating a shadow play around the pillars and archways. Old blues songs poured from Mango's portable speaker, and I listened eagerly to the band's touring tales while a pile of empty beer bottles grew at my feet.

A couple of hours in, I noticed that Liam and Ivy had disappeared again. A cold blade twisted in my gut as my mind flooded with visions of them together – his warm fingers caressing her translucent skin, her delicate limbs wrapping around him, swallowing him up. I shot to my feet, staggering slightly after the long night and the endless stream of beer.

"Um, where's the toilet, please?"

"Through there." Victor pointed to a hallway.

"Thanks."

The echoes of blues and laughter faded as I walked down the hall. A faint smell of mould filled my nose as I looked around the dark, dank walkways. Then, up ahead, I could hear muffled voices and giggles, and I walked gingerly towards them. A sliver of light poured out from a crack in a door. I prepared myself for the worst and slowly pushed it open.

It led into an old office lit by flickering fluorescent lights. Liam and Ivy stood by the desk, bending over a pile of white powder. Liam had a card in his hand, shaping a couple of lines. Ivy was holding a rolled-up twenty, waiting, when she heard me and swung around.

"Oh. Hey, Hazel," she said, her voice flat. I couldn't tell whether she was annoyed or indifferent at my interruption. In any case, my suspicions drained off me and I exhaled with relief.

Liam saw me and smiled. "Haze! Come on in. Want some?"

I looked at the lines, like drifts of newly fallen snow. There was no way I would say no and leave them to get high in their private club.

"Sure," I said, trying my best to sound nonchalant. Ivy handed me the twenty and I leaned in and took a line. "Thanks."

I passed the note back and sat down in an old swivel chair to await the rush. Ivy sniffed up a line, rubbed her perky little nose and claimed the other chair. Liam hoovered up two lines in quick succession, then jumped up to sit on the desk, leaning against the wall.

"So, Haze, your first full show," he said. "How'd ya like it?"

"It was fun! I wasn't too nervous, actually." I stretched my legs and the old chair squeaked under my weight. "And what a venue! I've never seen anything like it. It's gorgeous."

"Urgh." Liam groaned and wrinkled his nose, which made Ivy chuckle.

"Yeah, you must feel right at home," she said, smirking at Liam.

"It's a real comfort." He stuck a cigarette between his lips and fiddled with his lighter.

"Oh, shit, yeah," I said. "Your parents?"

He closed his eyes and filled the room with white smoke.

I looked at Ivy and back to Liam. "I'm sorry, I don't mean to pry…"

"Hey," Ivy said, "ain't no use gettin' moody." She grinned and looked over to Liam. "Tell her how you used to be a little choir boy!"

"No way!" I yelped. "For real?"

Liam's lopsided smile appeared as he shook his head. "Don't do this."

I tried to imagine Liam in a choir, with his tousled hair and long white gown, his tiny little voice. "Wow, I wish I could have seen it."

"You can!" Ivy squealed. The coke was coming at me like a bucket of cold water to the face, and I turned to Liam with inquisitive eyes.

He looked at Ivy and back at me, then sighed in resignation. "Fine." He pulled out his phone, unlocked it, and began scrolling.

"No… way…," I breathed, leaning in, waiting for the reveal. "This is too good!"

"There. Enjoy." He held up his phone. On the screen I could see little Liam standing between two other boys, his hair neatly combed and his mouth wide open in earnest song.

"Holy smokes!" I grabbed the phone and pulled it closer. "This little innocent boy! And look at you now." I tutted. "What a fall from grace."

I laughed and Ivy joined me with her giggles. It was a rare and curious feeling to laugh along with her as though we were best friends.

"Alright, ladies, hilarious," Liam said, although I could tell he enjoyed the attention.

I took one last look at that little boy, frozen in time, wondering what he was like, what his life looked like. Then I passed the phone back.

"Can I take another?" I said, pointing to the pile.

"Sure."

I picked up the rolled-up note and took a sniff. Then I got up on the desk and sat down next to Liam, energised by a wave of restless courage.

"What happened, though? Your parents were, like, super strict, right?"

He coughed out a bitter laugh. "You could say that."

Ivy's smile faded and she cast her eyes down.

"Well, what was it like?"

"You don't wanna know."

"But I do. I mean. You don't have to tell me, of course. But I would love to know."

He looked at me, frowning. "Why?"

"I don't know. I'm curious about you and your life." I shrugged. "I'm curious about everyone. I've been alone for so much of my life, I find it fascinating hearing people's stories."

"Fine." He exhaled a final lungful of smoke and stubbed out his cigarette in an old pen stand. "My dad is a mean bastard who raised me to be afraid of everything, including him and a god I don't believe in. Maybe my mom meant well, but she was scared, too. Scared of my dad, mostly. I was constantly negotiating a maze of rules and threats, and none of it made any sense."

I looked over at Ivy, who sat looking at her lap. She had clearly heard this all before.

"While I was still young enough to buy their bullshit, I spent all my waking time trying not to end up in hell. And a lot of things could get you into hell, believe me, at least according to their fucked-up version of religion. Music, for example. Unless it's gospel, which was never a favourite of mine." He scoffed. "Hanging out with non-believers, which was all of my friends. Drinking. Smoking. And don't get me started on sex. Even if I didn't believe it, there was always this feeling of guilt and shame."

"It was your dad, though," Ivy interjected. She turned to me and added, "This ain't like regular Christianity. If you ask me, I don't think it had much to do with religion at all."

"I know, I know," Liam said, frustrated. "My dad was just on this fucked-up power trip his whole life. His church was a way for him to act out his own demons. If he hadn't had that, he would have found something else. I know that, but still... Organised religion makes me sick."

"Wow," I said. "No wonder you're not a fan of churches."

Liam ground his teeth together. "Yeah."

"So your parents think you're going to hell?"

"Totally convinced, no question."

"Man." I tried to put myself in their shoes – to fully believe that we're all waiting for heaven, and knowing that your own child won't be joining you in eternity. I sighed and looked up at the mildew on the ceiling. "That's gotta suck."

"You've no idea."

"What about you, Ivy? Were your parents religious?"

"Oh, sure, my parents are *very* good Christians." She tilted her head and pursed her lips. "Except, they ain't."

"What do you mean?"

"Oh, it's a status thing, a matter of society and appearance. But if you asked them what it actually means to be religious, they wouldn't know what to say. They sure as hell wouldn't feed no poor people or do any of them things folks say Jesus did. My parents are mainly concerned with dollars and prestige."

I had figured she came from old money.

"Do you get along with them?" I asked.

"With my parents? Come on. Who does?"

"Enough of this," Liam snapped, jumping down off the table. "Let's get out of this hellhole. I need some air." He scooped up the coke and shoved the pouch in his pocket. "Come on."

"Leave me some, would ya," Ivy said. "I think I'll stay here with the boys. I'm not in the mood for one of your spontaneous midnight adventures."

"Suit yourself."

Ivy's eyes cut to me for a second before she shifted her attention to her nails, her face as unreadable as ever.

Outside, fresh winds were whipping through the streets, and I was glad to be out of that musty crypt. We walked down a side road with no traffic, just dim streetlights and walls decorated with elaborate murals.

"Not a lot going on out here," I said. "Where do you want to go?"

"You said you wanted to sightsee, right? Well, you still haven't seen the bridge."

He smiled and took my hand, and led me to a main road where he hailed a cab. "Take us down Fort Point, would ya?"

We climbed into the car and rode north. In the privacy of the backseat our bodies entangled once more, my incredulous heart pounding along with the radio and the flashes of orange that washed over us like strobe lights. Then Liam held a finger to his lips and, with one eye on the driver, pulled out the coke. As quietly as possible, we took a bump each, and a cocktail of cocaine and adrenaline sent me flying through the night.

We stopped by a narrow strip of beach that lined the dark water. The wind was rising and I spun around, my hair and dress fluttering in the breeze. To our left, the enormous structure of the Golden Gate Bridge rose into the sky, illuminated by blazing orange streetlights that reflected as a fiery flurry in the choppy strait.

I took a few tentative steps closer to the water's edge. "There it is," I said quietly, feeling strangely reverent. "Gosh, it's huge."

"So it is," said Liam, his eyes on the towering structure. We stood in silence for a moment, Liam's eyes on the bridge and mine on Liam. I wondered what was going through his mind, and whether he cared what was going through mine.

"Right," he said, snapping us out of that wordless space. "Let's go up on it."

We walked back along the shore until we reached some steps leading up a grassy hill. A steep path twisted its way upward, and suddenly I became uncomfortably aware of my rapid heartbeat. I stopped to catch my breath and put a hand to my chest, anxious about the effects of the coke.

"Where'd ya go?" Liam was further up the path, obscured by darkness. I hurried to catch up.

Traffic was rushing back and forth over the bridge, and I felt a little shaky as we stepped onto its footpath and started walking across. The entire structure seemed to wobble as passing vehicles crossed the bridge joints with loud clangs. Once I had reassured myself that it wasn't going to collapse under my feet, I looked up at the colossal tower and felt a little dizzy. This bridge was a familiar sight, sure, but it was also like nothing I had ever seen before.

I peered over the side and saw the dark sea rolling towards the shore, each wave frothing into a line of white foam. We were so high up that it seemed to be moving in slow-motion. Way across the bay I could see the glittering lights of the city centre, all those twinkling skyscrapers, all that buzzing life.

Liam was walking ahead of me, saying nothing. We reached the first tower, walked around it, and kept going. Then he stopped and leaned against the railing, looking down at the water way down below. A cheeky gust of wind lifted my skirt and I tried to smooth it down, my laughter dissolving in the gale. Liam just kept staring at the sea.

I sidled up next to him and looked over the edge, and an uneasy jolt of vertigo took me by surprise. It was such a long way down. I grabbed the railing and held on tight.

"They call it the Suicide Bridge," Liam said, raising his voice above the wind and traffic. "Did you know that?"

"No." I followed his gaze down to the ruffled surface. "No, I didn't know that. Is it a popular spot?"

"Most popular in the world, I think. Nearly two thousand people have ended their suffering here."

"Whoa." I imagined lifting my leg over the railing, then

the other, saying my last words, and falling to my death. I shuddered and tightened my grip around the cold metal. "I could never kill myself. I just can't fathom it."

"Well." Liam stood back and pushed his hands deep into his pockets. "Sometimes it feels good to have the option, doesn't it?"

"What option? Suicide?"

He shrugged. "I mean, I wouldn't. But sure, sometimes I fantasise about it." His eyes lingered on the inky water. "Just drink myself stupid and jump into oblivion."

My mouth fell open. "But *why?*" I didn't want to believe what I was hearing. I had finally found someone so out of this world, so full of magic and mystery. And for that person to wilfully end his own life – I couldn't bear to imagine it. When he didn't respond, I prodded him with my elbow. "Tell me, why?"

He yanked his hands out of his pockets and the swift motion made me jump. "Look around you, Hazel!" He drilled his desperate eyes into mine. "The world is falling to pieces! There's barely anything left. We've poisoned everything. All that remains is for us to take each other out, nations and neighbours. At least if we get on with it soon, the planet might still have a chance to recover." He bit down and turned back towards the sea. "I used to think things could change, but they're only getting worse. I see that now. All I'm saying is, it's good to know there's an end to it all. A way out."

It took me a while to gather myself from the shock of his words. I looked out over the black ocean and twinkling skyline, tasting the fresh, salty winds. It didn't seem all that bad to me.

"Come on, Liam. It's not all doom and gloom! The world is full of beautiful things, too. People who care about each other, who do good things. They just don't make the news, that's all! And you can't say that everything is falling apart.

Not while people still create art and write beautiful books and fall in love."

"Art is just escapism," Liam muttered.

"That's not true!" I said. "Art is the language we use to convey our unique experiences, a way to communicate the inexpressible. It's not escapism. It's truth."

Liam heaved a stubborn sigh. "It's just a way to make life seem more beautiful than it actually is. To lend it some kind of meaning that isn't really there."

"But what if it *is* there? What if life is more beautiful than you realise?"

He scoffed. "Open your eyes, Hazel. For so many people, life is nothing but pain, and I'm sick of being aware of it all. I'm tired of having to be fucking conscious all the time. Sometimes my head feels like a prison." A dark shadow had swept across his face, and the bubbly rush of the coke had transformed into something angrier, more sinister.

"Liam, please... It wouldn't be such a crime to let yourself be happy for once."

I tried reaching for his hand, but he pulled away.

"No, fuck it, Hazel. I'm sorry. I know you mean well, but..."

My hair was twirling all about my face and I pulled it aside, tucked it behind my ear. "But what?"

His jaw clenched and unclenched. "I've just—I've given up on all that. Being happy. It's not gonna happen for me. I feel like, even when things are going well, I'm still..." He scraped his foot against the railing. "It's like I'm always waiting for things to turn to shit. Like I don't deserve anything good, and nobody gives a shit about me."

"I give a shit!" I grabbed his shoulders and shook him, trying to wake him from his self-absorbed slumber. "Liam. I give ten shits. How about that?"

He swallowed hard, his gaze resting at some distant point

beyond me. Then he met my eyes and forced a placating half-smile.

"I'll take it. Thanks, Hazelnut."

He wrapped his arms around me and I pressed my face to his chest, to his wild beating heart. "Please don't kill yourself," I whispered, too quietly for him to hear over the howling wind. The traffic rushed ever onward.

* * *

Back at the house, I crawled into Liam's bed for the last time before we took off for LA. His skin felt warm and alive against mine, and I explored every curve and contour of his precious body, wanting so badly to fix all the hurt inside.

Afterward, I lay beside him, willing myself to sleep, but my heart was still beating its cocaine rhythm. I forced myself to lie still and relax my body, one limb at a time.

Then Liam stirred and whispered in the dark. "Hazel? You awake?"

"Yeah."

He was quiet for a bit, and I rolled over to face him. He held me with his big eyes, the streetlight outside faintly reflected in them like tiny fires.

"I did try."

"Try what?"

"To kill myself."

I pushed myself up on my elbow and looked at him. "When?"

He sat up against the headboard. "I was sixteen."

"What happened?"

"Pills. Lots of 'em. Woke up in the hospital with the worst fucking hangover of my life."

"Shit…" My throat felt dry and I swallowed hard. "Were —were your parents there?"

"No, they..." He snorted bitterly. "They left a message."

"A message? Saying what?"

He took a deep breath. "That I had brought shame on the congregation, and I should call them when I was back on my feet."

"What!" I sat up straighter. "You're kidding?"

"Afraid not."

"Oh my god." Tears began to sting behind my eyelids. "Did you call them?"

"Yeah. My dad was furious. Told me that God punishes suicides, but that it didn't matter since I was on a straight road to hell anyway."

Liam's eyes were faraway, lost in the memories. I moved closer to him, but he flinched at my touch.

"I'm so sorry, Liam. That's too awful."

He relaxed and let me put an arm over his shoulders. Slowly, he threaded his arms around me and buried his face in my neck, and I stroked his hair while whispering empty reassurances. He felt like a shard from a broken vase; forever cut off from the shape he could have been a part of, unable to find his place in the great puzzle, his edges dangerously sharp.

EIGHTEEN

And so we left San Francisco, heading south on Highway 1. The fog had cleared to reveal a blinding spring day, but my mind was still clouded over with Liam's confessions. I had hoped to cosy up next to him in a booth, but he disappeared into his bunk and stayed there all morning. Instead, I sat by the window opposite Lawson, quietly mulling things over in my sore head.

As we rolled into the Californian Hills, I felt a familiar flutter in my chest. It's so simple, the act of packing up and leaving a place behind. At your next destination you will arrive to another blank slate, another chance to be reborn. It's easier to be sad in a foreign place. Everything feels new and less real, and you can hold on to the illusion that all your problems will go away at the next stop; just keep going down the endless road, chasing the mirage.

To our right lay the Pacific Ocean, vast and brilliant, its ancient coastline rising in rugged cliffs that broke the foaming waves far below. And there, as we zoomed down the smooth road that lines the far edge of America, it occurred to me that I was the furthest from home I would ever get, at least on this continent. How far I had come from that dark place I used to call home, in both space and mind. How different my life had become in such a short time. Everything had changed, *I* had changed; I could feel it in my bones. My underlying structure was reshaping itself, my tectonic plates rumbling and shifting.

I thought of Mother in her studio. What was she working on now? If at all; maybe she was just munching pills and burying herself in books. Perhaps she was looking at photographs of times gone by while bemoaning the unfairness of it all. Weeping over her lost family and runaway husband, people she had fought so hard to push away.

And Amber, where had she gone to? What did her life look like? It had been over two years since I last saw her, when she snuck into the house to steal some of Mother's meds. She had done it before and would surely do it again, but she had made it clear that she didn't want anybody's help. I didn't even know where she was staying.

I leaned my forehead against the window and remembered my sister, before everything had become so broken. I knew she would be proud of me for what I was doing. Proud that I had finally left.

I heard Liam stir and clamber out of his bunk bed. I looked back and tried to catch his eye, but he wouldn't look at me. His hair was a spiky mess, his eyes hollow and lined with dark rings. He stared ahead as he walked right past me.

"There any coffee?" he mumbled.

"All out, bro," said Lawson. "You'll have to make some more." Liam groaned and began clattering with mugs and coffee grounds.

I looked at Lawson, but he just shrugged and turned back toward the sea. Once the machine was brewing, Liam sighed and rested his head against the cupboard. He seemed determined not to speak to anyone. As soon as the pot was done, he brought a cup to an empty booth and sat down in a sullen silence.

My mind started rummaging for reasons why he was acting this way. Had I said something wrong last night? Had I reacted poorly, or pushed him too far when asking about it? The questions kept spinning and I shifted restlessly in my seat, trying instead to focus on the wide open ocean; searching for that distant horizon.

* * *

"Picnic break!"

I jerked awake and looked around. Victor had parked the bus in a dusty car park and was already outside grabbing bags from the undercarriage.

"Picnic?" Ivy stood up and rolled her shoulders. "What you got planned this time, Vic?"

He stuck his head through the door. "You wanted the scenic route. What's the scenic route without a beach picnic? I didn't want to stop at any old roadside diner, not when we're passing right through Big Sur! So I packed lunch. Figured y'all would like it."

"Victor, you legend!" Mango howled, flying up from his seat. "Dining in the wild!"

"Now, first things first." Victor wagged a warning finger in the air. "We've got exactly two and a half hours before we have to get back on the road, so let's get organised."

"Ooh! Set your timers, folks!" Mango jumped around and threw some air punches in Victor's direction. "I'm pumped!"

We stepped outside into a brisk wind and the distant sound of crashing waves. The day was bright and warm and I fished out a pair of sunglasses, but Liam threw up his hood and kept to himself.

Victor handed us a bag each and led us away like a row of

goslings. "This way! Mind your step now, it's a rocky way down to the beach."

Over the edge of the cliffside, a breathtaking vista came into view. At the bottom of the slope the wild ocean had been tamed within a lagoon, the water sheltered and calmed by a circle of jagged rocks. A perfect, white-sand beach stretched along the edge, and clusters of pine trees decorated the hillside. Above it the sky formed a cloudless blue dome, with a burning sun hovering in the middle.

Mango whistled. "Victor, my man, you've outdone yourself again!"

"Just doing my job," Victor said, although he was looking rather pleased with himself. "I would have arranged a barbecue, but you know the rules for state parks."

"Well, *you* know the rules, and that's all we need!" Mango looked around with a big grin. "This is perfect."

We reached the foot of the hill and the others began setting up the picnic. Awestruck, I sank onto the soft sand, admiring the majestic scenery. It felt ancient and powerful, otherworldly.

"Beautiful, isn't it?" said Lawson, as he sat down next to me. "This is true Kerouac country. D'you ever read Big Sur?"

"No, but I love On the Road! And now, I mean... I feel like I'm living it, Laws. It's incredible."

"'There was nowhere to go but everywhere,'" Lawson said, his eyes to the sea.

I jerked my head around. "'So just keep on rolling under the stars,'" I added. "One of my favourite quotes."

"Mine, too." He gave me a warm smile, his big hair tumbling around in the wind.

I thought about everyone back home, all those people who never once thought about leaving Folkestone. "With so much world to see, it doesn't make sense to stay in one place."

Lawson's eyes lingered on me for a second, then turned back to the water. "You're right, it doesn't."

"My hometown is right by the sea, but it's nothing like this." I gestured at the insane surroundings and made a mental comparison to Kent's uneventful pebble beaches and barren caravan parks. "You yanks do epic very well."

Lawson laughed. "I guess we do. Especially around these parts. This is the best thing about California. Not the cities, not Hollywood or any of that. This, nature, the parks and coastlines. Having grown up in the cornfields of Madison, this stuff is the cream of the earth. Am I right, Liam?"

We turned around, but Liam was nowhere to be seen.

"Where is he?" I stood up and removed my sunglasses. "He was here a minute ago."

Lawson stood up and scanned the area. "Liam!" His voice echoed against the encircling cliff face.

"Leave him be," Ivy said. "You know what he's like."

"She's right." Lawson gave me a reassuring nod. "He disappears sometimes. He'll be back."

"Okay," I mumbled, unconvinced. I kept an eye on the foaming sea just beyond the lagoon, and the rocky slope that rose behind us, but there was no sign of him.

"Right!" Victor gestured at his served-up feast. "Tuck in, folks!"

* * *

We gorged on sandwiches, salads and snacks until we could barely breathe. Victor was right – this was way better than some greasy roadside diner. When my plate was empty, I peeled off my cardigan and stretched out on the sun-warm sand. Above me an endless sky, around me pristine nature, but my mind was full of Liam. I couldn't stop thinking about everything he had said the night before, all that talk of wanting to die. Suddenly I could see dangerous places everywhere – the surging sea ahead, the sharp cliffs, the long fall from the rocks above.

"Liam's still not here." I sat up and turned to the others. "Aren't you worried?"

"Nah." Ivy sat with her pale legs gracefully outstretched, her hair in a messy top knot matched with a chic, oversized jumper. "Honestly, Hazel, this is what he does. No need to worry."

"What do you mean, this is what he does?"

"Our Liam is a lone wolf. He needs his alone time."

I shielded my eyes and looked around. "But you're sure he's okay?"

She smirked at me. "Yeah, I'm sure. This one time he disappeared for, like, two days. He's always fine. Why, you feelin' lost without your rock star by your side?"

"What! No, it's not like that, it's just—"

Her tinkling laughter cut me off. "I'm fuckin' with you, girl!" She squinted at me, then gave me a friendly nudge. "Call him if you're so concerned."

I pulled out my phone but there was no signal. Lawson was polishing off the last of the potato salad, and I went over and crouched down next to him.

"Hey, Laws. Can I speak with you?"

"Oh, sure." He wiped his mouth and stood up. "What's up?"

"Somewhere private?"

"Uh, okay, yeah."

We walked down the beach, out of earshot of the others.

"I just thought I should tell you…" I searched for the right words, hoping I wasn't breaking some unspoken bond of trust. "Yesterday, Liam took me to the Golden Gate Bridge and told me all this stuff about—about suicide."

"Suicide?"

"Yeah, like, how he wants to die, or life is too painful, or whatever. And he told me that he tried to kill himself."

"When?"

"When he was sixteen."

Lawson nodded, unsurprised. "Yeah. But that was a long time ago, and he's not the same guy now."

"You knew about it?"

"Yeah, I was there for the whole thing, trying to help him afterwards when his parents were being assholes."

"Oh."

"After that, he pretty much moved out of home. Stayed at mine a lot, but mostly at Frank's. At least Frank was decent about the whole thing."

I remembered Frank's wise eyes and calm voice, and it warmed my insides. "I'm glad he had you two."

"Look." Lawson placed his hand on my shoulder. "Liam and I have known each other forever. I promise you, he wouldn't just up and kill himself like this, in the middle of a tour. It's sweet of you to worry, but there's no need." He looked around, searching for a distraction. "Let's go for a walk. I want to see what's behind those rocks over there."

The warm sand turned to rock under our feet as we reached the edge of the lagoon and started up the cliffs. The breeze was picking up, relentless waves launching against the rocks.

"So, how did you guys meet?" I asked, realising I knew so little about their past.

"In school."

"Oh, so, a proper long time ago?"

Lawson looked at me and laughed. "Proh-puh," he repeated in his silly Cockney accent. "Yeah, since elementary school. It was a strict religious school, and from day one, Liam and I became allies in the fight against the evil overlords."

I smiled at the image of Liam and Lawson as rebellious schoolboys.

"But the differences between us were obvious already then, at six years old. I didn't really care about the religious side of school, or the way they treated us, the lies and hypocrisy... I don't know, I guess I didn't take it seriously. I actually thought it was kinda funny. But not Liam. He was always so angry about it all. He just couldn't let it go."

I walked alongside Lawson, watching my step over the uneven rock.

"We've been through so much together," he continued. "As we grew older, we chose different paths in life. He's always been reckless and roaming, while I prefer to keep both feet on the ground."

He stopped to lift aside a drooping branch and let me pass.

"In our late teens, that's when he got into his drink and drugs. I tried a bit, as kids do, but he went all out. It scared me at first, and I tried to stop him, tried to change him. Figured I knew what was best for him. But I didn't. I don't. Who am I to say anything about anyone else's path in life?"

We had reached the top and could see the cliff face stretching into the distance, lined with white sand along the water's edge.

"But what about if you think he's doing harm to himself?" I asked.

Lawson paused, looking out over the ancient shoreline. "He's been in the game a long time. I just gotta trust him." He shook his head with a sigh. "It's not like I can stop him anyhow. Believe me, I've tried. Sometimes, we just gotta let people be who they are."

"I wish I had your patience. I hate being worried all the time."

"I've had a lot of practice." He flashed me a smile. "Anyway, what about you? You never talk about yourself. What's your story?"

"Oh." I let out a dismissive chuckle. "It's boring. Not much to tell."

"Somehow I doubt that. What was school like? I'm guessing you didn't go to a religious school. Or maybe you did?"

I looked up at him, at his kind and curious eyes. Good old Lawson.

"Well..." I sat down on the shrubby ground, and he sank down next to me. "I was homeschooled, actually." I squeezed my eyes shut, anticipating his reaction. When he didn't say anything, I opened them again but kept them on the ground, avoiding his gaze. "Not at first, but since high school. My mum thought it would be best for me, but..." I ground my teeth together until my jaw ached. "I think she was wrong. Sure, I learned stuff. I studied art and all those things I was supposed to be passionate about. But that's not really what school is about, is it? Isn't the point to learn about people and relationships, and to find your place in the world? I envied my friends. Their lives carried on, while mine just... stopped." I glanced over at Lawson. "Wow, that got real. I'm sorry. I've never told this to anyone before."

"Why not?"

"It's embarrassing! I mean, my classmates knew, of course. But it didn't take long before we all lost touch. And since then, well, it's not something I want to shout about. Makes me feel stupid."

"You're not stupid, Hazel! It's not embarrassing at all. It's totally common, at least in this country."

My face dropped. "Is it? I've never met anyone else who's been homeschooled."

"Well, I don't think it's a big deal. Actually, it's kinda

cool. You've had a unique experience. And school really isn't that great, trust me."

Lawson's easy laugh made me feel lighter. He didn't judge me. I filled my lungs with the salty air while my stomach slowly untied itself.

"Anyway, you turned out alright, didn't you?" His eyes glimmered as he grinned at me. "I'm honoured to have been privy to this highly classified information." He stuck his elbow in my side and I couldn't help but laugh.

"Thanks," I said. "For being nice."

"Any time, Jane Eyre."

I laughed again and slapped his arm. "You're such a dork."

He sat up straighter, looking a little concerned. "She's English, right?"

"She's a character in a book, but yes, she was English."

"Phew!" Lawson exhaled in exaggerated relief. "That was a close call. I best read up on my English literature."

I beamed at him, bright as the California sun. He held my eyes for a moment, then snapped to his senses and stood up.

"Hey, we best head back. If we don't get back on the road soon, Vic's motherboard will short circuit."

"Uh-oh! Then we might have to take over the clipboard."

"I'm sure none of us is ready for that kind of responsibility," Lawson said with affected gravity, and reached his hand out to help me up. We brushed sand from our legs and made our way back down the rocks.

As we approached the beach, I was relieved to see that Liam had returned. He was sitting on a rock by himself, picking at some leftover salad. I walked over to him, but he still wouldn't look at me.

"There you are," I said.

"Yep."

I sat down on the sand next to him, biting my lip,

wondering where the line should be drawn. But I couldn't help myself.

"I was worried about you. Where were you?"

"I'm…" He met my eyes briefly. "I just needed to go for a walk."

"Liam," I said, exasperated. "Have I done something wrong?"

"No." He swallowed hard, looking down at his food. "No, you haven't. I just… There's some shit I gotta figure out, okay?"

I waited for him to return my gaze, but he seemed fully concentrated on his salad. Eventually I gave up and looked out over the waves rolling in and spraying the rocks. "Okay."

It was a long six hours onwards to LA. I hoped that whatever Liam was trying to figure out, he would do it soon, and not kick me off the tour. My mind swirled as I watched the sun descend toward the ocean and ignite the horizon in a blazing display. In a flash it was gone, swallowed up by the sea, and everything turned a soft, peachy blue; like a perfect Californian postcard.

NINETEEN

I had almost imagined that we would roll into a red-carpeted city covered in spotlights and glitzy celebs, all overlooked by the fabled Hollywood sign. But the reality was quite different. From my window, night over LA looked busy, messy, down-and-out; a brimming concrete soup that seemed to go on forever.

Vic had booked us into a cheap hotel on Melrose Avenue, where I spent a lonely night in a single bed, wondering what I had done wrong.

We had two shows lined up in town, and the following day we gathered and made our way to the first. It was all beginning to feel familiar – the set-up, the soundcheck, the pre-show butterflies. But I still wasn't used to Liam's gagging groupies. I had missed him in my bed last night, and now they seemed to be closing in like vultures.

After the show I hovered outside, keeping an eye on them. Mango was in the midst of the chaos, trying to get in on the action. "Yo, Liam!" he yelled. "We partying tonight?"

"I dunno," Liam said over the crowd. "I think I need a break."

Mango pushed his way through the girls. "Hey, man, come on. These ladies want to party. We should show them a good time."

I stood eavesdropping from the sidelines, trying to look inconspicuous while waiting to see what they would decide.

"Nah, man, I don't know." Liam hesitated, scratched his head. Then, without warning, he looked up and caught my eye. I flinched and turned away, feeling my cheeks grow hot. "I'm not sure I'm up to it tonight," he added.

"Man, where's Liam the superstar gone, huh?" Mango attempted his most playful grin.

"Wait, one sec." Liam put a hand in his pocket. "Phone's ringing. Can you keep 'em busy?"

"This is the task I was born for." He clapped his hands together. *"Chicas, ven a mi!"* He grinned and heaved his arms around the shoulders of as many girls as he could fit.

Liam pushed away from the clamour over to a quiet corner and answered his phone. I took a step closer.

"Hey, man, great to hear from you! Yeah, we're doing good. In LA at the moment. Yeah, yeah." He covered his free ear and turned away from the noise. "You okay? Frank?" His gaze flitted over the crowd, pausing briefly at me where I stood a few steps away. "Hey. No worries... Sure, yeah, I'm doing fine. Hey, listen, Frank... You don't sound too good. Shouldn't you see a—" He stopped, then let out a frustrated sigh. "Alright, if you say so..." His eyes lifted to me again and stayed there. "She's fine, yeah. She says hi back. Alright, great. I love you too, man. Take it easy. Bye."

He hung up and stared at the screen, now black and silent. I took some hesitant steps towards him.

"Was that Frank?"

"Yeah."

"Is everything okay?"

"I dunno... He said he wanted to check in on us." Liam's

face was hard, his brow furrowed. "He asked about you. Sends his regards."

"Thanks..." I gave him an uneasy smile. I hoped Frank was okay, but a bad feeling had sprouted like black vines through my gut.

Liam looked down at the locked screen, scratching the back of his neck the way he did when he was mulling something over. Then he shook his head, slipped his phone back into his pocket and strode over to Mango. "Right, where's that party at?"

* * *

Liam and Mango headed over to the nearest bar with their groupies in tow, while the rest of us stayed behind to pack up our gear. Satisfied that every last cable had been rolled up and stashed away, Victor locked up the bus and we went to join the boys at the bar.

We found them sitting in a large corner sofa at the back, surrounded by champagne bottles, two bottles of rum, and several shot glasses. They had five or six girls on either side of them, and they seemed to be sharing touring stories with their rapt audience, who sat batting their eyelashes and punctuating the storytelling with tinkling laughter and gasps of astonishment.

I looked over at Lawson and rolled my eyes, but he just laughed and shrugged.

"I guess we're doing this," I muttered, and sat down and poured myself a glug of rum.

The bottles were drained and more were brought in, and the stories kept coming, but I didn't hear them. I tried to chat to Lawson, to have fun with the others. I even tried talking to Ivy, but my brain filtered out everything except the swooning *oohs* and *aahs* of Liam's gaggle. For each glass of rum I necked their eyelashes grew thicker, their cleavages more provocative, their lips a more toxic shade of scarlet.

Then a blond number to Liam's right leaned in and began stroking his hair. I wasn't sure how much he had drunk, but he was now swigging freely from a bottle in his hand. I waited for him to stop her, but he didn't. Something heavy slammed into my gut as she leaned closer and pressed her lips onto his.

"Fuck this," I mumbled, and staggered to my feet. "Where can I go for a smoke?"

I stumbled through the dark bar out into the beer garden, which felt like a sanctuary of silence and fresh air. I took a deep breath of the fragrant California night and willed my head to stop spinning. So, he was in there kissing a fan. So what? This must happen all the time. It was none of my business. But, no… It didn't feel right. I wrapped my arms around myself, black mould consuming my insides.

I sat down by a table in the corner, digging through my pockets for cigarettes but finding none. Then the patio door swung open and loud music spilled into the yard.

"Hazelnut, what's up?" Liam stood on the steps, a rum bottle dangling from his left hand.

I sighed and stared straight ahead. "Nothing's up. What's up with you?"

"Hazel, baby, don't be angry," he slurred, and walked over and sat down next to me.

"I'm not angry," I said, but my tone suggested otherwise.

He leaned in towards me, his eyes obscured by the veil of his fringe. "Nothing happened in there." His breath reeked of old booze and I turned the other way.

"None of my business," I mumbled.

He sat back and the bottle slid out of his hand, landing on the gravel with a *clink*.

"C'mon, baby. These things happen sometimes, but they don't mean nothin', I swear. It's no big deal."

I stared at the ground, chewing my lip, lost in the grey area.

"I'm sorry, okay?" He reached his hand out, his fingers grazing my thigh. "Look, it's great to have you on the tour. I... You're adding so much to the songs, and..." A hiccup took him by surprise. "I don't wanna fuck that up."

I closed my eyes and all I could see was the kiss.

"I'm fine," I spat. "Don't worry about me."

"Hey guys, you alright?" Lawson came out the door and walked up to us. "Everything okay?"

"We're fine, apparently," Liam said sourly. "She's fine, I'm fine, we're all dandy." He pushed himself to his feet. "You two have fun, then," he grumbled, and started towards the bar. I watched him out of the corner of my eye, my heart aching.

Then he stopped and turned around, and I couldn't help but look up and hope he was coming back for me. But he just picked up his rum bottle and, with shoulders slumped, wobbled back inside.

Lawson sat down next to me and leaned forward to catch my eye. "You okay, Haze?"

"Yeah," I said, trying to calm my breathing. "No. I don't know. I don't know what's happening."

"What do you mean?"

"I don't know where I stand with him, Laws. Like, we're together, but we're not *together*, are we? I don't think that's how he does things."

Lawson sighed and shook his head. "I'm sorry, Haze."

"Where does that leave me? Do I just sit back and let him snog all his fans, and go fuck Ivy whenever he feels like it?" I drew a shaky breath and looked up at the night sky. No stars could be seen, outshone as they were by the bright lights of Los Angeles.

"I gotta admit, though," said Lawson, "I haven't seen him like this in a while."

"Like how?"

"Like, so into someone."

"Really?" I felt my eyes grow big and hopeful.

"Really. He's got a thing for you, big time. And I—I think it scares him. He doesn't usually let people in."

I nodded, looking down at my rainbow shoes. "Some big walls around that heart of his."

"Exactly. He's a good guy deep down. He's just a bit messed up when it comes to things like this. Like, relation-ships and stuff. I think he gets a bit lost. But it's hard, I mean..." Lawson hesitated. "I've never seen him with, like, a girlfriend. You know?"

"Yeah... That's what I figured."

We sat in silence for a moment before Lawson stood up. "Wanna come back inside?"

"Be there in a minute. Thanks, Laws."

I was left with the hazy night and shrouded sky, around me a constant hum of traffic and the distant wail of sirens. Well, what had I expected? I was only here on loan anyway. My carriage would turn into a pumpkin eventually. Why not enjoy the ride while I had the chance?

Taking one final lungful of the night blossoms, I walked back into the sweat and noise. Liam stood by the bar talking to Mango, and I was relieved to see him away from the fangirls. He saw me walk in, said something in Mango's ear, then came up to me. He seemed a bit sharper than a minute ago, and I could guess why.

"Haze, can I talk to you?"

"Sure," I said, feeling less hostile now.

"I'm sorry, I was being a dick, okay? Please don't be mad

at me." He lowered his head and his fringe dropped forwards. "And I'm sorry about yesterday. I just… I was trying to sort some shit out in my head. It wasn't fair on you."

"What shit?"

"Just… my shit. Never mind."

I took a step closer and forced him to meet my eyes. "You can tell me."

He looked at me through the strands of his near-black hair. Then a lopsided smirk gradually formed. "Well, Detective Griffin," he said, shaking the fringe out of his face. "You got some strange hold on me. You won't have any trouble getting information outta me."

My heart twirled at his words and I tilted my head with a cheeky expression. "Well?"

His smile faded and he looked out over the bar. "I just don't do this sorta thing. I'm not used to it."

"What do you mean?"

"Like, tell people stuff. Private things. But you… You lure it out of me, somehow. It feels good to tell you things. Feels like you care. But yesterday, I dunno… It freaked me out a little. Also, remembering the whole thing, it still hurts. I just needed some space to figure things out." He looked back at me, his brow furrowed. "Does that make sense?"

I nodded. "It does."

He reached for my hand and weaved our fingers together. "I missed you last night."

His hand felt warm in mine and I gave it a squeeze. "I missed you too."

"So, we okay?"

The clock behind the bar chimed three times. The witching hour was upon us. I was beginning to feel like I didn't give a shit anymore about categorising and naming whatever was going on between me and Liam. Life – and my visa – felt too short to worry about silly disagreements. I looked up at Liam, drew closer to him, allowed myself to dive into his eyes and get lost in their surging currents.

"Fine," I said, narrowing my eyes with a mischievous grin. "On one condition."

He gave me a curious look, his crooked smile appearing. "What?"

"I've always wanted to see the Hollywood Sign." I grabbed his waist and pulled him closer. "Take me there?"

His smile grew wider. "Let's go."

* * *

We stepped out of our cab near the top of Mount Lee as the first glimmer of dawn bled into the sky. Liam took my hand and we walked up the sandy path that curved around the hilltop. We followed a bend and my breath caught in my throat as the glowing mass of Los Angeles came into view. And there, perched on the hillside were the iconic letters, inverted from where we stood.

I walked slowly, staring out over the city that stretched before us, infinitely vaster than San Francisco. Jagged hills rose out of the mountainside, framing an immense sea of orange lights that burned and pulsed under the slowly paling sky. The air felt cool and gentle, tinged with some exotic blossoms and dry desert sand.

We sat in the brittle grass and watched as the metropolis came to life under the rising sun.

"You're forgiven," I teased, giving Liam a poke.

"Easy," he grinned.

I leaned my head on his shoulder and rested my eyes on the sparkling vista.

"So, um, Haze, I was thinking..."

"Yeah?"

"What are your plans, like, after the tour? When do you go back home?"

I sat up, my heart sinking at the thought. Summer had only just begun, with its false promise of forever. But this adventure, like everything else, had an expiry date.

"Fourteenth September," I said.

"You got a ticket already?"

"Yeah, I had to get one as part of my visa."

He nodded. "Okay," he said, forcing a smile. "Just checking."

I ran my hand over the soft skin of his arm, then down along his charcoal jeans. He raised his eyes to me and I held them as I squeezed his leg, my hand edging back up his thigh. The future felt like a distant and intangible concept. All I had was the here and now, and I intended to make the most of it.

With a sly smile I lifted one leg and straddled him, my arms resting on his shoulders. He looked achingly beautiful in the faint morning light; his pale skin like a transparent layer which could never conceal the tinge of sadness that never seemed to go away.

Slowly, I leaned in and kissed him, tasting his lips and tongue and neck, and he grabbed my hips, pushing himself against me, and I felt him grow hard. He guided me onto my back and climbed on top of me, his soft hands tracing a treasure map over my body.

Beyond us, the vast chaos of the City of Dreams carried on glittering.

TWENTY

I'm not sure what time it is, and frankly I don't care. I was supposed to call Mother to let her know where I was, but we're having too much fun and I've decided to forget. The night is young and free, and so are we.

We've left Tom's house and brought the party to the local cemetery. Our voices echo over the graves, calling the ghosts to come join our midnight revelry. We laugh and holler, leaving a trail of empty beer bottles in our wake. Some of us have begun to pair up, and something crackles through the air.

We sit down by a mossy brick wall, and Lydia throws her arm over my shoulder.

"I've noticed Tom looking at you," she says, throwing me an overt wink.

"You have not," I protest, although I have noticed it, too.

"You should go talk to him!"

I look over and see Tom chatting to Finn and Lucian, hands in his pockets, occasionally throwing me a glance. I smile at Lydia. "Maybe I will."

"That's my girl! More beers over here, please!"

Petra pops open some bottles and passes them round. Someone has brought a portable speaker and starts playing music. Summer is just around the corner and the stars are out to play.

But our merriments come to a halt when we hear a stuttering siren approach, the surrounding headstones assaulted by a piercing blue light.

"It's the police!" someone shouts.

I stare in disbelief as two officers climb out of a patrol car.

"What's going on here then?" the female officer asks as they come walking towards us. Everyone freezes, their beer bottles dropping to the ground. The music stops.

* * *

"I'm sorry to disturb you at this late hour, ma'am."

My mother doesn't respond, just stands gripping the front door with bloodshot eyes.

"The kids were making a racket down at the graveyard, and we had complaints from local residents."

Mother turns to me, iron eyes drilling into mine. "Thank you for bringing her home," she says, her voice like granite. "I don't know what has come over her lately. I will see that this doesn't happen again."

The police car drives off to deal with the rest of my wayward friends, and I stand shamefaced in the hallway. Mother looks at me for the longest time. Disappointment sits around her pursed lips, and fury burns in her eyes. I curl my shoulders inwards to make myself small.

"It was no big deal," I say. "It was just a party."

"Just a party!" Mother repeats, exasperated. "Why didn't you call? Don't you understand that I worry about you? I've been up all night waiting for a sign of life."

"Come on." I sigh and roll my eyes, and for a second I feel like Amber. "You're overreacting."

"Have you forgotten that we're on our own now? You only have me *left, and the burden of raising you falls on my shoulders! You should be thankful that I even care."*

I stare at the floor. "Can I go to my room?"

"Are you drunk, too?"

I say nothing.

"That does it. Hazel, I'm pulling you out of that school. It's been nothing but a terrible influence on you. I barely recognise you anymore."

I raise my head slowly, gaping in shock. "You... You can't do that!"

"Yes, I can. If I believe it's in your best interest, I will do everything in my power to make it so."

"But... Where am I supposed to go? What school—"

"You'll be homeschooled. I've taken this under careful consideration, and I know what must be done. I'll get you a tutor to run you through the GCSEs—"

"What about my friends?!"

"Those people are not your friends," she spits. "They don't care about you. Look where they've got you. You have to think about your future, Hazel! You're going to be a successful artist, and you need to stay focused."

"But I hate painting!"

Mother gasps and puts a hand to her chest. "You don't mean that."

"I don't want to be an artist! I just want to be a normal kid."

"A 'normal kid' who gets pissed up in the local cemetery? A normal kid, who is escorted home by the police? Yes, I can see why."

"You can't do this," I mutter, crossing my arms. "I'll tell Dad."

"Oh, you think Mallory will care? You think he will abandon his new position and hop on the first train from Paris to make sure you get to stay in school? Leave his clients and his fancy events and come home to make sure his family is happy?" Something sour comes over Mother's face and she turns away. "I wouldn't hold my breath, dear."

An awkward silence hangs in the air. I am exhausted, deflated, and now terrified for my future.

"This is final. I will set it in motion tomorrow, and we'll start after the summer break. I will find you a suitable tutor, and this way we can put more focus on your artistic development. Imagine how far you can come! This is a great opportunity for you, Hazel. A lot of young artists would do anything to be in your position. You should be grateful."

I swallow hard, my eyes on the floor. Silent tears trickle down my cheeks and drip off my chin.

"This conversation is over," Mother says, wiping a tear from her own cheek. "Go to your room."

TWENTY-ONE

Over the next few weeks we weaved our way across the desert states, performing and partying all over the south-west. We slept in hotels, motels and our mobile bunk beds, partied with strangers and old friends of the band, and consumed more coffee and booze than we did food, but life was ours and the night was always young and so we kept going. Object Impermanence were beginning to feel like family.

On lazy afternoons, we'd find a shady spot to escape the dusty desert heat and play music. Ivy would bring out her glockenspiel and experiment with new melodies to suit our set. I learned some of the songs on guitar, too, and occasionally we'd try to write new songs, all of us together. Summertime, lie-ins and road trip life made the perfect recipe for inspiration.

Sometimes, Liam would let me sit with him as he composed a new song. It was a miraculous thing to behold, the way he reached into the ether and picked out the most exquisite verses, as though they were revealed to him like stars at twilight – one by one falling into place, twinkling with infinite mystery. Watching him create so freely reminded me of the feeling of a brush in my hand, in that safe space of my early childhood; making magic out of nothing.

* * *

When we finally left the desert, I was relieved to see the lunar landscape be gradually replaced with lush woods and open fields broken up by muddy rivers. We were entering the Deep South, bursting with life under a blazing July sun. I watched in fascination as we drove past desolate country churches, gun stores, roadside pawn shops and grand mansions in one big, glorious mix.

Our destination was New Orleans, where we would stay for a week in Ivy's aunt's summer house. All the drifting and drinking and singing had left me a little frayed, and I had needed some of Liam's uppers and downers to level me out. A whole week with a house to ourselves sounded like just what I needed.

The summer house sat in a breathtaking suburb of grand, wooden houses with wrap-around porches and perfectly trimmed lawns. Fairy tale oak trees sprawled across the sky and shaded the streets, their crooked branches draped in hanging moss like beards of wise old men.

But the heat was something else. The desert had been burning hot, but dry as dust. Here, the air felt close and clammy, enveloping us like cling film. We escaped inside where Ivy led us into a bright, airy kitchen, all high ceiling and wood panelling painted in sage and cream.

We dropped our bags and leaned against chairs and countertops, fanning ourselves.

"I don't know how you can wear long sleeves today, Ivy," I said.

She tugged at the bell sleeves of her silky top. "I mean, I grew up here, so I don't mind the heat."

Liam plonked himself down on a stool by the breakfast bar. "Don't worry," he said to me. "The evenings are much cooler. We'll just siesta all day and stay up all night."

Lawson chuckled. "Basically your dream come true, you nocturnal beast."

"Ain't that the truth." Liam put his arm around my waist and pulled me close, and I noticed Ivy giving us a sideways glance. Lately, Liam had been a bit freer with his affections towards me, and as much as it thrilled me, I still felt like an intruder. Nothing had been defined and so there were no clear rules – and I couldn't help but wonder what went on between them once I was out of sight.

She kept her eyes on us for a brief, uncomfortable moment, then headed for the hallway. "I'll go switch on the AC," she said, and after she disappeared, I could relax in Liam's arms.

"Right, onto more urgent matters," said Liam, grinning. "Where are the beers at?"

I looked around at our new home with an expectant smile. Through the large windows I could see a wild garden of thriving greenery, a Louisiana jungle at full bloom. When Victor opened the patio door, we could hear lazy birdsong and the gentle tinkle of a windchime. Despite the sticky heat I was already falling for the beautiful South, and I looked forward to some midnight magic in this enchanting town.

* * *

The following night, Liam and I headed out to explore New Orleans. We brought a beer each and wandered down Canal Street towards the riverfront. Streetcars trundled up and down the tracks in the middle of the road, alongside large palm trees that sat unmoving in the thick air, like rows of frozen fireworks.

Closer to the water, we dove left down narrower streets full of colourful cafés and houses with intricate balconies resting on thin pillars. We passed little curiosity shops full of Mardi Gras masks, antiques and crystal balls, and I pressed my face to the shop windows to better see what wonders lurked in the dark. As we walked on, we began to hear music spilling out of venues and bars, vibrant jazz and soulful blues, trumpets and trombones and tinkling pianos.

"This is the French Quarter," Liam told me. "Best part of town, hands down. Old buildings, great music, and the people are wild."

"It's unreal," I said, my eyes bouncing all over the place. It was like walking through a time capsule, except the past had been covered in lights and colour and glitzy makeup. Then I noticed Liam had stopped, and I turned around. "What's wrong?"

He stood looking at me with that lopsided smile, all mischief and roguery. "Come here," he said, and I walked up to him with a quizzical look. He leaned closer. "I know a way to make this night even more special."

I narrowed my eyes at him with an intrigued smile. "What are you up to...?"

He took my hand and pulled me towards a dark corner. After making sure no one was watching, he pulled out a baggie containing two little tabs with tiny pandas on them.

"Is that... LSD?" I asked, recognising the trippy squares from movies.

"Yeah." Liam's eyes twinkled. "You in? It'll be one hell of a ride."

I looked at the tabs, then back up at Liam. "Wow, um. I don't know, I've never tried it before."

"Don't worry, it'll be great. We'll have a magical time

together, just you and me. On our own secret fairground ride."

I looked up at the sky, a midnight-blue dome enclosing this fairy tale city. Above our heads, wrought-iron balconies jutted out over the streets, their railings twisting in labyrinthine swirls. Sprightly roots melodies floated at us from every direction. A damp breeze drifted in from the Mississippi, some foghorn blowing from far across its murky waters. I did want a magical, secret adventure with Liam. Of *course* I did. A girlish excitement came over me and I broke into a grin.

"Let's do it."

"That's the spirit!" Liam pried open the baggie and poured the tabs onto his palm. "Ladies first."

"What do I do?"

"Stick it on your tongue and leave it there awhile. Until the paper disintegrates."

I picked up a tab and placed it on the tip of my tongue. It didn't taste of anything. Liam licked the other tab off his palm and grabbed my shoulders with a broad smile. "We're off to Neverland," he whispered, and swallowed me up in a big hug. A shiver ran through me as all the stars in the galaxy reached through the murky sky and filled me with their ancient light.

"How long before we feel it?" I asked.

"It'll start soon, half hour or so, and then it'll build. You'll peak in about two hours."

"And how long does it last?"

"About eight hours total."

"Eight hours?!" My hands flew to my mouth, but it was too late to back out now. Liam laughed at me, a friendly laugh that let me know I needn't worry.

"Hey, babe." Holding my shoulders, he looked me square in the eye. "Our magical adventure, remember? You won't want it to ever end."

* * *

Night-time New Orleans was like a dream even before the acid did its work on me. The cool mist rolling in from the river mingled with the sticky night air, and orange street-lights dotted the area like glowing spheres. It felt like walking through some dreamy, mid-century movie set.

"What're you smiling about?" Liam asked, looking at me with a knowing smirk.

I was grinning helplessly, as though my cheeks and jaws had a life of their own. "I think I'm feeling something."

"Oh yeah? You like?"

"I think so. I feel all... tingly."

I had become hyper-aware of my body as it moved through the surreal setting, feeling my feet as they hit the ground, my steps echoing in a beautiful rhythmic pattern against the old walls. The colours of the buildings seemed brighter; their edges blurred. The balconies seemed to move and sway as we walked past them, subtly dancing along with us in the night.

I turned to Liam. "What are you feeling?" I needed to know that we were on the same level. I didn't want to lose myself completely, unless he was losing himself right next to me.

"Visuals are coming on." He looked thoughtfully around him. God, he had the most beautiful face, his skin like gold in the soft orange light. "Euphoria setting in," he continued. His smile, as usual, lured a smile out of me. "Feelin' good," he concluded, throwing an arm over my shoulders. I slid my hand around his waist, proud to be by his side, thrilled to see where this night would take us. To think that I had escaped the confinement of my childhood to go on this shimmering adventure, which had led me to a stroll through Neverland with the most beautiful boy in the world.

We walked up Decatur Street, the mighty Mississippi rolling alongside us. Each time we passed an open door, I couldn't help but slow my steps and peer in at the explosion of colours and tunes and lights, people having a grand time drinking and dancing, watching the musicians with their merry saxophones and raucous pianos. New Orleans seemed like one giant party.

We walked onward, while the world morphed into a dazzling kaleidoscope. Contours were bending and dancing around me, lights pulsating with life. I kept glancing at Liam, wondering what he saw and thought and felt, but he gave nothing away. We turned a corner and headed down a quiet side street, past rows of modest wooden houses painted in pastels and draped in fairy lights and whimsical windchimes.

"Everything looks like paintings," I murmured, as I surveyed my new, fuzzy surroundings. "What do you see? Does everything look like oil paintings to you?"

"Not really," said Liam. "Great place for tripping, though. Pretty."

"Those flowers look just like Monet, look! You can literally see the brushstrokes. This stuff is incredible." A small willow tree dangled her bashful branches at us and I had to stop and stroke it. "Ah, like the gardens of Renoir." I sighed and traced its shape with my fingertips. "Wow, I don't think I've ever really seen a willow leaf before. They're so long and graceful, just like the branches. Like each leaf is a tiny representation of the branch itself." I craned my neck upward towards the top of the tree. "Man, there are so many perspectives in this world."

Liam chuckled and shook his head. "You enjoying that acid then?"

"Whatever." I grinned at him. "Let's lie down on the grass! Can we?"

"Sure, whatever you want."

I lay down and let the rest of my life fall away. Everything past and painful and all the unknowns of the future pulverised before the magnificent present. Above me, I could see the night sky stretch all the way to the beginning of everything that ever was, and for a moment I thought I could sense its enormity in a way I hadn't before; as though I could reach out and touch the edges of the universe and find that they are linked in an infinite loop, and that all edges are nothing but illusions, and endings are really only beginnings seen from the other side.

Liam sat gently stroking the grass at his feet. I edged closer, feeling a rush from knowing that we were hovering in a secret dimension, just the two of us, here amid the backstreets of New Orleans. I sat up and smiled at my Peter Pan.

"How come your hair is so dark, huh?" I asked, stroking his neck. "It's almost black. Are you, like, part Native American or something?"

"No, not Native American. My mother is Romani, second generation. Her parents came here from Czechoslovakia after the war. Made their escape when the government decided that they would sterilise all the Romani women."

"Whoa, that's harsh."

"Yeah, people are assholes." He leaned back and looked up towards the boundless cosmos. "My grandparents descended from gypsy people, travellers. I like to think about my ancestors, forever roaming the earth, never content to settle anywhere."

"Sounds like you now."

"Ha, yeah... I suppose."

I grinned and pulled my knees to my chest. "You're making your ancestors proud."

Liam began stroking the grass again with a pensive frown. "I'm not sure it's that… It's just the gypsy blood. It pushes us to keep moving. Maybe there's something chasing us." Then he looked up and trapped me with his dark eyes. "I love it when you smile like that," he said. "When your dimples show."

My smile faded. "I hate my dimples."

"What? But why?"

I closed my eyes, but I was shocked by a vortex of swirling patterns and quickly opened them again. "I inherited them from my mum. When I smile I look just like her, and I don't like it."

"That's silly." Liam moved closer and put his hand on my cheek. "You're not her. It's not really fair on your poor dimples to despise 'em like that, because of something that's completely out of their control. Think how they must feel."

I pressed my lips together but couldn't stop myself from laughing.

"There ya go, that's better," Liam said, poking my dimples with his fingertips. I giggled and my skin sparkled and the whole wide world shimmered before our acid eyes.

Then Liam's ringtone pierced the air, and just like that, our little bubble burst.

"Laws, what's up? Now? Sure, why not. Text me the address. Great, see ya." Liam hung up and slipped his phone back into his pocket.

"What's going on?"

"The others are at a house party in Bywater, at some friends of Lawson's. I said we'd head on over. That okay?"

I grunted. "That sounds like a mission. Can't we just stay here?"

"There's nothing going on here, though."

"Exactly." I doused him with my most persuasive grin. "So nice and peaceful."

Liam smiled and stroked my hair. "Don't worry, it'll be fun. The acid is just keeping you in the moment, but you'll enjoy the next moment just as much. Trust me."

His big eyes tickled my face, my senses all jumbled up.

"Fine," I conceded. "I trust you."

* * *

A short cab ride later, we found ourselves in front of a two-storey house with a large front porch full of music and bottles and people. My head was lost in an acid maze and I had to squint to make out shapes. Goosebumps wriggled all over my skin, and my limbs seemed unable to cooperate. I steadied myself on Liam as we walked up to the porch, where I leaned on the railing and took some deep breaths.

"How you feelin'?" Liam asked.

"Um, like I'm in some mad circus, about to shatter into a gazillion atoms. Is that normal?"

He chuckled. "Pretty much. Hey, look at this." He crouched down and pointed to a large cobweb that stretched across the corner of the porch railing. Night dew had formed droplets all over the web, like perfect shiny beads that glowed with reflections of the nearby streetlights. Liam moved closer and squinted at the tiny marvels. "Isn't that amazing?"

"So pretty," I whispered. I leaned in to study the droplets, the way they seemed to expand and contract as though they were breathing. "My mother used to do that..."

"Do what?" Liam asked, and when we stood back up my legs felt more like tentacles than bones.

"Like, point things out. When I was little. Always challenging me to see things from a different perspective, to notice things."

"I thought you didn't get on with your mom?"

"I did... At first." I could see her in my mind, the idealistic artist she once was; and before I knew it, all the other memories came pouring in like a typhoon. The acid had ramped up my brain, which now flickered with a non-stop film reel of all the things I wanted to forget.

Liam rested his elbows on the railing. "When did it change?"

"I'm not even sure..." I clutched my solar plexus, trying to scratch a restless itch burning somewhere between my ribs. "You got a smoke?"

"Sure, yeah."

We lit a couple of cigarettes and sat down in an old porch swing, which squeaked gently as we rocked back and forth.

"She was the best mother when I was little. We had a secret, special bond, she and I. She raised me to become an artist, like her."

"You an artist? Hell, Haze, you never told me this."

"No, no," I protested, flustered. "I'm not an artist. Maybe I was, I don't know. But I'm not anymore. I haven't painted for years."

"Why not?"

I closed my eyes and watched images rolling by, flashing visions of paintings we had created, Mother and I. I could taste the turpentine on my tongue.

"It felt like she got angry at the fact that I was growing up," I said. "She didn't want me to live my life, but I had to, you know? She turned bitter and depressed, and everything just broke." I took a long drag off my cigarette and felt the smoke fill me, scratching at my insides. "It scared me to see how dark her world became. To watch her turn into this gnarled, isolated thing. I figured it was art that made her that way, the way she hid away for days on end with only her canvases for company. And the colours... She used to paint bright and bold, but gradually she reduced her palette to black and purple. Every single painting, just those two gloomy colours. It terrified me. And still she kept pushing me to become like her. I couldn't understand why."

I winced and took another drag while I sifted through my thoughts. Liam sat patiently listening.

"So, I stopped painting. It was too frightening, too painful. Instead I studied it, learned about all the great artists, but I could never again pick up a brush."

I paused, my mind tumbling through a wormhole of memories.

"My older sister was a piece of work, too. She would always pick fights with Mother. It was awful. Then one day, Dad got this promotion. He's an art dealer, that's how he met my mum. His new position required him to spend a lot of time in Paris, and I think he saw a chance to get out of it all. Just sort of drifted away, without an explanation. I mean, we all knew why, but still. He just gradually disappeared."

"Shit, Haze. That sucks."

"He finally divorced her just as I had finished school. I thought I would go to uni, get out of that town, but she needed me..." I drew a shaky breath, still gripping my chest. "She needed me. Fuck."

"What's wrong?"

"I just feel so guilty," I said, squashing my cigarette in a flowerpot. "For abandoning her."

"But you didn't abandon her. Like you said, she can't blame you for living your life."

"Yeah, maybe..."

"Not maybe. You can't be pandering to people who don't consider your needs, too."

"She *did* consider my needs, though. She made sure I always had everything I needed to develop as an artist. And my dad always put food on the table, even after Mother's paintings stopped selling. I had it good."

Liam scoffed and flicked his cigarette onto the lawn. "If you say so. Can I ask you one question though?" He turned and looked at me intently. "Did you feel loved?"

"I had everything—"

"Don't give me all that bullshit about a stable home or someone teaching you to paint. I mean, did you feel loved? Unconditionally loved, supported, seen?"

I stared at my shoes, the rainbow stripes burning bright, blending into each other.

"Thought so," he said.

I was a bit taken aback. I had never thought of it that way. If anything, my mother loved me too much, a love so overbearing it threatened to choke me.

"It's harder when everything points to a stable home. When, from the outside, everything seems fine. Makes it harder to see the abuse."

"Abuse?" I repeated, sceptical. "That's a bit strong. Well, maybe not in your case, I don't know..."

"Hazel, using your child to feed your own ego, be that suffering artist or self-righteous saviour, that's abuse." Liam seemed to be growing agitated, stomping his foot against the porch planks and flicking his lighter in and out of life. "Loving your child only on a narrow set of conditions, that's abuse. Emotional neglect."

The garden was swaying and breathing its acid dance before us. Everything shimmered with blurry streaks of green and red and blue, my mind like a prism splitting the world into its component parts. I was gazing into my past, turning over memories, re-examining events. Abuse?

Liam pushed himself off the swing and the change in balance made me jump. He leaned against the railing, facing away from me. A little unsteady, I got to my feet and stood next to him.

"Hey," I said, reaching my hand out until our fingers

touched. "Liam, what's on your mind? Do you want to talk about it?"

Little grooves appeared in his jaw as he clenched and unclenched it. Then, in one swift motion, he yanked his hand away and took a step back.

"Enough of this sad shit," he spat. His hard voice made me flinch. "I need a drink."

With that, he stormed inside. I went after him, his words echoing in my mind. While Liam spoke to some people in the kitchen, I was back in my childhood bedroom, hanging paintings on my wall. I was on Sandgate Beach, picking pebbles with Mother, naming every colour I could see in the ocean. Overcast days always had a very different palette to sunny ones. I was in my mother's studio, the smell of jasmine tea tickling my nose. Then, at the art gallery, watching as she received high praise from her many admirers, and sold painting after painting. I was there, wishing I was her, wanting nothing more than to grow up to become like her, to make her proud.

Someone bumped into my side and I tumbled into the kitchen counter, suddenly aware of my surroundings. I was being tossed like a corpse on a stormy sea between the here and now and the stinging memories of all that was lost.

I called Liam's name, but couldn't see him anywhere. The world throbbed and warped around me. "I want it to stop now," I mumbled, pressing my hands against my head to keep it from shattering.

I tried to find a focal point, but everything was moving and twisting before me. The music and laughter seemed to manifest into physical form, a black snake slithering through the air and bending the three dimensions into something unrecognisable.

I needed out.

Fumbling my way down the hall, I opened every door

until I found a bathroom and sank down onto the cool tiles. The walls kept changing colour around me, and sounds from outside were fluctuating and pulsating. I needed to focus on something familiar and reached for my phone to look for a soothing song.

But just as I was about to open it, I was startled by the shrill chiming of my ringtone, the vibration like a jack-hammer through my skull. The phone slipped out of my hands but kept ringing. I picked it up and squinted at the screen to see who was calling.

No.

Not now.

Mother.

TWENTY-TWO

I stared at the bright screen, unable to move. My limbs were fettered, my breath trapped in my chest. Why now, when my brain was swimming in a multi-dimensional soup I could barely see through? The ringtone ricocheted against the hard tiles and resonated through my bones, sounding an alarm deep inside me that said, *Don't answer.*

Then, another voice echoed through my head. *Maybe she needs you. You can't just ignore her. What if something is wrong?*

Then another. *I miss you, Mother. I miss who you used to be. Who we used to be.*

Something small and frail inside me was reaching out, longing to hear her voice – the soft and soothing tone it once had, before it became saturated with bitterness. Back when everything made sense and nothing was my fault.

The ringing stopped abruptly and all was black and silent. I swallowed hard, gripping my phone. I imagined her at home, alone, lost, needing someone, and the guilt wrapped its toxic vines around my heart. I knew I wasn't going to be able to let it go.

Leaning on the sink for support, I slowly got to my feet. I

opened the tap and splashed some water on my face, then switched on the light. I gave myself a hard stare in the mirror, my phone poised like a weapon.

"You can do this," I said to my warping reflection.

With a shaking hand, I unlocked the phone and went to call history. Pressed call back. Put the phone to my ear. Heard the familiar *ring-ring, ring-ring*.

"Hazel?"

It wasn't the honey voice of the mother I wanted to remember. This voice sounded frail and sharp-edged, like broken china.

"Hazel, are you there?"

"Ye-yes, I'm here." I maintained eye contact with myself, hoping it would help me focus. "How are you, Mother?"

"Oh, as can be expected," she sighed. "I'm becoming old and irrelevant."

"You're not," I heard myself protest, even though something stung my gut as I spoke the words. I was tired of refuting her self-pity.

"No, it's fine, it's what happens when you grow old. You'll see. And the world has tired of my art, it would seem. To think, Hazel. Once, I had a following of people who all wanted a piece of me. I had two children, and a loving husband. Somehow, I still ended up with nothing."

"Mother—"

"No, no, it's fine. I've come to terms with it." Her words curdled as they left her mouth, bitter as mugwort. "It's part of life's natural progression."

I pressed my lips together and there was a brief, painful silence.

"Where are you?" she asked. "Why haven't you called?"

I didn't know what to say. Because I couldn't bear the pain? Because it was easier to look the other way than to turn and face the guilt? Because I was finally enjoying a life of my own?

"I don't know, I've been really busy over here."

There was another silence, and then I heard a poorly disguised sniffle. My eyes rolled around in their sockets. Not this again.

"Hazel." Her voice was like that of a pleading child, and I didn't know why but it made me feel sick. Stomach-churning, near-gagging sick. "I don't have anyone. I can't stand the fact that you are so far away. That there is an entire ocean between us, Hazel. It's not right."

Four words bounced around my skull: *You made your bed.*

"Did you know that your father has met someone else?"

"Er, no. I don't know what he's up to."

"I saw a picture of them together. She's far too young for him, it's revolting. Some Parisian tart who calls herself an artist. No doubt she's using him for his money and contacts."

"Stop it, Mum," I said, leaning my forehead against the cool porcelain of the sink. *Just please stop it.*

"Don't you call me that. You know I hate that."

I stood back up and stared into the mirror, my pupils expanded into big, black pools.

"I'm just so lonely," she continued. "It's unbearable."

Her words, charged with years of twisted sorrow, poured into my ears like drops of belladonna, and my reflection began to morph before me. I leaned forward in shock as I watched myself age, sharp lines appearing around my eyes and mouth, and my irises fading to a pale grey. I pressed my palm to the glass. It was my mother's face.

"What's happening...?" I whispered, my breath caught in my throat.

"Hazel? Hazel, are you there?"

I couldn't respond. I stood frozen, gaping at the impossible metamorphosis. "No... It can't be..."

"Hazel? Are you talking to someone else? This is your mother calling you, can you please pay attention?"

"Mum, I'm not, I can't... I gotta go."

I fumbled with my phone and ended the call, but once again it slipped out of my trembling hands and crashed onto the tiles. When I picked it up, there was a fresh gash across the screen.

"Fuck!"

I needed to get outside.

I pulled open the bathroom door and stumbled down the hall, rushing to get out before the walls collapsed around me. In the living room, I elbowed my way through the mess of noise and colour and bodies, around me a sea of unfamiliar faces.

"Liam?!" I shouted, although I wasn't sure if anyone could hear me. "Has anyone seen Liam?"

I staggered sideways and landed on a coffee table. Someone asked if I was okay, but I couldn't answer. Instead I slumped onto the floor, covering my ears and squeezing my eyes shut. But in that quiet space other things crept to the surface: Mother's accusing eyes, the subtle insults, her never-ending pain; then Liam's voice, soft and sorrowful, his sweet promises and talk of dying.

"Stop, please stop," I whimpered, but when I removed my hands the music pounded in my head, my compromised brain scrambling it into senseless chaos. My stomach began to churn and my jaw was twitching. I had to get out. I couldn't throw up, not here.

I sucked in as much air as my lungs could hold and focused all my strength on standing up. Step by step, I made it to the kitchen, bumped into some people and mumbled an apology, found the back door and out, out into the cool night.

Fresh air filled my lungs and soothed my skin, and the thumping music became muffled and soft. Grass! I fell onto the ground and stroked the lawn with open palms, feeling its green softness tickle my hands, so familiar and gentle, damp with dew. I felt my stomach relax, the gagging reflexes ease up.

I swung my legs in front of me and removed my shoes, then shakily stood back up. Bare feet sweeping over wet grass, I started towards the back of the garden, to the farthest, darkest, quietest corner. *Just keep going, just get through the night—*

"Hazel!"

Huh? Did someone call me, or was it just in my head?

"Hazel, wait up!" I turned around and saw Lawson jogging towards me, his big, curly hair flopping with each step. Panting, he stopped and put his hand on my shoulder. "You made it! You okay?"

"Lawson... Hi."

He took one look at me and knew. "Haze, what did Liam give you?"

Embarrassed, I looked down at my bare feet. "Bit of acid."

He nodded. "How you feeling?"

I hugged myself and leaned in towards him. "Not good, Laws, I don't feel good at all. Can you help me? Just, can you please be with me?"

"Of course! Hazel, I'm always here for you. Tell me what's wrong?"

"I just feel like—like I'm losing grip of reality. Everything is warped, and terrifying, and I was inside and my mum called and it was awful. I got so overwhelmed and I thought I was going to be sick, so I had to get out, but it's really hard to walk..."

He opened his long arms and pulled me towards him. "Shhh..." He held me tight and stroked my hair, and the sensation was enough to distract me from all the mess in my head. "I'm here now, you'll be fine."

I sniffled, feeling pathetic and lost. "It's just, I thought Liam would be here…"

"I know, Haze, I'm sorry."

I pulled back from Lawson's embrace and looked up at him. He seemed even taller than usual, or maybe it was I who felt smaller. "Have you seen him anywhere?"

"I haven't, sorry. I'm sure he's around, but he can be a bit elusive, as you know."

"Yeah…"

"No need to worry, though. You'll feel better real soon. I've been there. The acid doesn't peak like this for very long. Water helps, I'll get you some. Stay right here."

He bounced off and swiftly returned with a bottle. The cool liquid felt like a cleansing river running through my body, returning life to my veins. I felt better already, lulled by Lawson's reassurances. But I wished they had come from Liam. *Our magical adventure*, he had said. Where was he now?

And, as always, there was Lawson, so sweet and kind, so sensible. He really was the opposite of Liam: an open book, selfless, straight-laced. I looked up at him and let a grateful smile come to my lips. He smiled back at me, holding my gaze steadily.

My brain was calming down and the spiralling, swirling world around me was slowing. As I studied Lawson's face, I noticed things I hadn't before – his soft cheeks, the curve of his eyebrows, and long, dark eyelashes, almost like a girl's. He was a very beautiful boy, too.

I leaned against his chest and it felt so warm, like a hot water bottle pressed against a painful tummy. His heartbeat was slow and regular, just like I had imagined it would be. I searched the sky for evidence of something other than us, but above was only black fog; not a star in sight nor planet nor galaxy. It was just us here, on this earth, with me so far from home, surrounded by foreign seas. Really, I had no one. I was on my own. But wrapped in Lawson's steady arms, I could breathe easy, at last.

I looked at Lawson again, surveying his features.

"Your eyes…," I began.

"Oh my god, are they still there?" He put his hands to his eyes, pretending to feel for them. I laughed and put my hands on his chest.

"Stop! I meant, I've never noticed their colour before."

He stopped teasing and looked right at me, giving me plenty of opportunity to study his irises.

"Green?"

"Well, they're aquamarine, but there's this brown bit around the pupils."

"Oh yeah, that."

"I've never seen that before. They look like islands in a sea. Something solid amid stormy waters."

We stood there, inches away from each other, both now knowing what was about to happen and both reluctant to stop it, even though we knew we should.

I tilted my head and stood on my tiptoes, and before I knew it our lips had met, and I fell into his soft kiss and the way his hand found its way onto my hip, so warm against my body, radiating heat. I had found an island in the storm, and I wanted to light a fire and set up camp. For the first time in what seemed like forever, I felt safe.

Then my feet slowly found their way to the ground again. Our lips separated but instead our eyes met, and we stood like that for a moment, looking into each other but saying nothing. Then Lawson lowered his gaze and broke the silence.

"I'm sorry…"

"For what?" I noticed his hand was still resting on my hip, and I wanted it to stay there.

"I've…" He looked out over the garden, then back at me.

"I've imagined that moment many times over. You have no idea. But I can't... You're Liam's girl. I can't do this."

"Oh..." His hand slipped away and I felt its absence like ice against my skin. My cheeks burned and I looked down at the ground. Had I got involved with the wrong guy? How typical, falling for the tragic anti-hero and neglecting to notice the wonderful boy-next-door.

"But just so you know," he began, and I slowly looked back up. "I've imagined that kiss for a long time." He held my gaze, showing a transparency and earnestness I had never seen in Liam.

Damn.

I still ached for closeness and took a cautious step towards Lawson. Gently, he enveloped me in his arms, and I leaned into the soft rhythm of his beating heart. As I closed my eyes, geometrical patterns danced on my eyelids, while my brain twirled like a pinwheel in a hurricane. *Someone, anyone, take me away, hold me close, keep me safe. I can't do it by myself.*

* * *

When morning finally came, the hallucinations had given way to a persistent headache. I had spent the remainder of the night chatting to Lawson, safe on our little patch of lawn. But as the sky paled and people began to disperse, I went again to look for Liam.

I walked slowly, keeping my head level so as to not aggravate the pounding. I realised it had been a long time since I had eaten anything, but hunger felt far off. I was so weary, my mind like shredded lace, torn and flimsy.

I found him in one of the bedrooms, sitting on the floor with a guitar, surrounded by a group of people. I couldn't help but notice the pretty girl by his side.

"There you are!" he said, standing up to greet me. "Where have you been?"

"Where have *you* been?" I countered, hugging myself to keep my molecules intact.

"Oh, sorry, Haze. We've just been in here chatting and playing music."

"Cool," I mumbled, eyes to the floor.

"Guys, this is Hazel, she's in the band."

"Hi." I gave them a pathetic wave, then turned to Liam. "Can we please go? Everyone else is leaving."

"Oh, sure…," he said, looking surprised. "Um, twenty minutes?"

I sighed. "Fine."

I waited for him to wrap up. When we walked outside to get a cab, I didn't speak. What was there to say? The world looked sad and lonesome, all its colours watered down by the bleak dawn.

"You okay?" Liam asked, a little hesitantly.

"I'm fine," I muttered.

"Babe, please. Don't be pissed."

I shook my head, looking down at the pavement. "I just… I needed some help earlier, it was pretty scary."

"I know, I'm sorry. I got distracted."

"Yeah."

He looked down at his feet and scratched his neck. "Look, Haze. I was feeling a bit off earlier. All that shit about our parents, and… I don't know, it got too painful. I just had to switch it up, focus on something else." He threw me a remorseful glance. "It's no excuse, I'm sorry. I didn't mean to lose you all night."

I stood holding myself, chewing my lower lip. "You could have told me."

"I know, I know," he said, impatiently. "But I didn't know how to talk about it, really."

He shuffled his feet, looking at me through his dark fringe. Then he took a step closer, risking an arm around my shoulders.

"Don't be mad, Hazelnut."

"Liam, I'm tired."

He thought for a moment. "I know what will fix this."

Our taxi rolled up and Liam leaned down to speak to the driver.

"Hey, man, could we make a detour to Café Étienne?"

We got in and our driver stopped a few blocks away, outside a small bistro.

"Wait here," Liam said, and disappeared inside. I didn't understand how he had all this energy still; I could barely muster enough to nod. A few minutes later he re-emerged with two takeaway cups. As he stepped inside, the smell of roast parsnip filled the cab.

"Soup!" he grinned. "It'll fix you right up."

I hadn't thought I was able to eat, but it did smell delicious. I took the hot cup and held it in my hands, breathing in the comforting scent of root vegetables and oil.

"Truce?" Liam asked, giving me the puppy eyes.

I rolled my eyes but couldn't help but smile. "Fine."

The soup slipped down my throat with a soothing warmth that spread from my tummy all the way to my fingertips and toes. The muscles in my neck relaxed and my mind began to ease. I leaned into Liam and pressed my face against his chest, which smelled of sweat and smoke and a fruity tinge of cologne. He wrapped an arm around me and held me tight, and I stayed very still, wishing he would never let go.

TWENTY-THREE

I woke in twisted sheets, hot and sticky. Through the window I could see heavy clouds obscuring the sky, and the humid air felt dense in my lungs. I turned around, but Liam was already out of bed. I could hear soft strumming and crawled forwards to the edge of the mattress. He was sitting on the floor in the corner, cradling his guitar, searching for new melodies.

"Hey," I said, my voice dry and cracking.

He looked up with faraway eyes, lips in a thoughtful pout.

"You okay?" I asked.

He nodded and returned to his guitar, his fingers deftly plucking the strings as though they were an extension of his body. His lips were quietly mouthing words, looking for the right combinations. This was comedown Liam; I had seen it before. When he felt like this, all he could do was play guitar or take coke. I was glad he had chosen the guitar today.

My stomach grumbled and I realised how hungry I was, but I couldn't bring myself to move. Instead, I curled up into a ball and let my mind drift back to memories of the trip. It felt like a shimmering dream and a distant nightmare all at once, now slipping back into my subconscious. I was glad to find my mind somewhat intact again.

"I'm hungry," I whispered at last, looking over at Liam. He didn't respond. Slowly, I rolled off the bed and gently stood up. "Okay," I breathed through a sudden headrush, "I'm fine. I'll go get something to eat."

I didn't know why I spoke. He wasn't listening anyway.

* * *

Everyone else was already up. Ivy sat in lotus position on a chair, sipping a glass of orange juice. Mango lay lazily draped over the chair opposite, munching on a bagel. Victor was buttering bread, and Lawson was making coffee.

"Morning, guys." I felt brittle, like I could shatter at any moment.

They all looked up and greeted me, and Lawson's eyes lingered on me a little longer than the rest.

"You hungry?" Mango gestured at the brunch spread before him. I scanned it, looking for anything I could imagine eating.

"Hmm, yes, thanks... But first, coffee."

I walked over to the machine and Lawson handed me a fresh cup. Our hands touched as he passed the drink to me, and I held his gaze for a moment.

It didn't go unnoticed.

"Well, you guys." Ivy's languid voice floated through the kitchen. "I say, y'all got quite friendly last night, didn't ya?"

My face burned. What had she seen?

Mango's curiosity was piqued. "Oh, did you now?" He sat up straighter in his chair and rubbed his hands together. "Let's have the gossip!"

"Oh, nothing but a romantic kiss in the hanging gardens of Nawlins," Ivy cooed. "Not that I was peepin', but it was hard to miss." She shook her hair and sipped her juice, pleased with her observational skills.

I stood gaping in stunned shock when Ivy looked over towards the hallway, her smile widening.

"I don't suppose you've told ol' Liam, have ya?"

I swung around, and the air was knocked out of me when I saw Liam leaning against the doorpost with a puzzled expression on his face.

"Liam, it's not…" What could I say? I couldn't deny it.

He frowned and looked from me to Lawson. "You two?"

"Bro, it was nothing," Lawson protested, throwing his hands up. "We were drunk, okay?"

"I was looking for you, Liam." My stomach contracted at the memory of the hallway closing in on me. "I was freaking out, and Lawson looked after me."

I knew this was no excuse, but I wanted him to know.

"Oh, so that's fine, then," Liam said sharply. "If you can't find one, take the other!"

"Hey!" I snapped. "Who are you to talk?"

Liam backed away, his already hollow eyes full of disappointment and distrust. "Whatever," he muttered, then turned and walked back to the bedroom, slamming his palm hard against the wall.

I spun around and narrowed my eyes at Ivy. "Thanks a *lot*," I hissed. To my surprise, she wasn't smiling smugly as I had expected, but rather looked a little contrite. I put my coffee back on the counter, glanced briefly at Lawson, then headed to our bedroom to set things straight.

He was back on the floor, guitar in lap. I closed the door and stood opposite him, but he wouldn't look up.

"Liam."

He kept his eyes on the fretboard.

"Liam, for fuck's sake, look at me!"

Slowly, he lifted his eyes, red and raw, fuming. I hated seeing him like this.

"I don't know why you're so upset."

He let out a bitter laugh and returned to his strings. "Fine."

"Honestly, though, I don't. It's not like we're exclusive. You go round doing whatever you want with all your groupies, and god knows what you get up to with Ivy."

I could see Liam's jaw tensing, his left hand gripping the fretboard so tightly that his nails went white. Then he pushed the guitar away and shot to his feet.

"I haven't done a fucking thing with Ivy since we met, alright?"

I crossed my arms. "How do I even know if that's—"

"And the fans," he cut in. "I mean, come on. It's not like I sleep with them. Not anymore."

I pressed my lips together, my pulse throbbing in my temples.

"And Lawson, of all people? My best friend?!" He ran a hand through his hair and walked over to the window, his back to me. "What a fucking cliché."

Shame crept in and I looked at the floor while a heavy silence expanded through the room. I wrung my hands, holding my breath.

Then Liam let out a long sigh and leaned his forehead against the window. "What does it matter, anyway? It's not like this can last."

"Liam…" I wasn't ready for this to end, not now, not like this. "Don't—"

"No, it's fine." He turned to me with cold eyes. "You're better off with Lawson. He's a much better person than me."

"Liam—"

"Don't. It's true. Fuck it. I gotta get out of here."

He grabbed his phone and wallet and stormed out the door.

"Liam, wait!" I scampered after him and tried to reach for his hand, but he pulled away. In the kitchen everyone sat breathless, watching the disaster unfold. Liam strode past them without a word.

"Later," he muttered, and slammed the door behind him. We were left with a thick silence that filled my throat like mud. Tears were rising in my chest, but I couldn't cry, not in front of the others. I swallowed hard to force them back down, pacing my breathing.

Lawson took a step towards me. "Haze, you okay?"

I waited until I could speak again without bursting into tears, then stalked up to them and stared at Ivy with all the rage in me. "Happy now?!"

She just looked at me, her eyes wide, her mouth slightly ajar.

I stomped back to our room and fell onto the bed. My head had started throbbing again. I needed food, rest, recovery; not *this*. Hurt and confusion and crushed dreams filled my lungs until I couldn't breathe, and I writhed sobbing over the messy bed. The sheets smelled of Liam and I wrapped myself in them, pressed my face to the mattress and screamed until my temples threatened to explode.

After I was all emptied out, I lay on my back staring at the ceiling, wishing I never had to move again. There was a knock on the door.

"Go away," I said, assuming it was Lawson.

"Hazel?" It was Ivy's voice, light and tentative.

I didn't respond.

"Look, I'm sorry, okay? Can I please come in?"

Now, this was new. Ivy apologising to me? I had never heard her speak in that tone before.

"Please?" she insisted.

I sighed. "Fine."

She cracked open the door, slipped inside, and closed it quietly behind her. Then she walked up to the edge of the bed and motioned to sit down.

"Go ahead," I said, still laying on my back, my eyes stinging.

Ivy sat down and looked at me with earnest concern, and it was a little unsettling. I had never seen her like this before. She picked up a box of tissues from the bedside table and handed me one.

"Thanks," I said hesitantly, still waiting for the catch. I dabbed my eyes and blew my nose, then slowly sat up and leaned against the wall. Whatever lofty expectations I'd had of this life, of joining a travelling band and falling crash-boom-bang for their beautifully vulnerable, messed-up singer... It was a fairy tale, nothing more. Here I was, the ragdoll abandoned, stitches coming undone.

"I'm sorry, Hazel. I didn't mean..." She heaved a sigh. "I didn't know he would get so mad."

I shifted my sore eyes to her.

She lowered her gaze, fuzzy locks dropping forwards. "I guess he really likes you."

I was surprised to feel a sting in my chest, not for myself, but for Ivy. If what Liam had said was true – that things had ended between them when I turned up – then this must all have been so painful for her.

My face softened and I tilted my head. Ivy looked up and wrinkled her brow. "What?"

"It's just..." I felt a warm drop at the tip of my nose and swiped it with the tissue. "I'm just surprised, is all."

"Why?"

I pinched my lips together. "Well, you know. You don't like me much. I thought you'd be happy about all this."

She squirmed and sighed, the way you sigh over a familiar old problem. "I... I like you just fine, Hazel."

"You—you do?"

"It's just how I come across. Apparently people don't find me all that friendly." She let out a sour laugh.

"Right..." I wasn't used to having heart-to-hearts with Ivy, and I didn't want to say the wrong thing.

"I don't mean to be that way. It's nothing personal." She looked up at me, and I landed in the cool waters of her eyes. "Can I...?" She gestured at the space beside me, and I nodded. As she came closer, I noticed how small and fragile she seemed.

"You okay?" I asked. This shiny porcelain doll, this perfect specimen of a girl who could transfix anyone with her beauty and command a concert hall with her haunting violin. What could possibly be wrong in her life?

She tugged at the sleeves of her jumper, pulled them down over her hands. No matter the weather, she was always wearing long-sleeve tops. I had figured it was just her Southern blood that made her less susceptible to the heat, but now she sighed and slowly pulled her jumper over her head, and my breath caught in my throat when I saw her arms.

Their pale skin was sliced with brutal, red streaks; old scars from deep cuts that would never, ever heal. I stared at them for a long time, unable to speak. She cast her eyes down, awaiting my reaction.

"Oh my god, Ivy...," I managed at last. "What happened?"

"I happened. My life happened. It's awful embarrassing, but... this is me."

"What do you mean, this is you? You did this?"

"Afraid so."

"But... Why? I thought..."

I stopped myself, afraid to say something stupid.

"You thought what? That I had the perfect life, that I was pretty and rich and lived in a big house in the suburbs? That I had everything I could ever want?"

My cheeks burned. "I guess."

"Yeah, that's what everyone thinks. And not once has anyone asked me what it's *really* like, how I feel, what I want. None of it. They just assumed. And no one saw."

"Saw what?"

"Saw *me*. Saw that I was hurtin'. That I was lonely as hell." She leaned her head against the wall. "My parents didn't give a shit about me. Teachers were busy with louder kids. And everyone at school… They thought I was fair game. Untouchable. Like they could do or say whatever, and I would react like a Barbie doll. Meanin' not at all. Some were afraid of me, I guess, and some were outright mean. Jealous, maybe, or bored, I don't know."

She pulled her knees to her chest and wrapped her arms around them, gazing into some void in front of her.

"And I tried. I tried to be the plastic doll they made me out to be. I tried to not react. Put on a mask of indifference. But the thing is, once I had put it on, it was really hard to take it off. Like, impossible. I guess I never really managed to."

And she was right. As she was telling me this, her face was still held in that steely, icy expression – eyes cool, eyebrows unmoved, lips slightly pursed.

"Cutting helped me *feel* something. Seeing my own blood reminded me that I was a real person."

I sat quietly while I let this new reality sink in.

"Thank you," I whispered finally.

"For what?"

"For… sharing. Thanks for trusting me with this. I'm glad you told me."

"Yeah?"

"Yeah."

The girl I saw in front of me looked very different to the one I had been touring with the past couple of months. Her dainty features looked less sharp and superior, and I saw how vulnerable she was underneath that thin sheet of protective ice she always carried around with her.

"I'm glad to know you better," I said, and braved a small smile. She smiled back, a childlike simper I had only seen her give to Liam. I reached out my hand and gently squeezed hers. "I guess we're all fucked up in some way."

"Would be boring otherwise, no?"

"True, that."

There we sat, her hand in mine and our pains laid bare, like sisters. It struck me that her hair was the same colour as Amber's. But I had never felt as close to Amber as I did to Ivy that afternoon, as we sat side by side on those ruffled sheets.

* * *

I waited all day for him to get in touch. I thought about texting, but figured I should give him some space. Besides, I wouldn't know what to say. It all felt broken beyond repair. I crawled into bed early, feeling too small for the big bed, and hoped he was okay.

Around three in the morning, I was woken by clanging and crashing in the kitchen. I threw the covers aside and hurried over.

"Hey!" I hissed in the dark. "You're waking everyone up."

"I don't care." He kept rummaging through the cupboards until he found a bottle of whiskey, which he grabbed and then stumbled past without looking at me.

"Liam!" I followed him down the hall and into our room.

He sank to the floor and pulled out the cork. I walked up to him and yanked the bottle out of his hand.

"Give me that," I said, reaching for the cork.

"Fuck you," he spat.

"Hey!"

"Give me the bottle," he said, trying to keep a level voice. I didn't move. "Give me the fucking bottle!" He pushed himself to his feet and staggered over, grasping for the whiskey but missing as I swung my arm around.

"Liam, please. Can we just talk? You don't need any more of this."

"I need a hella lot more of that," he growled through gritted teeth.

I stood still, the bottle weighing heavy in my hand. There was nothing I could do. I was tired. Tired of the rollercoaster, tired of all the mess. I closed my eyes, my shoulders slumping in defeat.

"Fine." Reluctantly, I handed the bottle back to him. "But you're on your own."

I turned around and began picking up my clothes that lay strewn along the wall, shoving them into my backpack.

"What are you doing?" His voice sounded bitter and fed-up.

"I'm out."

"Out where?" he asked, knowing full well that I had nowhere to go.

"I'll ask Ivy if I can sleep in her room. I'll figure out the rest tomorrow."

I had to keep wiping my eyes so I could see where my stuff was. A hairbrush, my earphones, some old underwear. I pushed it all into my bag.

"You can't…," Liam began, looking unsettled.

"Yes, I can," I said, furious tears now streaming down my cheeks. "Watch me."

"Fine!" He threw the bottle against the wall, and I jumped as whiskey and shattered glass sprayed across the room.

"Jesus Christ! Liam, you're a fucking psycho!" I couldn't see straight anymore, my eyes burning bright red. "Get away from me!"

"Gladly! I don't give a shit anymore. As if I ever cared."

"Guys…" We both swung around and saw Lawson standing in the doorway. "What's going on?"

"It's nothing, Laws." I lifted my backpack onto my shoulders.

"You should fucking know," Liam said, and pulled out a coke pouch and a key.

I sighed. "Great. More coke."

"Yes, more coke! Like it's any of your fucking business!" His phone started chiming in his pocket, but he let it ring.

"Guys, please," Lawson said, helpless to try and diffuse the situation.

Liam sniffed his key and looked at me, defiance burning in his eyes. His phone kept ringing. I shook my head, unable to tear my eyes from his face, still so beautiful it made my heart ache. Why couldn't I just walk up there and put my arms around him and make everything okay again, like we always did? How I wanted to clean up his head and his veins and give him what he needed.

Then I turned around and walked out the door.

"Haze." Lawson searched for my eyes, but I slipped past him towards Ivy's room. Instead, he went to try and calm Liam down, and as I walked down the hall I could hear their voices, tense and fractious.

I knocked on Ivy's door. She opened it right away, her eyes damp and full of guilt. "This is all my fault," she whispered.

I shook my head. "No, it really isn't. Look, would it be okay if—"

I was interrupted by an anguished scream I knew so well from some of his songs; a raw cry that carried impossible weight and emptied all the air in his lungs. I spun around and saw Lawson appear.

"Hazel, you gotta come over here."

I hurried down the hall. "What…?"

Liam was sitting on the floor with his hands behind his head, eyes wide with horror.

"It was his mom on the phone," Lawson said, his voice shaky. "Frank… Shit."

My stomach lurched. "Frank what?"

Liam's breathing grew agitated, panicked eyes staring at nothing. "He's dead…"

My lungs contracted and I felt myself wobble. "No, no, no…" I stumbled over and wrapped my arms around Liam's trembling body.

He began frantically shaking his head. "It can't be… No, it can't be." Then he curled up into a ball and began sobbing into his jeans. "Fuck!"

"Oh, god, Liam. I'm so sorry." Everything else fell away, and all I could do was hold him as he lay there shaking. "I'm sorry for everything," I whispered, squeezing him tight. "I'm here, it'll be okay. I'm here…"

TWENTY-FOUR

Everything was put on hold. Liam became a ghost and we all did our best to keep him alive, if not sane. I sat with him when he let me, but mostly he wanted to be left alone. The rest of us retreated into a hushed stasis, treading carefully on the eggshells of grief.

One afternoon, I was in the kitchen making soup for Liam. Ivy sat perched on the countertop next to the cooker, keeping me company.

"He won't talk to me, Ives," I said, as I stirred the thick liquid. "He just sits there, staring into the void. I guess he's sick of me. Especially after what I did."

"It ain't about you, Hazel. He's grieving. Give him time."

I sighed. "But I want to help him."

"You *are* helping him."

"How? How, when we can't even speak to each other?"

"What is there to say? Frank is dead. There are no words that can change it."

"No, of course not, but... Doesn't it help to talk about things?"

"You don't always need words to connect. Sometimes all a

person needs is for someone to sit with them in the dark. To not try to define or refute their pain, but to just let it be." She tilted her head and her auburn topknot slid to one side. "You know how he is. When shit gets too painful, all he needs is silence."

"Yeah…" I sprinkled some black pepper in the pot. "And poor Frank. To die alone like that, and not tell anyone. How long had he been sick?"

Ivy shook her head. "I don't know… It's awful."

I closed my eyes and saw Frank's face, his kind eyes and cheeky smile, his wistful air. I thought of all the Franks he had been in his lifetime. How many facets there are to a single person: one for each of our ages, one for each of our identities, one for each person who knew us. What a great black hole we leave behind when we go.

Ivy noticed me wiping a tear from my cheek. "Hey, now," she said. "It'll be okay." She reached an arm out and gathered me in a hug, and I buried my face in her red locks, breathing in honeysuckle and bergamot. I was not yet used to this new dynamic between the two of us, but it felt good to have an ally. A sister.

We separated and I returned to the soup. "I can't imagine what he's going through," I said. "I've never known anyone who died. Have you? Lost anyone you loved?"

Ivy looked away for a moment, pursing her lips, then shook her head slowly. "I don't think I've ever loved anyone like that."

We looked at each other, her eyes wide and soft, like summer fields. "Me neither."

"Hey, guys." Lawson walked into the kitchen, looking tired and glum. There were no more of his quips, his silly jokes or nicknames. He glanced into the saucepan. "Smells good. Is he eating anything?"

"A little."

"Thanks for looking after him, Haze. You're doing great. And you too, Ives."

"It ain't me, I'm afraid," Ivy replied. "It's all Nurse Hazel here."

"I try," I said with a shrug.

"So, um…" Lawson shifted his weight and leaned against the countertop. "Our next show is in two days."

Ivy cut her eyes to me. I nodded and pressed my lips together. "Yeah, I know."

Lawson waited a moment before he spoke again.

"Could you please check with him… how he's feeling? See if he's up to it? We'll have to cancel otherwise, but the sooner we know, the better."

"If we need it," Ivy said, "I'm sure my aunt would let us stay here a while longer."

"I'll ask him." I turned off the hob and took two bowls from the cupboard. "I'll let you know what he says."

Liam lay unmoving under the covers, a burial mound of sheets and sorrow. I padded over to the bed and put my bowl on the bedside table, next to his pill bottles and a half-empty bottle of whiskey.

"Liam?" I sat down and held out his bowl. "Got some soup. Wanna try it? Please?"

He lay still for a moment, then rolled over and slowly pushed himself up and leaned against the headboard.

"Thanks," he mumbled, taking the bowl. He picked up the spoon and let it hover in front of him. His hair was a big, black mess, his eyes underlined with dark blue. I went to open a window to clear out the heavy air, then sat back on the edge of the mattress.

"So, I have to ask…," I began, trying to see if he was up for conversation.

Liam slipped the spoon into his mouth and turned his tired eyes to me.

"How are you feeling about the show? It's the day after tomorrow. Lawson was wondering if we should cancel, or…? It's entirely up to you, of course."

He swallowed another spoonful and wiped his mouth with the back of his hand. "We're not cancelling."

"Oh. You sure? Your health comes first, you know. It's important that you—"

"I'm fine, really. It's just a show."

I nodded, looking down at my hands. "Okay. If you say so. Just let me know if you need anything, okay?"

"Yeah."

I picked up my bowl and walked towards the door.

"Haze."

I turned around.

"Thanks for the soup."

I nodded. "Sure."

* * *

The day of the gig, we were all on edge. Liam stayed in the bus with his guitar and nobody challenged him. We went through the motions – sound-checking, forcing down some food, exchanging pleasantries with the supporting band. We didn't see Liam all afternoon, and I prayed he wouldn't bail on us at the last minute.

Ten minutes before our cue he walked in, guitar in hand, and we all fell silent. None of us knew what to say, but then Lawson reached over and placed a hand on his shoulder. Liam pressed his lips together with a sombre nod, and they exchanged a glance between brothers.

Out on stage, a rowdy audience welcomed us with a roar. They all seemed well into their drink already, and in my mind I pleaded with them, *Please, go easy on him today. He breaks so easily.* I kept one eye on him as he fiddled with his strap and strings and glanced at the new setlist. He had changed it around to include some of his most tortured songs, and I hoped it would be cathartic.

As the first riff sounded, I switched to autopilot. I let the melodies carry me away to some safe space not quite there, but not quite elsewhere. Maybe this is what Liam did, all those times when he performed and seemed to be hovering in a secret dimension. Was it just an escape, somewhere to hide?

We reached the final song, and after a deafening guitar-off between Liam and Lawson, Liam leaned into his microphone and a thousand exhilarated eyes stared expectantly at him. He hesitated for a moment, then spoke.

"Thank you all so much." He was looking at his fretboard, avoiding their stares. "I—I'd like to tell you something." He ran his fingers up and down the worn strap that held his guitar in place. "When I was a kid, I was afraid of my parents. They terrified me with their stories of hell and warnings of eternal punishment."

I stood frozen on the spot, stunned by this unexpected public confession.

"There were a lot of rules to follow, too many to keep up with. I could never go to them when I needed to talk or wondered about something. They would have just responded with judgement and discipline." He paused. "But there was one person who saved me, who showed me that life didn't need to be so rigid and empty. My mom's brother. His name was Frank."

The audience was beginning to see where this was going, and we heard some scattered *aaws* from around the venue.

"Frank knew how to live. My parents despised him for it, but I figure deep down they were just jealous. Envious that Frank decided to live free, the way he chose, according to his own rules."

"Yeah!" came some shouts of agreement from across the room.

"That's just it. Don't ever let anyone else decide how you live your life. No book, no teacher, no parent, no priest. You are responsible for you, and you make the rules for your own life." Liam was looking up now, straight into the crowd, the conviction of his words plain on his face. "Frank showed me the way. Tonight, we sing for Frank, and tonight we drink to him." He picked up his beer and raised it to the room.

The audience held out their drinks and yelled, "To Frank!"

Liam took a big gulp from his cup and placed it back on the floor. "I've got one more song for you. This one's for you, Frank."

There were shouts and whistles as Liam returned to his fretboard. The rest of us could only stand back and listen as Liam remembered his uncle, now immortalised in a haunting song.

* * *

Safely out of the spotlights, we let out a collective breath that we had been holding the entire day. Then another worry washed over me – what was to happen to me now?

The others gathered around Liam, and Lawson patted him on the back. "Well done, bro. That was amazing."

"What a beautiful song, man," Mango said.

Ivy walked up and embraced him, and they stood like that for a moment, his hands clutching her dress. "You did good," she whispered, stroking his hair. "Real good."

I looked away, my chest still aching with the memory of

our fight.

Liam sat down in an armchair and motioned for the others to sit on the couch. I tried to shrink into the wall, willing my skin to match the pattern of the wallpaper.

"So, guys." Liam looked at each of his band members. "The funeral is next week. We're going to have to cancel Memphis. But that's the only one. I'll come back for the rest of the tour."

"No problem, bro," said Lawson. "We'll take care of it. You do what you gotta do."

"Thanks, Laws. So, if everyone's alright with it, we'll head to Madison and stay there a few days, and then head back down to Kansas City."

They began talking about the whens and wheres of the remainder of the tour, and I slunk over to the corner to grab the bus keys. I had no place here anymore. My skin felt too tight on my body, my chest constricted. I needed a downer, something to take the edge off. My best chance was searching the bus.

I snuck out and began rummaging through Liam's bunk, looking for any kind of pharmaceutical comfort. Under his pillow, around his mattress, in the plastic bag on his shelf. Nothing. My heart was racing, and I took some deep breaths to calm down. Then I brought my blanket to a booth and curled up into a pathetic ball.

The bus felt like a cocoon, the calm in the eye of the storm. I leaned against the window and thought of home. Less than two months until it was time to go back. But where would I go, if I now had to leave the band? I pulled out my phone to search for buses and hostels, but my stomach turned at the thought of it. And worse yet – what would I do when I got back home? I couldn't go back to living with Mother. I was stuck between a past I wanted to forget and a future I couldn't fathom. I had no home anywhere.

The bus doors opened and my heart went to my throat. Liam's head appeared, and he looked down the aisle and spotted me.

"There you are. I was looking for you."

I sat up straighter, feeling like a trespasser. "Oh, sorry, I... Sorry."

"Hey, what did I say about all that apologising?" He gave me his best lopsided smile and sat down next to me. "You okay?"

"Yeah, I'm just... I was thinking about my plans."

"Oh." He looked down at his hands. "What are they?"

"Well. I guess the problem is, I don't have any. I don't know what happens next, or what I should do..."

"Maybe I can help you with that."

I looked up and met his eyes.

"Come with me?" he said.

"Come with you where?"

"To the funeral."

"What?" My mouth fell open. "To Frank's... With your family?"

"Please?" He lifted the corner of the blanket and burrowed closer. "I need you there, Haze. I don't know how else I'll get through it."

He needed me. He needed *me*. That was all I wanted to hear. I relaxed and pulled more blanket out from behind me, stretching it across Liam's shoulders.

"Okay, sure," I said. "If that's what you want."

His crooked smile glowed with reassuring familiarity. "Thanks, Haze. I owe you one."

That night, we were back together in his bed. There was no more fighting, no more sour words, no rehashing of past mistakes; just us, our bodies and minds, entangled like silver chains.

TWENTY-FIVE

And so we found ourselves once again in Madison, back in the studio where it had all begun.

It had been just a couple of months since I sat on those front steps, worrying that Liam wouldn't turn up. All the blossoms had gone from the trees, and the grass had turned dry and tawny in the baking July heat. My heart turned inside out at the thought of that day, the bittersweet memory of all that dizzy exaltation, all gone now, having to make room for this heavy grief. We dressed for the funeral in silence.

Liam looked the perfect picture of a tragic rock star when he emerged in a black suit that clung to his skinny frame, and a black tie with a shoddy knot around his neck.

"This okay?" he asked, pulling at his shirt cuffs. All throughout the night, the whole way to Madison he had sat by himself, staring into the dark. I wasn't sure if he had slept at all.

I walked up to him and straightened his tie, tugging at the knot until it looked passably smart. Then I reached out and pulled his fringe to the side, and let my hand linger on his cheek.

"It's okay," I replied, trying to balance the precarious line between warmth and pity, while also attempting to hide my own nerves. Today, I had to be strong for Liam.

I had tied my hair back in a solemn bun and put on the only black dress I had, together with a pair of black stockings. Presentable enough, I hoped.

Liam picked up his jeans off the floor, stuck his hand down the pocket and pulled out two little blue pills. Valiums. He held one out to me and I gratefully took it. Anything to soften the blow of this day.

But the edges of a funeral are not easily softened. My gut twisted as we walked up to the church. Liam was staring in front of him, his jaw clenching and unclenching, as though he was fighting some battle in his mind. As the Valium kicked in I could feel my lurching insides slow somewhat, and soft clouds drifted in over my mind.

The church was a large building, clean and beige, lined with plain windows. Just off its centre rose the bell tower, topped with a copper dome and a large cross that loomed above us. A chill nipped at the air and grey clouds hung in the sky, heavy and waiting.

Mourners were gathered outside in small groups, speaking in hushed voices. I felt Liam tense beside me, and he slowed his steps.

"You okay?" I asked, giving him a sideways glance.

He took a breath and surveyed the crowd. People he may not have seen in years – some whom he had once been close to, perhaps, and who had slipped aside as life got in the way; some whom he may have hoped to avoid for the rest of his life. That's family, isn't it?

I wished he would speak to me, but as always when something troubled him, he turned into himself, rolling up like a hedgehog, spikes pointing outward. I knew better than to try and poke him.

He swallowed hard, then kept walking. I had to pick up my pace to keep up.

I looked ahead at the mourners before us, and soon I saw the people Liam was steering towards. They were looking over at us: a dark-haired woman with a frail, anxious look, and beside her a tall man in a black robe and white collar, his mouth set in a grim line. Liam's parents. I took a deep breath, grateful for the Valium.

"Liam…," his mother began, and fresh tears filled her puffy eyes. Her hands were fidgeting with an already soaked handkerchief. She was small, a head shorter than her husband, and dressed in solemn black with only a modest silver cross resting on her collarbone. Her hair was thick and wavy, a shade of brown so dark it was almost black, just like Liam's. She radiated worry, and she held a hand out towards her long lost son, but stopped herself. There had always been, and remained yet, an impenetrable barrier between them, and she held her hand mid-air as though she was touching that wall and couldn't reach any further.

Liam didn't move towards her, but kept his gaze on his father, the dreaded pastor. The two stood still for a moment, sizing each other up. Mr Riley had not yet looked at me, so I stayed put, taking quiet, shallow breaths.

At last the pastor cleared his throat and held out his arm in a stiff greeting. Liam let it hang for a second longer than was comfortable. Then, with an almost imperceptible sigh, he reached out and shook his father's hand.

Mr Riley was an imposing man. His sturdy frame made Liam look small and weak; his flawless posture making a point of Liam's slumped shoulders. He still had a full head of hair, snow white locks perfectly combed, and contrasted against his dark, serious eyebrows. Even his nose looked noble, and I could picture his profile on some ancient coin. I felt myself shrink a few inches before him.

Then Liam turned to his quivering mother and gathered her in a tense hug. "Hi, Mom." Mrs Riley erupted into another wave of weeping. "This is Hazel," Liam said, gesturing to me. "She's touring with me." I lifted my hand in an awkward greeting. His parents looked me over, and Mr Riley gave me a grim nod.

"Pleased to meet you," he grumbled, in a tone that suggested he was anything but.

Liam scratched the back of his head. "Alright, well, we'll go inside."

Just before we walked off, I saw Mrs Riley reach her hand out, once again slamming into the invisible wall that surrounded the son she had always loved but could never relate to. The son whom she knew in her heart of hearts was going to burn in hell for eternity, condemned by a God she worshipped. The son who, she couldn't deny, had always favoured Frank over his own parents. Frank, her brother, whom they had gathered to bury. Frank, who was surely also going to hell. I tried to swallow the lump in my throat and hurried after Liam.

A soft murmur hung over the church, people finding seats, whispering greetings and condolences. We walked up the aisle towards the altar where the casket lay, and my heart nearly stopped when I saw a face appear. Open casket. My empty stomach lurched, looking for something to regurgitate.

I inched closer, Frank's chemically preserved face easing into view until I stood right by him. I had never seen a dead body before. He looked like a mannequin, polished and smooth, all those lines and dimples ironed out. My face twisted into a grimace and I forced myself to look away.

Liam stood next to me, his jawline hard. I imagined he wasn't seeing the stitched-up doll before him, but rather the Frank who had taken him in and guided him through a tough adolescence, who had always been there to lend an ear and a comforting smile. Frank, whom he had loved, and who had loved him, unconditionally.

We sat in the pews in the back, lurking like the two unwanted strangers we were. Liam's father began his sermon, talking about God's stray children and the forgiveness they must make themselves worthy of. I felt Liam stiffen by my side.

The pastor's mighty voice filled the space as he intoned some verse from the Bible. "But the souls of the righteous are in the hand of God, and no torment will ever touch them. Those who trust in him will understand truth, and the faithful will abide with him in love, because grace and mercy are upon his holy ones, and he watches over his elect."

Liam shook his head and squirmed.

Mr Riley closed the Bible with a loud boom that echoed between the stone walls. "Frank never turned to God. He never put his faith in God. We know that for those who fail to accept Jesus as their saviour, eternal punishment awaits. We pray that our Lord, in his almighty wisdom, will still find it in his heart to forgive Frank and welcome him into his holy kingdom."

"Oh, for fuck's sake," Liam muttered a little too loudly, and shot to his feet.

"Liam!" I hissed. Some people turned to look but he was already out the door. I whispered some apologies and hurried after him.

He was standing out front, his hands deep in his pockets, kicking at the white gravel that covered the grounds.

"Liam…"

"No, fuck this shit! I'm not going back in there. That self-righteous asshole! He doesn't know what he's fucking *talking* about. And he sure as hell knew nothing about Frank. What gives him the right to judge like that? And all those people listening to him, trusting him... He's poison, Hazel!" He kicked at the ground again. "Frank would be so fucking disappointed."

I walked up to him and quietly reached out a hand. Liam threw his head back in frustration, looking up at the empty sky above. Then, with a sigh, he dropped his head and took my hand.

We walked around the graveyard until we found the newly dug hole which was to be Frank's final resting place. We sat down next to the mound of damp soil and stared into the rectangular pit. A cool breeze rustled the leaves around us, and a solitary crow hopped from treetop to treetop, squawking mournfully.

"I should have stayed with him." Liam's hoarse voice broke the eerie silence. "I had a feeling something was wrong. Whenever I tried to mention doctors, he would just dismiss me. I wish he could have told me. Maybe I could have helped."

"Liam, you can't blame yourself. It was Frank's choice not to tell anyone."

He let out a small laugh, tinged with sadness. "He was always like that. Didn't like to cause a fuss. Probably felt like he wasn't worth it..." Liam's voice faltered and he looked down at the ground. "I should have known better. Should have *been* better. He was such a great man. And nobody saw it but me. That's the worst part. He was so lonely, the black sheep of his family, when really, he was the best of all of 'em."

He pulled out a flask and took a long sip, but when he offered it to me, I declined. I didn't want to drink with nothing but a sleeping pill in my stomach.

"I could have paid his fucking medical bills," Liam continued. "I could have... After everything he did for me." He slumped over, buried his face in his hands, and I could feel a few more cracks appear in my porcelain heart. I leaned over and put a hand on his back, stroking him gently. What else could I do?

The mourners eventually emerged, led by Liam's father and Frank's casket resting on the shoulders of six men. Liam and I stood in the back as Mr Riley declared Frank returned to ashes. Then they lowered him into the ground, and there was no sound except quiet weeping and the strain of the ropes. The wind was picking up, and dark clouds were sweeping in over Wisconsin.

* * *

As people began to make their way to the reception, I noticed Liam was already slurring, his eyes glazed and disconnected.

"Are you sure you want to go?" I asked, hoping I could convince him to stay away. "Why don't we just head back to the studio and chill?"

"What, and deprive my father of a chance to castigate his degenerate son?" There was something devious and defiant in his eyes, and I had an uneasy feeling. I held his gaze to see if he would come to his senses, but he seemed determined.

"Okay," I said at last. "If you're sure."

"I'm sure. Don't worry, baby." I had seen this kind of reckless, plastered-on cheeriness before. It poorly masked the turmoil beneath, and it never led to anything good.

We joined a solemn crowd in Liam's childhood home in the suburbs. The living room was lined with tables neatly covered in paper cloths, holding an impressive buffet of coffee, cakes, bread and fruit. From the kitchen, we could hear Mr Riley's booming voice.

I glanced over at Liam. His face was damp with sweat, his hair a tousled mess, and his tie was coming undone. I had to stop myself from reaching over to wipe his forehead and straighten his outfit. *Just please, let this be over soon.*

"Just coffee?" Liam said, as we walked alongside the smorgasbord. "Hey, Dad! You not serving anything stronger?"

Pastor Riley appeared in the doorway, staring down at his disappointment of a son.

"No, Liam," he barked. "There's plenty of coffee, and there's juice in the fridge. You can help yourself to anything you want."

"But what I *want*," Liam said, leaning on the table and nearly knocking over the stacked porcelain cups, "is *whiskey*. Where's your whiskey, *Father*?"

"How dare you! How dare you come here, drunk and high and the Lord knows what, behaving like a child at your own uncle's funeral!"

"Look who's talking!" Liam snarled.

"I'm warning you...!"

Mrs Riley appeared behind her husband, wringing her hands with a teary expression. Liam stopped, and put his hands up in defeat. "Sorry, Ma," he said, stumbling backwards just in time for me to catch him.

"Please excuse us," I mumbled, and led Liam towards the hall. "Hey, Liam, let's go outside for a minute, yeah?"

A few people were out on the patio with coffee cups and cigarettes, and we pushed past them into the garden. The wide lawn was lined with beautifully maintained rose bushes and hydrangeas. Everything was dark blue, the sun setting somewhere behind the heavy clouds. A summer storm was brewing and the air felt thick, desperate for a release.

I walked beside Liam, who was heading towards a shed that sat under a cluster of conifers at the back of the garden.

"What was that all about?" I asked him.

"My hypocrite Dad, that's what," he muttered. "Hey, come see this."

He pulled aside a large tree branch and crawled in behind

the shed. Bemused, I crouched down and followed him. Against the fence was a small, shoddily assembled wooden structure, and Liam bent down and removed a makeshift door.

"This was my hiding place," he said, and gestured for me to enter. I looked behind me to see if anyone had seen us, and then I got on all fours and crawled in through the little doorway.

Inside smelled of dust and damp. Liam fished out two block candles from a rusty tin box and set them down. He lit them both, along with a cigarette for each of us.

"This is amazing," I said, looking around at the perfect little den. "You built this?"

"Yeah." He pulled his legs to his chest and leaned against the mossy old wood. "I needed somewhere to hide, some-place that was my own."

"Hide? From your parents?"

"My Dad, mostly." He sat for a moment, lost in thought. Then he shook his head and looked up at me. "And look, I'm still doing it." He laughed bitterly. "Oh my god, he's such an *asshole*. Lecturing me about being drunk. You should have seen him when I was a kid."

"Oh. Did he drink a lot?"

Liam scoffed. "I barely saw him sober for the first fifteen years of my life. A drunk, abusive shithead. Apparently the righteous can do God's punishing for him."

I felt the air leave my lungs. "I'm—I'm so sorry, Liam. That's awful."

"Yeah, well. Now he's sober and thinks he's so high and mighty, he gets to judge everybody."

I imagined little Liam curled up in his secret hideout, covering his ears and wishing for another life. It broke my heart.

We smoked in silence while the candle flames flickered,

creating warping shadows that danced over the creaking walls.

"Hey," I said, as I put my cigarette out on the damp ground. "Do you think we should head back to the studio?" I hoped we could escape without another run-in with his parents. We had had enough complications for one day.

Before Liam could answer, a voice sounded by the entrance. "Knock, knock!" Liam broke into a grin and leaned over.

"Jared! Come on in, bro!"

A straw-blond guy crawled in and sat down in the corner. "Sorry to interrupt, but I saw you guys walk over here, and I remembered the old den! Legendary." He looked at me. "Hi, I'm Jared, Liam's cousin."

"Oh... You're not, um, Frank's kid, are you?"

"No, cousin on the other side of the family. Frank didn't have any kids."

"Oh, yeah, of course. I'm Hazel."

"Hazel. Well, you must be in Liam's good books if he's showing you the secret headquarters!"

Liam laughed, a kind of boyish laugh I hadn't heard from him in a long time, and it sounded like the sweetest music.

"Hey, listen, I'm so sorry about Frank, man. He was such a great guy."

"Thanks, Jar. Appreciate it."

"I'm sorry, guys," I said, "I need the loo." I wasn't in the mood to be friendly to strangers, and it sounded like Liam could do with some boy time. I got to my feet, hunching under the low ceiling. "I'll see you in a bit, okay?"

Outside, I brushed pine needles and soil from my dress before I walked back to the house. I tried to make myself invisible as I grabbed a bread roll from the buffet, which I wolfed down on my way to the toilet.

In the bathroom mirror, I smoothed down my hair and

wiped the mascara from under my eyes. *Nearly over*, I told myself. I took a few deep breaths and walked back out to get some coffee. Praying no one would talk to me, I quietly took a cup and pressed the thermos lid, and the bitter scent of bottled coffee wafted up at me.

"So, you're Liam's girl?" A voice came from behind me and I felt my muscles go rigid. Looking over my shoulder I saw a woman, about fifty, with strawberry blonde hair that framed her face like ocean waves on a sunny day. Her dark purple dress stood out from the sweeping sea of black, and around her neck she wore an ankh pendant, dangling at the end of a long silver chain.

"Um, yeah, I guess. Do I know you?"

"No, but I think we may have some things in common, you and I. Frank was my, well… My partner, I guess. For a while."

"Oh…" My shoulders relaxed a little, and I took my coffee cup and turned towards her. "I'm so sorry."

"It's okay, we weren't together when he… When he died. We broke up about a year ago. But still…" She lowered her red-rimmed eyes. "The loss hurts."

"Of course."

"I'm sorry." She offered me a warm smile, her eyes framed by faint crow's feet. "I'm Vanya." She reached out a hand, decorated with bangles and rings, and I shook it.

"Hazel."

"Nice to meet you, Hazel. Want something stronger with that coffee?"

We sat down in the conservatory where Vanya fished out a small flask of vodka from her handbag. She poured a glug in each of our cups and raised hers to me.

"To complicated men, and their understanding women," she said, with a wry smile.

I chuckled hesitantly and clinked my mug against hers. "To that, why not."

Vanya leaned back in her chair. "So, did you ever meet Frank?"

"I did, yes. Only once, but we had a lovely chat. He was very sweet."

"He really was." Nostalgia shaded Vanya's eyes and she looked down at her cup. "Not without troubles, though. But what a precious soul."

"How long were you together?"

"Eight years." She let out a weary exhale. "Eight years of ups and downs. But I don't regret any of it. He was an incredible man. He just didn't know how to love. Or to be loved."

I bit my lip and thought of Liam. Like uncle, like nephew. A brief silence hung in the air.

"And you? How long have you and Liam been an item?"

"Oh, I don't know. We're not really an item. I joined their tour a couple of months ago. I sing with the band."

"That's fantastic! Sounds exciting." She began running her thumb over the ankh necklace, sliding it up and down its long chain. "You know, I saw them a few times, a few years back when they performed in town. Little Liam, he was such a star."

The image made me smile. "He still is. But... Yeah."

"But what?"

"Oh, nothing."

Vanya gave me a knowing look. "They're very much alike, aren't they?"

"Who?"

"Liam and Frank. It's always been that way." She took a thoughtful sip of her drink. "As Liam got older and they started spending more time together, the similarities became even more apparent. That aloofness, the walls they build around themselves. It can be hard."

She spoke slowly and emphatically with that same Midwestern melody, soft around the consonants and lazy on the vowels. I looked up at her and braved a smile, a strange sense of validation untying my stomach.

"Yeah," I said finally. "It can." Her eyes lingered on me and I shifted awkwardly in my seat. "So, um, do you live in Madison?"

"Me? No, I'm over on Lake Michigan, just outside Chicago. I have my studio there."

"Studio?" I couldn't help but sit up a bit straighter. "You an artist?"

"Ceramicist."

"Oh, right." I nodded, relaxing back into my seat. "Nice."

She tilted her head and fine lines appeared around her smile. "Why do you ask? Are *you* an artist?"

"I used to paint, yeah."

"A painter, how lovely." She looked me up and down. "It suits you."

"I don't anymore, though." I took a sip of my drink, grimacing as the vodka stung the back of my throat.

"Oh? Well, you know. Once an artist, always an artist. I don't think that's something you ever lose. Even if you try." She narrowed her eyes at me. "You ever done murals?"

"Murals...? No."

"I've been looking for someone to paint my studio wall. I need a mural to brighten up the building some, add colour to that drab bit of concrete." Vanya nodded at me. "Maybe it's a job for you."

I let out an uneasy laugh.

"Who knows," Vanya said, her bangles jangling as she lifted her cup. "Maybe I'll see you there one day." She looked at me as if she knew something I didn't. I nodded nervously and downed my spiked coffee.

"Huh. Maybe."

"Hazel!" Liam was calling me from the living room.

"In here!"

He came through the door with Jared in tow. His face lit up when he saw us, and without hesitation, he strode up to Vanya and grabbed her in an eager embrace.

"V! How are you? It's been so long!"

"Liam, honey." She closed her eyes and held him tight, stroking the back of his head. "How wonderful to see you. I'm just fine." She pulled back and looked at him, eyes sad but full of benevolence. "Missing your uncle, though."

"Yeah… Me too."

Vanya kept her hands on his arms while surveying his face. "Oh, honey, you're so pale. Are you doin' alright? Are you eating enough?"

"I'm fine, V," Liam mumbled, then turned to me. "I see you met Hazel."

"I have." Vanya gave me a warm smile. "She's a good girl, Liam. You take care of her now."

"I try." He scratched his neck and flashed me a crooked smirk. "Mostly it seems to be the other way around, though."

Vanya shook her head. "Why does that not surprise me?"

Liam shrugged and the two of them exchanged a glance, some sweet and nurturing understanding between them.

"So, Haze," he said to me. "Jared's just leaving, and he can give us a ride. Wanna get outta here?"

"Sounds good," I said, relieved that it was finally over. I turned to my new confidant. "It was lovely to meet you, Vanya."

"Lovely to meet you too, Hazel."

I nodded and turned to leave, but she stopped me.

"Hey, wait." She opened her handbag and pulled out a card which she handed to me. "If you ever need anything," she said, bright eyes piercing me, looking right through me.

I pinched the card between my fingertips. "Thanks."

"Or if you change your mind about that mural."

"Ha, right. I'll think about it," I said, just to be polite.

"Great to see you, V," Liam said. "I'll see you around, okay?" He hugged her once more, and then we walked out of the Riley residence, leaving behind childhood trauma, a sullen pastor and slowly staling bread.

* * *

We waved goodbye to Jared and stepped out into the humid night. Dark clouds loomed above us, and the sound of crickets pulsed through the air like an alarm nobody could turn off. As we walked up to the studio, lightning crashed over the sky and brought an echo of rolling thunder.

"Oh, shit," Liam mumbled as he felt through his pockets.

"You're kidding?" I groaned. "No key?"

"Ah, fuck... Maybe it's back in the den."

He went to look for a way in, and I felt the first few raindrops on my forehead. Liam tugged at the windows, one by one, but they were all locked.

"The bedroom window must be open, I never lock it. Where's the ladder?"

A loud thunderclap cracked just above us, initiating a violent downpour.

"Oh god! Liam, what do we do?"

"Don't worry, I got this!" Liam put his shoulder to an old cellar door and forced it open. He slipped inside and quickly returned, triumphantly carrying a stepladder over his head.

"We're saved!" he yelled above the roaring rain. "I'm gonna need your help, though."

He stopped underneath the bedroom window, unfolded the ladder and leaned it against the wall. "It's not nearly long enough. Can you get on my shoulders?"

"What!" I looked up at the window, high above. "You must be joking?"

"Ah, it'll be fine, you're tiny! I'll carry you on my shoulders and climb the ladder, and then you can pry the window open and jump inside."

"You're crazy!" It all felt ridiculous. An unexpected bout of laughter bubbled inside me, a welcome relief from the heavy day we had survived together. I looked from the ladder to the window. It seemed to be our only option. My dress was now completely soaked and clung to my body like seaweed, and I could feel my hair coming loose from its bun.

"Okay, then," I conceded, laughing in the deluge. "Let's try it."

Liam stooped down and I clumsily climbed up, placing one leg on either side of his head.

"Here we go." He started to stand up, but instantly his knees buckled and he stumbled sideways. I held my hands out and landed against the wall, crumbling into a fit of giggles.

"Liam!" I howled. "Steady, please!"

"My apologies, ma'am!" He tightened his grip around my legs. "Okay, ready, set, go!"

I held onto his head and balanced myself as best I could, and he managed to stand up. I reached out and grabbed the ladder for stability.

"All good up there?"

"Yep, still alive!" The rain was pounding down on us, but I didn't feel cold anymore. "Okay, I've got the ladder, come closer... That's it." I felt like a slapstick cartoon character as we tottered back and forth.

"Ready?" Liam asked, putting one foot on the bottom rung.

"Ready!"

Rung by rung, we got closer to the window. Liam felt

steady now, fully concentrating. I carefully leaned in to counterbalance his weight until I could reach the window. I grabbed the edge and pulled it out.

"It's open!"

Liam took one more step, which enabled me to hang my arms over the edge. Safely hooked, I was free to break into another giggle fit.

"Careful!" Liam said, and I quickly collected myself.

"Okay, push!"

He put his palms against my thighs and heaved me upwards. I pulled myself up just enough so I could swing one leg in, then crawled over the ledge and landed on the floor in a wet pile, howling victoriously. I got to my feet and stuck my head out the window. Below me, Liam stood squinting against the rain.

"Go to the front door," I said. "I'll open it for you!"

I hurried downstairs, leaving a wet trail through the hall. I turned the key and opened the door, and there stood Liam, soaked to the bone, his long fringe hanging in wet streaks across his face, his eyelashes glittering with raindrops. We looked at each other for a moment, his lopsided smile back in place. I was still panting with the break-in effort, and a small pool of rainwater was forming at my feet.

Liam took a step towards me and pushed me inside, up against the wall, and for the first time in what felt like forever he pressed his body against mine, his lips against my neck, his tongue tracing rivulets of rainwater. Hot shivers shot down my spine and sparkled deep inside me. He grabbed my wrists and held them above my head, and as he did so, I felt the most amazing flood of relief, a great weight dropping from my shoulders. The strength I had tried to display these past few days, the bold front I had struggled to maintain, it all crumbled as he resumed control of me, of himself, of us. Finally, I could let go.

He kissed me long and hard while guiding me back towards the living room, until we reached the dusty old sofa where we had played together that afternoon a lifetime ago. Fumbling hands removed wet clothes until we stood skin to skin, his body like a radiator I wanted to wrap myself around. He pushed me onto the sofa, and it was the sweetest sensation of not having to decide, do, or say anything; just be there and let him do to me what he wished.

Lightning lit up the room and thunder clapped and rumbled through the sky. The rain was coming down in sheets, rattling the windows. I opened my legs and pulled him towards me. He ran his hand up my neck and grabbed my hair, pulling it down as he thrust hard into me. My moans dissolved in the drumming rain as I gave in to the blinding pleasure of having Liam inside me; the way he could take away the whole world and make me forget who I was, even for just a moment.

With his jaw clenched shut, he kept his burning eyes locked with mine as he fucked me harder than ever before, as though he was trying to release all the frustration and pain and ache that spilled from his heart.

I held onto him and prayed that it would work.

TWENTY-SIX

Moments before dawn, a noise snatched me out of sleep and my eyes flew open. I lay still for a moment, listening. There it was again, a distressed mumbling. I turned around and saw Liam snared up in the covers, whimpering in his sleep.

"Liam?" I whispered.

"No, no, no…" He turned his head to the side, clenching a fist against his chest. I put a hand on his shoulder and felt his skin, hot and damp with sweat.

"Hey, Liam, wake up!"

He jerked awake, panting, his eyes darting around the room.

"Hey, now," I said, trying to catch his flitting gaze. "It was just a dream."

He sat up and took some shaky breaths, then wrapped his arms around his knees. "It was my fault," he croaked.

"What was?"

"I know you're gonna tell me it wasn't, but it's not true. It's not true…"

Already we were haunted, and not by the kind of ghost

you can exorcise. I sat up and leaned against the headboard. "Liam, what were you dreaming about? Talk to me."

He swallowed hard and looked off into the distance. "I was pushing him into that hole."

"Frank?"

"He was standing in front of me, looking how he always looked, alive and healthy. And I…" Liam squeezed his eyes shut. "I put my hands on his chest and pushed him into his grave. His fucking grave, Hazel!"

He covered his eyes with his hands as if trying to shut his vision out, but I knew the images that hurt him the most lived right inside his own head. Looking at him made my insides ache, his sorrow like radiation poisoning the both of us.

I stroked his arm helplessly. "It was only a dream…"

He groaned and leaned over to pick up his bag off the floor.

"What are you doing?" I asked, even though I had a sinking feeling I already knew.

He pulled out a pill bottle, his hands shaking as he tried to pop open the lid.

"Don't," I said, instinctively grabbing his arm. As much as I understood his craving, this had to stop. "It won't help."

He turned his damp eyes to me. "Hazel, please…"

"Just give it a little while, okay? I know you're upset, but this isn't a long-term solution. You've got to let yourself feel stuff, or it will never go away."

Liam pinched his lips, the pills rattling around in their bottle as he tipped it backwards, forwards, backwards. Then he squeezed his grip around them and sighed. "Fine," he said, and dropped them to the floor. "Can I at least have a smoke?"

We threw on some clothes and stepped outside. The storm had cleared the pressure from the air and the world felt cool and still. Above us the sky was paling, light peach bleeding into ash-blue like faded watercolours. I buried my hands in my sleeves and sat down on the porch steps next to Liam.

"Want one?" he asked, holding his pack of Luckies out to me.

I shook my head. "Nah. Thanks." Instead I inhaled the damp air, last night's downpour now rising in a soft mist that smelled of grass and dew and summer mornings. Crickets and birds were serenading the dawn, and the first glinting shards of gold cut through the trees.

Liam lit his cigarette and dropped his head into his hands. We sat in silence for a while, nothing moving except a trail of smoke that rose from his right hand, broken occasionally when he took a drag. How I wanted to help him, to go inside his mind and sweep up all the broken glass and bring in fresh-cut flowers.

When he spoke, his voice was hoarse and hesitant. "Do you…," he began, mumbling into his chest.

I waited a moment, watching his shoulders rise and fall in shallow breaths. The birds seemed to be singing louder by the minute. "Do I what?"

He clenched his jaw, his face hard. "Do you think Frank's in hell?"

"What?" I leaned forward to try and catch his eye. "No! Of course I don't think he's in hell. Why, do you?" When he didn't respond, I cautiously put my hand on his back. "Hey. What's going on?"

He sighed and sat up, sucking on his cigarette while staring into the void. "I'm just… surprised."

"By what?"

"By my own thoughts. I thought I knew what I believed." Finally, he looked at me. Dark rings lined his eyes, and his face looked pallid in contrast to his deep-brown, dishevelled hair. "Now I'm not so sure."

"Well, you don't believe in hell, do you?"

"I don't know anymore." He shook his head as if trying to get rid of some irritating bug in his skull. "I can't stop picturing Frank in some awful place where his pain never ends. I know my parents thought he was sinful or whatever, but he doesn't deserve that."

"Of course he doesn't."

"But what if it's true?"

"Hell?"

"Yeah."

"It can't be!"

"How do you *know* that though?" Liam snapped, and I flinched. A tense pause thickened the air between us before I spoke again.

"When I was a kid," I said. "I used to spend all day on the beach."

Liam stared at the ground in front of him, but I could tell he was listening.

"I'd sit and watch the horizon, the dividing line between land and sea. I'd watch day turn into night. I'd look at the sky and see space contrasted against mass. I noticed there were polar opposites everywhere. Land and sea, day and night, male and female, all the way down to protons and electrons, the tiniest pieces of life. This world, this entire life, is made up of duality. If heaven and hell exist, I think they're here on Earth. Death probably looks very different."

Liam took a drag and filled the morning with white smoke. "Like, how?" he said, his voice charged and tense.

I thought for a moment. "If life is the universe divided, maybe death is the place where the opposites combine. Where we can be whole again."

He scoffed. "Wouldn't that be nice. But there's no way you can know that for sure. Nobody knows anything. What if I've been wrong all this time? What if *they're* right?!" He threw his cigarette butt onto the lawn and started rubbing his temples. "All my life they forced their ideas into my head. My parents, my teachers. They wanted us to be so goddamn afraid all the time. And we were. We listened to their stories of hell and damnation, and we learned to live with the nightmares." He balled his hands into fists, his arms trembling. "Why did we have to be so fucking afraid? Who does that?" He flashed a pair of burning eyes at me. "Who wants their kid to be afraid all the time?"

I shrugged helplessly. "I don't know…"

He pulled out another cigarette and lit it.

"They said music was the devil's work. How is that even a thing?" He shook his head again, scraping his untied Converse over the grass. "You know, they made me burn my CDs."

"What…? Who did?"

"My parents." Liam's face was expressionless now, his eyes hooded, and beneath that calm exterior I could sense a live wire twisting and sparking. "One day, they barged into my bedroom and made me get all my CDs and tapes. All of it. I raged and I cried, but it made no difference. They made me carry it outside and shove it all in a barrel and burn it. Said it was the only way to get that devil's music outta my head."

My heart dropped through the dew-wet ground. "What the fuck? Liam. That's awful! I'm—I'm so sorry."

"Well, it ain't your fault," he spat, and for a moment I thought I could see that barrel fire flickering in his eyes. He sighed and hung his head, his shoulders curved under the weight of the world. "Shit, I don't know why I'm telling you this stuff. I never talk about this with anyone."

I edged closer but he flinched and turned away.

"It's okay," I whispered, but I knew that nothing was okay and I had no idea how to fix any of it.

He tugged testily at his hair and then shot to his feet. "Sorry, Haze." Avoiding my gaze, he scratched his arms restlessly. "I'm sorry, okay? I can't do this."

He stormed off inside and I hurried after him. I found him in the bedroom, hastily downing a Xanax.

"Don't," he said, holding a hand up to block my protests.

"No, it's okay." I took a step closer. "I get it." I looked at the bottle and suddenly ached for the relief. The last few weeks had been too awful, and I was tired of all the grief and pain. Fuck feelings. "Can I have one?"

Liam hesitated. "Uh, sure…"

I took the bottle from his hand and fished out a tablet, long and rectangular like a Tetris block. A whole pill usually just put me to sleep so snapped it in two, swallowed one half and put the other in my pocket for later. Liam looked at me, perplexed, and I returned his gaze with a sudden, resolute indifference.

Finally he opened his arms and wrapped them around me, resting his chin on the top of my head. "I'm sorry, Hazelnut."

I closed my eyes and pressed my face to his chest. "I'm sorry, too."

It was just too easy. And why have it hard when you can have it easy?

But easy doesn't always come cheap.

TWENTY-SEVEN

"How do you even *do* that?!"

I was sitting opposite Liam on the sofa, marvelling as he pulled yet another song from the ether.

"Do what?" he asked, all casual.

"Write songs like that! I'm so jealous."

I felt fluffy and fired up, like a marshmallow over a flame. It hadn't taken long for the living room to explode into a mighty mess of beer cans, scattered powder and over-flowing ashtrays. The Xanax had turned my brain into cotton balls, and when Liam once again whipped out the coke, I had no objections. I knew it was a temporary bandage, but it was a relief to see his cheeks flush with life again.

He shrugged, plucking a slow melody. "I don't know, I was just born this way. I can't even help it. I couldn't stop if I wanted to."

"Wow. It's never like that for me. I wish I could be in such immediate communion with inspiration."

"What was it like when you were painting, then?"

"Oh, I don't know…" I squirmed at the thought. Of

course I remembered how it had once felt. But that was in a different lifetime.

Liam let go of the fretboard and tilted his head, studying me intently. "Did it sometimes feel almost like the painting was creating itself through you? That it wasn't coming from you, but from someplace else?"

"I—I guess..."

"And that you just couldn't help yourself. Whatever you saw or felt, your brain just converted it into paintings?"

"Yeah, actually, it was exactly like that. Not so much now, but back then, all the time." I pursed my lips and gazed into my past. "You know, I had forgotten about that. But I remember now, how I was always framing the world and looking for angles and perspectives."

He leaned back with a smug smile. "There's your answer, baby. There's your inspiration. You gotta keep doing it."

"But I can't..."

"Why not? Because your mom's too up her own shit? Fuck that. You need to do your own thing. Think of all those paintings still being converted in your head, and you're not putting them anywhere. That's one hell of a burden to carry around. If I didn't write all these songs that keep appearing in my head, I'd sure as hell go crazy."

Restlessness came creeping up my legs again and I leaned over the coffee table to sniff up the snow-white remedy. "I don't know..." I sniffled and rubbed my nose. "It was always her thing. I hated how it always felt like I was doing it for her."

"Well, maybe now is the time to start doing it for yourself."

"But it's been *so long*. I'm not even sure I can do it anymore."

"Course you can! These things never leave you." His face lit up and he shoved his guitar aside. "Why don't you draw something right now? I'm sure there's pens and paper around here somewhere."

Before I could say anything he was up and away, searching the house for art supplies.

"Here!" he yelled from the recording room. "Will this do?"

His sudden enthusiasm was infectious, and I jumped up from the sofa and went to survey his loot: an old notebook with ruled pages – not ideal, but it could work – and some old pencil stubs. I looked at Liam and saw a childlike joy I had never before seen in him, and it was rubbing off on me, too.

"Okay, on one condition," I said, taking the notebook and pencils from him. "That you let me draw you."

"Why, of course! With this pretty face, who can blame ya?"

I laughed. "I could never do it justice." I felt sharp and ready, taut like a drawn bow and arrow, just waiting for the *twang*.

"You get yourself ready, Imma roll a joint."

"Oh." I stopped, my hand gripping the pencil stubs.

"What's up?"

"Are you sure it's safe, like, to mix? Coke and Xannies, and now weed as well?"

"Sure it's safe, it's no big deal. You gotta stop worrying so much, Hazelnut!" He grabbed my sides and tickled me, which sent me howling and grappling for rescue, the pens flying out of my hand.

"Stop! Mercy!" When he let go I pushed him off to a safe distance, and held my arm there while catching my breath. "You…! I'm watching you!"

"I know you are," he said, flashing me a teasing smirk.

I suppressed a smile and slapped his arm. "Behave, or I'll find someone else to draw!"

His face dropped in mock shock. "I can't even bear the thought. I'm all yours. Where do you want me?"

I looked around, considering angles and positions. "That chair, please."

"Yes, ma'am." He stopped by the coffee table to pick up a grinder and some papers, then went to sit in the chair and started rolling.

"I'll get some more beers!" I skipped into the kitchen, my wild blood pumping in my veins. "Oh, and a line. Which to have first?" I leapt back into the living room, carved a line out of the pile and sniffed it up, felt the rush like a fresh wind to my face. Back to the kitchen, grab the beers. "You want one, yeah? Of course you do, what am I talking about? When has Liam Riley ever been known to turn down a beer!" Two cold cans in my hands, grab a kitchen chair, back to the living room.

"Who you talkin' to?" Liam asked.

"Just myself. Why don't you stop eavesdropping."

He smiled and shook his head. "My Hazel, she sure is a nut." He licked the paper and sealed the joint.

I gathered up the dropped pencils and positioned myself in front of Liam, capturing him at a slight angle. He lit the joint and a sweet, earthy smoke filled the room. Pencil to paper, quick double-take of his pose, here we go.

Slowly, the shape of Liam's head and torso appeared on the page before me. It felt strange and familiar all at once, and I found I hadn't forgotten how to do it, not at all. Rather, it seemed I had got better at it, even though I had neglected it for nearly a decade. And it felt wonderful – the soft scratching sound the pencil made against the rough paper, the way Liam eased his way onto the sheet. There was his face, not quite right, move that jawline, that's it. Now the hair, and some shading, and now there's depth. Where do his eyes go? Looking up, getting distracted, staring at his beautiful face for a moment, then back to it, get the eyes just right.

"I need colour!" I announced. Pencils weren't enough; I needed paints to make Liam come alive. "Do you have any paint here?"

"I don't think so." Liam took another drag off the joint, careful to stay in position.

"Don't move!" I rushed off on a scavenger hunt. Of course there would be no paints, I knew that, but maybe *something*, anything that could add some colour to my portrait. In the study I grabbed a couple of highlighter pens, orange and green; and upstairs in a drawer I found some old felt tip pens, dried up and nearly gone, but I brought them down anyway to see what could be done.

Passing the kitchen, I could hear the crickets through the back door, and they followed me into the living room, beating and strumming in a regular pattern, humming a low note in harmony with the sound of blood rushing through my ears.

"Got some!" I spread my findings on the table next to me, held my drawing up to compare the proportions. Took the green highlighter and let it dance over the page, then orange and red, and it looked more and more like my mother's abstract paintings, I knew that, but it felt like that's what the drawing wanted to look like. Then I held the faded felt tip over Liam's heart and drew a small grey circle, and another on top of it, a spiral swirling outward, spreading and sprawling all over the drawing. It wasn't me doing this; there was some other force moving my hands.

When it was done, I put it down on the table in front of me, and although all the pens were back on the table, I felt like I was still holding something – a phantom brush between my fingertips.

Liam looked pleased with himself. "Great work, Haze!

That looked intense. I get like that sometimes when a song comes out. I get all swept up."

I felt emptied, but in a good way; like my dam had burst, my reservoir free to receive fresh rain.

"Wanna see?" I went over and handed him the notebook, and he sucked on the joint while considering my work.

"It's me. I mean, really, it's *me*. That's my face. And all these crazy colours and shapes, they make total sense." He squinted at the picture with a dopey smile, then looked up at me. "This is beautiful, Haze. This is what you should be doing."

He held out the joint to me, but I declined. I had plenty going on already. I sat back in my chair, staring at the picture. I felt again like I had when I was eight and my mother had showered me with attention like water and sunlight to a seedling, willing me to grow and blossom. My chest expanded with a warm glow. How I had missed that feeling.

"Thanks for this, Liam." I looked up, and my thumping heart nearly stopped dead when I saw him slump over and slide out of his chair.

TWENTY-EIGHT

"Liam!" I dashed over and grabbed him just as he hit the floor. "What's wrong? Oh my god oh my god. Wake up, Liam, Jesus Christ!" I shook him, slapped him, his face looked so pale, was it always that pale?! When he didn't budge, I crawled to the side and positioned him on the floor so I could listen to his heart, his precious heart. It was beating, fast.

I froze. "What do I do? What do I do?" *Phone!* I fumbled for my mobile but my fingers wouldn't stop shaking. *Stop it! Calm down.* 999... Wait, no, 911—

"Huh..."

I turned around and saw Liam, foggy-eyed and confused, trying to pull himself up.

"Jesus fucking Christ, Liam, don't do that to me!" I collapsed in a heap, and then the tears came. My heart was beating fast, too, as though it was sick of being stuck in its rib cage prison.

"Hazel, baby, don't cry," Liam slurred. With some effort, he leaned over and took my arm, but I shook him off and hit him in the chest.

"You fucktard! You said it was *safe!*"

"Yeah, sorry…" He wiped his mouth and ruffled his hair. "I guess the Xanax is still in my system. Maybe I should go easy on the weed."

"Yeah, no shit!" I stood up on shaky legs, tears pouring down my cheeks, tears of relief and rage and shame. On the table lay the pencils and highlighters, and in one swift motion I leaned down and swiped them all off, sending them flying across the room.

Liam stood up, too, looking small and shamefaced. "Hey… It's okay. I'm fine."

I looked at my feet, sniffling an endless stream of tears and snot. "You're not, though," I said, and I felt myself falling down some dark well at the bottom of the world. "I think it's time for bed."

Liam didn't say anything, and I left the mess we had made downstairs and stomped up to bed. I wasn't tired; far from it. My heart was pumping fervently as though the night would never end. Helpless rage seeped from my pores and made my skin itch as I lay down. I turned to my side and curled up into a ball, hugging my legs.

After a while, Liam appeared in the doorway. "So, that's it? We're just going to bed now?"

"Yes," I mumbled into my pillow, refusing to meet his eyes. I didn't know why I was *this* angry, but my blood had turned into red hot fuming oil, flooding my organs with a searing fury. How could he do this? Why was he so reckless? So *stupid?*

I felt my heart racing again and took a few deep breaths. Liam came over and lay down beside me, but I edged away.

"Babe, I'm sorry, okay? It's just the downers, sometimes they make me a bit tired."

"A bit *tired?* I was about to call a fucking ambulance, for chrissakes!"

I huffed and wriggled around until I was facing the wall. Liam hesitated. I could hear him hovering, waiting, wondering what to do. Then he sighed and turned away. I wanted him to wrap his arms around me and promise never to do that again. But he didn't.

Sleep was not going to come easy this night. We lay like that for a long time, with restless limbs and eyes wide open, waiting for the poison to drain from us.

* * *

We must have drifted off eventually, because suddenly I opened my eyes and the room was flooded with sunlight. Liam was still out cold, curled up with his arms around his pillow. The air was thick and hot and my head was pounding.

Something was buzzing. My phone lay silent on the floor next to me. I craned my aching neck around and saw Liam's phone by his side, his screen lighting up. I groaned and stood up slowly, so tired that my very bones might give up holding me together. The phone went silent and I stopped, but then it started up again.

"Jeez, okay, I'm coming..." My temples throbbed as I leaned down to pick it up. Incoming call from V. Who was V? Oh, was it...? I slid the answer button and walked over to the window. "Hello?"

"Oh, hi! Is that—Hazel?"

"Er, yeah... Vanya?"

"Hi, sweetie. I was just calling to check in on Liam. I was gettin' this awful feelin' and I thought I'd... Is he alright?"

I looked over at him, his rhythmic breathing, his arms gripping his pillow. "Yeah, he's fine now."

"That's good. I know he was so close with Frank, I'm sure he's going through a very tough time."

"He is…," I said, my voice frail and shaky. I wasn't sure how much I could tell her.

"Hazel? What's wrong?"

"Well…" I hesitated, then walked further away from Liam and covered my mouth. "He's just, you know. He's doing a lot of drugs. I don't know how to stop it. He keeps saying he's got it under control, but I'm not so sure anymore."

There was a brief silence. "Oh, honey…" A sigh floated down the line. "Don't take it upon yourself, okay? I know some about what you're going through. Have you talked to him about getting help?"

"Not really… Something tells me he's not going to be too keen on the idea." Somehow, I couldn't picture Liam voluntarily walking into rehab and spilling his guts in a support group.

"Well, all you can do is ask," Vanya said. "He's going to have to make those choices for himself."

I looked over at him, curled up among the covers. Maybe I could convince him. Whatever we were doing certainly wasn't helping. I had to at least try. "I'll bring it up, see what he says."

"Okay." There was a brief silence, then another sigh. "Oh, darlin'… This ain't easy on any of us."

I tightened my grip around Liam's phone, pressing it closer to my ear. There was something soothing about Vanya's emphatic speech, her sing-song accent. It felt good to confide in a grown-up, I thought – although wasn't I supposed to be a grown-up by now?

"You okay?" she asked.

"Yeah…" A sniffle caught me by surprise. "I think so."

"Well, you got my number and my card. Anything you need, please don't hesitate to call, alright?"

"Okay. Thanks, Vanya."

"Nice to speak to you again, Hazel."

"You too."

There was a click and Liam's phone went dead. I padded over to his side of the bed, and I could see he hadn't stirred. I was glad I hadn't woken him up; he needed the rest. I put the phone back as quietly as I could, then shuffled down the stairs, one step at a time, holding onto the railing. Past the mess in the living room, through the backdoor and out, out onto soft grass.

I stretched out on the overgrown lawn. Here, the world felt spacious and fresh, away from that fusty house with all its complications. The earth felt solid and compassionate beneath me, the treetops soothing and swaying, flickering sunlight tickling my eyes. An airplane hummed past high above, out there where life was still happening everywhere. I felt my neck relax and my head soften, the clean breeze clearing my lungs.

* * *

"Haze?"

I opened my eyes, blinking away a foggy dream. I looked up and saw Liam standing in the patio door. The playfulness of last night had been washed from his face like badly cleaned makeup; ashen skin, dark-ringed eyes, pale lips.

"What're you doing out here?" he asked.

I sat up, thankful that my headache had eased. "I needed some air." I shielded my eyes against the midday sun. "You okay? How you feeling?"

"I'm okay." He stepped out, bare feet in the long grass. "Look, I'm sorry again about last night. I didn't mean to scare you like that."

"Yeah… I'm sorry I got so angry." I swallowed, a knot forming in my stomach. "Look, Liam. I was just talking to Vanya—"

"What? Where?"

"She called while you were asleep. We wonder if, maybe…" I clumsily got to my feet and felt my chest tighten. "Like, maybe it's time for you to get some help?"

"Help?"

"Like... Rehab. Or therapy."

"No, no…" He held his palms up and took a step backwards. "No, fuck that. I'm fine, Hazel. I'm not… I'm just dealing with some shit, okay?"

I pressed my lips together, mustering some more courage. "I think it would be good to work through it properly, though? Like, with a professional."

"I'm not going to some fucking psych quack, okay?"

My heart sank. "Why not?"

He jerked his head to the side. "Look, I had enough of that shit when I was a kid. My parents dragged me through this psycho-bullshit after I tried to off myself. Forced me to go see this so-called doctor for over a year, some self-righteous ass tryin' to tell me how to live my life. Fucking waste of time, it was."

"I didn't know that. But it could be different this time. Wouldn't it be good to—"

"Haze," he snapped. "I don't wanna hear it. I gotta go, okay?"

"Go? Go where?"

"I gotta go back to my parents', see if my keys are in the den."

"Oh, okay. Do you want me to come with you…?"

"No, no. You stay here. I'll be back soon."

I bit my lip, nodding. "Okay."

He disappeared inside, and soon I heard the front door slam. I watched his skinny shape as he walked down the street. When was the last time he ate anything? Tomorrow,

Lawson and the others were coming to pick us up. It was time to clean up our act.

I headed inside, grabbed a bin bag from the kitchen and filled it with empty cans and bottles and tissues. I emptied stinky piles of cigarette ends and old joints into it, swept spilled tobacco and ash and empty baggies from the coffee table. On the floor lay all the vinyls, pulled from their covers. I sat down and paired them all up and stacked them neatly along the wall. Bin bag outside, wash up glasses in the kitchen, spray everything with pine-scented cleaner. There. That's better.

Upstairs, there was more to deal with in the bedroom. On the floor by Liam's side of the bed lay a tangle of old T-shirts, boxers and socks. I grabbed a carrier bag and began shoving all the laundry into it, but stopped at the foot of his bedside table. There was a bag, half-open, and I could see some pill bottles poking out. Slowly, I peeled it open to reveal the rest of the contents: some pouches of cocaine, a clear baggie containing some tablets and capsules in various shapes and colours, and another baggie with some crumbly substance I didn't recognise. I sat on my knees and stared at it for a long while. All this shit he kept cramming into his body, and for what? It was never going to help him.

"Fuck it." I twisted it shut and hid it in the hallway cupboard, way up on the highest shelf. Then I brought the laundry downstairs and put on the washing machine, and finally I went to put on a pot of coffee.

I was standing by the machine, waiting for its final sputters, when Liam burst through the front door.

"Fuck! Fucking shitbags!"

I ran into the hallway and found him kicking off his shoes. One got stuck and he flung his leg frustratedly until it slipped off and crashed into the corner.

"Whoa, whoa, what's wrong?"

"My fucking douchebag parents, that's what!"

The door was open behind him, and he turned and slammed it so hard that it bounced open again.

"Hey, hey…" I walked over and grabbed the door before he could assault it further, and closed it slowly. "What happened?"

"They've already sold his house," he spat. "Just like that. With all his stuff in it, too! There's nothing left. I can't believe how heartless they are. Just erased him off the face of the earth. Now, it's like he never existed!"

Liam stood shaking, his hands balled into fists. I swallowed hard and searched for something to say, when he snapped into motion and rushed past me up the stairs. I had a feeling he was going for something in particular, and my heart flew to my throat as I scurried after him.

"What the fuck…" He looked around the bed, lifted the covers, threw his pillow aside. Bewildered, he turned around and searched the floor, yanked open the drawers in his bedside table. Then he stopped, and for a brief moment the whole world stood still. He twisted around and fixed me with burning eyes.

"Where's my stuff?"

I stood wringing my hands while thinking of what to say.

"Where is it?!"

"Liam, please… Can't we just take a moment—"

"This isn't funny!"

"I know it isn't."

I looked at him with all the seriousness in me. He glared back at me, his face pinched with everything that was on the verge of exploding.

"Can I have it back, please?" He was snarling through clenched teeth, as though it took everything in him to not lash out at me. My stomach was bending and twisting, my ears ringing.

"Liam, I can't imagine what you must be feeling right now, but please... This shit is fucking with your head. I know you think it's helping, but it's only making things worse." I paused for a second, trying to find the right words. "I care about you too much to let this shit ruin you."

He stood staring at me, his breaths sharp and rapid.

"Do you even know what you're running from?" I braved the distance between us, taking a step closer. "If you just stop for a second, you might realise there was nothing chasing you to begin with."

He took a step back and started pacing back and forth, scratching his arms like a restless prisoner. Then he whirled around and slammed his fist into the wall. "Fuck!"

I flinched, breathing shallow breaths, fighting to stay calm.

"Fuck," he said again, quieter this time, shaking his hand and rubbing his bloodied knuckles. "Please, Hazel... I'm begging you." His face softened and tears filled his eyes. "Don't do this... I'm not worth it."

"What do you mean? Don't even say that!" Now I was crying, too. Why did we always come back to this?

"I'm nothing, Haze! I'm just a selfish piece of shit who wrecks everything I come into contact with. You're wasting your time."

I started backing out of the room. "Stop... Don't talk like that. I'll go get us some food, okay? You've barely eaten in days."

"I don't want any fucking food!"

"Okay, well," I said, ignoring him. "I'll go to the store. I'll see you in a bit, okay?" I turned and hurried down the stairs.

"Hazel!"

His roar faded as I slipped outside into the balmy afternoon. *All he needs is some food and some rest*, I told myself. *I'll take care of it.*

Halfway to the store, I pulled out my phone. No messages. I hoped that was a good sign.

I thought about the others, Lawson and the rest. We had only been away from them for a few days, but time had stretched and warped in our strange little bubble. I scrolled through my contacts and called Lawson. As it rang, I carried on walking down the summery street, so bright and peaceful. What a jarring contrast. The sun felt warm on my face; a nice, clean heat, not sticky like in the South.

I heard Lawson answer. "Hazel! How are you?"

"Hey, Laws. I'm okay, I think."

"So good to hear from you. How did the funeral go? I haven't heard anything from Liam. I guess he's still mad at me."

I closed my eyes as I recalled the kiss and the fight and all the pain I had caused.

"Yeah, um… It went as expected, I guess. But, well, there's been some trouble with his parents. They got into a fight at the funeral, and now he's just found out that they've sold Frank's house, along with all his stuff."

"What the hell?" Lawson sighed deeply at the other end of the line. "Jeez. How's he doing?"

I stopped at a big crossing and waited for the light. "Not great," I admitted. "He ran straight for his drugs, but, um…" I felt a little embarrassed about my crude attempt at cleaning Liam up. "I, uh, I hid them from him."

"You hid them? His drugs?"

"Yeah…"

"Wow, okay."

I waited for him to say more, but that seemed to be it. My stomach began to sink again. Had I made a mistake?

"You don't sound too enthusiastic."

"I mean. It would be awesome if he could, you know… not be high all the time. I'd love that. We all would."

247

"But...?"

"I dunno, I'm not sure what is the best way forward. Where are you now? He's not there with you?"

"No, I've gone to get us some food. He's barely eaten anything."

"Okay... Well, good luck with it, Haze. Let me know how it goes."

"Will do." The lights changed and I carried on walking. "Um, so, see you tomorrow?"

"Yeah, we'll come pick you guys up around ten. That good with you?"

"Sure. Looking forward to seeing you all again."

"You too, Mary Poppins."

I pressed the phone to my ear and smiled at his stupid nicknames. Good old Lawson.

In the store, I picked whatever looked vaguely healthy – fruits, cereal bars, soups, smoothies; anything that looked like it could nurture us back to health – and brought it back to the house. I lingered for a moment on the front steps, worried about what awaited me inside. Then I gently cracked open the door.

"Liam?" I slipped out of my flip-flops. "I'm back. I've got some snacks for us."

He didn't answer. I carried the shopping bag into the kitchen and placed its contents on the countertop.

"Hey, Liam? Wanna come see what I got?"

I heard a soft groan from the living room and stopped, a bunch of bananas frozen in mid-air. "Liam?" I put the bunch down and walked into the living room. Liam lay on the sofa, half-leaning, half-sleeping, an unlit cigarette hanging from his lips. On the table in front of him sat an orange pill bottle, its lid off, next to a large glass of whiskey. A cold pang shot through my gut.

"No... Please, no."

His eyes wandered around the room until they landed on me. "Haze…"

I couldn't hold it together anymore. "Fuck's sake, Liam!" I strode over and grabbed the bottle and hurled it into the corner, pills flying. "Look, I know you're hurting, but you can't keep doing this!"

His gaze drifted aimlessly through his temporary lobotomy.

"Hey!" I snapped. He didn't move. I kicked the coffee table, scraping it over the floorboards. No reaction.

Next to the sofa, Liam's guitar sat in its stand. His precious instrument that no one could compete with; the thing he loved more than anything or anyone. In a flash of madness I grabbed it and raised it above my head, poised to smash it into a thousand pieces, like he had done to my heart so many times.

But I couldn't. I held it there, waiting for a reaction, but Liam was too far gone into his Xanax fog. Slowly, I lowered the wooden body, the strings twanging slightly as I placed it back into its stand.

"You know what, you're right," I said, my face covered in tears and resignation. "Maybe you're not worth it."

I went to the hallway and pulled out his stash from the cupboard. He could do what he wanted; it wasn't my problem anymore. I stormed into the living room and threw the bag at him. It took a moment for him to react, then he slowly picked it up and held it to his chest.

"Thanks, baby…"

"Don't you fucking call me that. I'm packing my things. The others are coming for us tomorrow morning, and you best be stage-ready by tomorrow night."

I gathered my belongings in a huff and shoved them carelessly into my backpack, then pulled wet clothes from the washing machine and pressed them into a bag. In the kitchen, I found the food I had put out for Liam. What an idiot I was. He was never going to eat any of it, I knew that. He was going to destroy himself and I had no say in the matter.

Furious, I swiped it all off the counter, apples and boxes and bottles tumbling onto the floor. Then I took my backpack and went upstairs into one of the spare bedrooms and closed the door behind me. I put my bag on the creaky old bed and lay down next to it, hugging it tightly as I cried and cried and almost wished for home.

TWENTY-NINE

I spent all night lost in feverish nightmares, warping visions of Liam and my mother holding hands and staring at me like the *Shining* twins. When I tried to scream nothing came out, and I woke in a cold sweat gasping for breath, clinging to my bag.

Hunger clawed at my insides, and I thought of all the food that now lay rotting on the kitchen floor. *Stupid.* I didn't want to go downstairs and risk bumping into Liam, so I stayed put, eyes to the ceiling and stomach growling.

Around nine, I could hear him moving around the house. I lay very still, while the fights and nightmares replayed over and over in my head. I still felt furious, but I wasn't sure if I had any right to be. After all, he was grieving, and I knew that addiction was more illness than choice. But still, I felt like a discarded cleaning cloth – wipe the mess, rip and tear, out with the rubbish.

Just before ten, I heard the familiar sound of the rumbling old bus engine as it crept closer and sputtered to a stop out front. I shot to my feet, and through the window I saw Liam walk towards the bus. Its doors opened and Lawson hopped out and gingerly approached his old friend, some muffled words exchanged. Then they met in a brotherly embrace and I felt my shoulders drop with relief.

Lawson took Liam's bags and shoved them in the luggage compartment. He said something to Liam, and they both turned to look up at the house. I ducked, embarrassed to be lurking in the shadows. I grabbed my bag and headed downstairs.

I could see that Liam had tidied up some of the mess, including the groceries I had left on the floor. But in the living room the Xannies still lay scattered in the corner. When I saw them, the slam of Liam's fist hitting the wall echoed in my mind and an uneasy flutter shot through my chest. I went over and scooped them into their bottle and shoved them in my bag, then went out to meet the others.

"Hey, lady!" Lawson said, walking up to me with long arms outstretched. Liam's eyes met mine but he quickly turned away. I gave Lawson a tense hug, the memory of the kiss poking at my mind. He pulled away and looked at me, searching my face. "You okay?" he mouthed. I nodded. This was not the time or place. "Right," he said, then, louder. "Let's hit the road. Ready to roll?"

"Let's do it," Liam said, and went to lock the front door.

Lawson took my backpack and motioned for me to board. "Ladies first," he said, smiling. My gaze lingered on him for a moment, the weight in my chest lifting a little.

In the driver's seat, Victor greeted me with a small salute. Mango and Ivy were sitting in opposite booths and I walked up the aisle towards them.

"Hey, guys," I said.

"Hey!" Mango sat up straighter. "How did the funeral go? You guys okay?"

I looked over to Liam, who stood behind me. "Fine," he muttered.

Lawson stepped onboard and Victor pulled a lever, closing the doors with a hiss.

"I'm so sorry, man," Mango said, looking a little uncertain.

"We all are," Ivy added.

"Yeah, well," said Liam. "It's over now."

He squeezed past me to the beds in the back, jumped into his bunk and pulled the curtain. Everyone's eyes turned to me. I looked down and shook my head with a shrug.

"It's been a bit of a rough time," I mumbled, and they all looked at me with awkward compassion.

Alone in a booth, I curled up and blocked out the world with my earphones. I watched as the shabby studio house grew smaller and smaller, finally disappearing as we turned left and away from Madison for the final time.

* * *

Kansas City looked dreary and uninviting under a cover of grim clouds. The evening's venue was a nondescript concrete building, and we parked out front and unloaded our gear. Liam remained in his bunk and we knew better than to bother him.

Once we were set up and ready, I went with Lawson to find something to eat. We got some burgers from a market and brought them to the riverfront, where the muddy waters of the Missouri River were rolling by before us. A crack had appeared in the clouds, spilling slices of light from the slowly setting sun. We sat down on the grass to enjoy our dinners.

"So how did he take it?" Lawson said, wiping burger sauce from his mouth.

I chewed slowly, looking out over the murky water.

"Not great," I said finally.

"What happened?"

"You know when you called? Well, when I came back home, I found him half passed out on the sofa with a bottle of Xanax. He must have had some spare."

Lawson nodded like he wasn't surprised.

"I just lost it. Went and got his stash from the cupboard and threw it at him. Haven't spoken to him since."

"Oh." Lawson stretched his long legs out on the grass. "Do you want me to get you a separate room at the hotel tonight?"

The bit of burger I had in my mouth suddenly felt too large and I struggled to swallow it. Was this it? Were we over now? I couldn't see how we could patch this up. We had broken into too many shards, crumbled into too much dust; it felt impossible to glue back together. Reluctantly, I nodded.

"Yeah, I guess..."

"No problem, I'll sort it out. Vic has booked us into a decent hotel for once. We figured you guys could use a nice place to stay after everything you've been through."

"Thank you." I gave him a half-hearted smile, then sighed and hung my troubled head. "I don't know what I'm doing, Laws. I know I can't change him, but I can't stand to watch him destroy himself like this."

"Hey, it's okay," Lawson said. "Give it time. He'll probably get back on his feet now that the funeral is over and he's back on tour."

"Yeah, maybe..."

When I didn't say anything else, I could sense Lawson grasping for something to cheer me up. "Hey, did you hear about the meteor shower tonight?"

"No?"

"It's supposed to start around the time we're on, but we might see some after the gig. That is, if these clouds clear up."

"I've never seen a meteor shower. What's it like?"

"Just loads of shooting stars. It's pretty epic. I love space stuff."

I looked up at the sky. It felt comforting to consider a world outside my own, an infinite void around my troubles. Something so much bigger than me.

"I hope we can see some," I said, my eyes locked on the sky above.

We finished our food and got up to walk back to the venue. The sky grew darker, and the indifferent river kept on rolling.

* * *

Backstage, I helped myself to a beer while I took a look at the set list. It felt like a long time since I had performed. I hummed the tunes and reminded myself of my harmonies, pacing around like a trapped songbird. My voice felt like sandpaper and I tried some warm-up exercises, reaching for higher notes but getting frustrated when it didn't sound right. I stopped and gulped another load of beer, forcing myself to relax. I felt edgier than usual, frazzled. The last few days had done a number on me.

"Okay." I shook my hands to release nervous energy. "I've got this."

I started from the top, but stopped mid-note when I heard the door open. I turned around and saw Liam looking at me with a mournful half-smile.

"It's so weird," he said.

I swallowed. "What is?"

"Hearing you sing my lyrics. My words in your voice... It always amazes me."

"Oh." My muscles softened and I folded the setlist. "That's... good, I guess." I waited a beat. A shifting foot, a hesitant smile.

"I…" Liam pursed his lips. I waited for more, but he just sighed and looked at the floor. "I'll see you out there," he said, and before I could say anything else, he had closed the door behind him.

Out on stage, my hands clutching the mic stand, I fell back into it effortlessly. How I savoured that feeling of losing myself in the blinding lights, and the intimate act of wrapping my voice around Liam's. When we couldn't speak, at least we could sing.

But tonight, his performance felt edgy and irritable. He sang louder and angrier, slamming his strings. After a couple of songs, he let his guitar hang from its strap and leaned into the microphone.

"Thank you, you're too kind," he said over the applause. "But really, doesn't anyone wonder why the hell we bother with any of this?"

I felt my stomach knot. In my periphery I noticed Lawson glancing over at me, but I remained facing the audience and tried to keep my face neutral.

Liam continued. "Don't you know all songs have already been written? There's not a fucking new thing under the sun." He picked up his beer from the floor and drained the cup, and when he hurled it out into the room, the crowd cheered and whistled. Then he returned to the mic, pressing his lips against the mesh. "All stories have been told already. We're just running on repeat."

He heaved his guitar aside, pulled the mic from its stand and sat down right in front of the audience, dangling his Converses over the edge.

"Who here thinks they're *happy*?" he asked, his voice contracting with contempt. There were some scattered shouts and claps. "Well, I'll let you in on a little secret. It's all just a temporary illusion. Don't fall for it. You might win, but then you'll lose again. Count on it."

The crowd stood rapt, soaking up his angst.

"You think you have people who love you? Who understand you?" He twirled the cable around his hand. "Here's the thing, though. That's impossible. No one can ever truly know another person. We're all stuck in our own fucking heads." He pressed his knuckles to his temple. "We're all just fucking alone. Anything else is a lie."

"Liam…," I whispered, leaning away from my mic.

He turned and looked up at me, surprised, as if woken from a dream. The entire venue held its breath. Then he looked back out over his adoring fans, and brought the mic to his lips once more. "Fuck it. We may as well keep singing, right?"

The room erupted. Liam got back on his feet, stuck the mic in its stand and slung his guitar back over his shoulder. He counted *one, two, three* and we launched into the next song, but my mind was caught up in what he had said. How I wished he wouldn't feel that way. If only he would dare to open up and be vulnerable with us, he wouldn't have to feel so alone.

The rest of the show passed without incident, and I heaved a sigh of relief as we stepped off the stage. In a tense silence, we packed up and rode to the hotel.

As we walked across the car park Lawson stopped, his neck craned upwards. "Hey, look!" He was pointing at the now cloudless sky with a boyish grin on his face. I followed his gaze and saw a shooting star, then another; tiny sparks flying through the night, without a sound.

"Oh, wow!" I stopped next to him, my face turned towards the deep black universe above us.

"Beautiful," the others agreed, as they paused one by one to look up.

The six of us stood there for a moment, all our troubles evaporated before this silent sky spectacle. I glanced over at

Liam. He stood looking up, his face blank. There was no telling what he was thinking. I wished he would look over at me, but he stood unmoving, staring into the void.

* * *

My hotel room felt sad and cold and lonesome as I got ready for bed. I pulled on a T-shirt and brushed my teeth, my mind raging like a tornado across the wasteland of my life. How had I ended up here? And Liam, my Liam, was there any saving us? I brushed too hard until my gums started bleeding, spitting red toothpaste into the hotel sink. My face looked ashen, thin and weary in the mirror, my hair a matted mess. I sighed and turned out the lights.

In bed, I contorted my body into all kinds of positions, but I couldn't get comfortable. The bed felt too big and I felt too small, too fragile, too alone. A thousand thoughts banged against my skull, determined to keep me awake. The air conditioner whirred and the room felt too cold, but under the covers my body was overheating. I fluffed up the pillow, then pushed it down again.

"Fuck it," I whispered. Should I? Why not. I threw the duvet aside and padded over to the door. I needed something to help me sleep. Liam would have something for me. His room was just across the hall, I could go over there right now. It would be so easy.

It was probably a terrible idea, but I had grown accustomed to making bad decisions. I grabbed the door handle and was just about to pull the door open when I was interrupted by a knock.

I froze. It was way past midnight. It could only be one person.

The door felt heavy as I pulled it open, and my heart twitched at the sight of his boyish face and tousled hair.

"Liam...?"

"I'm sorry, Hazel. You're right. This shit isn't good for me." I looked down and saw that he was holding his stash. "You're going home soon, and I don't want to mess with our last few weeks." He held the bag out to me. "Take it. I don't want it."

Oh my god. I felt my heart make a hopeful twirl.

"Wow, okay. That's—that's great, Liam. Thank you." I took it from him slowly, as though I expected him to violently change his mind. But his arms dropped and he just stood there, drowning me with those waifish eyes.

"Haze..." He looked at me pleadingly, his head slightly tilted, half-obscured by that bit of hair that always hung down in front of his eyes. "Can I stay?" he said quietly, his voice cracking. "Please?"

The moment he spoke those words, I realised that was all the relief I needed. I wasn't sure how many more times I could sellotape my heart together, but standing there before him, his eyes on me, his fringe just begging for me to tenderly sweep it aside, I was as helpless as I ever was.

I put the bag down and stepped aside to let him in. He exhaled with relief, his lopsided smile returning. He walked up to me and took my face in both his hands, then kissed my forehead, my cheeks, and finally my mouth, while golden confetti rained inside me. He wrapped his arms around me and pulled me closer, and began kissing my neck while gently tugging at my hair.

"I'm sorry," he murmured between kisses. "I'm sorry I'm such an asshole."

His hand found its way up the side of my waist, setting off tiny explosions like sparklers over my skin, and my breathing grew heavier.

"You're not an asshole," I whispered, pulling his T-shirt over his head, running my fingers through his dark locks.

"I am, though," he insisted, as he pulled me towards the bed. "I don't mean to be. I promise I'll do better…"

"Shush, now." He lifted my shirt up and tossed it on the floor, and I gathered his skinny torso to me, pressing my face to his chest. "I love you…"

The second those words left my mouth, my heart stopped. As did Liam's wandering hands. He stood frozen, holding his breath. Ashamed, I lowered my gaze and mumbled some apology.

Liam didn't move for what felt like the longest time. Then he slowly dropped his hands to his side.

"Don't, Hazel. Don't say that."

"Liam, I… Just forget I said it, please. It doesn't mean anything."

"No, no, it does." He shook his head and took a step back. "You don't get it, Hazel. I ruin everything. I don't want to ruin you. You deserve better."

"But I want to be ruined," I said abruptly, surprised by the determination in my voice. I didn't care anymore in what ways he could hurt me. All I knew was that I didn't want him to leave. I didn't want to go back to bed alone, hugging a backpack and wishing for sleep that never came.

"Hazel, come on…"

"Liam," I said, my voice suddenly hard with impatience. "If you want me, take me. What I do or do not deserve is none of your business."

He looked stunned, his mouth open, as if waiting to see if I was being serious.

I tilted my head and ventured a teasing smile. "Go on and ruin me. I dare you."

He clenched his jaw shut and made some decision in his mind. Then he took a step forward and looked down at me, swallowing me up with those chocolate eyes. I stood my ground, staring back at him, showing my resolve.

"You're impossible," he said, his breath faster now.

"So are you," I whispered, a strange courage rushing through me.

"What does that make us?" he asked.

But he wasn't expecting an answer, for then he was all over me and we were on the bed and our heartbeats synched to a perfect rhythm, and above us meteors fell towards the earth and went up in swooshing flames, tearing white burning streaks across the sky.

THIRTY

I woke, unsure for a moment where I was. Then the memories of last night came flooding in, and I stretched like a purring cat, grinning from ear to ear. Liam was still asleep next to me, his face half-buried in his pillow. He seemed relaxed, his features soft, his breathing regular. I had never seen him look so peaceful.

Careful not to disturb him, I eased off the bed, picked up my T-shirt off the floor and pulled it over my head. From the desk I grabbed a piece of paper and a pen and sat down on the floor next to the bed. The wall felt cool as I leaned against it and began to draw the outline of Liam's body, all burrowed up in pristine hotel sheets. His head became a tousle of heavy, black lines, then the curve of his shoulder down to his narrow hips, where his legs bent slightly.

There was not a sound around me, as though the whole world was asleep. I felt protected in a safe little bubble, all my senses focused on the image appearing on the paper. The drawing carried the serene atmosphere of early morning, and I added soft lines around the main contours, like an energy field surrounding my sleeping beauty.

Then he stirred, twirled, and looked up at me from under his unruly hair. He blinked as he slowly came to his senses. When he saw that I was drawing, his lips curled into a bright smile.

"Sorry," I said with a coy smirk. "I couldn't help it."

He tilted his head, squinting morning eyes glittering. "My raw allure inspired you to create art, and you're *sorry?*"

That made me giggle. "Okay, no, I'm not at all sorry. Quite the opposite."

He laughed and sank back into his pillow, eyes to the ceiling. Then he turned back to me, still with that curious smile. "I just had the best dream."

"What about?"

"I'm not sure... I just remember vague images, but the feeling... I don't know. I was excited about something." He frowned, searching his subconscious for clues. "I usually have really fucked-up dreams, so it was a nice change."

I beamed at him. Seeing Liam like this felt like it had all been worth it.

He crawled closer and gestured at my drawing. "So, let me see what you've got." I took one last look to make sure it was finished, then handed it to him. "Mmm..." He nodded, taking it in. "I love this fuzzy edge you sketched around me." He stroked the paper gently, tracing the contours. "You can tell I was having happy dreams."

"You did seem really peaceful."

"Can I keep it?"

"Sure." I was surprised but delighted that he liked it so much. He turned and put it on his side table, then reached out an inviting arm to me.

"Come here."

I crawled back into bed and let him envelop me, nuzzling my face into his neck, breathing in his citrus hair. We lay back on the plush pillows, a tangle of limbs and love. He pressed his lips against my forehead, stroking my hair.

"Thank you," I mumbled into his neck.

"For what?"

I raised my head and looked him in the eye. "For what you did last night. For handing over your... stuff. It was a brave move. I think it will be really good for you."

He pressed his lips together and gave me a small nod. "Sure."

"We're all here for you if you need anything. You know that, yeah?"

"Of course, yeah." His face seemed to stiffen, but then he pulled me to his chest and held me there. "Thanks, Hazelnut."

If only I could have stopped time right there, preserved us in a little glittering snow globe, perfect forever.

* * *

"Hey, Liam!" Lawson's voice was coming from the hall. I woke from drifting dreams and unwrapped myself from Liam's warm body. "Where you at, bro?"

"In here! One sec." Liam rubbed his eyes and ruffled his hair, then got up to open the door.

"Wait, what?" Lawson stood outside, holding his phone up to show Liam something. He looked over Liam's shoulder, and when he spotted me his mouth fell open.

"Oh..." He took a step back. "I'm sorry, I didn't know..."

Liam looked back at me and smiled. "It's okay, dude. What's up?"

"Well, uh..." Poor Lawson was all flustered at the sight of me, half-naked in bed. I crawled further down under the sheets, unable to wipe the giddy grin off my face.

Liam laughed. "Did you want to show me something?" he asked, pointing at Lawson's phone, poised in mid-air.

Lawson tore his eyes from me, and then seemed to focus all his efforts on *not* looking at me. "Uh, yeah, Vic and I were just planning the route to Chicago…" His screen had gone black, and he unlocked it again and began tapping away. "But, um, we thought since we've got an extra day, we could head out to Mark Twain National Forest for a little excursion. Figured a bit of nature time would do us all some good." He held up a map and Liam leaned in to take a closer look. "See, it's just south of here."

"Sounds great," said Liam. "Let's do it."

"Sweet." Lawson locked his phone and put it in his back pocket. "I'll see you, uh, I'll see you both downstairs in a little while, okay?"

"Sure thing, man."

"Thanks, Laws!" I gave him an awkward wave, and with rosy cheeks he gave me a quick nod and disappeared down the hall.

Liam closed the door and turned to me, and he shook his head with a chuckle. "I think they're struggling to keep up with us."

* * *

The afternoon was bright and warm when we stopped the bus in a small car park, lazy after a long and winding drive through increasingly thickening forest. I jumped out the door with a squeal of delight, stretching my bare arms into the blue sky, breathing in the scents of sun-warm soil and thriving greenery at the height of summer.

"Aaah…," I sighed. "It's so beautiful!"

I was wearing a sundress with thin straps, a tucked-in waist and a breezy skirt that flowed about my legs. The boys were all in shorts and T-shirts, except for Liam who never changed out of his skin-tight jeans; but poor Ivy was dressed in another long-sleeve top and hovered alone in the shade of the bus.

Victor heaved a load of barbecue supplies onto the ground. "So, who's up for a swim?"

"Me!" I chirped, throwing an eager hand into the air.

"Me first!" Mango grinned.

"Good, 'cause according to the map, there should be a natural spring just behind there," said Vic, pointing towards a cluster of trees.

"I'll show you, guys," said Lawson, and began leading us down a grassy path.

"Yes! I can't wait for a dip." Mango grabbed two bags and headed off with Laws. I picked up the barbecue trays and skipped after the boys, my face doused in dapples of sunlight filtered through the lofty trees.

As we approached the spring the terrain grew craggier, and soon the ground opened up into a large pool of turquoise water. The sky, clouds and surrounding treetops were perfectly reflected in the calm surface, and not a sound could be heard except the occasional squawk and flutter from the birds above us. Around the water rose an edge of grey rock that provided diving access from every angle.

"Wow, check this out!" Mango hollered. "Nice find, Kowalski!"

"It's stunning!" I added. Lawson smiled and stuck his hands on his hips, looking pleased with himself.

We put our supplies down and, without further ceremony, Mango pulled his T-shirt over his head and cannonballed straight into the water.

"Hey!" we howled, backing away from the spray.

Mango resurfaced, panting rapidly. "Holy shit! It's so cold!" He pulled himself back up on some rocks, rubbed his arms to warm up, and then jumped right back in, this time with a more graceful dive.

"Brave man!" I yelled when he bobbed back up.

He rubbed his eyes and shook the water off with a gleeful grin. "The sooner you jump in, the sooner you get used to it."

I looked down at the rippled surface. "Yeah, you may have a point..." Sitting on the edge, I pulled off my sandals and dipped a toe. "Youch! That *is* cold."

Then I felt two hands on my back, and before I knew it, I was swallowed up by the freezing water. The shock sent a rush of adrenaline through my veins, and I resurfaced squealing and laughing. I looked up and saw Liam standing by the edge, his lopsided smile full of mischief.

"You! I'm going to get you!" I crawled over to the rocks and pulled myself up, my dress clinging to my body. Liam was already halfway around the spring, but whenever I darted one way to try and catch him, he went the other.

"Lawson!" I howled. "Help a girl out!"

"Gladly." Lawson grinned at me, and together we managed to corner Liam.

"Okay, truce, truce!" Liam yelled, holding his hands up to try and fend us off. But two on one, it was the easiest thing to grab his arms and swing him into the water with a mighty splash.

"Holy shit!" he spattered, and quickly swam over to the rocks and heaved himself over the edge. "Okay," he said, smiling. "I deserved that."

I walked over to him but he edged away. "Hey! We're even!"

I laughed. "Don't worry, I come in peace."

I sat down next to him, our soaked bodies slowly drying in the afternoon sun. Mango was still in the water, swimming back and forth and exploring little caverns in the surrounding rocks. Our barbecue gear was piled up and waiting for us, and Lawson and Victor were getting ready to jump in. Then I noticed Ivy sitting in the shade, her long sleeves telling a story that nobody knew. She was watching me and Liam with a sullen look on her face. I swallowed hard and looked away.

As the sun began to drop we gathered around a crackling campfire, leaving our clothes to dry on some nearby rocks. I'd pulled a cardigan over my wet underwear and edged closer to the flames for warmth. Drinks and grilled meats and veggies were passed around our circle, and our talk and laughter rose up among the trees. It felt like it had during those first few weeks, back when everything was new and whole and full of promise.

Liam sat by my side, glancing over at me with glinting eyes, and I was surprised by how openly affectionate he was with me. He played with my hair and let his fingertips dance over my neck and back, sending shivers down my spine like a spray of gold dust. And on the sidelines sat Ivy, occasionally looking our way with a hint of sorrow in those green eyes of hers.

"Alright!" Mango stood up and did some ridiculous pretend-stretches. "Let's not get lazy! Another swim, anyone?" A little less eagerly, the others got up to join him.

"I'll be over in a bit!" I said, and walked over to Ivy. "Hey, Ives, you okay?"

"I'm fine," she said, although she was looking at her beer can and not at me, and that said it all.

"Wanna go for a wander?" I suggested. "It's so beautiful around here."

She puckered her lips for a moment, then gracefully rose to her feet. "Sure, why not."

We strolled away from the quarry, down a path illuminated by slanting amber from the setting sun. The evening was balmy and the air felt soft as cotton.

I glanced over at my troubled friend. "So, Ivy... What's on your mind? You seem a bit off."

She let out a dismissive laugh. "Little Miss Fix-it. I said I'm fine."

I raised an eyebrow at her. "Come on, Ives. You're not *that* good at pretending, no matter what you think."

She didn't respond, just looked down at her feet as they swept over the grassy ground. With her eyes pointed downward, she didn't notice a toppled fir tree that hung low over the path. Before I could warn her, her hair had got caught up in the prickly branches.

"Ouch! Sweet Jesus!"

She twisted around and tried to pull herself free, while I crumbled into a fit of laughter.

"I'm sorry!" I gasped. "But you look so cute right now!"

"Holy hell!" Trying to break free, she pulled her head this way and that while barking a string of colourful, Southern curses. "Hazel, don't just stand there and laugh! Help me!"

Trying to contain my cackling, I went to disentangle her from mother nature's loving hand. I pulled gently at her locks, but the branch was sticky with sap and it wasn't easy. "What a mess," I said, poorly suppressing my giggles.

There, with my arms in the air and my hands in her hair, my cardigan falling open to expose my half-naked body, Ivy once again took me by utter surprise when she leaned in and kissed me, her soft, coral lips pressed against mine.

I stopped, blinking, staring at her. She looked at me, waiting for a reaction.

"Ivy, I..." Shocked, I lowered my arms, leaving some of her hair still caught in the tree. I had not seen *this* coming.

"I'm sorry," she mumbled. "That was stupid."

"No, no. I was just surprised, is all." I grasped for something to say while she lowered her gaze, looking even more downcast than before. "Hey…" I put a hand on her arm and tried to catch her eye. "What's going on, really?"

"I don't know, I'm all confused." She sighed and began to tug carelessly at the tangled locks.

"Here, let me do that." I pulled free the final strands and guided her away from the greedy fir. When I put my arm around her shoulders, I noticed she was trembling. "Hey, why don't we sit down?" I led her over to the edge of the path, and as soon as our bottoms hit the ground she burst into tears.

"I just want what you've got," she sobbed. "What you've got with Liam. You guys seem so happy and loved-up and sweet with each other, and I don't…" She snivelled and caught her breath. "I don't understand it. How do you do it?"

"Um. Do what, exactly?"

"I see you with the others, and you're so easy-goin' and open." Her breathing had calmed some, but tiny tears still trickled down her freckled cheeks. "I want that. I wish I could be more like that."

"Well… maybe you can?"

"I don't think so," she said bitterly, kicking at the pinecones around our feet. "I'm just cold and nobody likes me."

"That's not true," I protested, although I knew that she wasn't entirely wrong.

"Don't lie. You hated me for ages."

"Only because I thought you hated me!"

She looked over at me, her doleful eyes like jade marbles. Then a reluctant smile found its way onto her lips. "How stupid."

"I know!" We looked at each other and started laughing. "Look," I said, more earnest now. "The more I got to know you, the more I loved you. Don't be so afraid of showing people your true self. You have to let them in and give them a chance to love you for who you really are. And those who don't get it can go fuck themselves. They don't matter, anyhow."

She glanced at me through the dangles of her fringe. "Really? You mean that?"

"For sure! There's nothing not to like about you, Ivy. You're sweet and talented and interesting. And you have a fascinating past. It's not something you should hide away. We're all broken in our own ways, and it helps us to see each other's flaws and scars. We all have them, in one way or another."

She looked out over the darkening woods, hugging her legs to her chest. Her hair was still tousled around the top, and I reached out and smoothed it down.

"Maybe it's time to remove those long-sleeve tops of yours," I said. "It's way too hot for them, anyway."

"But… It's so embarrassing."

"No, it's not." I leaned forward and steadily held her gaze. "It's not embarrassing. It's just part of who you are. Of who you were. And we all have our shit, trust me."

I took her hand and smiled at her, wider and bolder until she had no choice but to smile back.

"Come," I said. "Let's go for a swim."

We got to our feet and started back towards the spring.

"Sorry I kissed you," she said, flashing me a smirking pout.

"Hey," I said, grinning. "I regret nothing."

Back at the spring, the boys were still hallooing and diving into the water. Ivy walked up to the edge, hesitated for a second, then slowly peeled off her top, exposing her carved-up arms. Liam was the first to notice. His face dropped, and he silently treaded water while keeping his big eyes on Ivy. He had of course seen her scars before.

Even with those angry marks across her arms, she looked

the perfect goddess in the scarlet twilight; auburn locks falling about her ivory face, her eyes bashful and tentative, waiting for us to accept or reject her.

Then Mango saw and swam towards her. "Oh my god, Ivy, babe." He hooked his arms over the edge and looked at her with earnest compassion. Ivy stood still, her shoulders slumped. Lawson and Victor stopped, too, and swam over to us. I sat down and let it play out.

After a moment's silence, Lawson spoke in a hushed voice. "When did you do it?"

"Back in my teens," Ivy said quietly. I'm sure they all had more questions, but they knew there was no use, and that wasn't what she needed anyway.

Mango pulled himself up and gave her a big, wet hug. "You know you're always safe with us, right?"

Ivy let out a long, shaky breath, as though she had been holding it for years.

"Of course," Lawson and Victor agreed, gathering around Ivy.

"Thank you," she whispered.

"So you're coming for a swim with us?" Mango asked, his big grin back in place.

"As ordered by Hazel." She looked at me with a sly smile; a smile between sisters, a smile of in-jokes and secrets.

"No time to waste!" Mango bellowed, and jumped back into the now-black depths. Lawson smiled at Ivy and patted her on the arm, then turned and dove in. Victor followed, then me. Last was Liam, who walked up to Ivy and, without a word, enveloped her in a long hug. Then he gave her knotted hair an affectionate ruffle and turned to the water.

"Ladies first," he said, and Ivy, standing there stripped down to her underwear and secret shame, took a step forward and dove into the water, smooth and graceful as a young swan. Liam jumped in after her, and I watched with glee as they all howled and laughed. I lay back and let my body float on the cool surface, feeling weightless beneath the darkening sky. A near-full moon had just appeared above the treeline, and the stars were beginning to peer down at us. It was a perfect moment, with deep nature all around me and the sound of my friends laughing and splashing, alive and wild and free.

THIRTY-ONE

After our forest sleepover, we set course for Chicago. It was a long journey and Liam seemed twitchy and restless all the way. He paced the bus aisle, making endless cups of coffee, sat in one booth, moved to another. I watched him out of the corner of my eye, hoping against hope that he wasn't going through some sort of withdrawal. I tried asking what was wrong but he insisted he was fine, so the rest of us tried to keep the conversation going while Liam did whatever Liam had to do.

Clouds loomed over us as we chewed up mile after mile of unchanging interstate. As we got closer to the city the roads got busier, cars clogging up every lane. Then, at last, we took a sharp left turn and Chicago's skyscrapers came into view, cutting into the thick afternoon.

Pressing my face against the window, I traced the trajectory of an airplane coming in to land at O'Hare. "I can't believe it's been barely four months since I first arrived here," I said, mostly to myself. "It feels like a lifetime ago."

Lawson, who sat opposite me, looked up from his phone.

"I know… I can't believe the tour's nearly over, too. Endings always suck."

"I wish we could keep doing this forever," I said, my eyes bouncing over the approaching city. "I don't want it to end."

"Well, there'll be more tours," he said, "if you can get another visa."

Oh. I hadn't thought about that. Sure, I would have to go home, but I could always come back. Hope tingled in my chest and I broke into an expectant smile. "You know, I'd like that."

Lawson gave me a pensive look. "So, when's your flight? Soon, huh?"

My face fell. "Three weeks, more or less." Three weeks to soak up the remainder of this journey. Three weeks to say goodbye to my dear friends. Three weeks to figure out what the hell I would do with myself when I got back.

Lawson shook his head. "Too soon."

"I know," I said, barely a whisper.

"Qué dices?" Mango poked his head out from the booth in front, where he sat opposite a snoozing Ivy. "You leaving us so soon?"

I hadn't spoken about it because I hadn't wanted it to be real. But it was. Summer always fades eventually, and all adventures come to an end.

Liam groaned and I glanced over at him. He was fiddling with the stereo system, frantically going through all the radio channels and dismissing each within seconds. His frustrated sighs had grown louder, his body language more jittery. I wondered what was going through his mind. God, how I wished he would just talk to me.

I turned and, with a wistful sigh, looked out over the approaching city. "Yeah, it sucks. I wish I could stay."

"Ay, what a shame. We'll miss you, *chiquita.*"

"We really will," Lawson agreed.

"Fucking piece of shit!" Liam yelled, slamming the stereo system and then hitting the power button so hard that he missed it three times before it went silent. All eyes turned to him, wide and concerned. He spat a few more curses and stormed off to his bunk.

I turned to Lawson, who shook his head with a shrug.

"Okay..." I stood up and gingerly approached Liam's bed. The curtain was drawn, and I held my hand up, a gentle touch against the soft fabric separating us. "Hey, Liam? You okay?"

He grunted in response.

"Can I... er... come in?"

There was a brief silence, then a sigh. "Not now, Haze."

"But—"

"Just... Please, leave me alone."

I closed my eyes, my hand lingering on the curtain, imagining my fingers tracing the curve of his neck, stroking the fine hairs on his arms.

Then I lowered my hand and headed back to the booths.

* * *

We rolled into the vertical mass of Chicago and onwards to a motel on North Side, close to the evening's venue.

"I thought you all had apartments in this city?" I asked Lawson, as Victor wiggled us into a parking spot.

"I do, and Liam and Ivy. Mine's not far from here but Liam's is almost an hour away. In any case," he added with a smirk, "I prefer to keep all my sheep together till the tour's over."

I smiled at him. "We'd be lost without our shepherd, clearly."

The moment Vic turned off the engine, Liam emerged

from his cocoon. Without a word he strode past us, jumped off the bus, crossed the road and vanished.

"Where is he going?" I asked. But Lawson just shook his head, his brow all furrowed. Suddenly I wanted nothing more than to be back by the campfire in the woods, with Liam's fingertips bringing goosebumps to my neck.

We checked in, showered and freshened up, then grabbed a late lunch. When we arrived at the venue there was still no word from Liam, and we were all growing tense. Victor kept checking his phone. Lawson was unusually quiet. A dull ache had settled in my stomach, but I wasn't sure if it was worry or anger or both.

"Our boy is getting lazy," Mango remarked as we hauled an amplifier across the stage. "Why isn't he here helping us?"

"I don't know," I sighed. After we had lowered the amp into position, I pulled out my phone. "I'll try calling him."

As I pressed dial his photo popped up, his beautiful face sliced in half by the crack on my screen. Each time I saw it I felt a little queasy, remembering Mother's phone call on that hard bathroom floor; my mind scattered over the tiles.

I shook it off and put the phone to my ear. Waited while the dial tone sang its monotone song. *Hey, it's Liam, leave a message.* Hang up, redial. Voicemail again.

"Liam, it's me. Where have you gone to? We go on in less than two hours. We need you here to help set up. Can you please come or call me back?"

There was a lot more I wanted to say, but I had to stop myself. Instead, I reluctantly lowered the phone and hung up.

When it was time for sound-check we all stood dejected, waiting for a miracle.

"Jeez," Lawson mumbled, pacing up and down the stage in great long strides, his phone pressed to his ear. "Come on, buddy, pick the fuck up." I had never seen him this agitated.

With a defeated sigh, he lowered his phone and glanced over at me. "He didn't say anything to you?"

"No, nothing."

"I mean, I know he's going through a tough time, but this is unacceptable."

"I know…" I stood wringing my hands and compulsively checking every entrance around the venue, hoping he would pop his head in any second. But he never came.

Ten minutes before the doors were to open, Lawson called it.

"Alright, we're gonna have to go ahead without him. I'll tell everyone that he's become suddenly ill. Hazel and I will do the vocals, and we'll refund people half the cost of their tickets. I don't know what else we can do."

"Oh, man…" Mango hung his head. "They won't be happy."

"Oh, hell, Liam," Ivy sighed. "Well, we'll just have to do what we can. And make sure he never does this again. We'll chain him to the bus if we have to."

"I'll take care of the reimbursements," Victor said, jotting things down in the tiny notebook he always kept in his shirt pocket.

"How could he do this to us," I mumbled, my stomach twisting. "Just fuck off and leave us with this mess."

"I know," Lawson said. "But right now, we gotta stay focused. We'll deal with Liam later." His eyes drifted downward for a moment, his mouth pinched in a grim line. Then he shrugged and looked up with a brighter expression. "Let's do this, okay? Let's have fun with it, let's not get all beat up about what we can't change."

The others nodded hesitantly, mumbling tense agreements.

"And Hazel, you and me, we've got this. We gotta bring the energy, we owe it to the fans. You with me?"

"Okay!" I gave him the best smile I could muster. "I'm with you."

* * *

It was awkward at first, but Lawson was an expert at managing the disappointed crowd. After explaining, apologising and promising refunds, he somehow managed to turn the atmosphere on its head and rile everyone up for a party. Even I got carried away, and together we put on quite a show.

Afterwards, we gathered backstage and Lawson gave us all a high five. "Object Imperfect, maybe, but it worked!"

"You did great, man," said Mango, patting Lawson on the back. "Could *not* have pulled that off without your showmanship!"

"Why, thank you," Lawson said, his faux-smug smirk in place. But then his smile faded and we all fell silent. "Anyone heard from him?"

Each of us checked our phones and shook our heads. My head was still spinning from the show, but now my stomach tightened with worry. Lawson noticed, and put his hand on my arm. "No need to panic yet. I'm sure he'll turn up soon. C'mon, let's pack up, guys."

A grim silence hung over us as we each grabbed as much as we could carry. I took two mic stands, their rolled-up cables draped around my neck, and headed out back. Thick, orange clouds hung over the city, obscuring the night sky. A chilly breeze nipped at the air, smelling of damp soil and city dirt. As I walked across the parking lot, I realised just how tired I was. Tired of all this drama, the uncertainty, Liam's unpredictable outbursts. I was tired of fighting, tired of trying. Tired of feeling like his dog, waiting like a loyal idiot while he tossed me aside, choking on the leash that he had woven from words and passion and a fire that had I so desperately craved.

But the flames were growing faint, the cold encroaching.

As I approached the bus I saw a dark shape huddling on the ground, and I thought for a second that someone had left a guitar case behind. But then I got close enough to see and my face dropped.

There he was.

THIRTY-TWO

Liam sat on the cold asphalt, leaning against the bus with his knees pulled up and his hands buried in his sleeves. Glazed eyes peered up at us from under his hood, and I noticed he was shivering. I just stood there staring at him, dumbly clutching the mic stands.

Ivy spoke first. "Sweet Jesus, Liam, you scared the shit outta us! Where have you been?"

He opened his mouth as if he was about to say something, but nothing came out. Then he lowered his head and began rocking back and forth, breathing in shallow bursts until he was hyperventilating.

"Alright," Lawson said. "Guys, go back inside, I'll deal with this." He went over and crouched down next to Liam. "Hey, bud, what's wrong?"

The others hesitated before they backed away and reluctantly walked back inside. But not me. I couldn't move.

Liam pressed his forehead to his knees and grabbed his head with both his hands, his rapid breaths turning to sobs.

"It's done, man," Lawson said. "It's over. Hazel and I had to do the vocals." He waited a beat. "Where were you?" I could tell he was trying to sound patient, trying hard to hold back all the pent-up frustration and accusations.

Liam balled his hands into fists and hit them against his head.

"Stop that," Lawson said, his voice flat and fed-up.

"I'm so sorry," Liam said finally, his voice thick and slurred. "I can't... I can't believe I missed the show." His face scrunched up again and he carried on slamming his fists to his temples. "I can't do this... There's some—something not right with me... I'm fucked up, Laws."

Lawson cut me a tired glance. An overwhelming sense of hopelessness washed over me and all my churning emotions came pouring out. I put down the mic stands and crouched down on the floor, stumbled sideways and landed on the cold, hard ground, weeping uncontrollably.

Lawson shot to his feet. "Hey, hey now..." He picked me up off the ground and wrapped me in his long arms. "It's okay. He's fine, everything will be okay."

Still wearing my necklace of cables, I sobbed like a lost child into Lawson's jumper, mumbling through my tears how I was sorry but I just was so fucking tired of it all, although he probably couldn't make out any words through my racking sobs.

Then I felt a hand on my arm, and I looked up and saw Liam. His eyelids were heavy, his eyes glassy, and he was struggling to stand upright. He held my arm and tried to focus on my face.

"Haze, baby...," he mumbled, staggering slightly.

"No!" I shook him off and took a step back. "Just fuck off, will you?! I'm so sick of this!"

He stood stunned for a moment, his mouth slightly open. He looked like he was about to cry again, but instead he squeezed his eyes shut, and when he opened them again his face was stone cold. "Where're my drugs?"

My mouth fell open and I stared at him, tears burning my eyes. "Are you fucking serious right now?"

"Just gimme my stuff. It ain't yours and you've no right to keep it."

"But you—"

"Fine, I'll go get 'em myself."

He swung around and pulled the bus doors open, stumbled up the steps and disappeared inside. My head dropped and fresh tears dripped onto the asphalt. How stupid I had been to think that things could change. Lawson put his arm around me and gave me a squeeze, but nothing could lift the black weight in my chest.

When Liam reappeared he was carrying the bag I had stashed in the back of my cupboard. Not a genius hiding place, but I hadn't had much choice. He held onto the doors as he climbed down, then glared at me and Lawson.

"Well, you two are gettin' on well," he grumbled. "That's just great. I'm sorry I fucked everything up. I'm out."

Lawson let go of me and took a step towards him. "Bro, don't do this, please. We can still fix this."

Liam's tired eyes drifted over the parking lot. "No, man, I —I can't do it. I'm… Fuck. I'm sorry. I'll be at the motel."

Before Lawson could respond, Liam turned and walked off, clutching the bag to his chest.

"Shit!" Lawson exhaled sharply, clenching his jaw. He pinched the ridge of his nose and dropped his head, curls falling forwards. "This time it's bad."

I swallowed hard as I watched Liam disappear around a corner.

"I'm sorry you've been dragged into all this," Lawson said.

"No, *I'm* sorry," I whimpered. "I feel like I've made everything worse, which is the last thing I wanted."

"We can't go round blaming ourselves. In the end, it's his choice."

"I just don't know what went wrong," I said, snivelling. "I thought he was doing okay…"

"Fuck it," Lawson said, through gritted teeth. "Let's go pack up."

* * *

Close to midnight, we finally got to the motel. I was exhausted and couldn't wait to lie down and forget about everything. But I could sense a restless night ahead, and before facing my reeling mind I grabbed Lawson, and we sat down on the brick wall that lined the parking lot. The winds were picking up and I shivered in my thin cardigan. Nonetheless, it felt comforting to sit outside, where the world seemed limitless and malleable, fresh winds blowing in from the north, wiping away all our woes.

We sat resting our heads against the rough bricks, looking up at the turbulent sky.

"What do you think will happen now?" I asked. "Will he hold it together for the remaining shows?"

Lawson exhaled slowly. "I don't know… We only have three more to go. It may be best if we cancel them. I don't know what he's going through right now, but I think this is beyond my abilities."

It was all coming to an end. I turned my attention to the buttons on my sleeve. They seemed to have no purpose, just put there for decoration. I tugged at them until I noticed one was coming loose. I let it hang from its thread and looked up at Lawson, his eyes lost among the clouds. "What about you?" I said. "What will you do after the tour?"

"I think I'll head back to Madison for a bit. My parents are remodelling, figured I'd help them out. It'll be nice to spend some time at home after all this running around. I'm starting to feel a bit tired."

"I bet."

"Then, I guess we'll start on the next album. We've got some new songs already, and Liam's keen to get them recorded."

My mind flooded with images of their studio; the whirlwind of ups and downs that had taken place in that house. "It's so weird how you guys get to carry on with everything, and I'm just going home." I poked Lawson's thigh. "Don't have too much fun without me, okay?"

He let out a small laugh tinged with something heavy. "We couldn't possibly."

Just then, the clouds had enough and began releasing their load over the world. Raindrops pelted the asphalt, heavy and persistent.

"I guess that's our cue," Lawson said. He jumped down off the wall and reached his hand out to me, and my hand felt small as he wrapped his long fingers around it and helped me down.

The rain was coming down hard, my hair already sticking to my face. Yet we stood there for another moment, me looking up at Lawson, his well-meaning smile warming me and shielding me against the cold.

"Well," he said finally, "I hope you'll sleep okay. Try not to worry too much about him, okay?"

"I'll try." I crossed my arms over my chest, shivering. "I feel like I should check on him, though. Do you think I should go talk to him?"

"Sure, if that's what you want. It's never good to leave things on a bad note."

"Do you know which room is his?"

"One fourteen."

"Thanks, Laws. What would we do without you?"

He didn't respond, and I didn't like the way his brow furrowed and how his eyes drifted towards the corner. I missed his cheeky grin and ridiculous nicknames. I reached up and ruffled his hair, which had flattened into sprawling curlicues across his forehead. "Gosh, you're so wet! I'm sorry I dragged you out here. Go find shelter, mister." I gave him my best smile as he walked off to his room.

One fourteen was up one floor and I trudged up the stairs, which ran along the outside of the motel building. I hugged the wall as I looked for Liam's room, the rain coming down harder by the minute. As I approached his door, I could hear voices and my breath caught in my throat. Had I got the wrong room? But then I heard his unmistakable voice, dry and soft like sun-warm sand. I tried the door. Creaking, it pushed open.

"Hazel!" Ivy's green eyes popped over at me, staring in shock over Liam's bird's nest hair. He had her up against the wall, his arm around her back, his lips on her neck. I drew a sharp breath as all my veins turned to ice.

No, no, no...

Liam turned his glassy eyes to me, his face blank. I stumbled backwards, fumbling for the door behind me, unable to tear my eyes from the sight I had imagined in my head countless times.

As soon as I regained control of my limbs, I bolted down the stairs and back out into the pouring rain. I ran as fast as my legs would let me across the dark and sorry parking lot, while the heavens did their best to wash away all our sins, but it would never work. We could never be clean again.

In my mind I saw Liam the first time I had seen him on stage back in Madison; his timid demeanour, his hunched shoulders, the way he slipped into that secret space as he sang and how his lyrics had wrapped themselves like chains around my heart. I saw the wildfire burning in his eyes as he leaned in to kiss me for the very first time, after he had chased poor Max away. I saw his tiny body curled up in apology after throwing up all over the motel floor. His sorrow on the Golden Gate Bridge. His warm hands on me, his furious tears, his bright smile as he encouraged me to go after my dreams, his posing and teasing and laughing and screaming. His heart, buried under so much grief and pain that no one could ever reach it.

"Hazel, wait!" I could hear Ivy calling me from across the lot, running after me. I kept going until I reached the brick wall on the other side, and then I didn't know where to go or what to do, so I just bent over, my chest heaving, lungs burning.

Ivy reached me and slowed her steps.

"Stay... away... from me," I panted. Chunks of hair clung to my face and neck and my clothes were soaked through, but I didn't feel cold.

"Hazel, you gotta believe me, I had nothin' to do with what you saw in there! I was jus' tryin' to get him to calm down and stop doin' so much of that damn cocaine, I swear to you. And then he just came at me, and I was just so shocked."

Her voice was squeaky and pleading, her Southern accent brought to its knees by her frantic rambling. I kept my eyes to the ground, but I knew in my heart that she was telling the truth.

"I mean, it's not like he was goin' to hurt me or nothin', it wasn't like that. But he's... He's really messed up tonight. I don't know what's gotten into him. He seems so broken, Hazel. I'm scared for 'im."

I swallowed hard, then slowly raised my head.

"Please, Haze." Ivy tilted her head, her face crinkled with concern. "Please, believe me. I'd never do nothin' to hurt you."

I closed my eyes and nodded. "I believe you."

She exhaled with relief. "Thank you. I couldn't bear…"

Her voice trailed off and I looked up at her, squinting against the rain. "I don't know what happened, Ives. I thought he was doing better."

She hesitated, her lips in a pensive pout. "I mean…"

"What?"

"I know he's been through hell, what with Frank 'n all… But now, this is somethin' else. I think he's been triggered, being back in town. The tour's comin' to an end, we're all going back to our lives… He dun't always take it so well."

I nodded, remembering when he had told me the same thing, under San Francisco's grey skies. Puddles were forming around us, reflecting blurry spheres of orange street-lights. I straightened up and swiped wet hair from my eyes. There was no more time to waste. We had to sort this out. "I need to talk to him."

"Right now? You sure that's a good idea?"

"Fuck good ideas. I have to."

An iron determination hardened my edges and sheltered me from the icy rain as I walked back across the parking lot and up the concrete stairs. The door to Liam's room was still ajar, and I pushed it open. He was sitting on the floor, fidgeting with a rolled-up note in one hand, the other frantically scrolling through his phone. His right foot was thumping a regular beat against the carpet. On the desk next to him lay several lines of coke and some scattered tablets.

"Liam."

He looked up with bloodshot eyes. "Hazel! Want some?" He held the note out to me.

"Stop it."

"Sorry, sorry, sorry…" He had taken way too much. He was twitching and jittery, bobbing his head back and forth, grinding his jaw.

"Liam." Leaving a trail of wet footprints behind me, I walked over and crouched down in front of him. "What the hell happened with Ivy just now?"

"Nothing," he snapped. "Nothing happened. It was stupid."

"It didn't look like nothing to me. You're hurting me, Liam. I thought... I thought we were good, no?"

He dipped his head into his lap with a long sigh. "Why do you even care?"

"What do you mean, why do I care? Why wouldn't I care?"

He jerked his head back up and glared at me with black eyes. "'Cause you're leaving!"

I flinched, his glare like a drawn weapon.

"You're leaving." He kicked at the chair by the desk. "So what's the fucking point?"

"You can't put this on me, Liam, that's not fair."

"I'm not *putting* anything on you, jeez. It's just the goddamn truth." He hung his head and took a few deep breaths, and his jitters began to ease up. "You're leaving," he said, eyes to the floor. "And I will miss you so fucking much, I don't know what to do with myself."

His words hit me like a knife to the heart, cold metal slicing me in half.

Still staring at the carpet in front of him, he continued. "It's no excuse, I know... I don't know what I was thinkin'. For what it's worth, I'm tryin' to find a way to deal with this. Tryin' to protect myself as best I can."

I stood up, my knees aching, my head pounding. "You can't keep doing this, Liam. You can't go around hurting people because you're not big enough to face your feelings."

He shot to his feet so suddenly that it startled me, and I instinctively took a step back.

"What about you?" he barked. "You can't go round tryin'

to fix all the broken people, just 'cause you're too fucking scared to look in the mirror!"

I stared at him, speechless, barely recognising him. "What... the fuck?"

"Why do you insist on hanging around all us broken people? Do you really feel so shitty about yourself that you need us to make you feel big? Like that shit you pulled with Ivy by the lake. Does that make you feel good, huh? Does that make you feel like more of a person and less of a beat-up fuck-up like the rest of us?" He grabbed the chair and knocked it against the desk. "And why did you waste your entire life looking after your fucked-up mom? Did that make you feel good, too?"

I felt like I had been punched in the gut, and I had to force myself to take a breath. "No, it made me feel like pure shit and you know it!" I backed away from him, hot tears burning my cheeks. His eyes were on fire, a poisoned river flowing through his veins, unleashing his demons and turning him into this unbearable monster.

"You have a *life*, Hazel. You have fucking purpose. And you're pissing it all away because you're so set on being a victim of your circumstances. Truth is, you're shit scared of looking in the mirror and facing all that shit you keep denying."

"Look who's talking!" My throat burned, my eyes stung, and a cold, hard frost had settled around my heart. "You know what, I'm so sick of this. You've been the best and the worst, Liam, but I... I can't take it anymore."

He stood staring at me through his dark fringe, his lips pressed together in angry anticipation, breathing through his nose in sharp bursts like a bull waiting to attack.

"Lawson—Lawson says you're going to have to cancel the rest of your shows, because you can't be trusted. So maybe I should just do us all a favour and leave now."

My voice faltered, the final words trembling. I wanted him to stop me. I wanted him to walk over to me, for those black eyes to turn brown again, his chocolate fondue eyes. For him to blink and wake from this nightmare and tell me it was all a bad dream, that he wanted me to stay forever and that I never had to go back home.

But he just looked at the floor, clenching his jaw. "Go ahead. What difference does it make?"

I waited a moment, hoping he would change his mind. But he just stood there, pinching the rolled-up note between his thumb and index finger.

Then all my senses sharpened at once, a red rage rising in my chest. "Fine!" I spun on my heels and stormed out, slamming the door behind me, and the world blurred as I ran to my room and grabbed my bag.

"Hazel!" Ivy appeared in the doorway. "What did he say? What are you doing?"

Sobbing, I heaved my backpack onto my shoulders and pushed past her.

"Where are you going?"

I didn't answer her. I couldn't answer her. I didn't know where the fuck I was going or what I would do.

"Hazel, wait!"

But I didn't wait. I just kept running.

THIRTY-THREE

I raced down the street in the pouring rain, my feet pounding the pavement. My backpack weighed heavy on my shoulders but I had to keep going, even though I was struggling to breathe. I had to get as far away as I could.

When my legs began to buckle under me, I finally stopped and frantically caught my breath. What the fuck just happened? What had I done? What had *he* done? I fell to my knees and sobbed into the deluge as I realised that I was all alone. I had nowhere to go. It was cold and wet and dark, and I was lost at a crossroads somewhere in Chicago.

Maybe Nathan could come get me. Or I could get a bus back to Madison, wrap myself in the familiar comforts of his easy jokes and designer coffee, and I could forget all about this mess. Nathan could make everything okay.

My clothes were already soaked through and now my bag was getting drenched, too. I had to find cover. I whirled around and spotted a bus shelter down a sideroad. On shaky legs I stood back up, steadying myself against a lamppost, and hurried over.

Safely out of the rain, I sat down on the hard bench and

rested my bag against my legs. Then my phone began to ring, and I hated that I wanted it to be Liam. But it was Ivy.

"Ivy, I can't… I gotta go. I've got all my stuff, I'm going to call my cousin."

"Hazel, don't leave like this! Can't we talk—"

"I'm already gone, Ivy. Please tell the others I'm sorry. Tell Lawson…" I could feel my lips begin to quiver again. "Tell Lawson I'm so sorry, and I'll call him soon, okay?"

"Hazel…"

"Bye, Ivy."

I hung up and scrolled for Nathan's number, blinking away tears so I could see. Pressed dial, leaned back, tried to control my breathing. I felt so lost, so alone, so unbearably stupid for having gone along with it all.

"Hazel?"

"Oh my god, Nathan." It was so good to hear his voice.

"What's wrong? You crying?"

I didn't know where to begin. I covered my mouth with my hand and succumbed to another flood of tears.

"Hazel, what's going on?"

"Nathan… I don't know what to do."

"What happened?"

"I had to leave, Nath. I had to leave the tour, and Liam, all of it… And now, now I'm sitting somewhere in Chicago, in a bus shelter with my bag and I don't know what to do."

"Shit, Hazel, I'm so sorry. But hey, don't worry, okay? You can always come back here, right?"

"Right?" I sniffled and wiped my nose with my sleeve. "I was thinking that, too. It would be so good to see you again, to come back to your place and just hang out like we did, before, before…" Sobs rose in my throat and I struggled to speak. "It's all so messed up, Nathan. First, it was so beautiful. I mean, *so* beautiful, I couldn't believe it. It was like a dream, Nath…" I closed my eyes and gave way to the memories that came pouring in – sunrise over Los Angeles, New Orleans magic, sharing the spotlight with Liam, waking up in his arms... "Where did it all go wrong?"

"Hey now, ladybird, you'll be okay, you'll see. You're always welcome here."

"Thanks, Nath." My nose kept running and I began rummaging through my bag for tissues. "I prolly shouldn't have run out of there like that, with no plan, but I just had to —" I stopped talking when I felt a small, hard piece of paper. Vanya's card.

If you ever need anything.

Vanya knew what I was going through. I felt like she understood more than anyone. Nathan was over two hours away in Madison, but hadn't Vanya said that she lived just outside Chicago?

"Haze? You still there?"

"Never mind," I mumbled, staring at the card pinched between my fingers. "I think I know where I'm going."

"Yeah? You sure? Hazel, you sound weird. Should I be worried?"

"No, no. I... I've got somewhere I can go, I think. Thank you, Nathan. I'll call you soon, okay?"

"If you say so, ladybird. Take ca—"

I had already hung up the phone and dialled the number on the card. There was no answer on the landline, so I tried the mobile number.

"Hello?" Vanya's warm voice came crackling down the line.

"Vanya?"

"Who's this?"

"It's Hazel. Liam's, um... Liam's friend."

"Of course! Hazel." She sounded a bit groggy and cleared her throat.

"I'm so sorry, I must have woken you up."

"Don't worry 'bout that. Are you okay? You don't sound too good."

"I… I think I need some help. You said I could call whenever…" I hung my head as doubt came creeping in. What was I doing? The rain kept hammering the plastic shelter roof. "I hope this isn't weird."

"Not at all, sweetie. What's wrong?"

"I had to leave…" My throat seized up as more tears came. "I couldn't stay with him anymore, Vanya, I had to go…"

"Aw, honey, it's okay, you'll be alright," Vanya said, her soothing lilt releasing the tightness in my chest. "Where are you now?"

I took another look around at the dark, wet street. "I'm not sure," I whimpered. "Northern Chicago somewhere."

"Oh, you're not far then. Why don't you share your location on your phone and I'll come get you."

"Really?" My lungs contracted with relief. "You'd do that?"

"Sure! I bet you're not even a half hour drive away. Just stay put and I'll be there as soon as I can."

"Wow, Vanya, I can't… I don't know how to thank you."

"Don't worry 'bout it. I'll see you soon."

I closed my phone and let out a long, shaky breath. I had somewhere to go. I wasn't alone. That was at least a start.

It felt like a long time before Vanya arrived. I rested my head against the cool Plexiglas, watching streaks of raindrops trace their diagonal paths across the shelter, its steady drumming against the roof enveloping me like white noise.

At last, a white pick-up truck rolled up and stopped in front of me. Without hesitation Vanya jumped out into the rain, getting soaked as she approached me with arms outstretched.

"Oh, honey," she said, and I was surprised at how easily I fell into her embrace and let myself be held. She smelled of jasmine and beautiful things, and I hugged her tight, crying into her shoulder.

"It's okay, let it out," she said, gently stroking my hair.

When all my tears were emptied onto her fleece, embarrassment came over me and I pulled away, eyes to the ground. "Thank you so much for coming," I mumbled. "I don't know what I would have done..."

"I'm glad you called, Hazel. Let's get you in the car, shall we, and you can tell me what happened."

She picked my bag up and put it on the backseat, then got behind the wheel. I opened the passenger door, hesitating. "I'm going to get your car all wet."

She let out an easy laugh. "It's only water."

I sat down, and when I closed the door the world became soft and muffled. The engine purred into life and we rolled down the street and took a left.

"So, how comes you've found yourself lost and alone in a rainstorm?" she asked, but there was no urgency in her voice, just that same, gentle kindness I had felt when I first met her.

I curled up, safe in Vanya's warm truck with late-night jazz floating out of the speakers, presented by a honey-voiced radio DJ, and I told her everything. How I had met Liam and fallen so hard for him, how I had wanted to be like him and heal him and love him, all at once. I told her all about his escaping into drugs and how I could see that he was hurting, that there was this big gaping hole inside him where his parents' love should have been, and how I feared that hole was never going to close up, ever, even when that's what I wanted most in the world. I talked about how I ended up getting high with him, how thrilling it had felt at first, but how it had spiralled into something far less pleasurable, something closer to survival; and still, how he had absolutely refused to get help. I also spoke about the way he encouraged me, willing me to draw and follow my passion, and teaching me his songs.

I cried and laughed and drifted away with my memories as we zoomed down the highway. Vanya sat there, listening in the same way Frank had – quietly, earnestly, without judgement – as we made our way through the downpour, her wipers beating away the rain in their rhythmic dance.

When we turned off the highway into tree-lined suburbs, the rain finally let up. Soon, we were driving down a narrow, winding road in the pitch-black night, which led to a house surrounded by tall woods. Vanya turned off the engine and everything went quiet.

"Well, it sounds like quite an adventure." She turned to look at me. "You're a good person, Hazel. I see much of myself in you. We want to help people. We want to fix situations. But you can't help those who don't want to be helped. In the end, the only person you can really help is yourself."

With that, she got out into the newly washed world and led me inside. Hers was a modest but beautiful home, all terracotta tiles and olive walls, woven rugs and beeswax candles. On every spare surface sat ceramic bowls and sculptures.

"Did you make all these?" I asked, gesturing at the pottery.

"Most of them, yes. Some are from students or friends of mine. You hungry?"

"No, I'm okay, thanks."

"Alright then. Guest room is over there. I'll go get you some sheets. You get yourself out of those wet clothes and I'll throw 'em in the dryer for ya."

I changed into dry clothes and together we made up the bed.

"Anything else you need?" Vanya asked, an easy smile on her face.

"No, I'm… This is all wonderful. Thank you so much."

"You're very welcome, honey. Stay as long as you need."

After she left, I sat on the bed and surveyed my new environment. The walls were a soft copper tone, and two large windows opened up to the blackness outside. My new bed was wide and comfy with plush feather pillows. In the corner, an open door led into a small ensuite bathroom. All this cosy comfort, and still I felt queasy with isolation, suddenly aware of how far away I was, stranded in this remote darkness.

I heard a toilet flush, a door click, and then all I could hear was my beating heart. I pulled out my phone to text Nathan. There was a message from Lawson and my stomach knotted. I missed them all so much already.

Ivy told me you left?? Haze, whats going on? Please let me know where you are and if you're OK. You're welcome back to us whenever, you know that right?

I held my phone to my chest and pictured Lawson's warm smile, his desert island eyes.

I'm sorry, Laws… I should have said goodbye, but I wasn't thinking straight.

I paused and looked out into the black night, where the world was still and silent.

I'm okay, I'm with Vanya, you know, Frank's ex? She came to pick me up, said I can stay here awhile. I don't know what my plans are, but O'Hare is so close, I might stay here until I go home.

Poor Laws. He deserved better than this.

I'm sorry it had to end this way. And I'm so sorry if I've made things worse. I hope you'll be ok… All of u xx

Then I opened my conversation with Nathan.

I'm at a friend's house. I'll be fine, please don't worry. Sorry I called you in such a state. Will call soon, hope ur ok xx

I sank back into the pillows, but I couldn't relax in this strange room. Feeling restless, I got up and pulled some clothes from my backpack, which I folded and put on the sideboard. I put my toiletries in the bathroom, and my jewellery and hairbrush on the bedside table. It was starting to feel more familiar, a bit more like home.

I dove back into my bag and found the drawing I made of Liam at his studio, with his black heart spiralling outwards. A nostalgic smile came to my lips, which quickly faded as I remembered how that night had ended. For a split second I wanted to tear it to pieces, but then I held it to my chest and suddenly it felt like my most precious belonging. Beside my bed, I found an old nail which I used to pierce the paper so that Liam could hang there, right next to me.

Thinking I might as well unpack all my things – something I hadn't done once since I arrived in America all those months ago – I systematically pulled everything out and placed it around the room. For each item that landed somewhere beside me, I felt comforted, soothed.

When I pulled out my hoodie, it unwrapped a pill bottle which flew up and landed on the floor next to me, rattling and rolling to a stop.

Liam's Xanax.

I had forgotten I had that.

I bent down and picked it up, read the label, felt the weight of the tablets inside. *I could have one now.* I ached for the moment when the pill kicked in and that soft tiredness came over me and things began to matter less.

Then I stopped myself and shook those thoughts away. What good would it do? This wasn't me. This was exactly why I had left. I considered flushing them, but in the end I just stuffed them in my makeup bag.

My backpack was nearly empty now, and all my things were out on display or folded onto shelves and in drawers. My own room. It felt strangely comforting; solid and permanent. Like I could relax and just be, if just for a little while. At least for the moment there was nowhere I needed to be, nowhere I had to go in the morning, no gig to play in a city a hundred miles away. A break, time to breathe.

I grabbed my now considerably lighter backpack and held it upside down, shaking out the last of its contents. An envelope fell to the floor, an envelope I recognised so well but hadn't seen in nearly four months. My mother's letter.

I fell to my knees and picked it up, held it in my hands. A single sheet of paper, yet it weighed on my heart like a ton of bricks. I read her words over and over, let them pour over me like hot tea on sugar, dissolving me into a sticky mess. My probation was over, the prison guards calling me back.

I scrunched up the letter and shoved it on the bedside table. Then I crawled under the covers, stuck my earphones in and opened Object Impermanence, and let Liam's spun-sugar voice seep into every forgotten corner of my mind until, finally, I drifted off.

THIRTY-FOUR

A gentle knock pulled me out of a deep sleep.

"Hazel?"

I sat up, squinting in the light while last night's events arranged themselves in my memory. A stabbing ache hit my gut as I realised it hadn't all just been a bad dream. But seeing the bright, warm room and my neatly organised belongings filled me with a sense of calm, despite everything.

"Hazel, can I come in?" It was Vanya's voice.

"Um, sure." I smoothed down my hair and pulled my legs into lotus position.

The door cracked open and Vanya appeared with a tray full of bread, fruit and fresh coffee. At once, the room smelled of early mornings and sunny kitchens.

"Sorry to wake you, honey, but it's nearly eleven. I thought you might be hungry."

I breathed in the soothing scent of freshly baked bread. "That looks amazing, thank you."

I made room for Vanya to sit on the bed next to me. She placed the tray between us and I gratefully grabbed the coffee. Sun poured in through the window, setting Vanya's golden locks alight as she looked around the room.

"I see you made yourself at home."

Nose in my mug, I could feel embarrassment flush my face. "Er, sorry… I just, I felt like it would be nice to have—"

Vanya laughed. "I like it. You made it cozy."

I lowered my cup into my lap and looked up at Vanya. "It's the first time I've unpacked since I left home, months ago. With the band, I was always on the move."

"I get it. It's nice to have your own space, especially after being rootless for a stretch." Her eyes landed on my drawing of Liam, dangling from its rusty nail. "Hey, what's this?" She leaned in to take a closer look. "Did you make this?"

I nodded.

"It's very impressive. You've captured his features really well, really brought him to life."

"Thanks…" Shyness came over me and I buried a bread roll in my mouth.

"I'd love to see more of your work sometime."

I turned to the window, eager to change the topic. We seemed to be surrounded by dense woodland, everywhere a sea of leaves on the edge of autumn. "This place is beautiful," I mumbled between bites. "Seems very peaceful."

"Yeah, that was the idea," Vanya said, her eyes drifting out over the turning treetops. "I came here after Frank and I broke up. Needed a fresh start, some purpose. Bought this place and fixed it up. Feels like I belong here."

"What, um… What happened between you and Frank?"

Vanya's lips curled into a wistful smile. "I think some men aren't made for relationships. I tried with Frank for a long time, but he never let me all the way in. It was like I could never truly know him, like he kept a part of himself from me. And whenever I reached for that part, he shied away like a spooked animal."

"That does sound familiar," I mumbled.

"It's a lonely life, living with someone like that. It's like you're never really together. No matter what they say, you can just feel the distance, that wall they keep up. I think you know what I'm talking about."

I nodded grimly.

"After many years of going back and forth, I gave up trying. I left everything behind, Frank, my job, and came here. Found a way to literally transfer my pain into mother earth, into the clay and mud. Now I teach classes, too, in my garden studio. The one that needs the mural painting." Vanya gave me a teasing smile. "Lookin' at your drawing, it's clear I picked the right girl for the job."

I felt my stomach contract. Was that why she had brought me here? I couldn't possibly paint a mural. I was so far removed from all of that, I couldn't even begin to conceive of it.

"I'm sorry, Vanya...," I began uneasily. "I can't paint it for you. I don't paint anymore."

"I remember you said when we first met. Thing is, though." She tilted her head, beaming all her warmth at me. "I just don't buy it."

"But—"

I was interrupted by my phone buzzing. I glanced at the screen and saw a text from Ivy. Seeing her name, I felt a familiar weariness come over me. Wincing, I drained the rest of my cold coffee and placed the mug back on the tray.

"Can I ask you something?"

"Anything, honey."

"Have I made the right decision?"

"Which decision are we talking about?"

"Leaving Liam behind. It's like you said, they shut down or hide away, but in the end, they need someone, don't they? I—I wish Frank had had someone when he... you know."

Vanya looked right at me, her steady gaze void of regret.

"We can give and give to someone, give everything we have and more, until there is nothing left of us. And then what good are we? To anyone?"

I turned and looked out into the bright sun. "Yeah, I suppose…"

"We empty ourselves into a bottomless well and then rage when it won't give us water. It's just not sustainable." I felt her hand on my knee. "I think you made the right choice, honey. The only choice."

I sighed, eyes dropping to my lap. "I hope you're right. But I can't help but feel responsible."

"Responsible? Darlin', we're only responsible for ourselves and our own actions. Liam's got himself to worry about, and you've got you, okay? Don't ever take responsibility for anyone else's moods or actions. That'll only bring you trouble."

I hugged my legs to my chest with a sigh. "I always do this," I mumbled.

"Do what?"

"Become people's helper. Liam was right. I don't know how to fix myself, so instead I just try to fix everyone else."

Vanya tilted her head questioningly, her long locks falling to one side. I didn't know how to explain any of it. Finally, I reached over to Mother's letter, now a scrunched-up piece of trash on my bedside table, and handed it to Vanya.

Without a word, she solemnly straightened it out and read it, considered it. A rising sense of shame took me by surprise, and I tried to swallow it back down.

When she finished, she carefully folded the letter and put it back on the bedside table. "I see. So that's why you no longer paint."

I nodded. "I just can't… Just the thought of holding a brush makes me feel sick."

Vanya looked at me then, her gaze gentle but scrutinising.

"Well," she said at last, a knowing smile on her lips. "I may have a remedy for that."

"What?"

"All in good time." She stood up and gestured at the breakfast tray. "Why don't you finish up here and then I'll show you around. Later, after dinner I'd like to take you someplace. And bring your mother's letter, okay?"

"Wait, what do you mean? Where are we going?"

"Oh, you'll see."

* * *

I took a long shower, washing away the rain and sorrow of the night before, and then Vanya brought me outside to show me her studio.

We walked down a stone path towards a gorgeous space at the back of the garden, surrounded by silver birches. The studio had a front terrace with terracotta slabs, on top of which sat a wrought-iron garden table with matching chairs. Above it, dreamcatchers and candle jars dangled from the drainpipe. To the right sat a small apple tree, and from its branches she had hung several tiny shards of mirror glass. As they spun they reflected the sunlight, making them flash like fireflies. There was not a sound except gentle birdsong and a soft whisper of the autumn breeze.

"This felt like the perfect place to rebuild myself after Frank," Vanya said, her long skirt billowing as she walked up to the studio entrance. "I had also spent nearly fifteen years working as a high school counsellor, which had taken its toll on me. I needed someplace where I could just be by myself, and for myself."

She pushed the door open and we walked into a large space bathed in light. Three of the walls had windows

305

looking out over the wild woods all around us. Several spin tables sat in a cluster, covered in stains of dried clay. At the back was a large, black chamber which I assumed was the kiln. Along the walls stood several shelves, all full of pottery in various stages of production.

"I've never been in a pottery studio before," I said. "So much stuff!"

"Yeah, as always, creativity demands a lot of tools," Vanya chuckled. "And speaking of which, here are yours, if you ever change your mind." She pointed to a tarpaulin on the floor, on top of which sat an array of paint buckets. "There's brushes, too, just behind 'em. Come here, I'll show ya."

She led me outside and around the studio, to the one wall that had no windows. It was a large concrete rectangle; its rough, grey surface a stark contrast to the soft colours surrounding it. She was right. It was aching to come alive.

"What would you want painted on it?"

"I don't mind at all. As long as it has lots of colour. I bought all that paint, just waiting to be used. For the right person to come and fulfil its potential."

I stood looking at it for a while. Tried to force myself to think of a motif, a pattern, anything I could imagine to decorate the wall. But I didn't have it in me. Some things we just have to leave in the past.

* * *

Vanya served up a spicy lentil stew, the worn old dining table bedecked with lit candles and wildflowers. Then, as instructed, I took my mother's letter and got into Vanya's truck.

"Where are we going?" I asked, but Vanya just smiled. Occasionally there was a bump in the road or a sharp turn, and I heard something rattle in the back. I glanced over at Vanya, but she kept her secretive eyes firmly on the road.

We drove through woodlands and suburbs until we could see Lake Michigan, ice blue beneath the setting sun. Vanya steered left and we drove north along the shore until we reached a small, desolate stretch of beach. There, Vanya stopped the truck and we stepped outside.

Soft, white sand sloped gently towards the calm water, around it a border of wispy grass bending with the breeze. A small falcon sailed above the lake, jerking its head left and right in search of dinner. I filled my lungs with the crisp air, tasting the wildness of the place. But why had Vanya brought me here?

She hovered by the car, looking at me with her Mona Lisa smile. I turned and walked onto the beach, my rainbow shoes sweeping over the fine grains until I reached the water's edge. The lake seemed to go on forever, vast as any ocean, calm and resolving.

Vanya appeared behind me and dumped a bulky bin bag by my feet. I looked at the bag, then up at Vanya, her long locks twirling in the wind.

"What's this?"

"This, my friend, is your salvation." She bent down and poured the contents onto the ground. It was pieces of pottery – ceramic sculptures and bowls and figurines. "Discarded pieces from the studio. I want you to smash them."

My jaw dropped. "You what?"

"You heard me."

Dumbfounded, I stared at the pieces, scattered over the sand.

"This is what we need, people like us. We take on the entire world and never feel like we have the right to our own feelings. So it builds up inside you."

"What does?"

"Rage. When we don't allow ourselves to express our anger, it remains inside us like a black hole that will consume us until there's nothing left. You're angry, Hazel. You're angry with Liam, and with your mother. I'm not saying it's their fault necessarily, but you still gotta let yourself feel and express your frustration. It won't leave you until you release it, honey. That's just how it works. Holding onto anger is only hurting yourself."

"You're being serious..." I crouched down and picked one of the pieces. It was a rough shape of a person curled up into a ball. I ran my fingers over its coarse texture.

"Young people walk around like they'll always be young, like their lives will last forever. But one day you'll wake up and wonder where all the time went. And that day, the one thing I don't want you to regret is not letting go of the pain when you had the chance. You mustn't waste your life on old grievances that don't need to hurt you anymore." The wind picked up slightly, ruffling the lake's pale surface. "Trust me on this. That sculpture you're holding. Stand up and throw it against that rock."

"But I don't feel angry," I said, feeling more than a little stupid.

"Sure you do. Remember how you felt after your fight with Liam? And your mom. Where's that letter?"

I hesitated, then reached into my pocket and pulled out the envelope.

"Read it," Vanya instructed. "I'll go for a walk. I'll be back in a little while, okay?"

With that, she turned and wandered off along the shore. I watched her for a long time, until she was nothing but a rosy speck on the horizon. Then, reluctantly, I read the letter again.

I pray to the gods that you will never feel the kind of pain you have caused me.

Such eloquent venom, such a clever disguise. But it was nothing more than a self-pitying guilt-trip dressed up in elegant script. I felt the urge to cry, but no – I was done crying. I was tired of being a victim of these sick people. Their burdens weren't mine anymore. My arms started to tremble, ferocious energy animating my nerves. I crumpled the letter once more and a scream rose in my throat, a scream for all the wasted tears, for all the fucked up years, for all those times I'd had to bite my tongue and force it all back down; all at once it came out into a great roar of release, as I raised my arm and threw the clay figure against the rock and watched it smash into a thousand shards.

I stood stunned for a moment, looking at the pulverised aftermath, and I noticed a flutter of elation in my chest. I bent down and picked up another piece, a mug with a broken handle. Without hesitation I slammed it against the rock, flooded with a strange relief as it disintegrated before me. Next, and next; one by one I destroyed the sculptures, and I barely noticed the way I screamed and cried as the pile of shards grew around my feet. Memories assaulted me like a swarm of bees – each time I had to give up a piece of myself to try and please her, every lie she had told in order to keep me chained, all those times I had blindly trusted that she was somehow omnipotent and that every part of me belonged to her. And somewhere in that onslaught of clarity I remembered all the cruel remarks she had made about Amber, the way she had put a wedge between us and deprived me of my only sister. How she had drained all the colours from our lives.

My screams echoed over the lake while the sun went up in flames over the horizon. Now Liam's face came to my mind and fresh rage erupted in me, and I threw the last of the pieces while cursing him all the way to the hell we didn't believe in, crying all the tears I had been afraid to show, saying everything I hadn't dared say, until I had nothing left and fell to my knees, sobbing among the wreckage.

Exhausted, I lay back on the sand and caught my breath, my eyes drifting over the pale evening sky. As my chest slowed its heaving, a strange serenity washed over me. The sky looked so beautiful, the way it darkened as it slowly gave way to night; and the air felt clean and fresh in my lungs. A soft wind combed through the tall grass around the beach's edge, whispering some hushed secret to me. I put a hand to my chest and noticed that something was missing – an old, heavy ache, which seemed to have floated away on the evening breeze.

After a while I could hear Vanya approaching and sat back up.

"Attagirl!" She walked towards me with a wide grin. "Now, how did that feel? Tell me honest!"

I broke into a goofy smile. "Good. Stupid, at first. But then it felt… great."

"Marvellous work, honey. Well done."

I let out a bubbly chuckle. "Is this how you used to treat students when you were a counsellor?"

Vanya laughed. "Not exactly. Although, in some ways, yeah. It is a universal thing, allowing ourselves to feel whatever we're feeling. But the pottery treatment is a recent invention of mine, I suppose." She smiled then, an earth mother smile that could warm oceans. "Only one thing left to do."

"What's that?"

She pulled out a lighter and handed it to me.

"Burn that fucking letter. That shit ain't yours to carry around no more."

I looked from the lighter to Vanya, then shrugged and took it. "Fuck it."

"Fuck it," Vanya repeated, matter-of-factly.

"Fuck it!" I yelled, and the echo over the lake sang my words back at me. I couldn't help but laugh. What pseudo-psycho nonsense. Never mind. It felt wonderful.

I flicked it into life, picked up the letter and watched as the flame began licking it, curling and browning the paper, then consuming it until there was nothing left but ashes.

THIRTY-FIVE

September sunlight poured in through every window in Vanya's studio. I sat by a pottery wheel, my foot pumping away to keep it rotating, while my hands attempted to create a shape out of a spinning lump of wet clay.

"Hold steady," said Vanya, who was standing behind me. "Now, gently press your thumbs down in the middle to create a hollow."

Slowly, I could see a bowl forming in my hands. I stared at the centre, hypnotised by its continuous twirls. It felt good to make something so immediate and tangible. I increased the pressure of my thumbs, but suddenly the clay collapsed and skidded across the wheel.

"Oh, shit."

"Don't worry," Vanya said. "It's all part of the process. Just knead it and start again."

* * *

I spent three days covered in clay, sometimes joining Vanya's classes, and gradually filled a shelf with wonky bowls and brittle mugs. They would probably end up in the smash bag, but that didn't bother me. It felt nice to create something with my hands; and while my hands were busy, my mind was quiet.

Every morning I walked past the pile of paint buckets Vanya had bought for the mural, but she never brought it up again. Instead, we talked about other things; about Vanya's wild twenties in San Francisco and her early years with Frank, and I told her all about Liam and Mother and Amber.

The clay kept me busy during the days, but late at night, alone in my room, a thousand thoughts came storming in. I couldn't get the band out of my head. I missed my friends, my Liam, the road. I kept checking their site and feeds for any updates, and saw that they had cancelled the rest of the shows. But no further announcements had been made and nobody had posted anything, so I had no idea how any of them were doing.

One night I was out on the porch, a chunky quilt around my shoulders to keep the chill at bay, and I started looking through photos on my phone. I scrolled backwards past my failed attempts at pottery, Vanya's studio, the shores of Lake Michigan, until I saw his face. My heart, as always, tumbled at the sight of his eyes – dark and sad and, somewhere in those deep pools, seeming to cast a murky reflection of myself.

I carried on swiping through pictures from the woods, our gigs, silly selfies in kitchens and on the tour bus and in busy streets in cities all over, and my insides ached.

As if guided by some outside force, I saw myself opening my text conversations and tapping on Liam's name. There were our previous chats, sweet words and pictures and banter. I scrolled upward while the ache intensified. Then I started typing.

Hey Liam. How are you doing? I hope things are ok. I've been think

Wait. What the hell was I doing? This was most definitely a bad idea. I closed the screen and held the phone to my chest for a long time while my heart slowed. Loneliness and isolation itched under my skin, and when I unlocked my phone again I opened my list of contacts. Right at the top was Amber. I brought the screen closer and squinted at the tiny profile picture. Her hair was as red and wild as ever, although she was smiling and looking healthy, which was new. Last active this afternoon, it said. So she must still be using the same number.

Images came to me of her on the swing, her bright ginger locks flying through the air, her little legs pushing us higher and higher. She had only ever tried to protect me. I felt like such an idiot for not having seen it sooner.

I was overwhelmed by an urge to contact her, but as I opened the keyboard I realised I had no idea what to write. Mother and I had shut her out, left her to her own shaky devices. Abandoned her. What words could ever make up for such a betrayal?

Hey, Amber. It's me. How are you?

Ugh, how inane. Delete.

Amber, it's me, Hazel. Sorry I haven't been in touch for so

Delete.

Hey! How

Delete.

Hey Amber, you ok? I'm in America and I miss you.

Delete.

Amber. I know now. I know it was mum's fault. I know it wasn't you. I'm so sorry.

Delete.

I've been thinking about that day on the swing. In the snow. Don't know why.

Delete.

Sadness welled up in me like a river after the rain, full and fierce. I tried to hold back the tears but there always seemed to be more; more sorrow, more regret.

There's nothing I can say. I know it's my fault. Or mum's fault. Does it make a difference?

Then my phone went *ping* and I nearly fell off the porch chair. It was a message from Amber.

It says you've been typing for ages. What's up?

I stared dumbly at the screen for a long while, trying to think of what to say. Then it started to ring, and a sudden panic tightened my throat. Shaking, I pressed the green button and put the phone to my ear.

"He-hello?"

"Hey, Hazel, what's going on?"

My sister's voice, so familiar and yet so foreign. She sounded bright and upbeat, which I hadn't expected. I swallowed hard, still choking on guilt.

"Oh my god, um," I stammered.

"Everything alright? I thought you might be on your deathbed, struggling to type goodbye with gnarled fingers or something."

I let out a nervous chuckle. "Not exactly, no... I'm in America."

"Yeah, Dad said. How are you finding it?"

"Great, mostly. It's been a crazy journey."

"You been out there finding yourself or what?" I recognised her teasing voice, and it made me smile.

"Yeah, pretty much," I said. She was quiet for a moment. I took a breath and closed my eyes. "Look, Amber. I'm so sorry. I just wanted to say that. For everything."

A crackling silence trickled at me from across the Atlantic. My chest felt tight, my bra suddenly too constricting around my ribcage.

"I've come to see things differently. And I see now…" I swallowed hard. "I see what Mother did. What Mum did. How she turned me against you."

Amber was still silent, and a thousand needles pricked my skin. I couldn't bear it if she wouldn't accept my apology.

"She had no right," I continued. "She's messed up, I see that now. But I didn't back then, I just didn't. I thought—"

"Hazel." Amber's voice sounded hoarse. "It's okay. It's not your fault."

"But I should have seen—"

"You were only a kid. She was using you. I saw it all along, and she couldn't have someone there who saw through her act. That's why I left. I was always sorry to leave you behind, but I knew I had to wait it out. For you to see for yourself. You were never going to take my word for it. You can't blame yourself. It's all her."

Tears were rising in my throat and I had to force myself to take long, slow breaths. "I wish things had been different…"

"They still can be."

They still can be. Something warm and gentle poured through me, releasing my hold on myself. Maybe it wasn't all too late. I pressed my phone to my ear, realising just how much I missed her. "Where are you now?"

"In my flat in Canning Town."

"Oh, you're in London?" I snivelled and pulled the quilt tighter around me. "You live alone?"

"No," she said, leaving a little pause of suspense. "I'm with my boyfriend, and, well…"

"Well, what?"

"We're having a baby, so I guess technically she's here too."

My jaw dropped. "Holy heck. Amber! You're having a—a *baby?* Shit. I had no idea! When?"

"In twelve weeks, if she arrives on time." I could hear Amber grinning at the other end of the line.

"Amber. Oh my god. Congratulations. I'm so happy for you." I couldn't imagine my reckless sister as a mother. But we had all got older, and hopefully a little wiser.

"Cheers, Haze. We're dead excited. And terrified."

"I bet. Did you say it's a girl?"

"Yeah."

"Wow…" The thought of a little mini-Amber filled my heart with hope. New beginnings to look forward to. "So, who's the dad?"

"His name's Matt. We met in NA, actually. But we're both clean now, and he's been so good for me. And I for him, I think."

"Honestly, Amber, that's so great to hear. I'm so… I'm proud of you. Hope that's not a weird thing to say."

"Not weird. Thank you. We've both worked hard for this. And sounds like you have, too."

"Me?"

"Well, yeah. You sound like a different Hazel to the one I remember."

"Yeah… I guess I am."

I could barely picture the girl I had been when I left. Even less so, the girl Amber had last seen. So many incarnations of me, it made me dizzy to think about.

"You'll have to tell me all about it. Your trip, I mean. And everything."

"Oh, I'd love to. It's been such a rollercoaster, I won't know where to begin."

"When do you get back home?"

"In a couple of weeks." It didn't matter how many times I checked the calendar or counted the days – it didn't feel real.

I heard a male voice calling Amber in the background. "Well, Haze, I gotta go. But, hey, it was good to talk to you."

"You too," I said. "And thanks, you know, for understanding. And everything."

"See you soon, yeah?"

"Sure, yes. See you."

She wasn't angry. She didn't blame me. I could feel every part of my body and soul relax with relief.

There was a *ping* and I saw another message from her.

Really good to hear from you. Glad we're both doing well, finally. If you want me to pick you up at the airport when you get back, text me your flight details and I'll be there x

I leaned back in the creaky porch chair and let out a long breath. For the first time I had something tangible to look forward to when I got back home – I would see my sister again. Having been estranged from her for so long, the thought made me nervous. We would have to find a way to start over.

I put my phone down and stood up, stretching in the chilly night. Pockets of stars were peering out between the clouds, and a web of cricket song pulsated around me. I stepped off the porch and onto the lawn, dew-wet grass between my toes, and looked up at the sky. A white flash of light made me jump; a tiny star shooting through the night, just like the night of the meteor shower.

Then my ringtone cut through the peace and I spun around. Was it Amber calling again? I padded back through the grass and reached over to pick up my phone. But it wasn't Amber.

It was Liam.

My heart jolted. Instinctively, I pressed the answer button, then held the phone mid-air while I tried to calm my frenzied mind.

"Hazel? You there?" I could hear his voice, distant and electronic.

I put the phone to my ear and he spoke again. "Haze?"

"I'm here," I said, my voice cracking.

He let out a lazy laugh. "Hazelnut." Immediately, I could tell he was high. Not coke high, Xanax high.

"Liam, are you okay?" My voice sounded more pleading than I had intended, my gut pinching with a familiar worry.

"I'm fine, baby, I'm fine." I heard some clattering noise in the background. "Missing you, though. A lot." A loud, scratchy noise hit my ear and I heard muffled cursing. "Sorry, dropped my phone. You still there?"

"Yeah," I said, my insides twisting. "I'm still here."

"Where are you, baby? You with Vanya still?"

"Yes, did Lawson say? I… I hope it's not weird, but I had to—"

"S'okay, Hazelnut. I understand." His voice was thick and slurred. "But… I wanna see you before you go home. Won't you come back? Just a few days? I'll pay for your ticket, whatever you need."

Of course I wanted to see him. But hearing him like this made me break all over again.

"Are—are you in Chicago?"

"Yeah, I'm at home. This fucking city… Drivin' me nuts. I'm really missing touring."

My lower lip started quivering and I could feel my resolve begin to dissipate. "Liam… I miss you too. But I—I don't think I should go back."

"Baby, come on. Don't be like that. We have something, don't we?" He paused, then heaved a tired sigh. "I fucked up, I know that. I'm sorry."

There was no anger left in me; only concern, and something like love. I had to go see him.

I took a breath and closed my eyes. "I'll come."

"For real?"

"I will. I'll come to your place."

"I'm so happy to hear that, Haze."

Something twitched in my chest and already I wondered if I was making a mistake. But life is full of mistakes, and if we didn't make them, we'd never get anywhere.

"Just, be careful, okay? I'll see how quickly I can get over there, but hopefully see you tomorrow. I'll text and let you know."

"My Hazelnut's comin' to see me," Liam sang down the crackly line, to the melody of *My Bonnie Lies Over the Ocean*. I heard glass against glass, like he was pouring himself a drink.

"Liam. Take care, okay?"

"Always, baby."

There was a click and he was gone.

I stood in stunned disbelief for a moment, the stars tickling me with their ancient light. Then I folded up the quilt and went inside to tell Vanya. She sat in the living room with her nose in a book. Phone in hand, I stood in front of her, wondering where to begin. She looked up at me, then slowly put her book down.

"You okay, hon? What's wrong?"

I swallowed. "Liam called."

"Is he alright? What'd he say?"

"He wants me to come see him."

"Oh, honey… You sure that's a good idea?"

"I don't know what's good and bad anymore, Vanya. I've no clue. All I know is that I miss him so much, I can't see straight. And I don't want to go back home not having seen him again. He didn't sound too good over the phone, and I—I just want to make sure he's okay."

Vanya looked unconvinced but came over and wrapped me up in a hug. "Whatever you think is best, Hazel. I trust your decision."

"Thank you," I said, sniffling. "Also, um, do you think you could, um…"

"Of course I'll drive you, sweetie. When do you wanna go?"

"Tomorrow morning?"

Vanya laughed and shook her head. "Young love. Consider it done."

I said a thousand thanks to Vanya for everything and headed to my room to pack. As I bagged up all my carefully laid-out possessions, I could feel my trepidation slowly give way to exhilaration. I was going back! I would to see Liam again, hold him and kiss him and never mind all the things that had gone wrong and all that had been lost or ruined; it would be us two again, even for a short while. *There is only now.*

After a long night of restless anticipation, Vanya served up our final breakfast which I rapidly shovelled down, eager to get on the road. I texted Liam to let him know that I was getting a lift and that I'd be there in about an hour. He hadn't replied yet, but he was probably still asleep. Nevertheless, I couldn't wait to be close to him again.

Outside, a sparkling sunrise had painted everything in a glimmer of gold. The surrounding woods were draped in a hazy mist that smelled of sap and earth and wet leaves, and above us a host of birds trilled their morning song. I took one last big lungful of the healing forest air, then shoved my backpack into Vanya's truck.

"All set?" Vanya asked on her way to the driver's seat.

"Yep, all se—oh, wait, my phone's ringing." I stopped and pulled it from my pocket.

"Is it Liam?"

"No…" I pressed answer and held the phone to my ear.

"Hey, Laws! Did you hear I'm coming back? Are you in Chicago, too?"

"Hazel…" Lawson's voice was dry and heavy like gravel, and in an instant I knew something was very wrong.

"Lawson. What is it?"

"I've got some… some bad news." He sounded choked, like he was holding back tears. I had never seen Lawson cry. I felt my body freeze, cement spreading from my feet to my legs all the way up through my body, swallowing up my heart, turning all of me to stone.

"Liam…" Lawson hesitated, cleared his throat. "I found him this morning…"

Cement in my lungs. I couldn't breathe. I couldn't speak.

"It, uh… It seems like he choked in his sleep, bad mix of pills and alcohol. Looks like it was an accident, but they're gonna need an autopsy."

The world had stopped, every clock on the earth ceased to tick.

"Shit, Hazel, I'm so sorry."

Black tar pouring over my skin, burning, searing. This couldn't be real. It was a joke, surely. But I could hear Lawson sobbing down the phone and I knew it was no joke.

"Hazel, you there?"

"No. Please, no…" I staggered sideways and landed against the side of Vanya's truck. It looked so white and clean, how could it look so impeccable when the world was made of chaos? My head started spinning and I pressed my forehead against the cool metal, and I heard Vanya say something, or was she yelling? I couldn't tell. My mouth felt dry and I wanted to scream but I had nothing in me, nothing but black tar and cement and whatever it is that burns in the centre of the earth, and I noticed the sky was ice blue as my head banged against the cold, hard ground and then there was nothing.

THIRTY-SIX

Days and nights bled into each other. I lay in Vanya's guest bed, drifting in and out of consciousness. My bag was left untouched in the corner, the walls bare, the shelves empty. I lay glued to the mattress, counting cracks in the ceiling while a thousand regrets charged through my mind. When I had the strength, I picked up my phone to call him, because surely this was all just a bad dream.

Hey, it's Liam, leave a message.

Each time I heard his voice I realised that he was never again going to answer his phone, and it felt as though the entire weight of the universe came crashing down on me, choking me. I couldn't move, and I couldn't lie still. I couldn't think, and I couldn't switch off. At times I lay motionless as a mannequin, wishing my breath would leave me once and for all, anything to end this torture. Other times I writhed wailing in my sheets until nothing remained of me but an empty shell, and then I would plunge into more fevered nightmares.

Vanya was there, urging me to eat something, to talk about it, but I couldn't engage with her or with Lawson and

Ivy who were calling and texting somewhere in my periphery. I had escaped into a haze where nothing seemed real, and that was all I could cope with.

I listened to his songs over and over, pressing the earbuds as deep as they would go until my ears burned raw because I desperately wanted his voice so close to me that I wouldn't be able to distinguish between him and myself. His voice sounded so clear, so real, as if he were right there next to me and I could hold his warm body and smell his citrus hair. But he wasn't. If only I had gone to him sooner. What if I had never left? I could have prevented this. No, *he* could have prevented it. I raged at myself and then at him but then realised it was all pointless because it was done and we could never take it back, and then I tumbled into another pit of the kind of despair you can't reason with and all I could do was keep breathing.

Once in a while my brain played cruel tricks on me and he came to me in my dreams; we were together again and no irreversible horrors had occurred and no death was on my conscience, and I never wanted to wake up.

At first, all I could remember were his lopsided smile and full moon eyes, his soft touch and the way I had fallen into him like a bottomless well each time he opened up and allowed me a glimpse of his marvellous and troubled soul. But after a while, other images started to elbow their way into my head: his raging eyes, his averted gaze, his vanishing and cheating and toying with everyone. And always there was the torture of knowing that it was all over, that I would never again see his face; that those teddy bear eyes were now life-less, yellowing spheres of nothing slowly turning to dust. That, somehow, seemed the most unfair of all.

* * *

One afternoon, after a blur of days or maybe weeks, I was just beginning to contemplate actually eating something of substance when I received a text from Lawson. A little foggy, I rubbed my eyes and squinted at the screen.

Hey Haze. How are you doing? It's been so weird over here, we're going through his stuff and talking to his parents. It's messed up. Anyway, we all miss you. You're flying back soon, aren't you? We're all in Chicago, I thought maybe you want to come see us before you go? Would feel weird not to see you again... Lemme know – either way I hope you know you can call me anytime. Love, Laws

I stared at his message for a long time. What date was it today? I opened my calendar app and saw that my flight was four days away. *Shit!* I scrambled out of bed and twirled around a few times in a panic. Four days! I had lost all sense of time but now reality sharpened in an instant, yanking me out of my prolonged nightmare.

Through the large windows in my room I could see a bright autumn sun shining through the yellowing trees. Lawson, Ivy, my friends in Chicago. Go see them? The thought turned my stomach at first, but when I read Lawson's text again I could feel my frostbitten heart begin to thaw around the edges. For the first time in days, I could picture something other than Liam's face, and think about something other than bitter regret.

I had to pull myself together. A little shamefaced, I smoothed down my greasy hair and pulled on my least dirty jumper, then padded out into the hall to find Vanya. She was sitting by the wood burner writing in a notebook, and she looked up and greeted me with her earth-mother smile.

"Oh, hey there. How are ya?"

"Hi," I said, wringing my hands. "I, um, I think I could maybe eat something now, if that's okay?"

Vanya closed her notebook and stood up, strawberry hair

tumbling down over her orange cardigan. "Of course! Come, let's find you something. What are you in the mood for?"

I followed her into the kitchen and sat on a barstool by the island, beneath the warm light of naked bulbs dangling from a large piece of driftwood.

"Let's start with some tea, shall we?" she said, pulling out jasmine leaves and a teapot from the cupboard. "Want some bread?" She gestured to the homemade loaf resting on a chopping board. "Help yourself."

I cut myself a slice and nibbled hesitantly at it, while Vanya boiled water on the stove. When she placed a steaming mug in front of me, I looked up at her with puppy eyes.

"I'm sorry," I mumbled.

"For what?"

"For... all this. I never meant to become your inpatient."

"Don't you say that. I'm glad I could be here for you, it's such a traumatic time." She lowered her gaze, mournfully shaking her head. "Little Liam..."

I pinched the bread between my fingers, my appetite suddenly shying away.

"He was a special soul," Vanya continued. "Just like Frank." Sadness glazed over her eyes as she took a sip from her tea.

"How did you get through it?" I asked, my voice shaky. "How can a person ever deal with this?"

Mug in hand, Vanya sat down on the stool next to me. "Time," she said plainly. "All wounds take time to heal. You just gotta hold on, and remember that you won't feel like this forever."

I chewed on my lip while considering my next question. I hated what it implied, but I had to know. "All that stuff you said, about not being responsible for other people. I get it, but still... Did you really not feel guilty about leaving Frank? When he..." My voice trailed off.

Vanya lowered her head, looking down into her mug. "Of course I did. I had all kinds of thoughts about how I should have stayed, should have tried harder, been more patient. But, you know, we can't always trust whatever thought pops into our heads. Should haves and could haves, they're not helpful. They're nasty little tricks, fooling us into thinking we're in control. But we're not. What's done is done. We only end up punishing ourselves for no reason." She took another sip and placed her mug on the countertop. "As I was processing everything, I came to understand that the best thing I could do for both myself and Frank was to try and move on, do something positive in this world. Because after all, we're still alive. Don't we owe it to the dead to make the most of it?"

I sat quietly for what felt like a long time, willing myself to swallow a dry piece of bread. *The dead.* Not our boyfriends or exes or bandmates. The dead.

It was so terribly final.

Somewhere below my ribcage I could sense a dull, black ache spreading like an oil spill. I glanced over at Vanya. "Did you know that he tried to kill himself when he was sixteen?"

"Gosh, no, I didn't." She furrowed her brow and I knew what was going through her mind – the impossible thing of trying to picture a young boy, desperate to end his life. "What happened?"

"He told me once, he took a bunch of pills and ended up in hospital. And his parents…" The anger that erupted inside me took me by surprise and I grimaced, my body trembling. "Those fucking people…"

"What did they do?"

I ground my teeth together. "They left a message for him, saying they were ashamed of his behaviour and that God punishes suicides, or some shit like that."

Vanya closed her eyes. "Oh, Liam…"

The window of relief had closed and I was once more dissolving into helplessness. The bread tasted like gravel in my mouth, and more tears burned behind my eyelids. "I don't know what to do!" I yelped. "Where do I go from here? How can we live our lives knowing that any time anyone can just disappear like that? It's too awful, Vanya, I can't take it…"

Vanya reached over and placed a hand on my shoulder. "You can. I know it doesn't feel like it now, but you can take it. We all can. It sucks and it hurts, but we get through it day by day, minute by minute until we're out the other side."

"Other side of what? I don't see the point anymore." I groaned and shoved my bread onto the countertop, where it landed next to my untouched cup of tea. "It all feels so empty."

"You know what, you're right." She folded her hands in front of her. "We're here, and then we're gone, and nobody knows why. But you know what I've found? Acceptance is the key to peace. If you can make friends with the emptiness of life, you don't need to run from it any longer. Whenever you get the feeling that everything is meaningless, don't be afraid of it. Turn around and face it head on. Embrace it. The moment you say yes to hopelessness, you'll find hope. I know that sounds strange, but it's true. Life is just one big paradox."

I tried to wrap my head around her words but the spilled oil was spreading inside me, covering everything in a helpless, sticky black. I needed to be scrubbed clean. Or switched off. There was only one thing that could help.

"I—I gotta go," I said, stumbling off the bar stool, tears blurring my vision as I rushed off to my room.

"Honey, wait…" Vanya came after me, but my mind was warped by a tunnel vision guiding me towards the bathroom, to my makeup bag, to the Xanax bottle. I could take just one, just to get a break from all this pain. Just one…

Then I felt Vanya's hand on my arm.

"Hazel, please, don't go there. Just take a moment. Whatever you're feeling, it's okay. It hurts, but it won't kill you."

I stopped, my fingers wrapped tightly around the orange bottle. The scene felt painfully familiar – except, last time I had been on the other side of it.

"Sweetie, I can't tell you what to do," Vanya said in a level voice. "But I just want to ask you, do you want to end up like Liam? Do you want to follow in his footsteps, or your mother's? I'm only asking, hon, because the choice is yours."

I slumped sobbing onto the floor. Vanya crouched down next to me, and sat there quietly while I cried and cried.

Once my sobs had faded to hiccups and sniffles, she gestured at the bottle in my hand. "Do you want me to take care of these?"

My arm was trembling, the tablets rattling around. The memory of Liam's glazed eyes flashed through my mind and a wave of nausea rolled through me. Slowly, I handed them over to Vanya.

"Good job, hon. I'll go put these away, and then I'll fix you some real food, okay? I noticed you barely ate anything."

I nodded, feeling flatlined. She gave me another pat on the shoulder and walked down the hall. I sat for a long time, listening to the sounds of pots and pans coming from the kitchen. I had to find a way to take another step; I couldn't sit on this bathroom floor forever.

Eventually I grabbed the sink and pulled myself up, but was startled by the sight of myself in the mirror. Who was that girl looking back at me? I could barely recognise her anymore. All those things I had seen and said and done, and all I had *not* done; everything I felt responsible for. *Should have, could have.* I winced and looked away.

But then I heard Liam's voice.

You're shit scared of looking in the mirror.

I stopped, glancing over at my reflection in the periphery.

"No, I'm not," I mumbled. "I'm not scared." But still I felt reluctant to turn and face myself. I forced myself around, leaning closer to that girl with the puffy face and weary eyes. Her face was the most familiar sight, yet still somehow unknown to me.

I squinted at her, trying to see beyond the two-dimensional image looking back at me.

Then, as if layers were being peeled and revealed, all at once I could see all the girls I had been, and would be, and could have been. I could see my mother's face there, too; her grey eyes looking back at me, the lines around her mouth, the slouch in her shoulders. But this time I didn't run away. And I saw Liam's eyes, too; their pain shining through mine. And, finally, tiny Hazel peered out at me with all the hope and innocence that spilled from her little heart. All of it, staring back at me as I began to well up.

Acceptance is the key to peace.

Could I do it? Could I accept the person I had become, and had been, and would be? Could I love her despite the wounds and scars, despite all I had been through, despite all those things I could never be?

I thought I could sense Liam laughing at me. A warm, friendly laugh, telling me I was being silly. The thought made me smile, which was a foreign sensation. And there were my dimples, but as I tilted my head and studied my reflection, forcing my smile to remain, it was as though, for the first time in my life, I could see them as my own.

There it all was: Mother, Liam, me.

"I dare you." My whisper filled the silent room. "I dare you," I repeated, staring at myself in the mirror. "I dare you to love yourself, despite all of it... No, *because* of it all. This is who you are. Everything you've done, everywhere you've been, *this* is it." I leaned closer, my hazel eyes drilling into me. "I fucking dare you."

I couldn't save anyone except myself, but maybe that was my only job.

An overwhelming wave of energy washed through me. I gave myself one final, hard stare in the mirror, then I spun on my heel and strode out through the kitchen where Vanya stood chopping carrots, but I didn't stop. I had to keep going.

"You alright, hon? Where are you..." She put her knife down and followed me as I walked out the backdoor and down the stone path that led to the studio. The air was still and crisp, as though I could cut right through it with a blade. Everywhere green and yellow and brown, the earth in her seasons, always changing.

"You okay?" Vanya asked, following closely behind me. "Where are you going? Hazel!"

My gaze was fixed on the wall, blank concrete calling me, waiting to be filled. I felt a steely determination surge through me, dyeing my blood a deep blue. I strode over and pulled open the studio door, over to the corner where Vanya had piled the paint cans onto a tarpaulin. I grabbed the edge of the tarp and pulled it backwards, across the studio floor and out the door. Vanya had stopped, and stood still to the side, watching me. I didn't care. This had to be done, and now. I used the back of a small brush to pop open the cans, one by one, their lids flying through the air, splattering paint over the ground.

I picked up a wide brush and drowned it in black, the deep dark black into which I had fallen and in which I had become so lost with Liam, pulled black oil from my chest and *splash* onto the wall, great big strokes, my arms moving of their own accord. I crouched down and covered the corner in black strokes, feeding them outwards, spreading them across the wall like a murder of crows opening their wings, taking off into the sky.

My blood pulsed through my veins and I twisted around, looking for blue paint that would match my dark blood. I sat down, my knees digging into the grass, and as I dipped the bristles into that thick royal blue I thought of Liam and Frank, together again, singing their blues, blue afternoons, blue like the infinite sky, and I poured it onto the wall, and the world softened through my burning tears but I had to keep going. I spread the paint over the concrete surface, watching its every crease and crack fill with blue and streaks of black.

Liam, you were so beautiful. Blue waves, arm twisting. *You taught me so much.* Blue mixing with white, light blue like a summer lake and then a blueish white like a bleak morning and then pure white, white all over the top of the wall, my arm stretching as high as it could go. *I wanted to help you. I tried. But I couldn't. You didn't want to be helped. I'm sorry, Liam. I'm so sorry. Where are you now? And all those songs you carried around in your head, who's singing them now?*

I reached for the red and it completely choked the white, blood dripping onto fresh snow, bright bold red in streaks of fury. *Why did you have to be so fucking stubborn? It didn't have to turn out this way.* Through the fog and sobs I could hear myself mumbling, and I was vaguely aware of Vanya standing behind me but I didn't care if she heard, didn't care if she thought I was crazy, I had to keep going. *Oh but, Liam, we had some fine times together, did we not?* I found the green paint, sat down by it, held the bucket in my hands. Green like the grass we had made love on, green like the fields we had driven through, green like the jealousy I had felt and overcome. *I wouldn't have missed it for the world. What adventures we shared, my beautiful, messed-up Liam.*

I dipped my brush gently, held the bristles against the can

and watched as the paint dribbled back into its container. Like the green of the earth that comes and goes, and comes again. I raised my hand and swept some green across the middle of the wall. *Comes and goes, and comes again.* Finally, I went back to the white paint, white like all the colours combined, white like the stars we watched together at night, white like the star Liam had now become, and I reached up and put those stars onto the wall, the stars we had been wondering about and longing for, the stars that made us and the stars that sustained us, bright white dots scattered all across the top, and then I dropped the brush and fell to my knees, panting, trembling.

Vanya appeared behind me and her hands were on my shoulders, warm and steady. She whispered something, shushing and pulling hair from my face, her sing-song voice like an ebbing ocean.

"Attagirl," she cooed. "It's beautiful."

I leaned into her chest and let myself be held, and she rocked me gently back and forth.

"I miss him," I croaked, sobbing.

"I know you do," Vanya murmured. "I know you do."

And I would have to find a way to be okay with that.

THIRTY-SEVEN

The concrete vastness of Chicago felt both daunting and comforting where I stood with my backpack, watching Vanya's truck disappear down the road. *Bye, V. Thanks for everything.*

The September sun hung low and pale to the west, its slanting autumn rays filtering through the tall buildings. I propped my backpack up against a wall and looked out over the parking lot where Lawson had said to meet. The noise of Chicago sounded all around me – honks, sirens, hammering and drilling from nearby roadworks. I tried to imagine Liam's life in this city, wondering about the places where he used to hang out, the people he knew. It was hard to picture him outside of touring, the only world in which I had ever known him.

Then I heard the rumbling old engine as it approached. There was no mistaking that sound. I jumped to my feet and lit up as it appeared from around the corner. There it was – the teal-painted wonder vehicle, the Interstate Marvel; my enchanted carriage rolling up to me and coming to a stop with a loud hiss. Lawson was behind the wheel, and he was out within seconds, loping over and swallowing me up in a big hug.

"Hazel," he said, his voice like a sigh of relief.

The familiar sights of the bus and Lawson brought up pain I thought I had worked through in my weeks with Vanya. I held him tight, pressing my arms into his back as my tears spilled onto his T-shirt. He squeezed me back, whispering my name into my hair, and when we separated I saw that he, too, was crying.

I put my hand on his arm and rubbed it gently. "It's so fucked up."

"I still can't believe it," Lawson said, his usually jolly eyes saturated with sorrow.

"Have you been back to his place yet?"

"Yeah, we've been over there talking to the super, and we started going through some of his stuff. It's just too surreal."

I looked over to the bus but couldn't see anyone.

"Yeah," said Lawson, reading my mind. "They're all at the beach already."

It felt reassuring to see Lawson again. Like it hadn't all just been a dream. I pulled him to me once more, and then we stepped onto the bus.

Lake Michigan lay vast and flat as ever, lined by Chicago's bulky skyline. We drove along a stretch of white sand until we reached the end of the beach, where the others were already sitting on chairs around a campfire. I swallowed hard as I looked at them through the bus window. They looked different, surrounded by a strange new aura; the suffocating blanket of grief. And most tangible of all was the void Liam had left behind. Victor and Mango sat next to each other, their shoulders slumped, Mango with a beer in hand. Ivy sat by herself, her bright locks outshining the fire as they danced about her face in the brisk winds.

It felt wrong, being there without Liam. He had been the glue that held us all together, the sun tying us to his solar system.

Lawson got up from the driver's seat and walked over to my booth. "You okay?"

I hesitated. "I don't know... I feel nervous seeing them all again."

"Don't worry. It's weird for everyone. You'll be fine." He attempted a smile, and I gingerly got up and followed him off the bus.

Mango was first to come up and offer me a hug, and Victor next. Mango's usual bright mood had been replaced with a quiet gloom, and Victor's face looked more serious than ever. I didn't know what to say. Finally, Ivy appeared behind Victor. She stepped forward with eyes downcast, hugging her arms. I placed my hand on her shoulder, and slowly she raised her head until her algae eyes met mine, and there was an understanding deeper than words. She released her arms and our fingers laced together, and we stood like that for a moment, joined in mutual grief.

Lawson pulled out a chair for me and we sat down, and for a long time nobody spoke. The setting sun cast long shadows across the smooth sand. Gentle waves licked the shore, and the odd boat went past. Picnickers packed up for the evening, walking past us with sunburned faces and bloated bellies. Planes came in and out of O'Hare, their contrails leaving a criss-cross pattern burning white in the light of the sunset.

Eventually, Mango stood up and looked at us. "This just won't do. Liam sure as hell wouldn't want us all sitting here sulking in silence."

He went into the bus and came out with two guitars,

which he handed to me and Lawson. Then he disappeared again and returned with Ivy's glockenspiel and a six-pack. He gave Ivy her instrument and passed the beers around.

Lawson and I tuned our guitars and looked at each other, then over to Ivy. She thought for a moment. "How about *Echoes from the Basement?*"

We nodded and found our chords, and Lawson counted us in. Our voices felt small and insignificant before the immense lake, the notes dissipating into nothing across the wide open space. But it didn't matter. It felt important, holy almost, as though we were bringing him back to life by singing his songs. It felt simpler than silence, lighter than words.

We played until long after the sun had vanished beyond the horizon and the stars lit up one by one behind the patchy clouds. A chill came rolling in from the lake and when we were all sung out, we exchanged our instruments for cardigans, blankets, and more beers.

Lawson put another log on the fire and crouched down to poke around it, reviving the flames. Then he sat back in his chair and looked up at the sky, letting out a long sigh.

"Liam, you fuck."

We all turned to him.

"I've been so angry with him." He shook his head slowly. "I thought he was such a shit for dying on us like that. I blamed him for being a selfish asshole." He peered up at us from under his curly mop, waiting to see how we would react. Nobody moved. "I—I yelled at him. Like, not *at* him, but you know... Told him to go fuck himself." He looked down at his hands. "I feel so guilty about that now. I'm sure he didn't mean to do it. He was messed up, but it wasn't his fault, technically."

"Don't feel bad, man," said Mango. "It's normal to feel angry. Healthy, even."

"Yeah... Maybe you're right." Lawson shifted his gaze

back to the flickering fire. "But now instead I feel guilty that I let it happen. Like I could have stopped it."

"You tried," Victor said, looking at Lawson over the rim of his glasses. "We all tried, but you tried the most."

I leaned closer to Lawson. "You told me once that Liam was always going to do his own thing, that he wasn't going to change because of anyone else. I think you were right. I talked to him about getting help, but…" I shook my head. "There was no way. Don't blame yourself. We did what we could."

"I don't know…" Lawson gazed into the flames, his face furrowed with too many thoughts.

"Well, in any case," Ivy interjected, "there's no point in thinkin' like that. What's done is done. Liam made his choices. He lived as he wished. There's no use in passing blame." She pressed her delicate feet deeper into the sand. "At some point you just have to decide, do you want to create, or do you want to destroy?"

There was a brief silence, then a wistful laugh from Mango. "He'd call us all dorks for even talking like this."

Lawson chuckled. "Yeah, you're probably right. He'd be offended that we would take credit for anything he did."

Victor and Ivy laughed too, and I felt a smile on my lips. It was a rare and comforting feeling.

"He'd be up and about, raving about some party some-where," Victor said. "Or challenging us to drive all the way to Manhattan before dawn."

We all laughed and sipped our drinks, holding onto this flash of relief like a lifebuoy, our desperate hands clutching at it.

"Man." Mango shook his head and smiled. "I used to hate that, the way he was always so unpredictable. Like, out of nowhere he'd be up and changing the plans, having some new vision or a different idea of what we were going to do.

Like that time in Denver, remember? When he wrote a new song just before the gig and started playing it without telling us."

"Like he did with Frank's song," I mumbled, my eyes buried in the dancing flames.

"Oh, yeah." Mango nodded. "Like that. Except this time he told us to play along, like he wanted us to improvise 'cause it would sound more genuine, or something like that. He'd always pull that kind of shit, it used to really piss me off." He laughed again and shook his head. "But it always turned out great, no matter what he did. We never regretted any of it." He sat back and took a sip from his beer. "Our boy, he taught me to go with the flow."

"We sure lived according to his whims," Ivy said with a sorrowful smile.

"We never knew what to expect," said Victor. "More often than not I'd find myself cleaning up some mess he made, but it always felt worth it. He kept us on our toes. Life never got boring."

"He changed all our lives, for sure," Lawson added. "He was my comrade since we were little kids. And for that whole time, even though he frustrated the hell out of me, like a *lot*…" He turned and looked out over the black water. "I loved him to death, and I wouldn't change a thing."

"I'll drink to that," Mango said, and we all raised our beers.

"It's funny," Lawson continued. "I used to think that I was holding him together, but I'm starting to think that maybe it was the other way around." He fiddled with his beer can, pulled the ring tab off the top.

"Maybe it was a bit of both," I suggested.

"Yeah…" Lawson twiddled the tab between his fingers for a moment, then threw it in the fire. "Maybe you're right."

We sat in silence for a while. The wind had died down

and all we could hear was the crackling and popping from the fire and the distant hum of Chicago.

Then Ivy spoke. "He made me feel less alone." We all looked up at her. "He never once judged me for my scars, or my past. He was the first person who made me feel less like a doll and more like just a girl. That may not sound like much, but to me, it was everything." She pulled a strand of hair from her mouth and tucked it behind her ear. "He was broken, like the rest of us. But he was different 'cause he was trapped in his head, chained by his drugs and addictions. He never gave himself a chance to look outside his own mind." She reached out and picked up a branch, which she used to poke the fire. There was a hissing sound and fresh flames shot up, illuminating her pale face. "I wish just once he could have seen himself how we saw him. How we see him."

Her eyes met mine, and I could feel my heart tugging at my lungs, emptying them of air. Tears threatened behind my eyelids and I swallowed hard.

"When... When's the funeral?" I stammered.

"Not for a while yet," said Lawson. "Still waiting on the autopsy results."

"Hazel, you going back tomorrow?" Mango asked.

"Yeah." I nodded grimly. "In a way, I'm glad. I'm not sure I'd be able to cope. Back to the Rileys' to bury another... No, I've seen enough funerals for one trip." My chest tightened and I had to push it out to take a full breath. "I hope he would understand."

"I'm sure he would, Hazel," said Lawson. "You know how he felt about funerals."

"Yeah..."

I looked up at the sky, patchy cotton clouds scudding by, in turn obscuring and revealing the universe. I remembered that morning on the porch steps, talking to Liam about death. Where was he now? Had he returned to the place where the opposites combine? Was he whole again? And if so, was he still him?

"Do you…," I began, but hesitated. I had been afraid to ask this question, but it had reeled through my head since the moment I learned that he was gone. "Do you think he still exists, somewhere?"

There was silence as we contemplated a question that felt too heavy to hold in our minds.

"I think so," Mango said at last. "It feels like he does. I still talk to my *abuela* sometimes. God bless her, she's been dead nearly ten years, but I feel like she can still hear me. Somehow. I can't explain it, but at the same time I feel like it's not my job to explain it. I just trust my instincts, you know?"

The others began to hum and nod.

"And even if she isn't there, even if she can't hear me…" Mango turned and looked out over the lake. "I still prefer to believe that she is."

"I feel like he's around," said Ivy. "Somewhere." Her dainty nose pointed toward the heavens, as though she were trying to find the scent of Liam's soul on the wind.

"Definitely," Lawson said finally, a reassuring certainty in his voice.

I looked around at my fellow mourners, my bandmates, my friends. "Good." I sank lower into my chair, stretching my legs out in front of me. "Because I can't stand the idea that he's completely gone. It makes no sense. He has to live on somewhere, or the universe is just too fucking cruel."

I swept my feet left and right, creating a little crevasse in the sand. Then I sat back up, picked up my bag and fished out pen and paper.

"Guys, do you mind if I draw you?"

"Draw us?" Mango raised his eyebrows.

"Yeah, it's just, it's something I like to do. If that's okay. I just want to draw this scene."

"Oh, sure," said Mango, and the others nodded. "Go for it."

I picked up my chair and moved a little closer to the water, and positioned it where I could capture everyone, the fire, and the bus from a perfect angle. I leaned back and focused on the graphite as it scratched the paper, watched lines and shading appear out of nowhere. A strange peace came over me, and I only vaguely heard the others as they carried on talking, reminiscing, laughing with each other. Something among us had begun to heal, one tiny piece at a time.

When the drawing was done, with the fire in the middle and figures huddling around it, our beloved bus in the background, I put my pencil to the bottom corner and scrawled a message for Liam.

Liam, you infuriating, beautiful thing. We're on the beach talking about you, and it's awfully cheesy and heartbreaking and you would hate it. And we love you.

Your Hazelnut

I walked back to the group, took one last look at the paper, then threw it on the fire and watched the smoke rise into the sky, carrying it to wherever Liam was now. Soft waves lapped against the shore, the lake vast and black.

I turned to the others. "Who wants to go swimming?"

Unsurprisingly, Mango volunteered first. "Hell yeah!" He shot up and clumsily pulled his clothes off while jogging towards the water's edge.

The memory of our night in the woods filled me with a warm glow, and I raised my eyebrows at the others. "Well?"

Victor shrugged and stood up. "For the greater good," he said, unbuttoning his shirt.

Then Ivy got up. "I'm coming, too!"

The two of them walked off to join Mango, who was already splashing in the surf.

I turned to Lawson. Sadness lingered in his eyes, as it would for a long time, but there was a hint of a smile on his lips. I reached my hand out to him. "Come on, then."

He stood up and took my hand, and together we walked into the freezing water. After everything we had been through, there was no room for blame or regret. All we could do was forgive ourselves and others, and try our best to move forward.

Mango splashed us and we shrieked in protest before attempting to reciprocate his attack. Funny how it's possible to laugh, despite everything. In the distance, the lights of Chicago pulsed through the night, its host of twinkling skyscrapers reflected on the lake's surface. And somehow, the world kept spinning.

THIRTY-EIGHT

I slept the entire flight home. It wasn't until the wheels of the plane scraped against the Heathrow runway that I woke with a jerk. I looked up, foggy and disoriented, at the world outside the tiny airplane window. It felt desperately familiar, and yet strangely new. I leaned my heavy head against the seat in front while the crew prepared to let us out.

Past passport control, I was officially back in my home country. I trudged on to baggage reclaim and found the carousel spitting out bags from Chicago. As my backpack came rolling towards me I saw how beat-up and dirty it was, how well-travelled. It was a very different bag to the one I had left with. With a satisfied smile, I lifted it onto my shoulders and headed for the exit.

There it all was. The newsagents, the sandwich shops, the staccato of the British accent in stark contrast to the soft and lazy American speech. The world was a heaving hub of activity, full of people on their way somewhere. Like I had never left.

I walked past the throng of people that stood at Arrivals,

waiting for their loved ones. I had anticipated this moment, and I had known that I would walk out of here without Liam by my side. But never had I expected that when I got back home, Liam would no longer be in this world.

"Hazel!"

I jolted at the sound of my name and looked up, scanning the crowd.

"Over here!" A bright red mop was bouncing up and down underneath two wildly waving arms.

"Amber?"

She pushed her way forwards until she emerged in front of the waiting crowd. There was my sister like I had never seen her before – smiling, a healthy glow on her cheeks, and a big, round tummy full of new life. She lowered her arms, tilted her head and gave me a cheeky smile. I broke into a grin and walked up to her, and we met in a long-awaited hug. With my face buried in that nest of ginger locks, for a split second I thought it was Ivy I was embracing. My sisters.

When we came apart, I gazed in shock at her ballooning body. "Look at you, wow! You're huge!"

"Gee, thanks!" Amber laughed and put her hands on her belly. "She is getting heavy. I can only hope she won't be as much of a pain as I was."

"Oh, my god. This is really happening. You're having a daughter!"

"I am indeed!" She smiled brightly, but then her expression turned more serious. "It's a chance to start again, is how I see it."

I nodded, biting my lip. "I think that's what we all need."

"Well, it's great to see you! Little Hazel, all grown up. The car is out front, I'll take you back to ours." We started towards the car park. "I want to hear all about your adventures. I've been kind of housebound lately, so I'll have to live vicariously through you. Tell me everything."

And I did. I told her all about how I couldn't stay in that house where we had both grown up, how Nathan had offered to put me up in Madison, how I had ended up touring with a band and had the time of my life. How I had fallen in love with a poetic singer and had my heart shattered over and over. Amber understood when I told her about Liam's life and death, and shared stories about some of her friends from rehab who had met similar fates.

Then she told me about Matt, how they had found each other and built a stronger life together. How they had felt when they had first seen those two pink lines, and how they were both determined to do right by their little girl.

And soon we were reminiscing about old times, something I hadn't done with anyone in a long while. It felt good to have my sister back.

She drove us across London to Canning Town and brought me into their flat.

"I figured you could stay in here while you get yourself sorted," she said, as she led me into a small but bright room. There was a rolled-up mattress which I assumed would be mine for now. In the corner sat a crib and some bags of what appeared to be toys and teeny-tiny clothes.

"The nursery?"

"It will be," said Amber, looking at the blank walls. "It will need some paint, of course. And some nice pictures and things, maybe. I want it to be bright and safe, and super cosy."

I surveyed the space. "Maybe a soft pearl yellow," I suggested. "It would really light up in the afternoon sun, and it would complement the brick building opposite."

Amber laughed. "I forgot I'm dealing with an expert!"

I smiled and shrugged. "I'll help."

"Yeah?"

"Sure! I'd love to. We can paint it together, and pick out

some posters and things. I think it should have lots of colour."

"You're hired!" Amber said, her big belly bouncing as she laughed.

* * *

So I started again, or tried to. I unpacked my bag once more, this time in a spare room that was soon to become a nursery. But first, it would have to nurse me.

Occasionally I'd exchange a few texts with Lawson and Ivy, but that whole life had begun to feel like a distant dream. One day, Lawson messaged and asked for my postal address, but I thought nothing more of it.

As I eased back into everyday existence I realised that, although life was back to solidity and routine, this time it could be different. I began to look for work around London, sending applications to every art gallery and museum I could find. I felt I owed it to myself to at least try. After all, this was my life, here and now, and I was free to make the most of it. While we're still alive, anything is possible.

One morning, a letter slipped through the door.

"It's for you," Amber said. "From America."

I held my breath as she handed it to me. A memento, a voice from across the ocean, some tendril reaching out to me from that other life I had once lived.

Carrying it like a rare blossom, I edged out onto the balcony overlooking the streets of Canning Town, where I carefully tore it open. It was a note with Lawson's sprawling handwriting.

Hey Haze,

Welcome back home! Hope you're doing okay over there and that whatever bed you're currently sleeping in is at least half as comfortable as your bunk bed on the Interstate Marvel.

I just wanted to send you this. We found it when we were going through Liam's stuff. It was folded up inside his notebook, and I thought you might like to have it.

Don't forget about us. We love you and miss you. Come visit us sometime.

Say hello to the Queen for me.

Yours always,
  Lawson

A teardrop found its way down my cheek and onto the paper, blotching his signature. Good old Lawson. I took a shaky breath and peeled his letter aside to see what he had enclosed.

It was my drawing of Liam, sleeping in the hotel bed. A stabbing ache took me by surprise and I bent over from the sudden pain. I stumbled onto the balcony chair and leaned into my aching heart as I stared at the drawing. Liam lay in perfect sleep, dreaming beautiful dreams, surrounded by my wiggly lines; the forcefield that, ultimately, was not enough to protect him.

"Haze?" Amber appeared in the balcony doorway. "You okay?"

I pressed my lips together and looked out over the East London rooftops. Rows of laundry hung on the balconies opposite, and a couple of pigeons were courting on the railing. Laughter rose from the street below where some kids were riding bikes. In the distance, I could hear the faint chugging of a DLR train.

"Yeah," I said eventually. "I'm okay."

I handed her the letter and the drawing. She looked at them, and then sat down in the chair beside me. "It's beautiful, Hazel."

"Thanks." A melancholy smile formed at the memory of Liam that morning. How peaceful he had seemed. I could only hope he was like that now, carefree, surrounded by beautiful dreams. "He loved it when I drew. He was always encouraging me…"

My voice trailed off as I remembered that day in the studio, when he had gone chasing after papers and pens so that I could paint something. I chuckled to myself, and another tear escaped the corner of my eye. I wiped it away with my sleeve and was overcome by another memory: the mural, Vanya's insistent prods, and the immense relief that had washed over me as I poured all of my pain onto her wall.

I looked over at Amber.

"Do you know if there's an art shop nearby?"

An hour later, I boarded a double-decker to Dalston. A lingering summer warmth hung in the air despite the colour of the overhanging treetops, which had begun to rust and bleed with their autumn palette. The sun was high above the rooftops, and it caressed my face as I walked through the big-city hubbub.

I found the shop, and a small bell tinkled as I walked inside. In an instant, the familiar smell of turpentine flooded my mind with memories.

"Can I help you?" The check-out lady, blond and chubby

with a friendly face and thick, black glasses looked at me expectantly.

"Yeah, um." As I looked around at all the tantalising tools, I realised that I hadn't shopped for art supplies in many years, and never on my own. I turned back to the lady. "I need a canvas or two, and some oil paints, please?"

"No problem." She shuffled out from behind the counter and pointed down the aisle. "Canvases are over there. The big ones are on special offer this week." She threw me a wink. "If you're feeling adventurous."

I smiled. "I am. I'll take two."

"Wonderful." She picked up two canvases so large that they were difficult to manoeuvre, one at a time, and leaned them against the counter. Big, blank spaces, waiting to be filled. Waiting for their purpose.

"And paints, please? Oil, not acrylic."

"Yes, of course." She turned around and studied the vast array of tubes hanging on the wall. "What colours are you after?"

I looked at the canvas, then let my eyes drift over the rainbow splayed on the wall. I was alive, and the world felt immense and full of promise. My smile widened and I turned back to the lady.

"All of them."

ACKNOWLEDGEMENTS

Thank you to all the amazing people who helped me tell Hazel and Liam's story:

To my online writing group, Stine and Victoria, for always being one click away, offering sprints and creative energy and fuzzy-heart support. Without you and your brilliant insights and feedback, this book would not be what it is.

To my local writing group, Alice, Aladar, Nick, Lizzie and Ben, for all the write-ins and afternoon pints, your staunch encouragement, and for reading and offering your invaluable input. This journey would not have been the same without you.

To the shining star that is Dana Young for her beautiful cover art.

To NaNoWriMo for making me fall in love with writing again.

To my volunteer beta readers for reading and offering feedback: Zoe Beeson, Sarah Hathorn, Kara Jordan, Gretchen Midgley and Imelda Taylor.

To Ellen Hampton for her insight into fundamentalist religion.

To Rick Jackson for helping me figure it all out and build something better.

To Kimberley Burridge for the tireless optimism and grace she offers her students.

To Margaret and Phil Lancaster for your unconditional love and support. I am very lucky to have you in my life.

To all my crazy, beautiful, beloved friends and steadfast champions; you know who you are. Whether nearby or across oceans, you're never far from my heart.

Finally, to Mike; my rock, my jester, my world. Whether backpacking around the world or descaling the coffee machine, life with you is always a marvel. Thank you for being my first reader and brainstorm buddy, for always believing in me, and for your unwavering support of my various bonkers undertakings (writing career included). Needless to say, without you, this book would not exist. May we always create wonders together.